Erik and the Dragon

By

Sam Ferguson

This is a work of fiction. All of the characters, organizations, and events portrayed in this book are either products of the author's imagination or are used fictitiously.

ERIK AND THE DRAGON

Copyright © 2014 by Sam Ferguson

All Rights Reserved
ISBN:1943183031
ISBN-13:9781943183036

For Rachel

CHAPTER ONE	1
CHAPTER TWO	16
CHAPTER THREE	27
CHAPTER FOUR	32
CHAPTER FIVE	46
CHAPTER SIX	57
CHAPTER SEVEN	64
CHAPTER EIGHT	86
CHAPTER NINE	91
CHAPTER TEN	98
CHAPTER ELEVEN	123
CHAPTER TWELVE	136
CHAPTER THIRTEEN	151
CHAPTER FOURTEEN	173
CHAPTER FIFTEEN	210
CHAPTER SIXTEEN	226
CHAPTER SEVENTEEN	241
CHAPTER EIGHTEEN	251
CHAPTER NINETEEN	262
About the Author	272

CHAPTER ONE

The mouse was curled tightly inside the toe of the half-burned boot. It could still hear the raptors squabbling over the large beast that lay dead nearby, but at least the wolves had gone. Slowly, the mouse gathered its courage and crawled toward the opening. The mouse's forelegs ached and twitched under its weight, and most of its fur on its right side had been singed off, but that was the least of its problems now. A shadow passed over the boot and the mouse froze. It twitched its whiskers and sniffed the air, tilting its head up toward the opening. After a minute it climbed up the back of the boot and peeked over the burnt leather. A great beast lay nearby, with its scaly tail encircling the boot. A few buzzards ripped and pulled at it from the soft underbelly, making the corpse twitch unnaturally.

Beyond that was a field littered with bodies, many of which had been ravaged by the wolves during the previous day and night, but now the vultures were upon them, getting their fill. It was a grotesque sight, but at least the abundance of food might help the rodent escape unnoticed. It looked to the burnt house first and then to the stables. There was no sign of any person. One more quick glance back to the birds before the mouse gathered its courage and flopped over the side of the boot to land on the ground. It streaked across the dirt, running silently and as quickly as it could. It scampered into the smoldering rubble and tucked under a pile of wood. It hid there for a few moments, peering out from its hiding place and checking to make sure the wolves had in fact left. Once he was satisfied, he scurried out from the wood to find an open space. He then sat back on his hind legs and stretched up into the air, checking the scents.

He heard a low growl behind him. He turned quickly and saw a thick furry feline tail twitching from behind a large hunk of stone. The mouse extended its right foreleg and began waving it around in front of him frantically. The cat leapt out suddenly, mouth open and sharp fangs pointed for the mouse.

A flash of light ripped through the space and where the mouse had been, Peren sat naked and wounded. The cat landed in

1

his lap and dug its claws into his thigh. Peren stifled a yell and ripped the cat free of him, holding it out at arm's length by the back of its neck.

"I must say, I don't like cats," Peren told the cat as he roughly tossed it aside. He rose to his feet and ran his left hand over the right side of his face. It stung and was incredibly tender to the touch. Even the open air agitated him. He looked down and saw that his right shoulder was missing the first couple layers of skin as well. He had other minor burns over his chest and torso, but at least he was alive. He only barely remembered the moment before the firedrake had spewed its fire at him, but he could still feel the heat in his skin. He had only woken up a little before dusk the previous day in his mouse form, and there was no way for him to know how long he had been unconscious. For now, he was just happy that he was able to change form fast enough to save himself. Looking around the rubble, he could only hope that the others had escaped as well.

He shuffled through the ruins of the manor, looking for anything he could use to clothe himself with. He looked under fallen timbers, in burnt chests and wardrobes, and was eventually able to come up with a pair of scorched pants that fit a bit too tight around the waist and a pink blouse. After he pulled on the trousers and wiggled them up around his waist he held the blouse up in front of him.

"Of all the things to survive a fire," he muttered. "It would have to be bright pink with white lace at the end of the sleeves." He looked at it and then down to his chest. "Nope," he said. "I'd rather be naked." He tossed the blouse down and left the manor to find a pair of shoes. He walked toward the waist-high stone fence and climbed over with some difficulty. Putting any weight on his right arm was excruciatingly painful. So he turned to the side and kicked his left leg up and slid across the stone wall, plopping over onto the other side without using his arms at all.

He searched the dead soldiers and came upon a promising pair of boots. He stuck his foot out to measure against the boot's bottom and sighed when he realized his feet were bigger. He walked on until he found another fallen soldier. This time his right foot matched the boot and he went down to pull it off. The soldier's foot came with the boot and then Peren realized that it was a kind of prosthetic. He turned it around to look inside and found the boot filled with a "foot" made of wood which had a long stem that inserted into the warrior's leg below the knee.

Peren dropped the boot and agitatedly stroked the bridge of his nose with his left thumb and forefinger, trying to push back the urge to swear at the fallen corpse for not having boots he could use. After he calmed down he continued scavenging what he could until he finally found a pair of good, sturdy boots, albeit they were a mismatched pair from two different soldiers. He also managed to scrounge up a couple of copper coins, a decent sword, and a long knife.

When he had it all put on he looked down at himself and laughed. "Mismatched boots, scorched pants, skin that looks like I slept in an oven, and a sword hanging from my belt. Yeah, I look great!" he laughed to himself. "Fit for a king!" Then he turned around and surveyed the scene one more time. He thought about looking for a horse, but he knew that was going to be a fruitless search, so instead he started walking the long road to Drakei Glazei. The only bright spot that gave courage was the fact that he did not see Lepkin, Gorin, or Arkyn among the dead. He hoped he was going in the right direction.

*****

Erik hiked up the rocky hill with the others. Heavy plumes of smoke and dust hung low in the air above them. Beyond the hill, Erik heard the cracking stone and popping beams. He didn't have to reach the top of the hill to know what had happened to Valtuu Temple. Alferug and the other dwarves were rushing past on their cavedogs, shouting orders to each other as they zipped by.

Lepkin reached the top of the hill first. He set his fists on his hips and hung his head low. Marlin was next. The prelate fell to his knees and let his arms hang at his sides. Dimwater put a hand to her mouth and gasped.

When Erik finally caught up to them and was able to see, his heart ached within him. The pride and joy they had all felt after sending Tu'luh away with his tail between his legs was snatched from them now. The once great and mighty temple was laid low. They could see a group of other priests trying to douse the fires that Tu'luh had set, but their water spells were no match for the dragon's flames.

"Come," Lepkin said soberly. "We should help them and then see if we can find any survivors."

Dimwater summoned a great raincloud above them and called forth the water. A column of thick drops crashed down below, attacking the hissing flames vigorously. "You go and look for survivors," she said. "I will help them with the fire."

Lepkin reached down and scooped his left hand under Marlin's right armpit and hoisted the man up. "Come," he said to Marlin. "Let's go."

Erik, Marlin, and Lepkin rushed forward, with Jaleal silently running behind them. The higher parts of the temple had fallen over in the direction they were approaching, utterly obliterating the portion of the wall that stood there and granting them access.

Marlin was quick to point at a pile of rubble nearby. "There is someone under this," he said.

Lepkin and Erik quickly moved in and heaved the large section of wooden boards and plaster up, tossing it off of an unconscious priest that lay underneath.

"He is in bad shape," Lepkin said as he bent down and set a hand to the side of the man's neck.

"His aura is fading," Marlin agreed.

The priest's back arched suddenly and he exhaled for the last time.

Jaleal moved in close and stroked his beard. "I don't imagine many would have survived the collapse," he said.

Lepkin nodded and motioned for them to keep moving. The four of them picked their way through the rubble, stopping occasionally to lift a hunk of stone or some timbers that had pinned a helpless victim underneath. Each person they found was too near to death to help, and some expired before the team could lift the rubble off of them. As they moved in closer to the main portion of the temple the rain thinned out and the smoke cleared.

"At least the fire is gone," Lepkin said.

Marlin remained quiet, scanning the area. "I don't see any others," he said slowly.

The majority of the tall temple had caved in on itself, crushing everything down into the cavern below. A few portions of the temple's foundation still stood defiantly, but Erik could hardly recognize anything. The dwarves had gotten to this area a long time before the others, and they were busy carrying bodies out of the

Erik and the Dragon

deep hole. Marlin turned away and wept and he slumped back down to his knees.

Lepkin grabbed Erik's shoulder and pulled him farther into the rubble. "Come with me," he said. Erik glanced back to Marlin for a moment and then went down into the hole with Lepkin. The two of them hopped from one hunk of stone to another as they picked their way down to the bottom.

"Watch your step," Faengoril shouted out. "Some of this is still very unstable!"

Lepkin nodded and pointed to a space in the rubble that was too small for him to go through. "Think you can slip in?" he asked Erik.

"You want me to go in there?" Erik asked incredulously.

"There is a box somewhere down here. I need it."

Erik looked at the hole. Jagged, splintered timbers poked through like great spears and the stone was chipped and rough. He was not going to enjoy this at all. "Couldn't we just try to dig it out?" Erik asked.

Lepkin shook his head. "That would take a long time, even if all the dwarves helped us. We need to get it and then be on our way."

"Where are we going?" Erik asked.

Lepkin arched his brow and folded his arms across his chest. "We have a dragon to hunt." Lepkin's words stabbed at Erik's heart with the touch of ice and the boy swore his heart stopped beating for a moment.

Then, Erik looked to the hole again and nodded. He wasn't happy about it, but it was the next logical thing to do. Tu'luh was wounded, and on the run. If they were to succeed, then now would be the best time to go after the beast.

"What kind of box am I looking for?" Erik asked.

"It is about this big," Lepkin said as he held his hands out in front of him to mime a box about a foot and a half wide by a foot tall. "It is made of mithril, and has dwarvish runes across the top."

"Mithril?" Erik asked. He had heard of mithril weapons and armor, but never a box. "Why would someone waste that on a box?" he asked.

Lepkin arched a brow and pointed to the hole. "We can discuss it later. For now, go and find it."

Erik frowned. He would have thought that his recent deeds

would have earned him a better standing with Lepkin. He took in a breath of courage and slid down across a stone slab and went into the hole feet-first. He felt a sharp poke in his side and reflexively twisted away from a shard of jagged stone that jutted out from his left. He moved slowly, carefully planting his feet on any hold he could before going deeper and grabbing onto new handholds. The rain from Dimwater's spell made everything slippery, as if it wasn't difficult enough.

The rubble quaked and scraped against itself. Something from above fell and dwarves shouted out just moments before a heavy hunk of stone slammed down, sending vibrations throughout the tunnel Erik was in. Erik moved faster, hoping to avoid being crushed, but he needn't have worried. The stone and wood around the hole shook, but only a bit of dust filtered down from above.

As he went farther into the chute, it angled out horizontally and he was forced to crawl through on his hands and knees. A couple of the areas were extremely tight, so that he had to stick his arms through first and then squeeze and pull the rest of his body through. Despite his best efforts, he could feel sharp points scraping him as he wormed through.

Then the shaft ended abruptly and opened to a room of black stone. Erik looked down and saw some fallen timbers in a hallway below that led to the room he was above. On the other side of the black room was a door.

Erik flipped himself around and lowered his feet and legs over the edge. Then he inched his torso over until he hung from a heavy timber with his arms fully extended. His feet dangled at least eight feet above the stone floor, but there was no turning back now. He let go and tucked into a clumsy roll as he hit the floor. He jarred his back a bit, but otherwise he was fine. He straightened up to his feet and went to the door.

Unlike many other areas of the temple, this room was entirely plain, as was the door before him. It was made of oak, and reinforced with black iron bands, but there were no designs of ornaments of any kind to be found. Just an old, strong door. Erik put his hands on the iron ring and gave the door a pull. It didn't move. He pushed, but again it didn't budge. Frustrated, he yanked hard on the iron ring and the door creaked and groaned as it toppled over toward him. Erik backpedaled out of the way just in time as the heavy door fell over and broke in two on the stone floor.

A dazzling, golden light streamed out from the doorway. Erik slowly stepped through to find a wondrous room. Four golden lamps stood around a pedestal in the center of the room. Each of the lamps burned brightly, with a white blinding flame. Erik then looked to the walls and realized that they were shining and reflecting the light.

"Mithril walls?" he said astonished. He reached out and put a hand on the wall nearest him and felt the warm, strong metal. He then turned back to the pedestal, raising his arms to shield him from the blinding light and spy what was atop the pedestal. There he saw the box Lepkin wanted. The smooth mithril shone brightly, temptingly before him. He walked up to the box and took it in his hands. It was heavier than he had expected, but he managed alright. As he stepped back with the box the lamps died down until the flames were no brighter than those of candles.

The box hummed and vibrated in his hands. He looked down and saw the runes Lepkin had said would be on top the box. They each glowed blue. He turned the box over, looking for the latch, or a hinge, or any way to open it. He found none. He couldn't even see a seam or a keyhole. It wasn't a box, but a cube of mithril.

"Just what do you think you are doing?" a voice cried out from behind him.

Erik wheeled around to see a short, thin man in the doorway. He bounded into the room and held his hands out expectantly. "Give me the box, right now!" he demanded.

Erik stepped back and twisted away from the man. "No," he said.

The man pushed a pair of thick, blue tinted spectacles up on the bridge of his nose and he fixed his bright green eyes on Erik. "Give me the box!" he said again.

"Who are you?" Erik asked.

"Who am I?" the man repeated. "Who am I?" he snorted and set a large backpack down on the floor beside him. Then he ran a hand through his curly red hair and stuck a finger in Erik's face. "I am Tatev, the librarian."

Erik nodded and looked to the heaping pile of books about to fall out the top of the backpack on the floor. "Where did you get those?" he asked.

Tatev huffed impatiently. "I am the librarian, who else should have the books?" he replied. He stepped closer and held out his hands. "Now give me the box, you don't know what you have there."

"No," Erik said. "Lepkin told me to get it, and the only way you will put a hand on it is by taking it from me." Erik quickly thought of how he would maneuver around the golden lamps and get away. He guessed from Tatev's build that the man was not much for physical exertion.

"Lepkin?" Tatev repeated. He pulled his spectacles off and wiped them with the bottom of his smudged, cream colored tunic. "The Keeper is here?" he asked.

Erik nodded.

Tatev's angular jaw dropped and his mouth opened into a wide smile. "Oh my," he said as his eyes started to sparkle. "You must be him!" he said excitedly. He stuck a hand out to shake Erik's and then quickly realized that Erik wouldn't be able to shake hands while holding the box. "Sorry," Tatev offered as he turned back to pick up his backpack. "I didn't realize who you were."

Erik stood puzzled, watching Tatev. "Are you one of the priests?" Erik asked.

"Yes and no," Tatev replied. "I have been in the temple for…" he stopped and tapped a finger on his pointed chin. "Actually, I don't remember how long I have been here," he said. "Perhaps twenty years now. Maybe a couple more." He shrugged. "It is sure an honor to meet you!" Tatev said.

Erik wasn't sure what to make of the man, so he summoned his power to discern Tatev's intent. Even after he found no ill will in the man's heart, he still kept a bit of a distance from him. "If you have been in the temple that long, then why are your eyes normal?" Erik asked.

"I never took the test of Arophim," Tatev replied. "Someone has to be able to search the books, you know," he added. He then hefted the pack onto his shoulders and held the straps with his hands near his armpits. "Once someone takes the test, they lose their ability to read normal books," Tatev explained. "But don't worry, I can read the magical books too." He pointed to his spectacles. "These are the Eyes of Dowr. They allow the wearer to see the magical writings of the mystics. This way I can read both kinds of books and help the temple archive all of the knowledge in the known world."

Erik and the Dragon

Erik nodded as though he understood and started to walk out of the chamber. "We need to find our way out," Erik said.

"Yes, yes," Tatev said as he pointed to the hallway across the room. "I cleared the way while I was coming here. It will be easy enough to get back now."

Erik walked through the hall, ducking under a couple of cracked beams and stepping over a few fallen stones here and there as Tatev continued to talk.

"You know," he began. "The Eyes of Dowr have a unique history. They are made from Aluriyum crystal, and are the only pair in existence today. The Mystics created them, though it is uncertain why they did so since they could read magical writings as they were the ones who wrote them. It is thought that they could see into the future and knew that they would need to provide a pair of spectacles like these for someone like me, so we could retain the ability to read normal books after others take the Test of Arophim and lose their natural sight."

Erik looked back to the red haired man and opened his mouth to say something but Tatev just kept talking right over him.

"The rims are made out of mithril, which is peculiar as there are no known sources of mithril in the east where the Mystics lived. That would suggest that the elves perhaps traded with the Mystics and or that perhaps the two societies created the Eyes of Dowr together. No one knows for sure, and I would be the one to know as I have read all of the books on the subject, believe you me!"

Erik sighed and stopped when he emerged into another ruined room. He glanced around but could find no way up. A hall branched off to his left and another to his right, but he wasn't sure which way to go.

Tatev kept walking toward the hall on the right as he talked. "I never thought I would meet the Champion of Truth," he said. "Sure, I have read a lot of the books of prophecy, and I knew that Lepkin had found a candidate, but to think that I would actually meet you, here, now—it's astonishing!" Tatev stopped suddenly and looked back to Erik, who was still standing in the middle of the room. "Well, are you coming or aren't you?"

"Is that the way out?" Erik asked.

Tatev nodded his head and gestured for Erik to take the lead. No sooner had Erik stepped past the man than he started talking again.

"If you are interested, I managed to save the book that talks about the Eyes of Dowr, and the special crystals that form the lenses. It is really quite interesting. The Aluriyum crystal is only found in one mine to the east, where the Mystics used to live until they were wiped out by some mysterious plague. It's too bad too, if not for the plague, perhaps they would still be around and they could help us solve all the puzzles they left behind."

Erik sighed and tuned Tatev out as best he could. He walked through the rubble, occasionally stopping until Tatev would rest his tongue long enough to point the right direction before continuing on with his rambling lectures. The boy was only all too happy to get back to Lepkin when the two finally emerged from the rubble and the dwarves helped them climb up to the surface.

"Tatev!" Marlin shouted out as the two returned to the ground in front of where the entrance had been. Erik stepped aside while the two embraced and peered back into the pit. He could see Lepkin climbing over the rubble.

"Erik," Marlin said as he pulled Tatev along. "This is Tatev, our librarian."

"Yes, he told me," Erik said.

Marlin smiled wide. "Tatev is one of the most knowledgeable members of our order."

"I see he still has a great fondness for books," Lepkin said as he approached.

Tatev beamed with pride as he set the bag down in front of them. "I saved as many as I could!" he said. "You know, when the temple was first built…"

Lepkin held up a hand. "Perhaps we can discuss it later," Lepkin said. His voice was polite, but it was also stern enough to make Tatev blush and nod nervously.

Thank you! Erik thought to himself.

"Put the box in here," Lepkin told Erik as he held out a burlap sack. Erik angled the box in through the opening and Lepkin sealed it closed.

"What is this?" Erik asked.

Marlin sighed and walked away, frowning. Lepkin watched the prelate go and then turned back to Erik.

"This box contains Nagar's Secret," Lepkin said.

Erik's eyes went wide. "The book is in there?" he asked incredulously. "All this time Tu'luh was in the same building as the book he was after? Why didn't he just take it and leave?"

Tatev jumped in excitedly. "Time is of no importance to a dragon. Lesser drakes have finite lifespans, but a great dragon has no such worry. If the beast you fought really was Tu'luh the Red, then he was one of the most powerful Ancients, and is older than Terramyr itself!"

Lepkin held up a hand, silencing the eager librarian. Then he told Erik, "He was waiting because he was looking for you."

"To see if I would join with him," Erik said as he remembered the dragon's words and his mind swirled through the visions he was shown. "He wanted me to help him use the magic in that book."

Lepkin arched a brow. "Had I not seen the dragon with my own eyes, I would not have suspected he could have deceived so many."

"How did he get in the temple?" Erik asked.

Lepkin shrugged. "When I was chosen as the Keeper, it was Hiasyntar Ku'lai who emerged from the temple to find me."

"The Father of the Ancients," Tatev whispered.

Erik glanced to Tatev and then looked back to Lepkin. "So he was the dragon that was left behind? Why didn't any of the books mention that? The books Al had me read said he was dying."

"He was," Lepkin affirmed. "To put it simply, Nagar's Secret was worming into his mind and heart, killing him slowly as it attacked his very soul. He sent the others away and built a chamber in this temple to protect himself from the book, hoping that he would live long enough to administer the Exalted Test of Arophim and name the Champion of Truth."

Erik scrunched his brow into a knot over his nose. "Why didn't the book attack Tu'luh?"

"Tu'luh is the master of Nagar's Secret," Tatev said quickly. "He and Nagar the Black forged the magical book and created the spells that it holds. Because of this, they were always in control of the magic, and never affected by its blight."

Lepkin nodded. "We all thought Tu'luh was killed in the Battle of Hamath Valley, so we had no reason to suspect that anyone could control the magic."

"If the book was so dangerous, why keep it in the temple, near Hiasyntar Ku'lai?" Erik asked.

Lepkin nodded. "It was always the plan to do so," he

explained. "From the first Keeper on down to me, we have always kept the book in the chamber you found it in. We let others assume that we either had it on our person or hid it somewhere far away, but we never moved it away from here. We enclosed it in a mithril box, and placed it in a room with mithril walls to help diminish the book's influence on the realm."

"How did mithril help?" Erik asked.

"Oh, well…" Tatev started to explain but he stopped short and looked to Lepkin with eager eyes and anxiously bit his lower lip.

"Go ahead, librarian," Lepkin said with a relenting smirk.

Tatev smiled wide and nodded excitedly, pushing his spectacles up higher on his nose. "Mithril is not just a superior metal," he started. "It is a special ore that is mined deep in the bowels of Terramyr. The metal itself is pure, and has a dispelling effect on dark magic. So, when Nagar's Secret was encased in mithril, the box itself retarded the magic's power and helped stave off its effects. Then, when the mithril walls were erected, it further hampered the blight's power and it allowed all of the dragons to leave the Middle Kingdom and escape beyond the book's reach. You know, mithril is actually mined in two places in the Middle Kingdom. Roegudok Hall is the site of the first and largest mine, though it dried up in the year…"

Lepkin held up a hand. "That's enough for now," he said.

"Right," Tatev sighed.

"When did Hiasyntar Ku'lai die?" Erik asked.

Lepkin and Tatev shrugged. "It must have been fairly recently. Within the last twenty years or so, since I saw him before that. Though, I am not sure how the former prelate, or the current one for that matter, didn't notice the difference between the two dragons."

"It was dragons who gave man the gift of sight," Tatev said. "But our ability has never equaled that of the dragons. It is possible that a dragon could hide its true nature from the members of our order, especially since only the prelate ever dealt with him. In fact, I was the only other person to know about the dragon. The librarian has the responsibility to inform the new prelate of the dragon's existence, but beyond the two of us, no one else was ever aware, until today that is."

Lepkin put a hand on Erik's shoulder. "We have the beast on

the run. He is wounded, and he will need rest. We should go on the attack and finish what we have started."

Erik looked to the ground and shook his head. "How are we going to beat him? I was supposed to take a test and gain better powers, but instead I have nothing." He looked to the burlap bag. "I don't even know how to defeat the magic in that book."

"For now we will take it one step at a time," Lepkin said. "Instead of concentrating on what we can't do, let us devise a strategy that utilizes what we *can* do." The boy looked up to Lepkin's strong, reassuring gaze and nodded. Lepkin gave one of his few smiles and pulled the sword from his belt. "This blade was given to me when I became the Keeper of Secrets. Now that I have fulfilled one of my tasks, I give it to you, the Champion of Truth."

Erik's eyes looked at the blade and he took it from Lepkin's hands. "For me?" he whispered.

"Alferug told me that you have been able to summon the white fire. Even without taking the Exalted Test of Arophim, I know I have found the true champion. The sword is yours. Wield it in defense of truth, and light."

Erik was about to express his thanks, but he couldn't find the words before Marlin, Dimwater, Jaleal, and Alferug approached. The boy turned to them and could see they had some things on their minds.

"We have been thinking," Lady Dimwater said. "Perhaps we should decide how best to track the dragon and kill it."

Marlin nodded. "If he was able to deceive all of us, then we should not let this opportunity pass us by."

Lepkin nodded. "I agree. First, we need to hide this book again, and then we should seek the dragon, and slay it."

"Where will we hide the book?" Erik asked.

"Only one place to hide it," Lepkin replied. "We will take it to Tualdern."

"The city of the Sand Elves?" Alferug asked.

Lepkin nodded. "It was they who helped us forge the mithril box which holds the book. They have a better understanding than most of its dark powers, and they will be anxious to keep it hidden."

"Plus," Tatev put in. "I doubt anyone would think to look for the book in the place its magic was first used." Erik looked to the librarian questioningly and Tatev smiled and winked. "Tualdern is on the eastern side of Hamath Valley, it is where Nagar first used the magic."

"And it is where countless men, dwarves, and dragons fought tooth and nail over the cursed thing," Faengoril growled.

"It is the best option I can think of," Lepkin said. "The elves keep to themselves for the most part, and hardly anyone ever ventures into Hamath Valley anymore."

"With good reason," Marlin added. "It is not a very welcoming place anymore."

"True," Lady Dimwater said. "But it is the best choice."

"I should take our cavedogs north, back to Roegudok Hall," Faengoril said. "I will inform our king of what has transpired and seek his assistance in defeating the dragon." He turned to Lepkin. "After you place the book with the elves, where will you go?"

"To Ten Forts," he said.

"Right, right," Tatev agreed. "Tu'luh will go back to Demaverung, and Ten Forts is the best place for us to stage our assault."

Alferug glanced to Faengoril briefly and the two nodded sullenly. "We'll see you there as soon as we can raise the army," Faengoril promised.

"I will send my warriors to Fort Drake," Marlin said. "I have only forty men left, and they will be appreciated at Fort Drake. If I take them to Ten Forts, they will not be as useful. I will go with you, though."

"As will I," Jaleal said. "I am with you to the end."

"I am not letting you out of my sight," Dimwater told Lepkin. Her tone was half playful, but still it made Lepkin squirm a bit. The others walked away then, leaving Lepkin, Jaleal, and Erik alone together.

"You know," Lepkin started. "I noticed a few additional scars across my body. Mind telling me why you were so careless as to let someone stab my leg, shoulder, and stomach?"

Jaleal laughed out loud and clapped his hands together. "You should be thankful that you have scars!" he said emphatically. "Before I got to you, they were not so neatly healed."

Lepkin turned on the gnome. "Oh?" he asked.

Jaleal produced his spear. "Aeolbani has more than a couple of useful powers," he said with a big grin. "Why, if it wasn't for me, I bet you would have slept through the whole battle with the dragon." The gnome grinned proudly and stamped the butt of the spear on the ground. "Let's go dragon hunting!"

CHAPTER TWO

Al sat awkwardly in his royal armor, shifting his weight to keep the metal from sticking into his hips. Apparently the dwarves of old were not as well endowed with love handles as Al was. Not that he was fat, on the contrary he was quite stocky and thick, but most of his bulk was solid. However, he did carry just a little bit of fat around the hips.

At least he had talked his footmen into taking off his gauntlets so he could move his arms freely. Wearing the gaudy armor was bad enough, but eating while trapped with stiff arms would have been almost unbearable.

He glanced around the room, noting that most of his dwarves sat to his left around the several long tables that had been arranged in the dining hall. To his right there was a large empty space, and then King Mathias in his high-backed chair of iron and carved wood. Beyond him sat the senators and other members of the court that Al didn't recognize off hand. In the center of the room, between the two long tables, danced a trio of women. They wore midriff bearing shirts of purple silk, with small golden bells along the sleeves. Their baggy, sheer blue pants flowed out as they kicked their legs high and twirled around to the rhythm they made by clapping their hands and tapping their bare feet on the floor. They were entertaining enough, but Al would have preferred to watch dwarven acrobats. Now those were women that could hypnotize with their looks!

He took a sip of his wine.

"Pheasant, milord?" a sultry young voice asked from behind. Al struggled to turn his neck and had to turn his whole torso to see who spoke to him. It was a lady servant, holding a platter with roast pheasant on it. One of the drumsticks was already taken, but otherwise the bird was intact.

"I'll have the other leg," Al said with a sharp nod of his head. He thanked her after she placed it on his plate next to a half-eaten slice of buttered bread and a small hill of fried potato cubes mixed with thin green beans and onions.

Al used his fork to separate the onions from his other

vegetables before eating the potatoes. He knew it wasn't very kingly to be a picky eater, but he had never gotten used to the taste of onions, nor the sour breath they left him with the few times he had choked them down. Besides, what was the point of being a king if you couldn't at least choose to avoid the foods you hate without being reproached for it?

After he finished the last thin green bean he picked up the pheasant leg and took a huge bite off the thickest part. The skin crackled in his mouth and the savory juices ran over his tongue as he pulled the meat free of the bone. It had been a long time since he had enjoyed fire-roasted pheasant. He closed his eyes in delight and savored the bite. Then he washed it down with a swig of sweet red wine.

"Bring out the juggler," one of the senators called out from the other side of the hall. A couple others nodded their approval and shortly thereafter a tall, thin man came walking into the room. The dancing women bowed to King Mathias and then pranced out of the hall, their bells bouncing and sounding with each step.

"My king, and honored guests," the man said with a flourish of his hands and a bow so deep that his head nearly touched the floor. "It is my honor to bring you the latest trend from the jugglers in Hornbeak." He shook his right leg and three juggling pins fell out of his enormous pant leg. A few of the senators laughed, but Al just took another bite of his pheasant.

The juggler then clapped his hands and two assistants came running out to him. They were young, maybe in their early teens. They wore white face paint with black around their eyes and red around their mouths. Each one carried a long stilt, and one also had a stool with him. The juggler turned, climbed up onto the stool and then leapt atop the stilts as soon as the assistants had them in place. The juggler reached down and buckled his feet to the tops of the stilts and walked around the hall, making a show of kicking each stilt out before him.

A couple senators clapped. None of the dwarves did.

Then the assistants went to the three juggling pins and began to juggle between themselves. At the juggler's command, they turned and threw the three pins up to him and he began to juggle while walking on the stilts.

"Good show!" one of the women at the other table called out.

"This is nothing," the juggler explained. "The masters in

Hornbeak have taught me a rare secret in my time there, and now I show it to you!" Each assistant pulled another pin from their own pants and they struck matches to them, lighting them on fire. Then they tossed them up to the juggler on stilts and he incorporated them in with the other three. "Watch carefully," he said as he stopped walking in a circle. He tossed the pins up higher and higher, until they nearly reached the ceiling. Then he made a couple of them collide in air, lighting the others on fire as well and then catching them to throw them back into the rhythm. After all five were on fire, several senators whistled and clapped.

Al watched the fire, entranced by the yellow and red flames as they danced and swirled over the juggler's head. Then, as if on cue the juggler held the brim of his pants out in front of him and the flaming pins went down inside one after the other in rapid succession amidst gasps from the audience. The juggler smiled and snapped his pants closed as he walked around the room. Al watched intently, expecting the man's pants to erupt in flame, but nothing happened. The juggler made three circuits around the room, then he stopped in the center of the room directly in front of the king.

"Now, here is the finale," he said with a sly smile. The man bent down in a quick bow and flipped the latches of his stilts loose before launching into a graceful backflip. The pins flew out the bottom of his pant legs one by one, each reigniting and streaking through the air after him. The man landed on his feet and looked up just in time to catch the first pin and throw it back into the air. He caught each pin effortlessly before throwing it back into the rotation. He juggled them for a few cycles and then clapped his hands twice. Afterward he would wave a hand over each pin as he caught it and threw it for the last time. The instant his hand passed over the wooden pin the flames died. When all of the pins were extinguished he caught them and tossed them to his assistants, who would hold them.

When he finished several senators stood and clapped for him, and even some of the dwarves rapped their knuckles on the table in approval.

"Well done," King Mathias said.

The juggler bowed his head and turned to each table for another bow. As he turned to face Al, the dwarf felt something strange. There was something in the man's eyes that unsettled Al.

Erik and the Dragon

The dwarf king instinctively pulled his knife into his right hand.

The juggler then turned back to the king. "With your permission, I have one more trick," he said.

"Of course," King Mathias said.

The juggler stepped closer to the king and Al tensed. The man twirled around and smiled to the audience. "For the last trick, I need a volunteer," he said.

"I'll do it," Al said.

"Oh, no no no," the juggler replied with a pat of his hands. "I would not dream of it, I am not fit to work with kings, I only perform for them."

Al sighed and watched the man keenly.

"Something wrong," a dwarf soldier asked as he leaned in close.

Al nodded, but said nothing. He watched the juggler turn to the senator that had originally called him out.

"You sir," the juggler said. "Would you be so kind as to join me in the center here?"

The senator nodded and wiped the corners of his mouth with a cloth napkin before walking around the table to join the juggler. The two assistants rushed up and put one of the wooden pins atop the senator's head. Then they turned and gave another pin to the juggler.

"For my last trick, I will knock this pin from our dear senator's head," the juggler said. He paused for effect. "Whilst my assistants juggle flaming pins between me and him." He clapped his hands and the assistants began juggling the three remaining pins in a close circle in front of the senator's face. The juggler turned to the king. "One inch this way or that and I will undoubtedly hit one of my assistants' pins, which will then hit the senator." He walked close to the two assistants and passed a hand over each pin as it passed in front of him, reigniting the pins. Then he turned and walked close to the king.

"Shall we take bets?" one of the senators jested.

"Fifty gold says the juggler sets our dear senator on fire," one of the women said.

"I'll take that bet," one of the men shouted out.

"Are we ready?" the juggler asked. He held the narrow end of his pin in both hands. He glanced to his right and left, giving Al a sly wink as he caught the dwarf's stare.

Al slid his arm back and prepared to throw his knife.

The juggler wound up over his shoulder and gave a slight, almost imperceptible twist of his wrist. Then he turned wildly toward the king. Al sprang into action and threw his knife. It whistled through the air and sunk deep into the juggler's hand, throwing the performer's aim off. A dagger *clinked* off the side of King Mathias' chair and the juggler turned to run away but the dwarves and king's guard were upon him like bees on the first flower of spring. Within moments the man was hauled away to the dungeon screaming and shouting, with his assistants being dragged in chains behind him.

The senator in the middle shrank away, staggering back to the table. "It wasn't me, I swear!" he said. "I only knew that a juggler was hired, but I didn't have anything to do with this!"

"Take him," King Mathias said sternly. "We will find the truth of the matter." The king's guard moved in and took the senator away.

Al moved over to King Mathias and picked up a wooden handled dagger. "It was well made," he said as he set the weapon down in front of King Mathias.

"Yes," Mathias agreed. "Hiding it in the juggling pin was clever," he said.

One of the other dwarves approached and slid the dagger back into the pin and then gave it a twist to lock the dagger in place. "It seems your security has overlooked a very basic protocol," he said.

King Mathias shook his head. "I have employed this juggler before," he said. "We have never had any issues before."

"I will look into it," Senator Mickelson promised as he took the weapon and unlocked the dagger. He slid it almost all of the way out before replacing it inside and locking it again. "Clever indeed," he said. "You can hardly notice anything with the pin," he said. "The seam lines up perfectly with the paint, and would be extremely hard to see."

"Then perhaps it is time to call off the festivities," Al said curtly. "There is a war out there, whether we like it or not, and pretending it doesn't exist will only give the enemy more opportunities to strike."

Mathias nodded and sighed as he leaned back in his chair. "I will not spend my final days in hiding," he said wearily. "I am tired

Erik and the Dragon

of staying in my tower. I would rather go out by an assassin's blade than gagging on my own spittle in my bed."

Al looked to Mickelson and then put a hand on King Mathias' shoulder. "I understand wanting to escape the trappings of being king more than most," he said.

"Yes, but what about the trappings of being old and sick?" Mathias countered. "Every night I close my eyes wondering whether I shall see the sun again."

Mickelson turned away and motioned for everyone to leave. "The feast is ended," he said.

"Horse apples!" Mathias grumbled. "Call the dancers back in, sit down, and let's finish our meal."

Al sniggered to himself and shrugged to Mickelson. "Let's eat," he said.

The room slowly settled down as best as it could and they all resumed eating, though not with the previous merriment that had accompanied the feast before the juggler had come into the room. Even the dancers seemed nervous as everyone finished the meal in silence. After twenty minutes, King Mathias rose from his chair and left the hall without even wishing his guests a good night.

It was then that Al decided to take a walk. He went into an antechamber and had a couple of his footmen help him escape his ridiculous armor before he slipped out into the night.

He followed the winding, cobblestone road to a large, ivory colored villa. The gates were closed for the night, but the guard out front let him slip inside where another servant opened the front door and took him into the drawing room, where he found Braun and Lady Lokton sitting and drinking tea.

"Well met," Braun said as he rose from his chair.

"I am happy to see you again," Lady Lokton added. "Tea?" she offered.

Al shook his head. "I just came from the banquet, I don't think I should put anything more inside, else I might pop." He grinned and patted his stomach, making an effort to stick it out far enough to draw a stifled giggle from Lady Lokton. "Not a bad place to stay," Al noted as he looked around the drawing room. His eyes went to a collection of pinned butterflies neatly arranged inside a glass case that hung from the wall.

"King Mathias has been very generous," Lady Lokton agreed. "We are sharing the villa with another family, and a few of the masters from Kuldiga Academy."

"Really?" Al asked. "Who else?"

"Myself and Master Gorin," Lady Arkyn said from behind as the two of them walked into the room. The blonde half-elf bowed her head slightly. "I heard that since the last time we saw each other, you have been named king of Roegudok Hall."

"Bah," Al harrumphed with a quick, dismissive wave. Then he looked up to the mountainous man next to her and nodded at him. "I have heard tales about you and your hammer," Al said respectfully.

"I have a few tales to tell," Gorin grinned and slightly inclined his head toward the dwarf. "To what do we owe the pleasure of your visit?"

Al's face turned sour, the smile melting away to be replaced by a scowl forming under a knit brow. "Someone attempted to murder King Mathias during the banquet," Al said.

The others gasped and came closer to him in the room. "A juggler, claimed he was from Hornbeak, and then he tried to put a dagger through the king's heart."

"Who caught him?" Braun asked.

"I did," Al replied evenly. "I can throw a knife better than most." The dwarf shrugged. "Even still, it was close."

"I thought all of the corrupt senators had been destroyed," Lady Lokton put in.

Al nodded. "They were, but there are others who would love the chance at taking the throne."

"And now is the best opportunity to strike," Gorin said. "With the senate crippled and the king making a show of coming down from his tower as he tries to keep peace in the streets, it is the perfect time for any ambitious group to strike."

Al nodded. "Quite right."

The five of them sat in silence for quite some time. Each lost in their own thoughts, worries, and fears while looking for any thread of hope to latch on to. It was Braun who finally broke the quiet.

"What about Lepkin, and Valtuu Temple?" Braun asked.

Al shrugged. "Haven't heard anything as of yet."

"We should go there," Lady Arkyn said. "We could lend our support to Lepkin and the others."

"Sounds as though the king needs us here, what with people

trying to assassinate him and all," Gorin pointed out. "Though, truth be told, I too would rather be afield than stuck inside these walls," he added.

The door opened and a heavy pair of boots *thumped* across the stone floor, coming closer to the drawing room. Lady Arkyn and Gorin glanced to each other and then turned to watch the doorway, expectantly. In walked a captain of the king's guard. Dressed in his red-rimmed, black plate mail and carrying a small, rolled parchment in his left hand. He pointed the brass-capped scroll at Gorin.

"The king has requested your presence, now." Then he turned to Lady Arkyn. "You as well." The captain narrowed his eyes on Al for a moment before arching a brow. "You should come also, King Sit'marihu, the king would appreciate your presence for this next council."

"Council?" Lady Arkyn repeated.

The captain shook his head. "Not here, the king will tell you everything when you arrive. Please, you are expected immediately." The captain stepped back to the side and motioned for them to leave the room before him. Al glanced to Lady Arkyn and nodded.

"I'll call on you again," Al promised Lady Lokton. She nodded politely in return. Al and the others left the villa and went back to the king's tower. The captain led them into a small antechamber on the first floor furnished with a short, round table in the center surrounded by a few chairs.

"King Mathias will be in momentarily," the captain said as he was the first to pull back a chair and sit down. Then he motioned for the others to do the same.

Moments later Grand Master Penthal entered the room and took a seat next to Al.

Al leaned over and whispered. "Any idea what this is about?" Grand Master Penthal held up a pair of fingers and remained tight-lipped. Al could see by the heavy look in Penthal's eyes that the subject was not going to be pleasant.

King Mathias walked in, holding a couple of loose papers in his hands. Everyone at the table rose to their feet and the king motioned for them to sit. None of them did until he had seated himself. "I have received two disturbing letters," he began. "Grand Master Penthal, would you care to begin?"

Penthal nodded his head and leaned in on his elbows as he

cracked his knuckles in front of his face. Then he took a deep breath and let his hands fall to the table. "Tarthuns have been spotted in the north," he said flatly. "For now, our forces that remain in Livany have repelled them, but they will try again."

"How many?" Gorin asked.

"The first wave was only forty, but our scouts report that there are several hundred amassing near the base of the mountains, and possibly many more on the other side of the range. It is impossible to know for sure at this point." Penthal nodded to the captain, who instantly produced an old map and unrolled it across the table. "Livany is the first defense from this area," Penthal said as he drew his finger from Livany to the mountains in the east. "There is only one pass in the north that can accommodate any significant numbers wanting to pass through the mountains, and we will have the advantage. The problem, is that in order to keep the Tarthuns at bay, I and the other knights will need to return to Livany. We depart tonight."

"Then who will augment the king's guard?" Lady Arkyn asked pointedly.

"I will," Al guessed. The dwarf king glanced over to King Mathias. "I assume you would request my soldiers to remain here?"

Mathias nodded. "I was hoping you would allow them to bolster my men in the city, until the Tarthuns have been repelled."

Penthal tapped his finger on the map. "There are seven knights in my order," he said. "And we each command a company of spearmen and footmen. Altogether we have just over seven hundred warriors at our command. Most of them are veterans, so we do not expect too much trouble."

"If the Tarthuns have a sizeable reserve coming through the pass, then I could send more warriors to the north to reinforce Livany," Al said quickly.

"No," King Mathias said. "If the Tarthuns break through Livany, then it will be left to my soldiers to turn them back."

"With respect," Al started. King Mathias held up a hand and slid the other paper forward.

"There is another matter that will require the dwarves' attention," King Mathias explained. Al reached out and took the proffered paper. His eyes grew wide as he scanned the words and then he dropped the letter as if it burned his fingers.

"By the Ancients," he said in a barely audible whisper.

Erik and the Dragon

"What is it?" Lady Arkyn asked. Al just shook his head and his mouth drooped open.

"Tu'luh the Red has returned," Grand Master Penthal said. He pointed to the letter Al had just read. "This is from Valtuu Temple and it states that…"

Lady Arkyn jumped up from her seat and snatched the letter. She devoured its contents and then slumped back to her chair. "The temple is destroyed," she gasped. "How can Tu'luh be alive?"

"It matters not *how* he returned. It matters only that he *is* here," King Mathias said. "This is why I cannot ask the dwarves to come north. Lepkin and the others are going south to hunt the dragon. I would ask the dwarves to aid him in that quest."

"Erik wasn't able to take the test," Al said with a shake of his head. "What are we to do now?"

Grand Master Penthal laid a hand on the dwarf's shoulder. "My men will hold the north, and yours will go south and slay the beast. Lepkin and the others have him on the run, so now we go to finish him."

"There is more to it than that," Al said.

"Where do I go?" Gorin interrupted.

"South," King Mathias replied. "I want both you and Lady Arkyn to go south and help Lepkin. We must do all we can to slay Tu'luh."

"And what of the assassination attempt?" Lady Arkyn pointed out. "You have enemies here as well."

King Mathias nodded. "That is why the dwarves that are here in the city now will stay with me. I trust them, and they are worth four times as many regular guardsmen."

"Senator Mickelson suggested you name a steward," the captain reminded him. "Just in case."

"Why?" Al snipped. "There is no reason to change the line of authority now."

"Because if *anything* happens to the king, then we need a ruler," the captain pointed out. "Lepkin is needed in the south, Grand Master Penthal goes east, and the senate is not complete. There should be a steward appointed in case—"

"No," King Mathias said definitively. "I already said there will not be a steward. I am king now, and though I may not remember everything as well as I once did, I am still sound. To appoint any of the nobles as a steward would only cause a deeper rift in the kingdom. We all know there is only one noble family that can be fully trusted, and the head of that family is currently in mourning as we speak. I don't trust any of the others with the power and authority that would come with being a steward over the entire Middle Kingdom. Even if there was an honest enough noble, the others would turn on him. My heir is, and can only be, Master Lepkin. That is the end of it."

Al smirked and turned a hard eye on the blushing captain.

"As you wish," the captain said.

"I've been stubborn enough to live this long, I can hold out at least long enough for Lepkin to slay the great wyrm," Mathias added. "And you will see to it that after he is done, he returns to Drakei Glazei." Mathias pointed an old, thin finger at Al and the dwarf king nodded.

"I will get him here in one piece," Al promised.

"I leave within the hour," Grand Master Penthal said.

"I will have my warriors report to you in the morning before sunrise," Al promised King Mathias. "Then I will take Gorin and Arkyn out to Roegudok Hall. As soon as I am able, I will march my army south to Ten Forts."

King Mathias nodded. "Then all is ready. May the gods be with us."

CHAPTER THREE

Gilifan stretched his stiff back and walked up the creaky wooden stairs to the top deck. The salty, somewhat foul air assaulted his nostrils as he opened the door. He hated the smell of low tide, like that of rotting flesh and mushrooms mixed with fish. It always seemed to be low tide in Candlepoint.

"I won't be but an hour," Gilifan remarked to the captain as he stepped onto the gangplank.

"We'll be ready," the captain promised. "I'll have my men pick up some fresh eggs and pickles, and perhaps another crate of oranges."

Gilifan left the ship and stepped onto the newly replaced dock. The boards were strong and bright, much unlike the posts sticking up from the water which were dark, smothered in moss and barnacles, and lined with deep cracks that threatened to set the entire dock adrift if left unattended for much longer. The necromancer wasn't over fond of Candlepoint. The town was old, dark, and dingy. The foul smell hung low in the air even away from the beach. The gutters in the street were lined with brown and black stains and murky, stagnant water that made the low tide smell almost pleasant by comparison. A couple of fishermen mended nets in the street, but otherwise there was very little activity outside until Gilifan made his way deeper into the center of the city.

Candlepoint was filled with squat, brown houses in ill repair. Many had ivy crawling up the sides, winding and intertwining with loose wall boards or snaking under broken shingles along the rooftops. None of the building were very tall, maybe ten or twelve feet high for the largest of the houses. The shops were about the same, with pitched roofs and large beams sticking out the front with pulleys attached. By the looks of the rusty pulleys and the old, fraying rope, none of the shops had seen very good business in the last decade at least. Then again, Candlepoint was not exactly renowned for its trading.

The one building that stood out was the lighthouse that gave the city its name when it was founded some three hundred years prior. The lighthouse stood tall, and even from this distance Gilifan could see it was kept in great repair, as it should be. If the lighthouse were to cease operations, then all of the seafarers would bypass Candlepoint altogether, opting to travel around the islands in the north, up past Kuressar and docking in Fisheye, which was only a day's journey north of Drakei Glazei. The lighthouse, on the other hand, allowed the ships to pass in through the narrow waterway and access Cesvaine and Nurrf, two extremely rich cities that prior to the lighthouse could only be reached by land. Thus, as long as the lighthouse operated effectively, Candlepoint would survive as a community.

The only problem was that the lighthouse only employed one family, and the community had been planned as a trade hub, but that had failed. The seafarer's always found better prices farther along their travels, so other than outfitting and rigging supplies the sailors had little use for Candlepoint. When the hopeful merchant entrepreneurs realized this, they too picked up and left the city, leaving their shops for the less reputable businesses that attract sailors on shore leave. Since the erection of several gambling halls, taverns, and the occasional brothel, Candlepoint became a destination for some ships, but it never became the shining community its name might otherwise suggest.

It was exactly this fact that brought Gilifan here.

He walked through the dingy streets until he found the Red Rat, a tavern painted bright red with a large, dangling wooden sign hanging above the door in the shape of a rat stuffing its snout into a tall glass of mead. Gilifan pushed the door open and stepped inside. A few of the patrons looked up at him, but they hardly paid him any more notice than to glance at the newcomer. The necromancer looked around, eyeing each table briefly.

He saw burly, sea-weary sailors playing cards and nursing metal tankards, a group of merchants sitting in the back corner harassing the barmaid, and a mix of others that all seemed as though they probably should be in a cell somewhere rather than out free on the streets. In his quick survey he saw more daggers and knives than he cared to count, but he wasn't overly worried. He strolled past a large, bald headed man with a patch over his left eye and then snaked between a few of the tables as he made his way to the bar.

Behind the bar a short, stout man with hairy shoulders stood wiping a mug with a gray towel. The man looked to Gilifan and nodded. "What'll it be? Room, mead, or company?"

Gilifan shook his head. "I am here for a meeting," he said as he slid a small, polished hematite stone across the bar.

The barkeep looked down and plucked the stone up in his grubby fingers, eyeing the symbol on top before dropping it into his pocket. "Room three, on your left after you go up the stairs around the back."

Gilifan nodded and placed a pair of copper coins on the bar. Then he made his way through the smoke filled room amidst the patrons' laughter, jeers, and shouts. A few feet in front of him an angry man threw a bunch of cards into another man's face.

"You're a cheat!" the first shouted. "No one wins that many times!"

The second man reached down for a dagger and rose to his feet, but it was too late. The first reached across the table, grabbed the man by his hair and slammed his face down onto the table several times.

The necromancer paused and waited for the fight to play out before walking by. He knew better than to separate a pack of dogs squabbling over bones. A few moments later a trio of mountainous men grabbed everyone at the table and threw them all out through the nearest window, shattering the glass all over the street out front and sending cheers up from the other patrons in the tavern.

"Use the door next time!" the barkeep shouted over the din. "That window is coming out of your pay!"

One of the burly bouncers just shrugged and wiped his hands. Then they all disappeared through a doorway, ducking into a back room until they would be needed again.

Gilifan smirked and continued on his way around the back of the tavern and up the flight of creaky stairs. He found room number three and pushed the door open. The room was darkened, but he didn't mind. He had expected as much. He went in, closed the door behind him, and then snapped his fingers. A small orb of light appeared in the center of the room and illuminated the figure sitting behind a large table, staring at him.

The man was shirtless, but to say he was naked would be inaccurate. Across his upper body were various tribal tattoos. Some weaved into each other, and others stood alone depicting weapons, dragons, or skulls. The man's head was shaved, except for a thick lock of hair in the center of the man's head that was neatly pulled back to form a braided pleat that hung down past his shoulders. A pair of scimitars lay on the table before him and he drummed his impatient fingers near the weapons as he leered at Gilifan.

"So, you are the wizard?" the man asked.

Gilifan looked to the man's beady, black eyes and nodded. "I am," he replied evenly. "And you must be Nerekar."

Nerekar nodded. "I was promised thirty gold for listening," he reminded Gilifan.

The wizard smiled and produced a purse from the folds of his robe. "I have it with me, as well as the additional hundred gold as down payment for your services, should you accept."

Nerekar nodded and pointed to the table. "Put it here."

Gilifan walked to the table and set the purse down. He then pulled a rolled parchment from his left sleeve. The paper was bound with a single brown string, and sealed with a small, round bit of dried wax. "This is my offer."

Nerekar took the parchment and broke the seal with his left index finger. Then he unrolled it and read through the contents. "No," he said flatly as he set the paper on the table before him.

"No?" Gilifan asked. "I was told the great Nerekar never declines an assignment." The wizard's voice showed his displeasure.

Nerekar shook his head. "No one has ever asked for the head of Gariche before," Nerekar replied. He pushed the purse back. "Take your money, all of it, and go."

A pair of Blacktongues emerged from hidden doors in the wall and leveled bows at Gilifan. The necromancer smirked and conjured a quick spell. His orb of light threw small white bolts at each of the Blacktongues and froze them in place like crystal statues.

"What is this?" Nerekar said as he rose and took his scimitars in hand.

Gilifan snapped his fingers and a wave of air slammed into Nerekar, pummeling the wind out of him and making him gasp for breath. "I have little patience," Gilifan said. "Now, I can still release your comrades, though I should destroy them for even daring to raise arms against me. You and I have a deal, Blacktongue! Your people have a debt to repay, and I will see it paid in full. The master demands it."

"You ask too much!" Nerekar said.

Erik and the Dragon

"Is Gariche beyond your reach?" Gilifan asked pointedly.

"No one is beyond *my* reach," Nerekar shot back.

"Then take his head. He is an obstacle and must be dealt with. You will board the ship with me now, and fulfill your duty as you have sworn to do. Your king promised me his best assassin."

Nerekar glared up at him. "I will do this for my king," he growled. "But you will double my price."

Gilifan smiled. "That, I can do," he agreed. "In fact, I will triple it. Consider the extra a retainer. *If* you succeed with Gariche, I will have one more task for you."

"You question my ability?" Nerekar spat.

"Well, to be fair, none of your predecessors have fared well so far with any task we have given them. Lepkin and the boy still walk among the living. Add the fact that you just balked at this assignment and no, it doesn't inspire great confidence."

"I will kill Gariche, and then I would kill the boy too," Nerekar swore.

"That is what I was hoping you would say," Gilifan said with a smile. "Gather what you need and meet me at the docks." Gilifan released his spell from the others and cast a disparaging look their way. "Leave your friends here, I don't care much for them."

Nerekar nodded. In a flash he whirled on his fellow Blacktongues, slitting their throats before they could blink. Then he turned back to Gilifan. "You will not question my resolve again," Nerekar said resolutely.

"That was unnecessary, but I appreciate the sentiment," Gilifan said. He glanced at the two dead bodies and chuckled softly before leaving the room. "Blacktongues are so moody," he said to himself as he left the building and went back out onto the street, making his way to the ship. He pulled his cloak in tighter around his shoulders and grinned. Nerekar would be fun to work with.

CHAPTER FOUR

Erik shifted in his saddle and stretched his neck. He felt a bit awkward being the only person on a horse, but Goliath wouldn't let anyone else ride him and there was no point walking if he didn't have too. Lepkin reached up and handed him a waterskin. Erik took a drink from the waterskin and coughed abruptly when part of it managed to go down the wrong way. His eyes watered and he handed the skin back to Lepkin.

"Shouldn't drink so fast," Lepkin pointed out.

"Thanks for the tip," Erik sputtered with a final cough and a quick wipe across his eyes. "Just my luck, live through battles with warlocks and dragons only to die choking on water while surrounded by allies."

Lepkin smirked and took a quick drink himself. Then he pointed ahead. "Grobung is not far now," he said. "Once we go around this bend in the road, the trees will clear and you will see a dark wall surrounding a lot of buildings. There are some farms there too."

As they went around the bend in the road, it happened as Lepkin said. The thick forest on the left was cut away, giving a wide view of green fields dotted with workers and carts going about their business. A few of the farms also had large pens with sheep or pigs inside. The smell of manure hung in the air heavily, but it wasn't altogether unpleasant. There was something about it that put Erik at ease. Almost like a sense of coming home, though he had never been here before in his life.

The farms ended at the base of tall, stark walls made of black bricks. The iron portcullis was up, allowing free passage in and out of the city, and only a few guards stood near the gate. Erik started to count the soldiers he saw, but quickly gave up once they passed through the gate. It seemed the town was two thirds soldiers, and only one third villagers.

"The commander at Fort Drake is the governor here," Lepkin explained. "The town essentially exists to service the fort. The farms you saw outside the walls produce food for the soldiers. There is a large lumber industry here as well, with a mill a few hundred yards to the south of Grobung."

"Smiths are here in abundance as well," Lady Dimwater added.

Erik could already hear the ringing hammers pounding away the day's work, though he could not see any of the shops nearby. He dismounted from Goliath and hitched the horse to a post near the gate and then the three of them walked quickly to catch up with the group. A few of the townsfolk stopped and looked at them, but most paid them no mind. They were busy bartering with soldiers or carrying loads of wood or grains to and fro through the streets. The soldiers hardly looked their way at all, except for a group of younger recruits who pointed at Dimwater and whispered among themselves.

Erik looked to his left and saw a square building façade with red lamps in the window. "The Alley Cat," he read aloud as he looked to the wooden sign of a suggestively posed black cat.

"Keep your eyes over there," Lepkin said as he reached over, grabbed Erik's head in his hand and turned it away. "There's nothing you need to see in that building."

Dimwater nodded approvingly and they quickly pushed him along the road until they came to a large inn. Lepkin, Dimwater, and Erik broke off from the group and went inside, while Marlin and the others continued along into the center of the town.

"Where are they going?" Erik asked.

"To buy supplies," Dimwater said.

"And to send dispatches out to the commander at Fort Drake as well as another to King Mathias," Lepkin added.

"Shouldn't we go with them?" Erik asked.

Lepkin shook his head. "No, we have something else to do." The three of them pushed through the doors and the pleasant, savory aroma of roasting lamb washed over them.

Erik's stomach grumbled and his mouth started to water almost instantly. "Maybe some food?" he asked.

Dimwater nodded and led them to a secluded table in a quaint alcove with a bay window overlooking a small patch of garden in the back of the inn. No sooner had the three sat down than a short, older woman came over with a big smile and a small carafe of water.

"What can I get for you?" she asked as she gave Erik a wink.

"What's on the menu?" Lepkin asked.

"We have roast lamb with scalloped potatoes under melted cheese, or we also have a beef brisket with sweet yams and grilled asparagus."

"No pork?" Lepkin asked.

"No, I'm sorry dear, but the soldiers have taken the last of our roast pig."

"That's too bad," Lepkin said. He turned to Erik and then pointed out the window. "They have a special pit in the back where they bury the pig and cover it with hot coals where it roasts for hours with sweet peppers, onion, and garlic. It is to die for, and half the reason I was looking forward to coming here."

The woman sniggered. "Well that is half the reason the soldiers come here too," she said. "Then she looked to Erik and stifled her next sentence. "So," she said after regaining her composure. "What can I get for you?"

Lepkin looked to Dimwater. The sorceress looked to Erik and then back to the woman. "We'll have the lamb."

"Alright dear, and what to drink? We have ale, mead, spiced wine, and we have apple cider as well."

"I would like the cider," Erik piped in.

Lepkin held up a finger. "It's not like the cider you get at the academy," he said. "The boy will have water, or plain apple juice if you have that."

The woman frowned. "'Fraid we don't have any juice," she said. "That isn't a product we get asked for much, but I can bring another carafe of water for him."

"That will do," Lepkin said approvingly.

Then the lady turned and walked away, her black and gray pony-tail bouncing with each step.

"Like I said, this town exists to sell their products and services to the fort and its soldiers. She might call it cider, but it is basically beer made from apples."

"Sounds interesting," Lady Dimwater said. "Perhaps I will ask for a glass."

Erik sat back in his chair and looked out the window. He watched a bluebird light on the branches of a birch tree outside, dropping a twig into a nest-in-progress. Then the bird took off, only to return a few moments later with another twig and a bit of spider's web in its beak. As soon as the new material was in place the bird would fly away for a few minutes and come back with

Erik and the Dragon

more to work on its nest.

"A bit late for the bird to be making the nest," Lepkin noted.

Erik turned form the window and looked to his tutor. "Maybe his other nest got destroyed," he said.

Lepkin nodded. "He won't likely be able to have a mate this year," he pointed out. "Seems pointless to build a nest without having a mate, or hatchlings."

Erik shook his head. "I don't know, he may as well prepare now," he said with a shrug. "Perhaps he has a mate, or maybe he will have one next spring."

Lepkin smiled. "We are not unlike the bluebird," he said.

Erik narrowed his eyes and drew his brow together.

Lepkin nodded and looked back to the bird. "I don't know that his first nest was destroyed, but whatever the reason, he is building a nest now, so that he can have a better future. We are like that. We are trying to build a better future for the Middle Kingdom. One where we can each have the hope of resting safely."

"That's putting it very simply," Erik said.

"But the basic principle is the same," Lepkin countered. "The bird works for a future that he hopes for, but is not certain will come. He toils to make a safe place for that future. We do the same. We are hoping for a future that is better than what we now have."

"I didn't take the test," Erik said abruptly. "We don't even know if I am the Champion of Truth."

Lepkin tapped a finger on the table. "If you were not the Champion of Truth, then the sword would not burn white for you," he countered. "You are the champion, I am sure of it."

"But how will we win? I have no special powers. I can't even see auras like Marlin can. How will I defeat the magic, or the dragon for that matter? I am just a boy."

"Just a boy?" Lady Dimwater echoed sarcastically. "You accompanied me to Spiekery to defeat a shadowfiend, do you remember?"

"You fought the demon," Erik said.

"But you helped me confront him, and then you fought the swordsman as well. Not any mere boy would do that."

"Let us not forget about the tournament at Kuldiga Academy either," Lepkin said. "None of us helped you then."

Erik nodded. "But I was only fighting other kids."

Lepkin grew impatient and crossed his arms. "Well then, how do you explain turning into a dragon and laying waste to the corrupt senators in Drakei Glazei, or defeating the warlock who came to attack your home?"

"I only accessed your power," Erik countered. "And the warlock was asleep."

"Being humble is one thing," Dimwater said. "But you are being annoying at the moment. You should at least acknowledge the things you have accomplished. It is not any boy who could do the things you have done, even with our help."

Lepkin nodded and leaned forward. "You didn't access *my* power," he said.

Erik looked up quickly and met Lepkin's fierce eyes. He opened his mouth, but the words didn't come out. Lepkin arched a brow and nodded decisively.

Just then the serving lady returned with a large platter heaped with skewered lamb and scalloped potatoes with cheese. Erik looked at the food and somehow it seemed less inviting to him than knowing what Lepkin meant. As soon as the lady turned and left Erik looked back to Lepkin.

"What do you mean?"

"It was *your* power," Lepkin said casually as he took a piece of lamb and plopped it into his mouth.

"My power?" Erik repeated. "What do you mean?"

Lepkin grinned widely, which was still something that Erik was trying to get used to. The big man finished his bite and looked to Dimwater. She nodded and glanced to Erik. Lepkin returned the nod and wiped the corner of his mouth with his sleeve. "Have you ever heard of the Sahale?" he asked.

Erik shook his head. "What is a Sahale?"

"You," Lepkin said pointedly. "You are a Sahale." Lepkin ran his thumb along the edge of the table as he phrased his next sentence. "You remember why I said I chose you to be my apprentice?" he asked.

Erik nodded. "Yes," he said.

"Well, there was another reason besides what I told you." He was quick to add, "What I said about your character and experience was true. Those were very important factors in my choosing *you*, but there is something else that I was looking for as well. For you to understand, I need to explain a few things."

Erik and the Dragon

Lepkin pushed the platter of food toward Erik and motioned for him to take some food. Erik took some meat and scalloped potatoes while Lady Dimwater poured water into his cup for him.

"Thank you," he told her.

She smiled and dished herself some food as well.

Lepkin then continued. "The Sahale are a special race. Their origin is extremely unique. During the time of the Ancients, long before Nagar the Black ever was known in this realm, there lived a very beautiful woman. The tales say her hair was red as fire, and hung down to her waist. She was slender, almost like a she-elf, but much taller of course. Her eyes were green, like emeralds, and her skin was a light golden brown. When she sang, the birds would come from miles around to listen to her music. Well, one day, after her fame had spread throughout the Middle Kingdom, a dragon came to listen to her sing. He was so captivated by her that he came every day thereafter to listen to her. When she would stop singing, he would tell her tales of the lands beyond the mountains.

"The two fell in love, which was unprecedented. The dragon went to Hiasyntar Ku'lai, and the Father of the Ancients devised a magic that would turn the dragon into a human so he could be with his love. As time went along the two of them married and had many children. The Ancients had no way of knowing, but the dragon blood still flowed through the veins of his children."

Lady Dimwater swallowed a bite and jumped in. "The first one to change into a dragon was one of the couple's grandchildren. It happened on the girl's seventeenth birthday. No one knows exactly what sparked the change, but it happened."

"That's right," Lepkin said. "As you can imagine, the family tried to keep it a secret, but a secret like that can't remain hidden for long. As each of the children and grandchildren married and produced more children, the gift spread. After a couple of generations they began to be called the Sahale, which means the 'gifted ones' in elvish."

"I am a Sahale?" Erik asked incredulously.

Lepkin nodded and pointed behind his ear. "You bear the mark of the Sahale."

"What is that?"

"A small, crescent shaped birthmark behind your right ear," Lepkin replied. "Let me finish with the history, and then I will answer your questions."

Erik nodded and set his food down. He was too excited to be distracted by the food or the grumbling in his stomach.

"As is the way of all creatures, some of the Sahale were good and honest, while others abused their gift for power and glory. Eventually a council of mages was created to eradicate them all, declaring the Sahale to be abominations. The Ancients tried to persuade the humans, but at that time the king did not listen. He cast the dragons out of Drakei Glazei, declaring that any dragon that dared return during his reign would be deemed an enemy and killed on sight. He raised his armies to support the mages in their hunt of the Sahale and the Ancients left Drakei Glazei."

"Where did they go?" Erik asked.

"That is when they established Valtuu Temple," Lady Dimwater said. "A large group of humans defied the king and set up an autonomous region to protect the Ancients."

"Why would the dragons need protection?" Erik asked. "If there were many of them, couldn't they have just fought the humans?"

Lepkin nodded. "Some of them did, and most of them were slain. The Ancients, however, chose to flee rather than burn the kingdom they loved so dearly. The dwarves at that time acted as a buffer so no army could reach Valtuu Temple. The Ancients thought if they left the humans alone long enough, then they would realize their mistake."

"But they didn't," Dimwater said. "Not until most of the Sahale had been destroyed, that is."

Lepkin nodded sourly. "It is a dark day in our history," he said. "We killed most of an entire race, nearly wiping them all off the face of the land. All because a couple of them had abused their power and the king decided *all* of them were evil." Lepkin sighed. "A few did manage to live, of course. No one knows exactly how many survived the purge, but rumors and legend suggest that as many as twelve might have escaped. Of those who did survive, a few were able to have families and the gift continued to be passed down from generation to generation, though the families generally made every effort to conceal their true identity. On occasion, a person would come to Valtuu Temple, claiming to be a Sahale and asking for magic to make them normal, but there wasn't anything to be done. Hiasyntar Ku'lai vowed not to interfere anymore for fear of creating more problems.

"When the king of that time passed away, his son continued the hunting of Sahale. He put a bounty of one thousand gold pieces out on any and every Sahale. So, any time a rumor sprang up about a Sahale sighting, warriors and hunters would flock to the area and kill the Sahale."

Lepkin took a drink of water and arched a brow as he looked off distantly through the window for a moment. "The dwarves then went to war with the humans until they forced the royal family out of the Middle Kingdom and in their place they appointed a new king. The new king was a wise wizard, who most of the people loved at that time. He had, in fact, been one of the first mages to hunt the Sahale, but through the years he had recanted his ways and he was quick to end the hunting of the Sahale. Some say it is because one of his daughters married a Sahale, but no one knows for sure."

"The Ancients came back then, and eventually there was peace between the humans and dragons again," Lady Dimwater said.

"I never knew that there was a war with the dwarves," Erik said.

"It is a part of our history that we do not talk about often. We are not proud of it, and so we prefer to let it fade into the past," Lepkin said. "However, it was many centuries ago. I don't even think that Al's great grandfather was alive during that time."

Erik took a bite of food and chewed it quickly, washing it down with a swig of water. "And I am a Sahale?" he asked.

Lepkin nodded. "I am getting to that," he said. "You bear the mark, as I already said. This mark is a special way to identify the Sahale. Males have it behind the right ear and females have it behind the left."

"How did you learn about the mark?" Erik asked.

Lepkin grinned. "I am the Keeper of Secrets," he said with a smirk. "There are quite a few things that I know."

"The dragon who chose you to be the keeper told you then?" Erik guessed.

"Precisely," Lepkin said. "It is important that I know how to identify a Sahale, because the dragons knew that only a Sahale would be able to use the magic of Allun Rha to defeat Nagar's Secret."

Erik scrunched his brow. "How did they know that?" he

asked. "Allun Rha was a wizard."

Lepkin held a finger in the air. "He was a Sahale," he corrected. "He was a wizard, it is true, but there was something about him that protected him from the power of Nagar's Secret. During a battle before Hamath Valley, he fought with Nagar and Tu'luh. They tried to use the magic on him, but it did not work. So, after Allun Rha and his army forced Nagar and Tu'luh to retreat, he went to work on the counter spell. It is a magic that he wrote in a book called The Illumination. He managed to complete it before the Battle of Hamath Valley and it was there that he used it to protect our allies when they fought Tu'luh's army."

"But it wasn't perfect," Dimwater said. "It protected the army and gave them an advantage, but it did not destroy Nagar's magic. Worse still, Allun Rha was lost in the battle, as was his book. No one has been able to recover it."

"So, I am the Champion of Truth because I am a Sahale?" Erik asked.

"No," Lepkin said decisively. "Through the years, a few Sahale have been found. I myself found three Sahale before you, but I did not see in them the same potential I see in you."

"What do you mean?" Erik asked

"Something about the Sahale protects them from Nagar's magic. Somehow the mixture of human and dragon blood has created an inert resistance to it."

"The Sahale also have a great potential as magic users," Dimwater said. "Marlin clued me in to how your magic is different than mine, or another wizards, and it does have great potential indeed."

Lepkin nodded. "However, being a Sahale is not enough. I still had to look for the right one. Someone with character and the will to choose the right in the face of overwhelming temptation. Just because someone is immune to the magic does not mean that they won't choose to abuse Nagar's Secret the same way that Tu'luh and Nagar would."

"So that is why Tu'luh wanted me to join him," Erik said. "He knew the book couldn't force me, and he hoped that I would choose to use it."

"Precisely," Lepkin said.

"He showed me a terrible vision," Erik commented. "One where the world ends because of the wars and strife that flood the

Erik and the Dragon

lands. He said using Nagar's Secret would avert the end of the world."

Lepkin reached over and grabbed Erik's chin and turned his face up to look into his eyes. "What is better, to live as slaves, or to die as free souls?"

Erik sighed. "I don't know anymore," he said with a shrug. "When I was with Tu'luh it seemed clear. Freedom was the better choice. Now, though, I don't know."

"Nagar was not looking for peace when he created the magic with Tu'luh," Dimwater said.

Lepkin shot her a look but she waved him off.

"You tell him about the Sahale and don't want to explain who Nagar really was? The boy should know."

"Let's eat for now," Lepkin said. "We can join with Tatev after the meal and Erik can talk with him about Nagar."

Dimwater frowned, but she didn't argue. The three of them stopped talking then and worked at eating the mound of cooling food before them. The savory smells and flavors that had so intrigued Erik before now seemed hollow and stale as he contemplated what he had just learned. He didn't like the idea that so much had been kept from him. He could understand the reasons, but he still didn't like it.

What else do you know that I don't? Erik wondered to himself.

After the food was finished Lepkin wiped the left corner of his mouth and looked to Erik. "I know it is a lot to take in," he said. "I want you to know that I would not have told you if I didn't truly believe you were ready to hear it."

Erik nodded and finished his last bite.

"We are here with you, until the end," Lepkin said. "I will help you as best I can. As I also have the gift of changing into dragon form, I can tell you quite a lot."

Erik scrunched his nose and peered at Lepkin. "If you are also a Sahale, then how did Nagar's Secret change you at the temple?" he asked.

Lepkin smirked and shook his head. "I am not a Sahale," he said. "I have a gift, but it is not the same. My gift is a temporary ability given to me through magic. Yours comes from a direct lineage. Being a dragon is in your blood. That is the difference. You have the combined blood of human and dragon."

"It is like combining magics," Dimwater said. "Combining the blood of the two races has somehow created an immunity among the Sahale that prevent the twisted magic from subjecting your heart to its will."

"The other difference is I cannot pass my gift on to anyone," Lepkin said. "Whereas you may pass your blood on to your future children."

Children? That was an interesting thought.

"Enough for now," Dimwater said. "Let's retire for the evening."

Erik and Lepkin finished eating while Dimwater rose from the table and disappeared around the corner to go upstairs. The lamb was cold now, but still delicious. The hostess came back then with a small plate topped with dark red cherries and set it before Erik with a wink and a smile before turning away.

"She used to have a son," Lepkin said. "He died when he was about your age."

Erik looked at the cherries and then glanced up after the hostess. "How did he die?" Erik asked.

"He took ill one winter," Lepkin said. "I was here then, passing through on my way south. I left the town only a few days before he died. She has come a long way since then though," he said with an admiring smile. "It's hard to pick up the pieces after something like that, but she has done well."

"What of her husband?" Erik asked.

"Never had one," Lepkin said with a shrug. "Or if she had then I am not for knowing." Lepkin set several gold coins on the table. "But I am always sure to tip her a little extra whenever I pass through." Erik nodded, realizing that Lepkin was still teaching him what it truly meant to be a knight.

Erik ate the cherries, biting them in half and using his tongue to pluck the pit out from the fruit before he spit it onto his plate.

"Use your fingers to put the pit down," Lepkin said. "It isn't proper to spit it out onto your plate."

Erik blushed a little, but did as Lepkin instructed him.

"I hope you exhibited better manners while you were in my body," Lepkin said teasingly.

Erik smiled. "I guess that depends on what you consider to be good manners," Erik said with a stifled chuckle.

"Indeed," Lepkin agreed as he reached over and took a pair of

Erik and the Dragon

cherries by the stem.

Once the food was gone they went up the stairs and followed the hall to the end. Lepkin opened the last door on the left and found Dimwater chatting with Tatev.

"Ah, there they are," Tatev said with a quick wave.

"How long have you been here?" Lepkin asked.

Tatev shrugged. "A matter of minutes, not long," he said. "We were just discussing the Immortal Mystics, and where we might be able to find The Illumination," Tatev announced.

"Allun Rha's book," Lepkin noted with a quick nod as he motioned for Erik to go and sit next to Tatev.

"Precisely," Tatev said. "I was pouring over everything we had in the library on the subject, and I think I may have found a lead. I told Marlin about it, of course, but things kept getting in the way so that I never got around to actually checking it out before..." Tatev's words grew quiet and he gazed down at the floor for a moment. "Well, before the temple was destroyed," he said after a moment. Then he looked up again with a wide grin. "But I saved the books we need," he said emphatically. He raised a small brown book in his right hand and waved it gently in the air. "This is The Canyon's Heart, written by Magus Siriali in the year—"

Lepkin raised a hand. "What does it say?" he said.

Tatev bristled and snorted at Lepkin's impatience. "It mentions that Allun Rha passed through Gerharon on his passage east, and stayed at the monastery for many days."

"It says *that*?" Lepkin questioned. "It actually says that *Allun Rha* went to Gerharon?"

"Well, no," Tatev said with a frown. He crinkled his nose and pushed his thick spectacles up on his nose. "But it describes a man who matches Allun Rha's description and says that he spent many days in the monastery studying and inquiring about the 'wise ones' in the east." Tatev got up from his chair and then pointed to a passage in the book. "It also says that when he left, he took the form of a winged serpent and flew over the mountains in the east in search of greater knowledge."

Lepkin took the book from Tatev.

"Gentle!" Tatev rebuked. "It's very old, and it is the only copy we have in the Middle Kingdom. It took me a decade to find a book from Gerharon."

Lepkin nodded and patted the air with his left hand as his eyes coursed over the page. "You might be right," Lepkin said.

"Might be?" Tatev repeated. "I *am* right," Tatev insisted. "*I am always* right."

Dimwater put a hand to her mouth to hide her grin, but Erik noticed it and had to look away to keep from laughing himself. Lepkin handed the book back to Tatev and went to sit next to Dimwater.

"Either way," Lepkin started. "We will have to find Tu'luh before we go east chasing after stories. Especially if we are to go through Gerharon."

"What is Gerharon?" Erik asked.

Lepkin started to open his mouth but Dimwater put a hand on his knee and stopped the words in the man's throat. "We can talk about that when the time comes," she said simply. "For now, let's concentrate on the task at hand."

Lepkin nodded. "Tatev, where is Marlin now?"

"He is purchasing some supplies and preparing the others to go north to Fort Drake."

"The others?" Lepkin replied.

Tatev nodded. "Yes, I am staying with you. I have knowledge that will be useful."

Erik had to give Lepkin credit. He knew that his tutor didn't have much patience for Tatev, neither did he for that matter, but Lepkin was able to keep an impassive expression on his face as he nodded and lay back on the bed, stretching out behind Dimwater.

"Tatev," Lepkin began, "Erik has just learned some things about the Sahale race. Perhaps you would be so kind as to take him outside and discuss that in some detail." Dimwater nudged Lepkin with an elbow. "I would appreciate it if you could also illuminate Nagar's history for him, and explain why he joined with Tu'luh."

"Very well," Tatev said happily. "Any other specific aspects I should focus on?"

Lepkin shook his head. "If you are going to remain with us, then you can help Erik learn as much as possible that will assist him master his gift. I am sure you will hit all the relevant points."

Erik's shoulder slumped. He was more than a little curious about the topic, but he was not excited about the chosen tutor. Still, when Tatev turned to leave, Erik put a smile on his face and went out the door with him.

"You sure rushed them both out the door," Dimwater

Erik and the Dragon

commented.

"I have something to ask you, Lepkin," Lepkin said. Lady Dimwater turned around to look into his eyes and smiled warmly as she reached out and stroked his hair to the side. "We don't know what will happen when we find Tu'luh," Lepkin said. "But, for whatever life I have left, I want to spend it as your husband." Lepkin took Dimwater's hand in his. "We have already lost so much of what we could have had together. I don't want to miss anymore. Now that Orres is no longer an obstacle, I don't want to wait another day." Lepkin slid off the bed, cradling Dimwater's hand in his. His voice cracked nervously. "Will you marry me?"

"I am, and have always been yours," she said.

"Marlin could officiate the ceremony," Lepkin said. "He could do it tonight."

Dimwater shook her head and put her fingers on Lepkin's lips. "No, not here," she said. "In Tualdern. I always envisioned us getting married in the grand city of the elves," she replied.

Lepkin grinned quietly and nodded his head. He bent down to kiss Dimwater's hand, then he stretched upward to kiss her mouth gently. "In Tualdern then," he said. Then he gave her another, longer kiss, pressing into her lips firmly and wrapping his arms around her waist, pulling her body close to his.

Just then the door burst open and in walked Marlin. The couple startled and turned to see a smile flash across the man's face and he held his arms open wide.

"It is good to see you both reunited at last," he said.

Lepkin blushed.

"Impeccable timing," Dimwater said coyly.

"Oh?" Marlin asked as he strode into the room. "Was I about to miss something?"

Lepkin shook his head. "We have decided to be married in Tualdern," he said. "And you are going to do the honor of officiating."

Marlin folded his arms and shook his head with a big grin plastered across his face. "Well, it's about stinking time!" he said.

CHAPTER FIVE

Al woke early and dressed quickly. He crept through the halls quietly. He had already told his warriors what the plan was, and now he desired to leave without another one of them stopping him and insisting on being his bodyguard. *As if I need one!* Al thought to himself as he passed through the doors and into the early, cool morning light. He saw Gorin and Lady Arkyn waiting for him.

"Get enough beauty sleep?" Gorin chided.

Al arched a brow and tugged at his beard. "You do know you are speaking to a *king* right?" Al quipped.

Gorin shrugged. "I don't recognize kings shorter than me," Gorin shot back with a wide grin.

"That would be all of them," Al said as he eyed the tall, mountain of a man. Then he chuckled. "But, I guess that's your point."

Gorin smiled appreciatively and the three of them made haste for the gate.

"Grand Master Penthal left about two hours ago," Lady Arkyn noted as they wound their way through the streets.

Al nodded. "He was never one for procrastinating," the dwarf said. "I am just glad he is on our side."

"Will I fit in your mountain?" Gorin asked out of the blue.

Al huffed. Gorin's tone was joking, but the look on the man's face hinted that perhaps the warrior was seriously contemplating the question. "You aren't *that* tall." Al waited a moment and then added, "You will have to hunch over a bit through the first tunnel though."

Gorin grumbled under his breath, but Al let it go.

A guard hailed the trio and waved them over to the smaller side gate as they approached. He wished them safe journeys as they exited Drakei Glazei. They went to the stable and Lady Arkyn produced the charter given to them the night before and handed it to the king's guard there.

"How many will you need?" he asked.

"Just three," Lady Arkyn said.

The guard nodded and looked to Al. "Can you ride a full sized horse?"

Al folded his thick arms across his chest. "Is a frog's butt water-tight?"

The guard frowned sourly and turned away, then halted and looked back to Gorin. "I'll see if I have a draught horse for you," he commented wryly.

"A frog's butt?" Gorin asked after the guard was out of earshot.

Al nodded. "It's a common enough expression," he said.

"Where?" Gorin asked. Al started to respond but Gorin waved him off. "Nevermind, I don't actually want to know."

Al shrugged and the three of them waited quietly for the guard to return with the horses. When the man brought the steeds out they quickly mounted and settled what they could into the saddle bags. Lady Arkyn rode a chestnut colored horse, while Al sat atop a black and white paint horse. Gorin sat on a great brown draught horse with tufts of white fur flaring out from behind each hoof. The beast was almost as muscular as the hulking warrior, and only made him look all the larger as he straightened his back in the saddle and adjusted his warhammer.

"Wait for me," came the almost inaudible shout. The three turned and looked up the road to see a shirtless man running toward them awkwardly. "Wait!" he called out again.

"By the divines," Lady Arkyn gasped.

"Peren!" Gorin announced happily. He reared his mount in the air and the great horse neighed and turned to gallop off toward Peren. Lady Arkyn and Al urged their horses to keep pace, but inevitably the larger horse pulled away from them and reached Peren a few seconds before the others.

Gorin leapt down from his horse and went to crush the man in a hug, but he stopped short and kept his distance. "What in the name of Hammenfein happened?" he asked.

Al and Lady Arkyn glanced to each other when they saw the burns.

"I mostly managed to escape," Peren said as he lifted his arms and examined the burns.

"You should not be out in the elements with uncovered wounds," Lady Arkyn said.

Peren smiled. "I'm just happy to be walking among the living."

"How did you escape?" Al asked.

"Not sure," Peren said. "I was staring into the firedrake's gaping maw and everything seemed to blur together. It was as if time almost stood still as I reflected on my life. I called to mind all of the spells I could think of, but none of them seemed to be strong enough to reverse the firedrake back into his original form. Then, all I remember thinking about was how before it had changed into a firedrake, it had been a cat hunting a rat. Then I thought how ironic it was that I caught the cat only to end up being the mouse." Peren shrugged and shook his head. "The next thing I know I woke up in a mouse's body. Somehow I had changed myself into a mouse. I was inside my own shoe, and the battle was over."

"Figures," Gorin said. "If anybody would sleep through a fight, it would be you."

Peren shrugged. "I assume we won, if the three of you are here."

Lady Arkyn nodded. "We lost most everyone else," she said. "But we defeated the enemy."

"What of Lepkin?" Peren asked.

"He is well," Al said.

"There is a lot to tell," Gorin said. "But first, you need to tell us why the firedrake you made turned on our own men."

Peren shook his head emphatically. "It wasn't me," he said. "I turned the rat into a wyvern easily enough, but the cat resisted my spell entirely. It was someone else, someone with far greater powers than I have."

"No matter now," Lady Arkyn said. "We slew the enemy's army in its entirety."

"Save the two Lepkin allowed to escape," Gorin pointed out.

Peren nodded. "Where are we going?"

"We?" Al asked hesitantly. "You should probably go in and see the healers."

Peren shook his head. "I may have been a mouse for a while, but I am still a man, complete with backbone and ready to move on. Lady Arkyn here can patch me up as we travel." He thumbed at the blonde half-elf and grinned proudly.

"Perhaps you should stay and rest," Gorin said. "King Sit'marihu has a point."

"King?" Peren echoed curiously. "I thought your brother sat

upon the throne?"

"No longer," Al said.

"Interesting," Peren mused. "In any case, I'll be going with you. What is our mission?"

Gorin held his arms out to the side and shrugged to Lady Arkyn. "He's as stubborn as a mule."

"I can help with the burns," Lady Arkyn said. "But I won't be much use if you get infected. The burns cover a lot of your body."

"They are not as bad as they look," he said. "I have some healing ability myself, and I have worked on them as I traveled here."

"You will need a horse," Al said.

Peren pointed behind them. "Looks like he is bringing me one."

The others turned to see the king's guard pulling a fourth horse by the reins. "I was going to prepare a fourth anyway, in case you needed an extra," he said. "Looks like I was right."

"Thank you!" Peren said as he strode past the others and clambered atop the horse from the right side. The horse pulled away a bit and forced Peren to stretch his torso. The man grimaced a bit, but kept silent and didn't utter a single complaint as he struggled to get atop the mount.

"Usually you are supposed to climb up on the left side," Gorin pointed out.

Peren exhaled slowly as he straightened himself in the saddle and gestured for the others to take the lead.

Al nudged his steed and the others all fell in with him as he ran his horse south by south east, along the same road he had traveled not too long ago from Roegudok Hall. They rode steadily at a quick pace over the well-traveled dirt road as it wound its way through emerald forests and rolled over gentle hills of tall, olive colored grass littered with purple bonnets and red poppies under the azure sky. The bright, warm sun was tempered by the cool mid-summer breeze, making the journey pleasant and comfortable as could be hoped for. The few farms they passed came and went, some adding the odor of barnyard animals mixed with the scent of freshly hewn grasses or the late fruit blossoms that had come after the last freeze of the season.

When night came, they barely stopped long enough to eat before jumping back on their horses and continuing on. Al could see easily enough in the dark, as could Lady Arkyn. They forged the way while Gorin and Peren followed closely. The white crescent moon reached high into the night sky, darting in and out behind thick silver clouds that all but covered the light from above. Only then, when their animals drooped their heads low and their hooves began to slow and walk in zigzagging lines, did they stop and make camp. Lady Arkyn and Al quickly set about gathering boughs and low hanging branches from evergreen trees to fashion beds from while Gorin cleared the ground near a copse of birch trees.

Peren worked on his body with some of his magic, healing it as best he could, but it was obviously slow going, and the day's journey had not helped him any.

"You should have stayed behind," Gorin said when he finished clearing the space.

"What, and leave all the fun to you? I don't think so," Peren said. "I'm fine."

"Here," Lady Arkyn said as she and Al arranged the boughs on the dirt. "It isn't much, but it will help keep your body warm and the smell will be better than the dirt."

Gorin looked to the branches and put his hand on the soft, tender pine needles. "I prefer the ground," he said as he pushed his branches away. "You can take mine, Arkyn."

The half-elf shrugged and took the branches, adding them to her own pile. She saw Peren looking down at the branches with a long, unfocused stare. "In my saddle bag there is a cloak," she said. "You can lay it over the top to help keep the needles from poking your wounds."

Peren smiled slightly and nodded. "Thanks," he said. "But I think I will just lean up against the trees over there." He took the cloak from the saddle bag and gently placed it over his legs as a blanket and leaned back into a couple of the young birch trees.

"Well," Al started. "Glad to see our work is appreciated." The dwarf flopped down onto his bed and slid his hands under the back of his head. "We should be there before lunch tomorrow," he said. "Then we can prepare the army."

"The army?" Peren asked.

Al snorted. "Gorin, you take first watch, and fill Peren in while you are at it."

"Yes, King Sit'marihu," Gorin said tongue in cheek.

"See, you are coming around after all," Al chuckled. Then he promptly went to sleep.

*****

Al stirred and scratched an itch on his left shoulder. The movement took him out of a dream that he could not quite remember and he sat up in his bed of branches. A small fire crackled nearby with a pot sitting in the flames. The dwarf put a hand to shield his eyes until they adjusted and then he reached for his axe when he saw a man squatting near the fire.

"Easy friend," the man said as he held his empty hands out to the side. "I mean you no harm."

Al jumped to his feet and glanced around the camp. He saw Gorin sleeping on the dirt and Peren was still slumped against the birch trees. Lady Arkyn was nowhere to be seen.

"She went out after a wolf that was snooping around the camp," the stranger said.

Al gripped his axe and eyed the man warily. "Who are you?" he asked.

"The name is Ferishe, I am a trapper," he replied. He pointed over his shoulder to a pair of mules laden with furs and steel traps. "I was just passing through when I noticed your camp. I asked if I might put on a pot of coffee and share the space with you. Your lady friend said it would be alright."

Gorin snored loudly and turned onto his side.

"How was it sleeping next to that all night?" Ferishe asked.

"Not as bad as waking to find a stranger in my camp," Al replied evenly.

Ferishe nodded. "I can leave if you like."

"That isn't necessary," said a soft voice from the road. Al looked beyond Ferishe to see Lady Arkyn strolling back to camp. "The wolf is gone now," she said.

"You have my thanks," Ferishe said. "I could have chased him off myself, but I am more than ready to rest my bones." He drew back the hood to reveal a deeply wrinkled tanned face. Deep creases outlined the side of his mouth, and crow's feet extended out from the corners of his eyes. "I am a good trapper, but I like to steer clear of wolves, if given the choice."

Lady Arkyn nodded. "It was the scent, you didn't clean all of your hides as well as you should have," she noted. "The smell of blood is what brought the wolf."

"Thanks for the warning," Al said to Arkyn sharply. "I wake with you gone and a stranger leading wolves to our camp."

"Just one wolf," Lady Arkyn corrected. "I asked him to leave."

"Asked?" Al echoed.

Lady Arkyn nodded.

Gorin snored loudly as he sucked in a breath, then the sound stopped abruptly and all three looked to him, waiting for him to exhale.

"Should someone poke him?" Ferishe asked.

Just then the giant man exhaled noisily and rolled onto his back, smacking his mouth a couple of times.

"I apologize for the wolf," Ferishe said. He glanced back to the furs. "I didn't have the time I needed to clean all of my catch before I started my journey. I didn't mean to cause any trouble."

"No trouble," Arkyn said as she sat cross legged in the dirt nearby. "We are even, so long as I get a cup of coffee."

Ferishe nodded and bent over the pot to sniff the aroma. "Just a few more minutes," he said.

"You were in a hurry?" Al asked. "Why is that?"

Ferishe snorted and pulled back from the coffee pot. "Tarthun scouts," he said. "I spotted a few of them along a river that I lay my traps near. I usually work in the mountains to the east. I trap mink, beaver, and anything else the fancy ladies desire to make coats out of."

"Were you in the wilds?" Al asked.

Ferishe shook his head. "No, that's why I left. As soon as I saw the Tarthuns coming over the border to the Middle Kingdom, I high tailed it out of there faster than a spooked doe in spring." He pointed to his mules. "That's why I didn't clean my catch as well as I should have. I just grabbed what I could and fled."

"How many did you see?" Lady Arkyn asked.

"Well, I didn't *see* any of them," he replied with a shrug.

"Then how do you know they were Tarthuns," Al asked. "Could have just been rival trappers."

Ferishe shook his head emphatically. "No." He gathered his arms around his knees and dropped his head low as he looked into the flames. "There is a village in the mountains, well, a trading post really, but there are folks who live there. Or, at least there were folks who lived there," he said. "I came through to buy another steel trap. One of mine had rusted out beyond repair and the springs were broke. When I arrived, there was nothing left of the town. Doc Hamm's body was lying in the street in front of his burnt shop. Spears in the ground had severed heads set upon them near the town's entrance. Darmond, the butcher, was stuffed full of arrows like a pin cushion. His wife and their children were gone. The divines only know what happened to them." He stared silently into the flames for a while.

"Did anyone survive?" Lady Arkyn coaxed.

Ferishe slowly shook his head. "I found a hatchet, buried deep in Migorun's chest. He was the post commander. He used to be an officer in the army. Retired now, of course. Came out to the trading post town to help with security." Ferishe shrugged. "The only real problems the town ever faced before was from the odd bear here and there, or perhaps some goblin scout foolish enough to leave its cave in the wilds in search of greener pastures, as it were. They never saw the likes of Tarthuns before though. Migorun and his sons were no match for them. Hard to say how many came through the town, or where they went, but they left no one alive. If anyone did survive, I am not for knowing their fate, nor would I want to dwell on what the Tarthuns might do to any slaves they took." He sighed heavily and leaned forward again.

"The coffee is ready," he said, his voice cracking midsentence.

"So where are you going now?" Al asked, trying to change the subject.

"To Drakei Glazei," Ferishe replied. "Try to sell off my furs and then move farther west. There is some good trapping to be had in some of the forests. Not as good as the mountains, but likely safer."

"We have heard of Tarthuns coming from the north as well," Arkyn said.

Ferishe nodded. "They are like wolves," he said. "They smell blood in the Middle Kingdom and are coming to scavenge us."

"What do you mean?" Al asked.

Ferishe poured a cup of coffee and handed it to Lady Arkyn. "It's hot," he cautioned. Then he turned back to Al. "Even at the trading post we heard the news about the senate," he said. "We also heard about the different nobles fighting each other and squabbling over the throne like a pack of dogs over a soup bone. I knew it wouldn't take long for news like that to travel out to the Tarthuns. A divided kingdom rich for the taking, if you have the muscle for it."

Al nodded his head. "They won't be able to come over the mountains in large numbers," he said.

"Why not?" Ferishe countered. "The pass in the north is not the only one, nor is it the best."

"What do you mean?" Lady Arkyn asked.

Al spoke up. "The southern pass would go through Hamath Valley. The elves would not easily let Tarthuns through there. Tualdern would have to fall first. Besides, I hear there are others not so keen on the Tarthuns that live in the southern wilds. The only logical pass is the northern pass."

Ferishe shook his head. "Maybe a few years ago, sure," he said. "Not so anymore."

Al looked at him quizzically. "I am a dwarf of Roegudok Hall, I know of no other pass through the mountains."

"The dwarves have not been as vigilant in the last few years as they have been in the past," Ferishe countered. "There is another pass, albeit half of the pass is actually a cave. It was discovered about four or five years ago now, after the spring thaw was followed by heavy rains and numerous flash floods that poured through the mountains. The trading town I spoke of was nearly washed away then. I know, I was there. I went up with Migorun to scout the area. We didn't expect much, but we found that a new stream had sprung up, joining the river near the town. So, naturally we followed the stream to its source. The water snaked through the forest for miles. It was slow going at first. The ground was so wet and soggy that our boots were barely able to keep their traction. In a few places we sunk down to our knees. Eventually we found a sheer cliff. At the base there was a huge pile of shale and dirt. As we drew closer to it, we realized that a large section of the mountainside had simply fallen away. The stream was coursing out from a cave at the base of this cliff, pushing the shale and dirt out.

"The opening was huge. About seven feet high but at least four times as wide. We went into the cave and spent hours walking deeper into the mountain. The stream inside was shallow there, maybe only a few inches deep, but it was spread out over a large bed of smooth granite. The tunnel was so long that it took us two days to reach the other side. When we did, we saw an underground lake. No telling how deep it was. After walking four steps into the lake we fell deep into the pool and had to swim back."

Lady Arkyn handed the empty cup back to Ferishe and he poured more coffee into it. The man first offered it to Arkyn, but she shook her head. Then he offered it to Al, who also refused. Ferishe shrugged and took a sip himself.

"Then what?" Al said. "Did you find an opening?"

Ferishe nodded. "We walked around the lake and found a large chute, with a steep, but not impassable incline. There was a stream of water flowing down from there into the pool in the cave. We were able to hike up the chute on the left side of the stream where the ground was solid and dry. The chute was maybe two hundred yards long, and it opened out to the side of a mountain overlooking the wilds."

"How big was the chute?" Lady Arkyn asked.

"Big enough," Ferishe responded. "About eight feet high and perhaps fifteen feet wide, not counting the stream."

"Where was the water coming from?" Al asked.

Ferishe nodded knowingly. "There was a taller mountain butted up against the one the chute was in, and the stream came from there. It looked to be a very old stream, not just one that runs during the thaw, but one that runs continuously."

"But certainly the thaw and the rains could have enlarged the stream," Lady Arkyn said.

"That was our thought as well," Ferishe agreed. "After time the pool overflowed its bounds so heavily that it broke through on our side of the mountains and flooded our town until the water pressure was relieved."

"So," Al said grimly. "We have a new pass."

Ferishe nodded. "And they have already used it to scout out our side of the mountains," Ferishe said.

"If the Tarthuns come from an unknown pass, it could be disastrous," Lady Arkyn said.

Al nodded. "Especially if they have drawn the Lievonian Order to the north."

"Too bad the dwarves no longer come out of their hole," Ferishe commented. Then he double thought and put a hand up while he nodded sheepishly to Al. "No offense," he offered.

Al sniggered. "No," he said. "It's a good idea." Al walked over and nudged Gorin with his foot. "Get up, giant, we have work to do!"

Gorin snorted and snapped up, rubbing his eyes. "What?!" Gorin grumbled.

CHAPTER SIX

Tu'luh's wings ached with each beat of the cold wind. Sulfur and ash filled his nostrils and the air grew thick with dark clouds and pillars of smoke. The great beast swooped down low, veering left and narrowly avoiding a jagged, obsidian peak that jutted up spearing the sky. As he broke down below the blanket of smoke he breathed in deep. A feeling of warmth overcame him as he looked down and spied the familiar river of lava that coursed through Verishtahng.

He stretched his wings out, soaring over the lava and gliding along, mimicking its curves. The black and brown earth below vented smoke and shot embers into the air around him. A few of the hot specks collided with him, sparking wildly as they shattered against his scales.

A pair of wyverns squealed below as they caught his approach. The pair scattered off to the south, dropping the ridgebacked mouse they had managed to catch. Tu'luh hung his left foreleg down and scooped the ridgebacked mouse up in its claw and then flipped it up into the air and snapped his jaws around the animal. It wasn't nearly a large enough meal to sate his appetite. The ridgebacked mouse was only slightly smaller than the average house dog, with bony plates that jutted out over its spine and gave it its name. It would take scores of the creatures at a time to come close to filling Tu'luh's stomach, but it had been so long since he had tasted of the beast that he could not pass up the opportunity to snatch the kill from the skulking wyverns. Had they not been so quick to escape, he might have eaten them too.

His stomach grumbled as though great boulders slid and ground against each other in his gut. His nostrils flared and he caught the scent of something much bigger. He turned to the north, abandoning the lava flow and ascending back to the clouds of smoke above. The smell of sulfur grew more intense as he neared a hot spring. Occasionally he would drop his head below the smoke to peer at the ground below. He saw a pair of gorlung beasts, but he passed them by. He was after much larger prey.

He flicked his tongue out into the air before him like a snake, tasting the humidity that hung in the air in the northern areas of Verishtahng. He knew he was close. The trumpeting sound of great animals blasting each other with water sounded from below and the great dragon dropped from the clouds like a mighty eagle. He pulled his wings in close, allowing the air to course by him as he aimed for the bull water mammoth bathing itself near the bank of the hot spring. A herd of ten cows surrounded the bull, with some calves hiding near their mother's legs.

None of them noticed his stealthy approach until it was too late.

Tu'luh struck with his rear talons, piercing the bull through the back near the bull's neck and driving it down into the water. The water mammoth gasped and snorted as it was crushed down and Tu'luh created a massive splash of searing hot water. The nearby cows trumpeted their warning and started galloping away in all different directions, but Tu'luh was faster than all of them. He swept out with his massive tail and drove his spikes through a cow's neck. The animal crumpled down, tripping over its trunk and head before Tu'luh leapt over her and took two more with his front talons. A blanket of fire poured out from his open mouth, catching several of the cows and dropping them on the burnt, crisp ground. He reached out like a snake and snatched another cow in his massive jaws, ripping her from the ground and shaking her violently to snap her spine. Blood coursed into his mouth and woke his hunger to new levels.

The dragon devoured the cow, bones and all in only a few bites and then he turned to the others. From the rest of the cows he ate only the legs and the massive flanks. Then he turned lazily and stalked toward the half submerged bull. He saw the gathering crocodiles, but they kept their distance, waiting patiently for the left overs. The massive beast twitched its tail above its head and then slammed it down before it entered the hot spring for the bull water mammoth. He dropped his head down and ripped off the bull's legs and then chewed on the bull's side, tearing a few of the tender ribs free.

One of the crocodiles moved in quietly, but all it took was a warning snort from Tu'luh to send the croc slithering away.

When Tu'luh had his fill, he lumbered away from the spring and curled down on the ground. He watched lazily as the crocs made short work of the bull's remains. There was enough food for them that only a couple bothered to emerge from the water and pick at the other carcasses on the ground. His hunger finally sated, he let his head rest on his foreleg and allowed himself the pleasure of a short nap near one of the many vents in the ground that would periodically thrust steam and smoke into the air.

The dragon didn't wake again until he shivered reflexively against the cooling wind of dusk. He lifted his head to find several crocodiles sleeping nearby, obviously appreciative of both the food and warmth he had brought them. Tu'luh slowly stood, his stomach hanging low with its load. He strained to stretch his wings. The movement spooked a couple of the crocs. They hissed and slid down the bank to splash into the hot water.

Tu'luh lurched up into the air, a little shaky at first, but soon he was flying back toward the west. He couldn't fly as fast as he had been before, but at least he wouldn't need to feed again for several days and he would be able to focus on the task at hand. He blinked his eyes and winced sharply as the lid scraped over his torn left eye. The orb had crusted over with blood and goop. He hissed and emitted a ball of flame as he thought about Erik. *I should have killed the boy when he first came to the temple.*

At least the boy was still too young to realize his own power. That would give Tu'luh enough time to gather his army and strike, if he was quick. At least Gilifan had not failed with his task.

Just before the darkening horizon, a massive conical volcano rumbled and spewed lava up into the air. The sight pulled Tu'luh out of his thoughts and brought his attention back to the present.

Home, I am home. Demaverung, how I have missed you. Tu'luh increased his speed until he reached the familiar landing two thirds up the volcano. He lighted upon the black granite and twirled around in place, surveying the land before him. Glowing embers rose into the darkening sky beneath the clouds of steam and smoke, like minute stars celebrating their king's return.

Tu'luh curled his talons around the edge of the landing and let out a mighty, savage roar that shook the very ground and parted the clouds above him. His thunderous voice echoed off the jagged rocks and through the crags that scarred the valley before the great volcano.

"The master has returned," a subservient voice said from behind.

Tu'luh turned around to see a large, bald man emerging from

the great cavern. He was dressed in brown robes, carrying a wooden staff made of thornwood and topped with a ruby the size of a man's fist. "Takala," Tu'luh greeted evenly. "I thought you would have died by now."

The man nodded knowingly. "I have been able to prolong my life more than most," Takala replied.

"What brought a shadowfiend of the Black Fang Council to my home?" Tu'luh growled.

Takala planted the butt of his staff on the ground in front of him. "We have been working with the Wyrms of Khaltoun," Takala responded.

"All of you?" Tu'luh inquired skeptically.

Takala nodded. "All of us," he said.

"Where are the others of your order?"

"I have been here for about thirty seven years," Takala said. "My mate was here with me, but she was slain by a pack of gorlung beasts seven years ago. My brother, one of the best we had, was slain by a gang of orcish witch-hunters a few years before that."

"It appears you have fallen on hard times," Tu'luh noted.

Takala nodded. "But we are still strong. There are five of us that remain. One lives in AghChyor, another is in Och'tunga, with the orcs, the fourth is in the east wilds, and the fifth is in Stonebrook."

Tu'luh sneered. "In Stonebrook?" he repeated. "And he is ready to fulfill my commands?"

"She," Takala corrected. "And, yes, she is ready for your command. You have only but to say the word and I will communicate with her."

"Come inside with me," Tu'luh ordered. "There is much we can discuss." The dragon walked by the bowing bald man and into the cave. Rubies, garnets, and diamonds glittered and sparkled in the walls as he walked in. The hot, red light from the volcano's core illuminated every inch of the stone cavern. The sulfuric, blistering air felt like a long lost friend as it enveloped his scaly body. Smaller tunnels branched out from the large cave he walked in, some closed off with iron doors and other left open in their natural state.

Each step he took vibrated the ground a bit, and doors started to open as men and women in black robes emerged from the smaller tunnels. Each of them was quick to drop to their knees as

Erik and the Dragon

soon as they saw him.

"The Wyrms of Khaltoun," Takala said. "The order has grown since my arrival."

"You sound as though you wish to take credit for that," Tu'luh commented.

"No, my lord," Takala countered. "Simply informing you that the order has grown."

"How many?" the dragon asked.

"There are five elders, who each preside over ten acolytes. The acolytes in turn oversee up to three initiates each. Those initiates deemed unworthy of the gifts the order has to offer are either sacrificed or turned loose in the valley."

"I suppose you have used that to your advantage?" Tu'luh asked.

Takala nodded. "I have absorbed the life force of a few, but only if the elders all permit it. If they vote against it, then I stand aside and let them deal with the less worthy how they see fit."

"How often do the elders communicate with Gilifan?" Tu'luh asked. He knew the answer, but he liked drilling his subjects for information. He felt it helped reinforce his command status and authority.

"Every ten days, without fail, and on any occasion when Master Gilifan makes contact for special circumstances."

Tu'luh nodded. I will retire to my chamber, send the elders in to me there."

"As you wish," Takala replied.

Tu'luh stopped abruptly. "I will have some of the acolytes accompany you tomorrow into the valley. I have already sent out my call, but it will be good to send you to personally round up my subjects."

"You have only but to say the word, I stand ready at any moment." Takala bowed and then disappeared into a tunnel to the left through a heavy iron door.

Tu'luh then continued through the winding tunnel until it opened into the large chamber he had grown to love after his exile from the Middle Kingdom. He stopped just inside and listened with his eyes closed. The piles of gold and diamonds in the far corner hummed and sang a music that only he could hear. He rushed forward and smoothed out his treasure before laying in it and wallowing in the pure bliss the precious objects brought him.

He snuggled his muzzle into the gold coins and breathed in the sweet, metallic smell and let himself drift into a half-nap before he heard the pitter patter of several feet strolling toward him.

He opened his eyes to see five men with long, grey beards hanging low from their cowls. The black backgrounds of their cloaks reflected the warm, vibrant light of the lava chute on the far side of the chamber while the white fronts of their robes shimmered and took on orange hues.

"I always thought the tales of a dragon's love for gold was exaggerated," one of the elders commented wryly.

Tu'luh sighed and drew his neck up from the gold. "It is something lesser minds would not understand," Tu'luh rebuked.

"I meant no disrespect, master," the man said with a humble bow of his head.

"Everything in the world has innate intelligence," Tu'luh said. "The grass hums low, bending under the groaning wind. Rocks grumble and moan. Rivers roar far louder than human ears can discern, but the sweetest sound of all comes from gold and gems. It not only pleases the dragons, but it helps us heal. The music is food for our weary souls, and is the essence of life itself. You humans would waste it by beating gold into coins, but we dragons understand its true purpose."

"Thank you for the enlightenment," the elder said quickly.

Tu'luh knew the man wasn't really thankful. He was just being patronizing. The only thing the Wyrms of Khaltoun cared about was acquiring Nagar's Secret. It was precisely this reason that constrained Tu'luh from explaining the true power that precious metal and stones held within. That was a special knowledge, reserved for only the Ancients and the gods themselves. However, the dragon was willing to suffer the humans' petty greed and wanton ignorance so long as they served him and his purposes.

"Does Salarion live?" Tu'luh asked, changing the subject.

The five elders turned to themselves briefly and then back to the dragon.

"She does, my lord," one of them said.

"Where is she?" the dragon inquired.

"We don't know where she is at this time," the elder replied.

"Then how do you know she lives?" Tu'luh countered. He narrowed his right eye on the man and he shrank away from the dragon's gaze. "I have a war to fight. I shall need her here. Send for her and tell her to come to Demaverung."

"With respect, my lord, Nagar's daughter rejected our order."

"No," Tu'luh said. "She rejected *your* order. Tell her I offer her the same thing that I offered her father. Tell her that, and she will come."

"What is it you offered her father?" the man asked weakly with trembling hands held up before his face like someone might do if they expect to be slapped for their words.

Tu'luh arched his neck back and slid his tail up to curl around his legs. "She will know what it is," the dragon responded. "Now go, and do as I have asked. The Black Fang Council will gather the lesser drakes and the others. I expect that you will prepare your members for war. We will march forth on Ten Forts soon."

The elders looked to each other again and bowed several times as they backed out of the chamber.

Tu'luh sank back down into the pile of gold and let the sweet music fill his head again. He breathed in deeply, stretching his talons and forelegs through the coins and letting the cold, vibrant metal slither over him.

CHAPTER SEVEN

Erik was all too happy to stretch his legs while the others prepared an early breakfast. He knew the day ahead was going to be tedious and long. There were many miles yet before they reached Axestone. He walked to a small grove of birch trees and listened to the birds singing to the rising sun.

"Beautiful, isn't it?" Tatev asked as he approached from behind.

Erik sighed and closed his eyes for a moment. Ever since Lepkin had asked Tatev to tutor Erik, there was hardly a single moment where the librarian wasn't spouting off about some fact or another that Tatev would swear was "most important to the quest at hand" and had to be full understood.

The boy turned around and forced a smile on his face. "It is a nice morning," he said.

"Back in town, I was going to tell you more about Nagar, but we ran out of time when Marlin came out to announce Lepkin and Dimwater's betrothal."

Erik nodded and his interest perked up. At least this was a subject he *wanted* to learn more about.

"Nagar was a Sierri'Tai," Tatev said.

"A what?" Erik asked.

"A Sierri'Tai. The elves are broken into many families, just like humans and dwarves are. The Sierri'Tai are one of two races that we commonly call drow, or dark elves." Tatev took a drink of coffee from his tin mug before continuing. "Simply put, Nagar was a Sierri'Tai prince. They had a great kingdom in Tualdern. They erected a city there the likes of which had never been seen before in the Middle Kingdom. To the east, they traded mostly with the, the Pes'Tai, more commonly known as the sand elves. Over time, the Pes'Tai mingled with the Sierri'Tai. They never really intermarried of course, but the sand elves did purchase shops and land in Tualdern. Eventually, hostilities arose between the two societies. Some say that the Sierri'Tai kidnapped one of the Pes'Tai princesses from the desert, so the sand elves retaliated by laying waste to the city. Others say that the sand elves had intended to overthrow Tualdern all along, and slowly positioned themselves in Tualdern until the day came they were ready to strike. Other theories, which I tend to give more credence to, accuse Tu'luh of setting the two groups against each other. No matter which theory is accurate, the result is known all too well. The Pes'Tai utterly destroyed the Sierri'Tai in a great battle and forced the few surviving Sierri'Tai out of their homeland. Nagar then set to working on a magic that would not only conquer the sand elves, but pay them back for their treachery. It was then that he and Tu'luh created the magic that we call Nagar's Secret."

"They worked together?" Erik asked.

Tatev nodded. "Nagar's and Tu'luh combined their forces together, using the magic to crush any and all who would oppose them until finally they marched toward Tualdern. All those who had been subjected to Nagar's Secret now obeyed their every command. The dwarves, dragons, and humans joined forces with the sand elves in the Valley of Hamath. The battle was horrendous, carpeting the valley with scarlet corpses and ivory bones. So great was the army that Tu'luh and Nagar led that the battle raged for days without ceasing. It is said that as many as half of the dragons in the Middle Kingdom joined with Tu'luh. It was a very dark point in our history."

"Why did the other dragons join with them?" Erik asked.

"The vision you saw," Tatev commented. "The one where Tu'luh showed you the end of Terramyr. He showed the same vision to the Ancients long before he and Nagar created their dark magic. Knowing that humans were not prone to peace, Tu'luh said it was better to slay all of the humans and orcs to save the world. Hiasyntar Ku'lai rejected the vision, and Tu'luh's suggestion. He said it was not right to kill the races they had sworn to protect. Tu'luh relented and went away for a season. When he returned, he said he had discovered a magic so powerful that it could force living creatures to bend to their wills on a massive scale. He proposed forcing all creatures, not just the humans, to subject themselves to the Ancients so that the dragons might save the world. Hiasyntar Ku'lai loathed the notion and banished Tu'luh from the Middle Kingdom, along with any dragon who agreed with him."

"If Tu'luh wanted the magic to save the world, then why work with Nagar?" Erik asked.

"Because the magic only worked by combining the magic of the dragons with that of the elves," Tatev said. "There is a book, called 'The Arcane Abyss' which describes all of the magics that exist, and which races can use them. It also discusses the theory of combining different magics to make them stronger, or to create new types of magic. Tu'luh needed to combine his magic with that of an elf. More specifically, he needed the magic of a dark elf."

Erik leaned into a nearby birch tree and his mouth dropped open as it clicked for him. "So Tu'luh used Nagar," he said only slightly louder than a whisper. "That is why you believe Tu'luh orchestrated the attack on Tualdern."

Tatev nodded grimly. "No one has ever been able to prove it," he said. "But the most plausible event I have uncovered while studying various sources is that Tu'luh hired a group of Blacktongues to disguise themselves as Sierri'Tai and attack the Pes'Tai camps east of Tualdern. They succeeded in kidnapping the Pes'Tai princess, and the Pes'Tai were very quick to answer what they thought was an unforgivable offense. The sand elves had never been overly fond of the dark elves. It was exactly the spark that was needed to ignite the flames of war between the two civilizations."

"How did Tu'luh know that his plan would work?" Erik asked.

Tatev shrugged. "I don't know for sure," he admitted. "Perhaps Tu'luh whisked Nagar away to safety, or perhaps he sent the Blacktongues in to help him escape. Either way, the point is that he got what he wanted. He created a vengeful drow who was willing to do anything it took to exact justice for what he saw as an unprovoked slaughter of his people. As a prince, Nagar was one of the more powerful drow sorcerers of the time. Once he turned to Tu'luh and the dragon suggested combining their magics, it was only a matter of time before the dragon had what he wanted."

"He would have used me too," Erik said. "He wanted me to help him use the book, he said it was the only way to save the world." He shook his head as he thought it over in his mind. "Does Tu'luh need an elf now?" he asked. "I mean, does he need a drow to use the magic?"

Tatev shook his head. "Now that the magic has been created, and written into the evil tome, anyone who has enough magical aptitude can use the spells contained therein. That is why it is so dangerous."

"We are lucky that he never knew it was in the same temple he hid in," Erik said.

"I admit, I should have seen it. The plan is so obvious to me now, in hindsight. Tu'luh was lying in wait because he had his own plan. The book is not enough for him. He knows of the prophecy as much as anyone else does. He knows that there is one who can destroy the book. If the book is destroyed, then he can't recreate the magic without the help of another Sierri'Tai sorcerer. Since Nagar died in Hamath, the task of finding another Sierri'Tai willing to work with him to recreate the evil magic would likely be as difficult as killing you, if not more so."

Erik shrugged. "Everyone thought Tu'luh died at Hamath," Erik pointed out. "I suppose it makes sense to see if he could kill the one who could destroy the book before going directly after the book."

"With you out of the way, then he could have struck openly," Tatev agreed. Then the man tapped a finger to his chin and his lips curled into a tight smile. "I also now believe that Tu'luh may have been resting, trying to regain his strength. He was lying in wait as a trap, that is certain, but I believe there was more to it as well. By all accounts I have read, Tu'luh died by Hiasyntar Ku'lai's own hand. If that is not true, then surely the red dragon must have been gravely injured."

"So he waited for me while recovering from his injuries," Erik said.

"Precisely."

Lepkin whistled at the pair from back at the camp. "Let's get a move on, you two. Come finish your breakfast and let's get on the road!"

"We can continue this later," Tatev offered with a smile.

*****

Erik shifted in his saddle for the thousandth time, but it didn't help. His lower back was sore, his tailbone was all but numb, and his rump kept fluctuating between losing all feeling and having tingles from sitting far too long. He directed Goliath over to the side of the road and struggled to slide down. He shook his feet and rubbed his thighs trying to get the blood to circulate normally again. To his dismay the only thing that happened was his feet woke up with the sensation of one million tiny needles poking through the soles of his feet. Erik stamped his feet, trying to squash the feeling.

"Just walk normally," Jaleal advised. "That will help the fastest."

Erik startled and turned around to see the gnome leaning against the base of a tall pine tree. "You scared me," Erik admitted.

Jaleal grinned. "I am very, very sneaky," he said with a wink. "It's one of my better traits." He whirled his shiny spear around before him and then stuck the butt-end onto the ground next to his boot. "Come, let's walk together for a while."

"I thought you were supposed to scout ahead?" Erik asked, pointing to the trees.

"Already did," Jaleal said with a shrug. "I went about six miles out, didn't see anyone, so I came back." The gnome pointed off to the west. "A herd of deer is out that way." Then he pointed due south, the direction they were traveling. "Only thing I saw this way was a band of three merchants. They each had a wagon filled with pans and pots. Looks like they make the wares themselves."

Erik nodded, feigning interest. "So, where do you come from?" Erik asked.

Jaleal offered a halfhearted smile. "An island to the west," he replied. "I told you already about how we were driven out of our homeland."

"No," Erik said quickly. "I mean, where do *gnomes* come from?" The boy stopped and looked down at his friend. "Did the gods create the gnomes in the beginning?"

"Ah," Jaleal said as he stroked his long, wispy white beard. "*That's* what you want to know, eh?"

Erik nodded.

"You could just have asked Tatev," Jaleal pointed out.

"I am afraid if I asked him, I would never again get him to close his mouth," Erik said sheepishly.

Jaleal laughed. "Yes, he does seem to lack somewhat in communication skills, but his knowledge is impressive."

"I guess," Erik said. "I would rather ask you, though, if you don't mind."

"Not at all," Jaleal said. "Gnomes were not created in the beginning. We were created much later."

Erik and the Dragon

"But you aren't a Cursed Race, are you?" Erik asked quickly.

"No," Jaleal said. "We were not created by the fallen god either," the gnome clarified. "We were created after the gods withdrew from Terramyr. At the time when Atek Tangui rose to power and the bridge to Volganor was hidden from the mortal realm."

"The gods created you then?" Erik asked.

"No," Jaleal said with an impatient hand waving in the air. "We gnomes are one of the Natural Races, we were created by Terramyr itself."

"Natural Races?" Erik echoed. "You mean like minotaurs, centaurs, and merfolk?"

"Precisely," Jaleal said. "There are many more races besides those as well. There are satyrs, gryphons, and even vinnies, among many others."

"What are vinnies?" Erik asked.

"Humanoid plants," Jaleal said. "They are somewhat like spriggans, but they resemble vines in shape and flexibility."

"Spriggans?" Erik screwed up his face. "I thought the Natural Races were just a myth."

"The world beyond the Middle Kingdom is quite large, Erik, you would be surprised by what lies beyond your borders."

Erik nodded. "How did the world create the Natural Races? I mean, the way you talk makes it sound as if the world is alive."

"Ah, but it is," Jaleal said with a big smile. He stopped and swept his arms out to the side, indicating the forest around him. "You may not see it, but Mother Terramyr is alive, and gives us all the sustenance we need. She waters us with the rivers and the rain, she clothes us with the cotton from her fields, and she gives us breath from her forests and houses from her stone. Terramyr has its own heart, and its own consciousness. That's why she created gnomes, and the other Natural Races. When Atek Tangui forced the old gods away, Terramyr knew that she had to protect herself from the evil Cursed Races, or else she might be slain by their bloodlust."

Erik tilted his head to the side. "You can't kill a world," he said incredulously.

Jaleal nodded emphatically. "Yes you can," he insisted. "You most certainly can."

"How is that even possible?"

"There are several ways, actually. Some are slower than others, but it is possible."

"What are they?" Erik asked.

Jaleal shook his head. "I know them," he said, "but I am not allowed to discuss them with others who are not part of the Natural Races. Please, don't ask me again."

"Sorry," Erik said quickly. "I didn't mean to…"

"I know," Jaleal interrupted. "No offense taken, just making sure you understand. It is my duty to guard those secrets." Jaleal wrinkled his nose and scratched his forehead. "I will tell you, however, that you did catch a glimpse of a possible future danger that could destroy this world, and everything in it."

Erik knitted his brow, but it only took a second to realize what Jaleal spoke of. "You mean the four fireballs I saw when Tu'luh showed me the future?"

Jaleal nodded. "I dare not say more about them, myself, even with other gnomes we do not like to talk of them, but they are very real."

"And they are coming here?" Erik asked.

Jaleal shrugged. "I do not know, but if they are, then there will be nothing we can do to stop them." The gnome shivered then and rubbed his shoulders as if a blizzard had just blown past. He shook it off and went to the nearest tree. "I'll go on ahead," he said.

Something about his tone of voice unnerved Erik. "Wait," he said.

Jaleal stopped and turned back to Erik.

"Tu'luh said that without Nagar's Secret, the four fireballs would come. Is that true."

Jaleal shrugged. "It's possible," he said. "I can't say for sure."

"Well, can't you tell me how to figure it out?" Erik asked.

Jaleal shook his head. "Like I said, they scare us gnomes. We don't keep books on them, we don't study them. They are just something we talk about in the darkest corners of our most secure halls deep within the ground. I agree it is worth researching, but I will not be opening that secret with you. Try Tatev."

Erik watched Jaleal disappear into the tree only to hear leaves above rustling as the gnome used his magic to travel along the roots and branches from tree to tree faster than a galloping horse could sprint down an even road.

"I heard my name," Tatev said happily as he came up behind

Erik and placed a hand on his shoulder. "Have a question?"

Great. Erik sighed and nodded. "Do you know about the four fireballs?" he asked.

"The four fireballs? Hmmm..." Tatev rubbed his chin for a moment and then flipped his spectacles up to scratch his right eye. "You mean the four fireballs you saw when you were with Tu'luh?" Tatev asked suddenly.

Erik nodded.

Tatev rolled his eyes and clapped his hands together. "I don't know if Lepkin would want me to tell you about them," he said.

Erik's eyes went wide. He could hardly believe Tatev wasn't foaming at the mouth to spill all of his knowledge. "I don't see how it can be much different from learning about Tu'luh and Nagar's Secret," Erik pressed.

"Oh, it's different," Tatev corrected. "*A lot* different," he added. He shook his head and pressed on. "Come on, we are falling behind."

Erik snorted in discontent. Lepkin was treating him differently now, but given the totality of their history together, he doubted his master would want to discuss the issue if Tatev was not even willing to mention what the four fireballs were.

At least his feet had stopped tingling and he could feel his backside again. He walked at the back of the group, winding over the dirt road through the green forest. The smell of pine filled the hot, dry air, and occasionally a rabbit or squirrel would skitter through the underbrush nearby. The sun peeked through the trees above with its warm, golden light. Despite the lack of any breeze, it was a pleasant journey, just long.

It was near nightfall when they finally emerged from the forest to see a large settlement. This city lacked any walls or gates. A couple of towers strategically placed around the outside was all the defense the place appeared to have. A thin, red banner flew atop each tower, catching even the slightest of winds. The towers themselves were made of wood, held up by five heavy timbers and culminating in a platform encircled by a waist-high wall of flat pine boards that had long ago warped and cracked in the sun. A single wooden ladder stretched down from the platform to the ground some thirty feet below.

As they passed by the first tower, Erik noted there were three archers on the platform. None of them said anything, but they all kept an eye on the group. Erik wasn't sure whether he liked their silence. It almost seemed less welcoming than a slew of guards barraging them with questions before allowing them to pass through a gate. Something about the way they watched the group sent a chill down his spine. He could feel their eyes upon his back long after he put their tower behind him.

The buildings of the town itself were all squat, wooden buildings. Every now and again a house would have one or two walls made of stone, but even then they were heavily augmented with timber. Farther in the town great log piles stood stacked high near a river. Several lumber mills worked with men running up and down carrying logs to the giant saws that separated the logs in twain.

"Axestone is the premier lumber producing settlement in the Middle Kingdom," Tatev said admiringly.

Now he wants to talk. Erik just nodded and turned his face away from Tatev, trying to drop a hint that he didn't care. If Tatev saw the gesture, he obviously didn't care. He went on for the next several minutes about the founder of Axestone, how he could fell a tree in less than three swings of his mighty axe which is now enshrined in the mayor's hall. Then he talked about how Axestone provided lumber for the great siege engines that finally helped the humans overtake Oskarion. There were other stories too, but Erik ignored the rest.

He was only too happy when Lepkin pulled the two of them apart and Tatev decided to go for a stroll by himself.

*****

Tatev wound through the streets as comfortably as if he had been in Axestone all his life. In reality, he had never set foot in the city. He had, however, read several books about it and even kept two maps of the city in his room near the archives of Valtuu Temple. His face soured then and he rubbed the bridge of his nose. He hated thinking about all the knowledge that had been lost. He had saved what he could, but it wasn't enough.

He shuffled over the dirt road, craning his neck up at the two story row of buildings on his right. He passed the apothecary, a carpenter guild house, and Titan's Savings and Loan, before he found what he was looking for.

Erik and the Dragon

"There you are," he said. His blue eyes twinkled and his mouth turned up at the corners in a great smile. "Calphar's Reading Room." He started for the old wooden stairs that led up to the shop when all of a sudden a hand butted up against his chest and stopped him in his tracks. Tatev startled and stepped back from the large man. He hadn't even noticed the man's approach.

"Didn't mean to frighten ya," the man said through yellow and brown teeth. "Just wanted to ask fer a coin."

"Absolutely not," Tatev said as he lifted his left forearm over his nose to shield himself from the thick stench of alcohol on the man's breath. "I haven't any extra money, and if I had, you would only waste it on liquor. Now be gone."

"Hey, no need to be like that, mate," the man growled.

Tatev shook his head and deftly walked around the staggering man. He quickstepped up the stairs and burst through the door, paying no heed to the shouting drunkard below. A bell above the door announced his arrival with a loud, brass jingle. An old woman emerged from around a bookshelf with a smile.

"Welcome to Calphar's Reading Room," she said with a crackle in her voice. "Anything in particular you are looking for?"

Tatev closed the door, again setting off the bell, and then pushed his glasses up the bridge of his nose before flipping the lenses up.

"Ah, you must be from Valtuu Temple," the woman said as she shook a finger at him. "And you are wearing the Eyes of Dowr, are you not?"

"I am," Tatev replied with a smile. "I have long wanted to come here, but have never had the chance before now."

The old woman grinned and pulled her purple shawl tighter around her shoulders. "What can I help you find, dear?" she asked.

"I have quite a list, actually," he said. "I need the second edition of Vishel's Arcaneum, the complete set of Andor's Guide to Herbs, the fourth volume of Grelek's Curse, the Encyclopedia Magicka, by Herber Granovoir, a copy of Green is the Forest, as well as..." Tatev let his sentence hang unfinished when he saw the old woman shaking her head and holding up a bony hand.

"I am not as young as I once was," she said with a shrug. "I will have to write this all down."

"Don't bother," Tatev insisted. "I can find them myself and pile them on your desk." He bolted to the shelf nearest him and twisted his neck to the left so he could read the titles and author. "Are your books organized by the Veron system, or by Larcher's grouping?"

"Neither," the old woman said somewhat tersely.

Tatev spun around on her, squinting and peering down his nose while his mouth hung open dumbly. "What system do you use?" he asked.

"I use Alberot's method," she said. "We group them by category, then by author's last name. You will find the category written on the shelf in the middle. The letter on the left of the shelf denotes the —"

Tatev cut her off. "Yes, I know," he said quickly. He tore through the shelves faster than a dog retrieving game. Mumbling to himself as he piled books into his waiting left hand until he had at least five at a time before rushing back to the counter to stack them all. Within a matter of minutes he had seven neat stacks of five.

"Young man," the woman called out from behind the pile of books. "How do you plan on paying for these?"

"With coin, of course," Tatev said. "Do you have anything else?" he asked.

"Anything else?" she scoffed. "Did your library at the temple burn down or something?"

Tatev's smile fell from his face and he drew his brow together, blinking away the sting. "Actually, yes, yes it did."

The woman put a hand to her mouth. "Oh dear, I am so sorry, I didn't realize."

"It's alright," Tatev said. "Can we have these books delivered?" he asked.

"Delivered?"

Tatev nodded. "I want to send these to Fort Drake. I can pay for the service, of course."

The woman looked at him for a few moments and then shook her head. "I have a grandson here who owes me a few days of honest work yet. I will have him take the books up without extra charge. Glad to help the temple rebuild its library."

"Thank you, that is very kind of you," Tatev said.

"There is one book that may interest you," she said in a half whisper. "It is something I have had for a while, but never put on any of the shelves. Guess I thought I would read it myself someday."

Erik and the Dragon

"What is it?" Tatev asked.

"The Infinium," she replied. "I never actually had the courage to read it."

"The Infinium, where in the world did you get that?" Tatev asked.

"I wasn't always an old woman," she scolded. "I used to travel quite a bit, in search of rare books and a good tale to tell my own friends and family."

Tatev grinned.

The old woman pulled her shawl in close again and nodded her head as her eyes focused on a distant point. "I once traveled with a man named Asusa. We called ourselves dungeon divers. We probably went on a hundred different adventures, risking death at every corner, slaying foul beasts and seeking our fortune. We spent a lot of time in the wilds, and a lot of time across the sea too." She reached up to a sapphire necklace and stroked the gem with her thumb. "Thought he and I would get married, grow old together." She huffed and shook her head. "The gods had other plans, I guess." She held a finger up in the air. "Wait here." The woman disappeared around the corner and Tatev heard an old door creak open. A few moments later she returned and placed a large, blue leather book on the counter in front of him. A golden infinity symbol was emblazoned on the front.

"The Infinium," Tatev said.

"Asusa gave me this book one night after we had completed a particularly successful adventure."

"Do you know what this is?" Tatev asked excitedly.

"I do," she replied evenly. "That's exactly why I never mustered the courage to read it." She grinned and tapped her necklace. "Never could bring myself to sell it either, since it was the last thing Asusa gave me."

"I don't even know how much this is worth," Tatev replied honestly. "I have three hundred gold with me, but even if I wasn't buying the other books, I don't think that would cover the cost of this one."

The woman smiled. "Well, give me a moment." She took out a piece of parchment and wrote up the order, including all of the other books. She listed the price next to each title. Some were three gold, some cost seven, but only a handful of the books Tatev chose cost more than ten gold coins. Then she turned to The Infinium and sighed. "So far the total for the other books is one hundred and twenty seven coins."

Tatev nodded. "I have that." He reached up and pulled a small leather purse up from under his shirt, over his neck, and placed it on the table as he pulled the opening apart. He reached in and pulled out six coins. "Here you are."

"I have not seen the likes of these for many years," the woman said as she snatched up one of the coins. She turned it over in her hand, admiring the work.

"Each one is worth exactly twenty-five gold coins," Tatev assured her.

"Oh I know what the old republic coins are worth," she replied. "I am just surprised to see so many in one location." She held it up to the light. One side had a pair of crossed swords and the other side showed a dragon in flight. "Haven't seen more than a handful of these since starting my shop." She looked down to The Infinium and smiled. "Tell you what. Hand me four more of these and we will call it an even trade."

Tatev nodded happily. "Done." He plopped four more of the large coins out onto the table and then scooped up The Infinium. "I'll take this one with me, the rest can be delivered to Fort Drake."

"As you wish," the lady replied.

Tatev walked back to the door and then stopped abruptly. "Whatever happened to Asusa?"

"I don't know," the woman replied. "I never saw him again. I thought about him often, of course, even after I married and settled down. You never do forget your first, I suppose," she said longingly. Then she smiled. "But, I have had a good life. I have a family, and that never would have been possible with him." Then she waved and disappeared around the corner again.

Tatev silently wished her farewell and went down the stairs. He had already forgotten about the vagabond from before. His eyes traced the symbol on the book's cover and he could barely hold his excitement in.

"No money eh?" the drunkard growled. The man stood blocking the stairs. Tatev looked around. He was too high up to jump comfortably, and the man was too close to escape back up the stairs. The drunk pulled a knife. "Hand over your coin, or I'll gut you like a fish, book lover!"

Erik and the Dragon

Tatev did the only thing he could think to do. He cocked back with the thick book and swung hard, connecting with the man's face and knocking him back down the stairs. The knife fell from the drunk's hands as he tumbled down to land on the ground with a *thawuump!* The drunk groaned, but made no move to get up.

"Knowledge is power, brother," Tatev said with a shrug.

*****

Erik helped Lepkin move the pack mules onto the large, hefty barge. Neither one of the animals wanted to get onto the boats, so Erik pulled on the guide rope while Lepkin pushed from behind. In the end it took a small spark of lighting to each mule's rump from Lady Dimwater to get them onto the boat.

"You have to know how to convince them," she told Erik with a wink.

Erik rubbed his hands together, trying to stifle the stinging in his palms from the coarse guide ropes. He moved aside so Lepkin and Dimwater could board the barge. He smiled when he saw the two of them interlock their fingers and walk hand in hand.

"Even amidst all the darkness of the raging storm, there is light and beauty in life," Marlin said as he walked up and placed a hand on Erik's shoulder. "You have done very well to make it this far," the prelate said. "Very well indeed."

"There is still a lot to do," Erik said modestly.

Marlin nodded. "That there is, but look at them," he said as he gestured to the pair. Erik saw them whispering to each other and even from behind could catch glimpses of their wide smiles. "This is why we fight. Not for glory, or honor, or some vain hope of having our adventures written down and immortalized by some worshipping bard, but for love."

Erik nodded and put a hand to his father's ring that hung on his chest from the leather thong. "And for family," Erik added.

"Family is love," Marlin said. "A different name, but the same concept." He stepped forward, dragging Erik along with him as he snaked his arm across Erik's shoulders. "One day you shall see for yourself, and it will become all the more clear for you."

Erik turned his head up to look at Marlin. "Have you ever been in love?" he asked.

"Once, a long time ago," he said.

"What happened?" Erik asked.

"She moved away," Marlin replied. "We were only fifteen at the time. Her father uprooted their family in search for better work, and I never saw her again."

"You were fifteen?" Erik asked skeptically.

Marlin nodded. "We wrote each other a letter or two, but the distance made it impossible to keep up for long. Eventually she stopped answering my letters."

"Why didn't you go and try to find her?" Erik asked.

"Let's just say that her father didn't like me much," Marlin replied. "Thought I was too rebellious and ornery. Actually he called me 'ungodly' once and chased me with a stick when he caught me kissing her."

"You?" Erik asked. He tried to imagine Marlin, the Prelate of Valtuu Temple, as an unruly romantic, but couldn't even imagine it with a straight face. "I bet he would die now if he knew what you have become."

Marlin pulled his arm back and motioned for Erik to sit down on a wooden bench near the front of the barge. "I suppose he would."

"Do you ever regret it?" Erik asked. "Not going after her I mean."

Marlin thought for a while before answering. "I think about what might have happened if we had run away together. We talked about it, you know, before her family departed. But there isn't much use in daydreaming about the past. If you spend too much time looking behind you, you'll just trip yourself up in the present and miss the opportunities of the future."

Erik started to ask where the girl went, what she looked like, or what her name was, but Tatev arrived just then and flopped down beside him on the bench.

"You will never believe what I found!" Tatev exclaimed.

Marlin and Erik turned to see a thick, blue leather bound book with a golden symbol on the front.

"Is that what I think it is?" Marlin asked.

"Yes!" Tatev squealed excitedly. "The Infinium!"

"Wait," Erik said as he turned back to Marlin. "How do you know what it looks like?"

Marlin traced his finger over the golden symbol. "This is written with magic," he explained.

Erik and the Dragon

Heavy boot steps approached and Erik looked up to see Master Lepkin and Lady Dimwater standing in front of them.

"The Infinium?" Lepkin asked.

Tatev nodded sheepishly. "I was going to ask for your permission to read it for him, of course, but I got excited when I saw Marlin and wanted to tell him first."

"What is it?" Erik asked, noting the sour expression on Lepkin's face.

"I don't think he needs to focus on that for now," Lepkin said tersely. "The knowledge in that book will not help him against Tu'luh, and that is what we must concentrate on."

Tatev frowned, but did not back down as he normally did. He stood up, face to face with Lepkin and looked the warrior dead in the eyes. "I disagree," he squeaked. "The Infinium may not be entirely relevant, but it is relevant insomuch as it has information which can help Erik answer why Tu'luh showed him the visions at Valtuu Temple. It will help him understand the four—"

"Not another word," Lepkin said sternly. "He doesn't need to know about that, not yet."

"If this book will help me understand the four fireballs that Tu'luh showed me, then I want to know," Erik said quickly. "I want to know what they are."

Lepkin arched a brow and slowly turned to face Erik. "Why?"

"Because Tu'luh said that without Nagar's Secret, this world would be doomed. If that is true, and these four fireballs are destined to come, then I need to know that what I am doing now is worth it. I need to know that we are doing the right thing."

"Slavery to Nagar's Secret would be worse," Lepkin said.

"I want to believe that," Erik said. "And I do, for now. But I need to know for sure." Erik sighed and slumped his shoulders.

"What else?" Marlin asked. "Go on, tell us what else is on your mind."

Erik looked up with tears in his eyes. "So many have already given their lives," he said with a cracking voice. "If we are to fight Tu'luh, and destroy the book, then I want to know why these fireballs will come. I want to know if we can stop them."

Lepkin's hard face melted away into an expression of shock. He folded his arms and leaned back from Erik for a moment, cocking his head to the side and studying the boy. Lady Dimwater wrapped her hands around Lepkin's thick right arm and leaned in slowly, whispering something into his ear that Erik couldn't hear. Lepkin nodded and looked back to Tatev. "Very well, Tatev, you have until we reach the falls to study the book with Erik."

Tatev nodded. Lepkin and Dimwater walked away.

Marlin patted Erik on the back. "I am going to go and sit with them," he said. "Good luck with the research."

Tatev let out a relieved sigh when everyone was gone. He sat down quickly and his hands were shaking. "I thought Lepkin was going to eat me!" he said under his breath.

Erik laughed and sat down next to Tatev. For once he was actually looking forward to talking with the man. "So, this book can tell us about the fireballs?" Erik asked.

The curly red-headed man nodded enthusiastically, instantly forgetting about his nerves and wiping a palm across the front of the book. "The first thing you should know, is they are not fireballs. They are men, or something like men."

Erik screwed up his face. "Men?" he asked. "What kind of men appear as fireballs?"

Tatev paused tentatively with his index finger hooked under the cover. "We don't actually have a word for them exactly. We know only what they are called in their tongue."

"Which is what?" Erik asked.

"Cherusaphi," Tatev whispered quietly. "But we don't say their name very often, even amongst ourselves," he added quickly.

"So what should I call them?" Erik asked.

Tatev slowly opened the cover to reveal the first page. Erik looked down and saw four images. Each one was like a man, except a tall, slender pair of wings extended high into the air above them. Each man sat upon a horse made of fire, and each held a great sword in their right hand and a skull in their left hand. The librarian ran his fingers over the image. "We call them the four horsemen," he said.

Chills ran down Erik's spine. He glanced around him, half expecting to find a specter watching him. Nothing was there. He saw Lepkin and the others sitting on the other side of the barge, but the sight of his friends did little to assuage the fear that gripped his soul.

"So the fireballs I saw were their horses?" Erik asked.

Tatev nodded.

"And they will come to attack us?" Erik asked. "How can four

Erik and the Dragon

men destroy a whole world?"

Tatev closed the book and sighed. "It is difficult to explain in short," he said. "What do you know of Terramyr's creation?"

Erik shrugged. "The old gods created it, and everything in it."

Tatev nodded. "With the help of the Ancients," he added pointedly. "That is why Tu'luh is so bent on stopping these horsemen."

"What do you mean?" Erik asked.

"The four horsemen are said to come from somewhere where even the old gods themselves cannot go. They wield power that not even the gods can fathom. No one knows who sends them on their errand, but it is said that once they are sent the end is unavoidable."

"The end?"

Tatev turned to Erik and nodded. "They are sent to kill worlds. They strike at the very heart of the world, and kill it as easily as a warrior might kill a sleeping baby. They wield not only weapons, but famines, pestilence, and great magic."

"And they are coming here?"

Tatev pushed his spectacles up onto the bridge of his nose and nodded solemnly. "They might."

Erik leaned back on the bench and looked around him. There were several other men on the dock, preparing the barge to travel, and the barge master himself had finally arrived, barking orders and ensuring his cargo was all in order.

"Where is Lepkin?" the barge master called out to Erik and Tatev. The two of them pointed to Lepkin and the barge master trudged on, barely acknowledging their help with a slight nod. "You bring enough food for your mules?" the barge master asked.

Erik watched the man for a moment and then turned back to Tatev. "Why would the horsemen come here, do they destroy worlds just because they can?"

"Oh, no, not at all," Tatev said quickly. "According to everything I have ever read and heard about them, they are sent to destroy worlds that have become too corrupted. Some higher council sends them in an attempt to maintain order." He slowly opened the book again and flipped to the first page of text. "That is why the Ancients came to the Middle Kingdom," he said wistfully. "In the beginning, the Ancients came to Icadion, the All Father, and asked for permission to reside in our world. The All Father allowed this, and the Ancients in turn vowed to help establish a place on Terramyr where they might guide and watch over the mortals that the old gods would put in their care."

"I thought the Ancients created the dwarves in the middle kingdom," Erik said quickly. "I was reading with Al and the book said…"

"Quite right," Tatev confirmed. "They did, along with some of the other races soon thereafter, but they were not the first creatures in all of Terramyr. Those were simply the first members of the Blessed Races to live in the Middle Kingdom. The Ancients then helped establish the kingdom itself, and swore to watch over and guide all who lived in the Middle Kingdom."

"Until the battle in Hamath Valley," Erik said.

Tatev nodded. "The interesting thing, is that Tu'luh was one of the original dragons to come to the Middle Kingdom. I have read a lot about the Ancients, and I know that there were several who all came to Icadion during the creation period. Not all of them are named, of course, but there are several dragons that are named in the ancient annals. Tu'luh is among those that are named specifically as having spoken directly with Icadion."

Erik screwed up his face. "If Tu'luh knows Icadion, then why would he try to ally with Nagar? Couldn't he just turn to the old gods for help?"

Tatev raised a finger. "Therein lies the thorn that pesters his backside," Tatev said. "After Atek Tangui rose to power, the old gods cut off the bridge between this world and Volganor, the Heaven City. The Ancients were left to their own devices as the mortals in the world started to turn away from the old traditions. As the demigods rose in power, so the Ancients did wane in their influence. Only here, in the Middle Kingdom, were the Ancients directly involved in the matters of our existence."

Erik sighed. He was trying to keep up, but he couldn't help but feel slightly overwhelmed. Religion had never been his strong suit, and history was not much better in his opinion. "I don't know," Erik said after a moment. Tatev closed the book and placed it on Erik's lap. The tome was very heavy, as if made with pages of brass instead of paper.

"Think about it," Tatev said. "Tu'luh is Hiasyntar Ku'lai's son, a prince if you will. He was using the magic because he was trying to avoid the impending arrival of the four horsemen. He has seen it before, and is afraid of what will happen if they come here as well. He knows firsthand the danger that lurks in the great beyond."

"So he is trying to save us all, and if I slay him, I will be sentencing our world to death?" Erik asked. He shook his head. "It sounds like I am fighting on the wrong team."

Tatev grabbed Erik's chin forcefully and turned the boy's face to lock eyes with him. "No, no, no, no!" Tatev assured him. "We are on the right side, I am sure of that."

"How are you so certain?" Erik countered. "If the world ends, there will be no future at all. How is that better than letting Tu'luh use his magic to rule the Middle Kingdom?"

"Because," Tatev began, "it is better to die free than to live a slave."

"But is it better to have no life at all than to live as a slave?" Erik fired back. "It is not simply a choice between living as a slave and living free. The choice I see here is living as a slave or condemning all the world to death."

"Tu'luh is very wise, and extremely cunning," Tatev said. "But even he is not certain that the horsemen are coming. The vision he showed you was a mix of what might be in our future, and what has been in his past." Tatev took the Infinium back from Erik. "Either way, there is a rumor that the secret to avoiding the four horsemen is written in this book."

Erik looked at the blue leather book and then back up to Tatev. "Are you telling me that this book holds the knowledge to save the world from the four horsemen, and it was just sitting here in Axestone, and nobody cares about it?"

Tatev smiled and shook his head. "Not exactly," he said.

Erik slapped his thighs and let out a frustrated sigh. "I don't understand you," he said. "Most of the time you go on and on with such clear detail that I can learn everything about something like your glasses, but now, when the subject is so important it will help me decide whether or not I want to find Tu'luh and fight him again you talk in riddles."

Tatev frowned. "Alright," he said quietly. "The truth is that many people have tried to read The Infinium. All of those people have either been driven mad to the point that they killed themselves, or they have been turned to babbling idiots. The most anyone has ever successfully done is to read the first few portions of the book." Tatev turned the book so that Erik could see the edges of the pages. "The portions with these pages, the ones that look lighter in color, those anyone can read without problem." Then he rubbed a finger over the darker portions a couple times. "The portions that look brown, those are the dangerous parts." He opened the book to the first brown page.

Erik saw a strange golden cord tied into a bow over the page. He could see that the cord actually went through all the rest of the pages, sealing them shut. A small lock held the tied cord in place so it could not be accidentally undone.

"To open this portion, and look at its contents, is to tempt fate itself," Tatev said in a voice barely above a whisper. He stared at the golden knot for quite a while before closing the book. "As it is, there are many things I am hoping to uncover in the first portion. Things that will help us learn more about the vision Tu'luh showed you, and see whether it is an accurate depiction of what will happen, or simply a representation of what *might* happen."

"What if you find out that he is right?" Erik asked. "Then what do we do?"

Tatev shrugged. "Then I suppose we will have to open the bound portion of the book and see if we can't stare into the gaping black hole of fate to find the answers we are looking for." Tatev rose to his feet then and started to walk away. "Go back to Lepkin and Marlin," he said. "I have told you all I can for now. If I find something useful, I will come and let you know."

Erik watched the curious librarian walk away, shoving his nose deep into the first few pages of The Infinium and nearly stumbling every other step as he banged into crates or barrels on the barge. Erik was now feeling more confused than he had ever been. He kicked his feet out and stretched his legs while he leaned his head back over the top of the bench, letting his neck and head dangle ever so slightly. He couldn't help but feel powerless and trapped. Worse than that, he was starting to question Lepkin, which was something he had never done before. Sure, he had always found his master hard, difficult to study under, and extremely rigid and strict, but never in his wildest dreams had he ever imagined Lepkin to be *wrong*. Now that possibility was creeping full into Erik's mind, and the vision that Tu'luh showed him of the horsemen came along with it.

He thought about the title that he was supposed to have as the prophesied hero. The Champion of Truth. An interesting phrase now, it seemed. He closed his eyes and focused hard. What was truth, exactly? Before it had seemed so clear. Right against wrong, the dark and the light. But now? Now everything was gray, and the answers were no longer easy. He thought about all of the people who had fought with him at his home. Had they all died for nothing? Would he have been better off sparing their lives and convincing them to join the warlock? What good would it really serve to protect the Middle Kingdom from Nagar's Secret only to have these unstoppable horsemen come and destroy the entire world?

The barge lurched sideways and then the river's current pushed it downstream.

"Next stop, the falls above Hamath Valley," the barge master shouted.

Erik looked up and watched Axestone fall away from them as the current slowly built up speed and pushed the barge faster and faster on its way. He realized then that he shared a lot in common with the barge. Both were being pushed by forces much stronger than they, and the course of those forces seemed unstoppable regardless of any action he might take. In that moment he felt more prisoner than champion.

CHAPTER EIGHT

"Eldrik," Silvi said softly as the boat lurched to a stop next to some rocks. The waves rhythmically bumped the side of the boat into a large, algae covered rock and Silvi stretched her hand out in a vain attempt to steady them. "We are here."

"I don't want you to call me that anymore," he responded. "My name is Aparen."

Silvi nodded wearily. "I forgot," she said. "Come, let's go."

Aparen nodded and the two of them clambered out into the shallow water, *splooshing* down and sinking slightly in the sand below. They let the boat drift off and carried their belongings onto the beach. Aparen's stomach growled loudly.

"I have another piece of bread left," Silvi offered.

Aparen turned up his nose at it and shook his head. He checked that the emerald amulet was secure around his neck and then he adjusted his belt to straighten his clothing. "So, where do we go from here?" he asked.

"Follow me," Silvi said. She tossed her raven black hair behind her shoulders and trudged up the gently sloping beach. Sand and bits of shells clung to the bottom of her white dress and caked her shoes and legs. Aparen followed only half a step behind.

He looked up beyond the beach to where the great pine trees stood. They were each several feet in diameter. They were so large that he doubted whether even the two of them would be able to touch fingers if they both tried to hug around one of the trees.

"They are Elder Pines," Silvi said without looking back. "They only grow here in AghChyor."

"They're big," Aparen noted. He took in a breath of warm, salty air and could almost taste the rich, thick pine scent from the trees. As soon as he neared one he picked up a fallen pine cone and wiggled his fingers in between through the tough layers looking for seeds.

"I wouldn't do that," Silvi cautioned.

"Why not?" Aparen asked. "I eat pine nuts all the time back at home."

"Elder Pines are different," she said. "The nuts they produce

Erik and the Dragon

are bitter, and can make your stomach go sour if you eat too many."

Aparen shrugged. He plucked one nut out and plopped it into his mouth. He didn't see what the problem was. The nut was larger than other pine nuts he had eaten, but otherwise it still smelled the same. He bit into it and started to chew. For the first second and a half the taste was pleasant, woody with a hint of pine and a meaty texture. Then it turned extremely bitter the more he chewed. He noticed Silvi standing and watching him then with an "I told you so," look on her face. Aparen forced a smile and kept chewing until all the bits were just small enough to swallow without gagging.

"Worth it?" Silvi asked.

"Not horrible," Aparen replied. His face involuntarily jerked to the side and a shiver ran down his neck.

Silvi laughed and shook her head. "Come on, we have a long way to walk yet."

Aparen shuddered again and scraped his tongue against his teeth to make the aftertaste go away. He weaved around the lumbering pines, following Silvi's white silk dress and glancing around at his surroundings. The forest was not unlike the area around his home. The trees were similar, albeit much larger, and the ferns and bushes were all familiar as well. Yet, there was something about this forest that felt different. He kept scanning the plants, looking for what it might be, but he couldn't quite figure it out.

"Death," Silvi commented dryly.

"Excuse me?" Aparen said as he double-stepped to catch up to her side.

"That thing you are looking for, the thing that makes you feel uneasy, it's death," she explained. "Come this way." She motioned for him to follow her down a thin, fading path of old flagstone nearly buried in the underbrush and dirt on the forest floor. They walked for about ten minutes before finally stopping before a large mound of dirt covered in dead grass and rocks. She pointed to it. "The gnomes used to be the guardians of this forest," she said. "They were driven out. Many of their dead are buried in mass graves, like this one, others have their bones scattered about the island. Since their death, the balance in this forest has shifted. That's why it feels different to you than the forest around your home."

"You feel it too?" Aparen asked.

Silvi nodded. "This forest has great magic in it. With the gnomes killed and driven out, that magic has been left imbalanced. Imagine an eternal night without the promise of the dawn. That is how this forest is. The magic it produces no longer has its counterpart that created the balance here. Now there is only death."

"Who drove the gnomes away?" Aparen asked.

Silvi shrugged. "Dremathor is his name." She paused for a moment and then turned back to Aparen. "Dremathor is the shadowfiend we are looking for. He is the one who helped Gondok'hr."

Aparen nodded. "So there is no life on this island anymore?" he asked.

"Some," she said. "But not much. Certainly not the kind of life that used to exist while the gnomes presided over the Elder Pines."

The pair walked around several large mounds and then through a long forgotten settlement. A wall of stone roughly nine feet high stood before them. There was no gate, only an opening in one side that allowed them to enter through. Aparen noted that the walls were almost twice as thick as they were high.

"It must have taken a long time for gnomes to build this," he noted.

Silvi nodded. "They lived here for thousands of years. There are many villages like this one on the island."

Rectangular stone houses stood all inside the wall, rising just about as tall as the surrounding barrier, and topped with square, flat stone shingles. Lichen and moss grew on the stones now, but even still, Aparen could see that the gnomes had used colored stones in their building to create geometric shapes and designs on every outward surface. Between the houses were small pens of stone, with rotted wooden gates crumpling off to the side and weeds overgrowing the area. In the very center of the village stood a monolith about four feet wide by four feet thick. Its surface was polished smooth and it rose twenty feet into the air. A brass pyramid capped the top of the monolith, pointing to the sky above.

"How could gnomes lift something like this into place?" Aparen asked.

Silvi turned and shrugged, but she didn't slow her pace. She

Erik and the Dragon

continued on through the village and out the other side while Aparen leaned in to rub his hand over the smooth surface of the monolith. When he finally realized how far Silvi had gone, he hurried to catch up with her.

Outside the village, an old stone path led into a thick forest. They followed it, winding their way in between the massive oaks and pines that stood over them like silent sentinels. The silence unnerved Aparen. There were no birds, no rustling leaves, not even a wind. It was as if the land itself was nothing more than a quiet monument of the past.

Aparen glanced up to the trees, and then shook off the nagging fears that nipped at the back of his mind. The two of them walked for an hour before they came to a stream. Silvi pointed onward, and the two of them walked alongside it for a while. Neither of them made a sound until Aparen clumsily kicked a stick with his feet while looking above at the trees. The stick skittered across the ground and smacked Silvi in the leg.

"Sorry," Aparen said quickly.

"It's alright," Silvi replied. She bent down, raising the hem of her skirt a little to brush off her leg. He watched, admiring her curves as she rose back upright. If she noticed him watching her, she didn't show it. She just continued on. Aparen watched her walk away for a moment before moving to follow her.

"How old are you?" he asked her.

Silvi stopped and half-glanced over her left shoulder at him. "Why does it matter?" she asked.

Aparen shrugged sheepishly. "No reason, I just... I don't know. I was just wondering." The young witch turned around to face him and leaned in close. Aparen's heart thumped loudly in his chest when the two locked onto each other's eyes. "What I mean is..." Aparen stammered, and couldn't finish the sentence. He wasn't even sure what he wanted to say. There was just something about her that entranced him at times. He could feel the warmth from her breath as she sighed. Her lips were only a foot away from his.

"I am old enough to be your mother," Silvi said suddenly, breaking off the trance.

Aparen cocked his head to the side and studied the woman from head to toe. "I don't believe that," he said. Her skin was far too supple, her curves were tight and youthful. She didn't have any wrinkles in her face, and even her voice lacked the sound of age. He couldn't believe that she could be more than five years older than him.

"Believe it," she said with a short nod. "I have been a witch since three years before you were born. I joined the coven when I was fourteen."

Aparen mentally added the fourteen years to his seventeen, and then added the additional three years. *Thirty four.* He shook his head again in disbelief and looked her over once more. "That is not so old," he said after a moment. "My mother is much older than that."

She moved in closer and caressed his cheek with her left hand. "My magic has kept me looking the same since my twentieth birthday." She then smiled and moved her index finger to the corner of his mouth. "It will keep me like this long after the gray hairs have started to set in on you."

He was no longer listening. He leaned in with hungry, slightly parted lips. A strong palm is all he connected with as his face smushed against her hand. He backed away awkwardly, blushing. "Sorry," he offered.

"If you want me, I will be yours," Silvi said quickly. "But you have to want me for me, and not just for my appearance." She turned abruptly, swinging her hair into Aparen's face and walked away.

"How do I prove that to you?" Aparen shouted enthusiastically.

Silvi shook her head and laughed. "You are a young man, it is going to take a lot to convince me that your desire comes from above your belt."

He stopped mid-step, taking the words in for a moment and then he shrugged it off and walked after her. He wasn't sure how to convince her, but he was sure that he did want her, now more than ever before.

CHAPTER NINE

"We have made anchor," Nerekar said dryly as he peered out a small porthole.

Gilifan moved over to take a look and saw rock wall lined with wooden pikes protruding straight out two-thirds the way up. "This is Pinkt'Hu," Gilifan said. "Formerly an orcish stronghold, until the noble knights of the Middle Kingdom conquered it. Too bad most of the buildings were destroyed in the battle though, it was surely a much better looking city before the humans put their hands on it."

Nerekar grunted. "I am not concerned with such things," he said. "Will you need me to come with you?"

The necromancer shook his head. "No, I have a short meeting here. I won't need anything from you at this time."

"The men above are moving that large crate," Nerekar said. "What is in it?"

Gilifan shot a sour look at the assassin. "That isn't any concern of yours," he warned. "Just know that it is something the master holds dear to his heart."

Nerekar nodded that he understood and went to the cot that he had been using for the duration of the journey. He dropped onto it and slung an arm over his eyes.

Gilifan made his way up to the main deck. He stretched his left shoulder by pulling it around his back and gently tugging upward with his other hand. The waning light of the sun cast long shadows over the docks that stretched outward to the sturdy, tall buildings. He could see a lamp man walking on stilts, lighting street lamps with a hooked torch and pausing only long enough to ensure that each lamp was fully lit before moving on to the next. A few people moved along the docks, carrying boxes and crates from the other ships into large warehouses that lined the docks.

The necromancer heard soft, steady footsteps coming up behind him. He turned to see the captain. "We are ready to move the crate," he said.

Gilifan nodded slowly. "Do exactly as I instructed you," he warned. He wasn't all that worried about the egg being damaged.

Dragon eggs had thick, unrelenting shells that could withstand much more than one would expect. However, he did not like the idea of others discovering the precious item. He shuddered to think what might happen if word were to spread of a dragon egg in the Middle Kingdom.

The captain, sensing Gilifan's reticence, laid a hand on the man's shoulder. "How long have you known me?" he asked.

Gilifan turned and looked the man in the eye. "You are my late sister's husband," he answered. "Which is the only reason I have trusted you so far." The captain smiled and nodded contently.

"I will not fail you."

Gilifan sniggered indifferently. "Still, if you should fail me, or allow your men to be careless, I will end your life faster than a boy kills a spider on his kitchen table. Remember that." Gilifan turned and walked down the gangplank toward the dock, leaving the captain to contemplate his warning.

As he strolled into the city, a cold breeze came in off the sea, bringing with it the stench of salt and low tide rot. The odor mixed and swirled through the streets among the heavy wood smoke that stung the necromancer's eyes and assaulted his nostrils. A mangy, gray cat skittered across the cobblestone in front of him. Fast on its heels was a much larger, tabby cat growling and pouncing at the gray cat's tail.

Thin, waist-high fog rolled in from the sea with the next wind. Gilifan gathered his cloak about himself in an effort to keep the chill out as he strolled farther down the main thoroughfare. On either side of him merchants were packing up the last of their wares from the street and moving them into the stone and wood row houses lining the cobblestone road. They also pulled the wooden shutters in and Gilifan could hear the slight ring of metal hooks slipping into the eyelets to hold them closed.

With the sun sunken under the horizon, darkness fell upon the city quickly. The street lamps did their best to chase away the shadows, but with the fog growing thicker, it was becoming more difficult. Luckily, as Gilifan made his way closer to the looming manor at the end of the street, the streetlamps became larger and more frequent. He also noticed more people out and about in the street, though they were almost all guards or patrolmen. Walking in pairs, the guards wore black tunics over rustling chainmail with black, shiny greaves protecting their shins and thighs. Their

Erik and the Dragon

helmets were simple, open faced steel caps with a sheet of chainmail sloping down the back of their necks and a few inches down their shoulders. Most of them carried spears or halberds. An unnecessary show of power and strength in a city as well run and orderly as Pinkt'Hu was said to be.

Each pair that he passed watched him closely, but none of them stopped him. Even when he approached the wrought iron gate that sealed off the manor from the rest of the city, no one said anything to him. He stood for barely more than a moment before the gate was opened from the inside by a large, gray haired man.

"I will escort you inside," he said. "Lord Finorel has been expecting you."

Gilifan nodded and followed the large man up the gray slab walkway as it wound around a circular pool with a pair of cherubs spouting water in the center. The necromancer hardly glanced at the bubbling fountain. He just walked past it, keeping his eye on the grand, arched mahogany double doors and the trio of guards standing before them.

When the gray haired man waved, the three door guards all scrambled to the side, well out of the way. The burly guard barreled into the doors, hardly seeming to slow as he pushed his way inside. The light from the foyer was almost blinding. A rush of warm air, scented with lavender and vanilla wafted out to greet Gilifan.

He stepped onto the tan marble floor and a servant rushed in to close the doors behind him.

"May I offer you some tea, or perhaps a brandy?" the servant asked.

Gilifan shook his head. "I would prefer mulled wine," he said.

The servant cocked his head to the side and bowed slightly before backing out of the large entryway to disappear into a hallway on the left.

"Mulled wine?" the gray-haired guard asked. "Interesting choice."

"It's cold outside," Gilifan replied. "Besides, Lord Finorel always keeps mulled wine on hand. Has ever since I have known him."

The guard nodded and pointed through the arched hallway before them. "I can lead you to the drawing room."

"I can manage," Gilifan said sourly. He strode beyond the guard, down the marble hall. He passed ivory colored pillars alternating with busts and statuettes, mostly of famed warriors past. He walked beyond the first two doors on his left and then turned to enter the third. He pushed it open and moved quickly inside to take a seat in a red, high-backed velvet chair near the hearth.

A small fire crackled and popped, giving its heat to the room around and allowing Gilifan to thaw his legs and feet. He had only just relaxed into the chair when the door opened again. In walked the servant with a silver goblet. The smell of chives mixed with the aroma of warmed wine. The necromancer took the drink and offered a small nod of appreciation to the servant.

"Anything else?" the servant asked.

"I don't suppose Lord Finorel has any roast duck around?" Gilifan asked.

"I'm afraid not, milord," the servant said. "Duck has been rather scarce this season."

"I see," Gilifan said as he took another sip of his drink.

"I can offer mutton, or perhaps a cut of veal."

Gilifan shook his head and waved the servant out.

His wine was nearly gone by the time the door opened again and Lord Finorel walked into the room. The man was dressed as regally as ever. Black leather boots polished to a high sheen, laced with golden silk cords and topped with a pair of tassels. Billowing red pants swept out to the side, exaggerating the man's girth. A thick brown leather belt held the ridiculous pants up around Finorel's wide waist with a silver buckle prominently displayed over the man's bulbous belly. A maroon shirt fitted with two vertical rows of gold buttons clung tightly around him, straining to hold itself together. The sleeves puffed out like the legs of his pants, making his arms look as though they were fancily wrapped stuffed sausages. A high, ruffled white collar emerged from the shirt's opening to hide the man's thick, flabby neck and double-chin. Whatever wasn't covered with the collar was discretely buried under a reddish-brown beard which was always oiled and impeccably neat.

"I apologize for the delay," Lord Finorel said in his rough, husky voice. "There was some business which needed tending to."

"Pirates?" Gilifan asked nonchalantly.

Finorel closed the door and stomped over to the drawing table. "Heavens no," he said with a laugh. "Trade matters. We lost our main supply of iron ore last week to a cave in accident. I had put out the word that we were looking for new suppliers. For the last three days I have been negotiating with the four biggest mine operators in these parts. Just finished the deal a few moments ago."

"Who did you choose?" Gilifan asked as he rose to his feet and joined Finorel at the drawing table. He didn't actually care which mine Finorel got his ore from, but he had always found that the small talk helped make Finorel more agreeable when it came to discussing his own business.

"I went with Mackelrow. His mine is the closest, and he was able to cut me the best discount. Even said I could station a few of my guards at his mine."

Gilifan cocked his head to the side. "Didn't you have some of your men at your former supplier's mine?" the necromancer asked.

Finorel smirked and raised a thick finger up before his face. "It wasn't like that," he said. "It was a natural cave in, and I had no problems with my former supplier whatsoever."

The necromancer offered only a disbelieving gaze.

Lord Finorel chuckled to himself. "It isn't that I am not capable of such things, but really I had no problem with the former supplier. He was always on time, delivered good product, and charged fair prices. No reason for me to interfere there. The shaft simply collapsed. Killed the operator and thirty or so of his workers. It was a tragedy."

"As you say," Gilifan said. He then looked down to the map on the table. "What about our business?" he asked.

Finorel leaned over the map and pulled a monocle out from his right pocket. He held it up to his right eye and squinted down at the map. "Here," he said as he jabbed his fat left index finger onto the map. "This point here is an old orcish fortress. It is all but forgotten now. The entrance is half-buried and the bulk of the remains actually run into the side of the mountain. One way in, one way out."

"Temperature?" Gilifan asked.

Finorel nodded. "It stays hot and humid year round, just like you wanted. There are natural hot springs inside the fortress that prevent the winter's cold from coming in."

"That is good," Gilifan said. "It will be likely another year before the egg is ready. It will need to be kept warm through the winter."

"No worries," Finorel assured him.

"How do you propose to protect it?" Gilifan asked.

"You already met Bergarax, the gray-haired guard."

Gilifan nodded.

Finorel moved his left hand up to his beard and gave it a slight tug. "He is my half-brother. More importantly, he has taken the oath to join with us. He has a group of mercenaries under his command that are securing the fortress as we speak."

"Mercenaries?" Gilifan questioned. "Do you think that is wise?"

"They are good men," Finorel said with a sharp nod. "Besides, they only guard the entrance. My personal guard will protect the interior of the fortress, and only Bergarax knows what is inside the crate."

"What do the others believe it is?"

"Weapons, gold, the usual contraband, but no matter what they believe, they are my men, and they will not bother the egg."

Gilifan nodded. "How far is this from the city?"

"It is roughly a half day's journey from here," Finorel said. "I will have Bergarax pick up the item tonight, and he will march it out to the fortress before the sun rises."

"Is there still a curfew in effect?" Gilifan asked.

"Did you see any on the streets after sundown?" Finorel scoffed.

"It's astounding what the people let you do."

"The people don't *let* me do anything," Finorel retorted. "But, if I tell them that a curfew keeps them safe and helps me crack down on burglars and thieves in the city, they will go along with it. Fear is a powerful motivator, but you have to know how to employ it properly."

Gilifan nodded. "I would agree with that." He sighed deeply and then extended his hand across the table. "If all goes well, then Tu'luh shall be back for the egg next spring."

Lord Finorel took the necromancer's hand in his own and gave it a hearty shake. "You haven't mentioned what has become of Master B'dargen, how is he?"

Gilifan did his best to keep an expressionless face. "He has died, in the service of our master."

Finorel frowned. "That saddens me. I had hoped to see him again, when the war had been won."

"Worry not," Gilifan said. "He died well, and I am sure he will be justly rewarded when the master has conquered all."

"As you say," Finorel said with a slight bow of his head. "Is there anything else you require of me? I could offer a warm bed for the night."

"No," Gilifan said. "I should leave now. I have a long way to travel yet, and the Blacktongue waits for me aboard the ship. I should return soon. His kind are useful if well trained and kept in check, but they are somewhat like large, reckless dogs. If you leave them for too long they will chew up the house in their boredom."

"Of course," Finorel said with a shrug. "I have employed a few of them myself, when the occasion warranted such measures. I understand. I will send a pair of my personal guard to escort you back to your ship."

Gilifan arched his left eyebrow. "You think I need protecting?"

Finorel sniggered and shook his head. "No, but with the curfew in effect, it will look strange if you walk freely about the city. Best it look as though you are escorted officially."

"As you say." He turned and went for the door, then paused and turned back to Lord Finorel. "I heard duck has not been plentiful this season, is that accurate?"

Finorel nodded grumpily. "Very few have returned from the south this year," he said. "The orcs either suffered a harder winter last year, or their chiefs grew very fat."

"Well, then perhaps it is time someone stir them up with something to do. It would be a shame to see the orcs grow fat and lazy."

Lord Finorel snorted. "Best of luck to you, my friend. I hope to see you again soon."

Gilifan nodded and left as quickly as his feet would carry him.

CHAPTER TEN

Something slammed into Erik's foot again. He jerked awake to see the barge master kicking him.

"We're here," the man said, pulling at the ends of his moustache. "Come help me tie off."

Erik looked around quickly. Men were busy about the barge, moving to and fro with heavy, thick ropes. They yelled to some others who had already made it to the river bank and were busy wrapping the ropes around thick timbers stuck deep in the ground. The barge master dropped a chain into Erik's lap.

"This is for the gang plank," he said. "Go and hook it up." The man pointed to the gang plank and Erik quickly got up to help.

He bent down next to the plank and looped one end of the chain through an iron loop at the bottom end of the plank.

"Here, boy, toss it here," one of the crewmen shouted from the bank.

Erik stood, balled the rest of the chain together and heaved it up and out to the other man, watching the chain unravel like a snake thrown through the air. The chain splashed and jingled as it extended to its full length. The crewman caught the end, quickly jerking his head and face out of the way and then he pointed to the plank.

"Lift up the bottom end when I tell you," the man shouted.

Erik moved into position. He watched the crewman walk the chain around a heavy, sun-bleached timber that had a groove worn around the middle of it. The chain slipped into the groove easily and the man took up the slack.

"Now?" Erik asked.

"Aye, now, boy," the man said. Erik lifted the end of the plank and slid it up to the edge of the barge. "Now I'll pull and you keep the plank steady so it doesn't fall in the river before it's in place."

Erik nodded and grabbed the side of the plank.

The barge master came up then and kicked the top end of the plank with his boot. "Here, lad, come and hold the top." He

Erik and the Dragon

hooked a length of rope out from under the plank with the toe of his boot and pointed to it. Erik blushed and ran over to the rope. He bent down and grabbed it.

"Hold steady," the man on the bank shouted. Then he began to pull the chain around the timber, drawing the long plank out over the side of the barge.

"Mind the hooks, boy," the barge master warned.

Erik nodded, noting the thick iron hooks on the bottom of the plank, on either side of the rope. He peered around to see the slots the hooks slid into and did his best to line them up as the man on the bank continued to pull the chain. He had to take short steps to keep from bashing his knees on the plank, but the work was easy enough. The hooks slid right into place on the first try, ending with a slight *click* just before the man on the bank reached out and took the bottom end of the plank in hand and set it to the ground. Then the crewman gave the chain a quick yank for good measure before using an iron lock through the links to hold it, and the plank, in place on the bank.

"Well, if this whole dragon chasing thing doesn't work out for you, I might take you on as a deck hand," the barge master said as he clapped Erik on the back.

Erik smiled politely, choosing to simply acknowledge the comment rather than insult the man by saying how beneath him he thought that work would be.

Tatev came up then with a serious look on his face. "Actually," he started, "if he fails, then we will all likely be dead."

The barge master's eyebrows arched up and the man twirled the right end of his moustaches as he frowned down at the short, red haired librarian. "Well, perhaps he could help me navigate the stars then," he said with a smirking shrug.

Tatev frowned and pushed the golden spectacles up on the bridge of his nose. "I don't think…"

"Give it up, Tatev," Lepkin called out from behind. He and Lady Dimwater walked through the group and down the gangplank. "Come on," he said. "We still have a long way to go."

"Shall I get the pack mules?" Erik asked.

"My men will get them," the barge master said, then he whirled around and walked off barking orders at the crew members still on the barge.

"Navigate the stars," Tatev said under his breath as he

stepped onto the gangplank. "Have you ever heard of such a thing?"

Erik knew that Tatev wasn't really asking for an answer. The man was simply thinking out loud, another one of his more endearing traits that Erik liked about as much as the endless history lectures. He turned and went back to the bench he had been napping on and reached under it to grab his sword and backpack. He fastened the items to himself and then joined the others on the bank.

"Come, I want to show you something," Lepkin said. He put a hand on Erik's back and gently pushed him forward alongside the river.

Erik could hear the roaring water as it broke around the large boulders in the river to leap off over the edge. He and Lepkin walked right up to the edge, scanning the vast valley before them. Erik glanced behind him, looking at the green forest flanking the river and then turned back to the valley. He couldn't make sense of it. There were no trees. There were no bushes. He couldn't even see flowers or grass. Despite the mighty river dropping down into a large, tear-shaped pool and then flowing through the valley itself, the land was dark and barren.

"Is there no life?" Erik asked.

Lepkin shook his head. "Not here," he replied. "Hamath Valley was once a green, lush land with forests, farms, and grassy fields stretching from here to the edge of the Middle Kingdom. Now it is only a wasteland. Seeds unlucky enough to fall here are never able to take root. The soil is tainted with the blood of the ancients, and littered with the bones of men, elves, and dwarves. I wanted you to see this, because this is what we are trying to stop. If Tu'luh has his way, all of the Middle Kingdom would become like this. I know he showed you a vision, and I know that Tatev has been scouring that book of his, but I wanted you to see this for yourself, with your own eyes."

Erik nodded and scanned the scene before him. Off in the distance he could see the mountain ranges coming together, each dropping down to meet around a few towers and spires that Erik could only just see. "Is that Tualdern?" he asked.

Lepkin nodded. "The gate city of the elves. It is what separates the Middle Kingdom from the eastern wilds. It will take us the better part of a day to reach it, if we are lucky."

Erik and the Dragon

"Lucky?" Erik asked.

Lepkin crossed his arms. "Hamath Valley is not a place I wish to be caught in come nightfall," he said grimly. "The land is not only barren, it is cursed. Those who venture into it without the guidance of the sun are never heard from again."

"Why?" Erik pressed.

Lepkin shrugged. "Some say the ghosts of the fallen are doomed to repeat their battle, and claim the lives of those who are foolish enough to venture inside at night. Others assert there is a beast that has made this valley its home. Nobody knows for certain."

Erik looked back at the librarian for a moment out of reflex.

Lepkin shook his head. "No, not even Tatev knows what the true cause is," he assured him.

Erik's eyes widened and he turned back to the valley. "So how do we get down there?"

"There is a trail, but it is already too late today. We will make camp tonight here on the ridge. At first light we will go down."

Erik nodded. A chill ran up his spine. It was as if a pair of eyes were staring at him from somewhere below. There was something down there. He could feel it.

He and Lepkin walked back to the group and they went about clearing the ground and laying out bedrolls. Tatev and Marlin went to the river bank and began fishing. Lady Dimwater arranged a pair of fire pits and conjured up blue flames to keep the area warm.

The barge master collected the rest of his payment from Lepkin, bid everyone farewell, and then he and his crew set off up river. Erik watched the vessel, noting that it took almost all of the crew to propel the barge up stream against the current. Only the barge master and two others stood along the deck while everyone else either heaved and pulled against great oars, or helped steer the barge clear of rocks with long poles that they stabbed into the water to move the vessel accurately.

"Definitely not the kind of work I would want to do," Erik muttered under his breath.

"Why is that?" Lepkin asked curtly. Erik frowned and blushed. He didn't realize that Lepkin was close enough to hear him. "Is it because you think the work beneath you, or because you imagine fighting dragons to be easier?"

Erik sighed. "I am not judging *them*," he said quickly. "I just don't think I could do that for all the days of my life."

"Not adventurous enough for ye, eh?" Lepkin asked with a nod. "I can understand that, but believe you me, they make good money for what they do."

"Just seems too confining to me," Erik mused as he watched the barge steadily lurch upstream.

"I got one!" Tatev yelled from the bank excitedly. Erik and Lepkin turned to see Tatev pulling a shiny, two foot trout out of the river. "Oooh, he's a fighter!" the librarian said as he twisted the hand net around the fish and hurried up the bank with it flopping wildly and thrashing its tail about. Tatev pulled a small wooden club out from the backpack at his feet and smacked the fish over the top of its head. A sickening *crack* was followed instantly by a couple of small, jerky twitches from the fish. Then it was still. Tatev looked up, grinning wide, his deep dimples bookending his up curled lips and white teeth. "Erik, come I will show you how to properly roast a blue trout."

"Go on," Lepkin said with a nudge. "I'll finish setting up the camp."

Erik followed Tatev to the closest fire and Tatev set the fish down in a large pan. He pulled a knife and jammed it into the fish's belly and started cutting up toward the mouth. He then made a couple of short slices on either side of the fish's jaw before ramming his finger down the fish's mouth and pulling hard. The cartilage and bone split as the guts and innards came out in one slimy mess, dangling from the lower jaw. "Here," Tatev said as he handed Erik the fish. "Run your finger along the spine and squeeze out the rest."

Erik took the fish, turned it upside down and ran his right thumb down the spine. The cold meat slimed around him as he pushed out the mucky blood and gunk along the spine. When it was all out, Tatev pointed to the river.

"Now go rinse it while I get a few sticks to make a spit."

Erik got up and went back to the river. He clenched his left hand hard around the tail and tried to hold the head with his right as he swished the fish back and forth in the current. It wasn't until the fish was back in the water that he realized how slimy it truly was. He almost lost his grip a couple of times, but he managed to keep hold on the fish until it was clean.

Afterward, Erik went back to the fire and saw Tatev

Erik and the Dragon

sharpening both ends of a long, thick stick. One end he shoved into the ground outside of the fire pit. When Erik gave him the fish he promptly turned it upside down, so the tail was up, and jabbed the stick through it. He then wiggled the stick until the angle over the fire was just right.

"It has to be close enough to catch the heat," Tatev explained. "But, not so close that the flames scorch the outside before the inside is fully prepared." Erik nodded. Tatev pulled a small leather pouch out of a tin can and dumped a small amount of powder into his hand. "This is a mixture of salt, rosemary, and a hint of cumin." The librarian licked his lips. "Been a long time since I have had some good trout!" He rubbed the powder onto the outside of the trout and then backed away.

"Here," Marlin called out from behind them.

Erik and Tatev turned to see the prelate carrying a net with three more fish, all of them larger than the one Tatev caught. "Think you can clean them all?" Marlin asked.

Erik nodded reluctantly and took the net.

"How did you catch so many?" Tatev asked.

Marlin pointed to his eye. "I do have an advantage over you, my friend," he said. "I can see where the fish are hiding."

"That's cheating," Tatev commented.

Marlin shrugged. "There is no cheating in fishing," he replied.

Tatev sighed and took the net out of Erik's hands. "Come on, I'll help you," he offered.

Twenty minutes later the entire group was seated around the fire. Each took half of a fish to begin with, which left one additional fish over the fire. Erik and Tatev shared the fish that Tatev had caught because Tatev said his fish would taste best not only because of his special powder, but also because it was caught fairly.

Erik didn't know if cheating made the other fish taste bad, but he did know that Tatev's fish tasted heavenly. The outside skin was crispy and crunchy, yet the meat inside was soft and flaky. A hint of smoke flavor had mixed with the rub to produce one of the most mouth-watering meals he had ever tried. He scarfed the food down, hardly stopping to take a drink in between bites.

"There is more if you want," Marlin said.

Erik nodded and started to get up but stopped abruptly when a great, piercing shriek tore through the air above. He flinched, looking up to see the source of the sound when out of nowhere swooped down a massive eagle. Its talons ripped through the fourth fish over the fire and its mighty wings stirred the smoke and flames as it took off for the sky again, ripping the stick clean out of the ground and taking it along with the fish.

"Now, that wasn't fair," Marlin commented with his mouth half full of food.

Tatev turned and shrugged. "I thought you said there was no cheating in fishing?"

Everyone laughed.

*****

That night, as Erik looked up to the stars from his bedroll, a cold breeze rushed up over the cliff and wrapped itself around the camp. The blue fires hissed and crackled against it as they were bent low to the ground. Erik felt a shiver course down his skin and he pulled his blanket around him tighter.

Crrrack!

Erik nearly jumped out of his skin as he flipped around to peer out into the darkness in the direction of the cliff. He didn't see anything, but he could hear it.

Thawump!

His heart almost stopped. His breath caught in his throat.

"Don't let it get to you," Tatev whispered from nearby. "They don't ever leave the valley."

"What is it?" Erik asked. "Is it the souls of those who fought here before?"

Tatev frowned. "I don't know," he said. "All I know is I won't be caught in that valley before sunup or after sundown. Not for all the gold in the world."

A mighty roar rose up from the valley floor, like a great beast. It sent goose bumps down Erik's arms. The wind grew fiercer then, howling and wailing like an army of the forgotten dead. Erik looked around and saw everyone else was sleeping soundly. Lepkin and Dimwater were lying side by side, Marlin was a few yards beyond them. Jaleal was sitting with his back propped against an oak tree. Even Tatev drifted off into sleep after a few minutes.

Erik did not sleep. Even seeing his friends so peaceful and calm did nothing to allay his fears. He couldn't help but feel as though whatever was down there was about to come up over the cliff and devour them all. The few times he managed to close his eyes, his ears would seem to pick up more sounds. There was nothing he could do to calm his mind.

He gripped his sword, hoping it would give him courage to sleep. It didn't.

Finally, after hours of waiting for the threat to come after him, he had had enough. He rose from his bedroll and went to the edge of the cliff. He felt the same feeling as he had before, something was watching him. He could feel the cold, steely eyes upon him as easily as if he had felt a raindrop in late autumn fall upon his face.

He wasn't sure why, but he let his fear turn to anger. His hot rage slipped down his arm and lit his sword with the searing, white flames. Then he opened his mouth and shouted at the valley. A great ball of white light erupted from within him and illuminated the area below.

Misty figures flashed and streaked out of sight, fleeing from the light and howling in anger and fear. He couldn't make out most of them. They scattered so quickly that all he could see was their movement.

Then his eyes landed upon one image. A large humanoid stood at the edge of the tear shaped pool, staring up at Erik and smiling. It raised a misty hand and curled its sharp, taloned finger in a come hither motion. Then it snarled and Erik's light vanished.

Wailing and yowling erupted from the valley floor and a great wind rose up, wrapping around Erik and pulling him toward the edge of the cliff. His heart fluttered and a lump caught in his throat, stopping his breath. A cold, gripping fear coiled itself around his spine, sending shivers through his limbs as the magical wind drew him closer to the edge.

A strong, determined hand clamped down on his left shoulder and ripped him back from the edge. "We should wait for the light," Lepkin said sternly. "Those beings down there can't abide the sun."

Erik nodded twice, eyes wide and fixed on the cliff's edge.

"What did you see?" Lepkin asked.

Erik shook his head slowly. "I don't know. Maybe a man, maybe a ghost. I couldn't tell. But it was real, I swear!"

Lepkin sighed and pushed Erik farther away from the edge. "You don't have to worry about convincing me, Erik," he said. "I *know* they are real. That's why we pitched camp up here for the night. Some forces are best left alone, even for the Champion of Truth."

"I'm sorry, I just…" Erik's words trailed off. What had he hoped to accomplish? Why had he gone to the cliff in the first place?

"Don't beat yourself up over it," Lepkin said as if reading Erik's thoughts. "Come, I will keep watch for the rest of the night."

Erik saw Dimwater sitting up in her bedroll, watching them as Lepkin moved to sit at the edge of the camp, planting himself between Erik and the cliff. Dimwater brushed her hair over her left shoulder. She glanced up to Lepkin, who simply nodded at her and she offered a slight smile.

"Erik, come lay over here in Lepkin's bedroll," she said.

No sooner had he managed to squirm under the blanket and lay his head down than he started snoring loudly.

"Thanks," Lepkin said.

Dimwater smiled with a quick nod. "He should sleep soundly now until the morning," she said.

"I didn't think they would call to him like that," Lepkin said.

Dimwater sat silently for a moment. "They have been waiting a long time," she said after a moment. "I am sure they can sense the power he carries."

"We will have to be careful tomorrow," Lepkin said. "Do you think they will stay hidden from the light?"

Dimwater shrugged. "I am not sure," she said.

"Everything I have read says they cannot abide the light of the sun," Tatev put in quickly from the side.

Lepkin turned to regard the curly haired red head. "Have you read anything about being able to pull victims over the cliff?" he countered.

"Well…no," Tatev said with a frown.

"It's Licenien," Dimwater said. "I would wager my life on it."

"Licenien," Lepkin repeated. "The battle mage?"

"No," Tatev corrected. "Licenien was the Tarthun priest. He led two hundred zealot warriors into Hamath valley. He was considered Nagar's most loyal ally by many, and some even say that he was one of Nagar's trusted advisors." Tatev rubbed a weary hand over his face, wiping a long yawn away and shaking off the night. "He died in battle."

Erik and the Dragon

"But not before cursing the valley," Dimwater said.

Tatev nodded. "He swore that he would get his revenge on all the living foolish enough to tread in his grave."

"We will need to keep our wits about us tomorrow then," Lepkin said.

"It would be simpler if we could just use magic to get there," Tatev said with a hopeful look to Dimwater.

She shook her head. "I have never been to Tualdern, and even if I had, the city has powerful wards against all kinds of magic. I would only be able to put us in the valley anyway."

Tatev sighed and shrugged. "I am going to try and get some sleep, if that's possible after talking about Licenien." The little man wriggled into his blanket and pulled it tight around him.

"You should get some sleep as well," Lepkin said.

A howl came up from the valley below.

Dimwater rose to her feet and looked over to the cliff.

"What are you thinking?" Lepkin asked.

Dimwater answered with a sly smile. "You are not the only one with tricks," she said coolly. "I want to see what is down there."

Lepkin reached out as she walked by and seized her arm. "I can't let you do that," he said.

She smiled at him and bent down to kiss him. The moment her lips touched his, Lepkin's body went limp and she used her magic to guide his sleeping body down to the ground. She gave him another kiss, this time on the cheek, and then continued toward the cliff. She looked down into the darkness. Something within her breast stirred and she instinctively turned her head slightly to the right. A glimmer shone in the darkness on the valley floor. A smile crept over her face.

"Come down," a harsh, gravelly voice whispered from the darkness.

Dimwater turned away from the cliff and walked several yards away without answering the voice.

"Do you fear me?" the voice taunted.

"Not hardly," Dimwater muttered as she picked a spot on the grass and sat down cross-legged. She kept her back to the cliff and whispered the words of a powerful spell. She closed her eyes and felt the energy rush through her body. Her skin tightened with gooseflesh, her neck and spine shivered, and her heart beat quickly in her chest. It felt as though a whirlwind was born inside her chest, stirring up her insides and pulling at them. After a moment, she opened her eyes and pushed up to stand again. The others still slept, just as she had wanted.

She rubbed her right hand over her left forearm and felt a tingly, warm sensation course over her. Then she turned and saw her body still sitting on the ground. A silvery-blue cord extended faintly from her body and feeding her spirit with the energy it needed to maintain the out of body spell.

"Now, I will come," she told the voice. She floated above the ground, quick as a sparrow yet as graceful as a butterfly. She went out over the edge of the cliff and gently descended down to the valley floor. It was still dark, as it had been before, but now she could see scores of silvery spirits and beings watching her. One of them looked particularly unpleased.

"You are too cowardly to come in the flesh?" he taunted.

"I think the word you are struggling for, is clever," she replied evenly. She dropped onto the ground in front of the being and glanced around at the other hungry eyes around her. "Without my body, you have no power to attack me."

"Then be gone," the ghoul said. "You have no place here."

Dimwater stepped forward and reached into the being, gripping it where its spine should have been. "Licenien, I know it is you," she said evenly.

The ghoul's eyes flashed red and he opened his humanoid mouth to reveal sharp fang-like protrusions. He bent forward to bite her, but she held him firm and kept him at bay. "Body or no body, I will rend your spirit apart and devour your energy."

A multitude of ghouls rushed forward swiping and biting at the cord connecting Dimwater to her body. Silvery twinges of pain ripped through her. She whirled on the ghouls and dispersed them with a flick of her wrist. They shrieked in pain as her magic ripped them asunder.

Licenien backed away cautiously, the fight gone from his eyes. "How can you command such power?" he asked.

"As I said," Dimwater began. "Without my body, you have no power to attack me. Furthermore, I know you, and I know your curse."

"You know nothing," Licenien hissed. "Why have you come to torment me, witch?"

Erik and the Dragon

"I am no witch," Dimwater replied evenly as she stalked around Licenien.

"Only a witch could command this kind of magic," Licenien said.

"Let's just say I am not exactly human," Dimwater said.

Licenien studied her then and nodded after a moment. "I can see it now," he hissed. "You are demon-born."

Dimwater laughed. "Well, if you can see that, then you should know that in this form I am more powerful than you."

"What are you going to do, kill me again?" Licenien laughed. "You have nothing to scare me with?"

"What if I told you that I could banish your spirit to Hammenfein?" Dimwater asked. She watched the ghoul's face turn sour and then flashed a sly smile at him. "Or, perhaps we could come to an agreement, what do you think?"

Licenien floated away and then back, as if caught by a sudden breeze. "What kind of agreement?" he asked. "What do I have that you could possibly want?"

"Suspend your hunting," Dimwater said without hesitation. "Cease praying upon mortals in the valley for a time."

"Ah, you seek to travel through my valley," Licenien growled. "No, you know my vengeance must come upon all foolish enough to descend into Hamath valley. It is mine, and so is every soul that ventures into it."

"Four days," Dimwater said. "That's all I ask."

"No," Licenien said. "I saw the young man atop the cliff. I smelled his blood, I felt the energy in his soul. He, and all the others with him shall die if they come down."

Dimwater floated to him and gripped the ghoul again. "Then I send you down to Hammenfein, and all the souls that now follow you will be free to pursue their own peace." She lifted her left hand and a bright green flame grew above her silvery form. She inched it closer to Licenien. He tried to struggle away from her grasp, but he couldn't escape her grip. The flame licked his form and he jolted suddenly.

"Stop!" he cried. "By Icadion's beard, stop!"

Dimwater pulled the fire away. "I know the true power of your curse," she said. "You subjugate all the souls in the valley to you, and force them to serve you, but none of them can save you from me. More importantly, none of them can save you from

Hammenfein. With you gone, they will be loosed from your control, free to seek peace, and you will be forgotten."

"Licenien will never be forgotten," the ghoul hissed.

"They will tell your story around campfires for a few years, to be sure, but after a while, when Hamath valley is traveled freely once more, no one will remember your name. You will be forgotten, and your soul will be lashed to the pillars of the fourth level of Hammenfein, where you will waste away forever."

"You want four days?" Licenien asked.

"Four days," Dimwater replied. "After that, you may retake your valley and do as you wish."

Licenien looked over his back, farther into the valley and then he grinned slyly. "Alright, you may pass through the valley for four days. After that, I will hunt again."

Dimwater released Licenien and stepped out over the water of the tear-shaped pool.

"Who is the boy?" Licenien called out after her. "He must be quite special for you to risk your life like this."

Dimwater stopped and turned, debating whether to tell him. "He is the Champion of Truth," she said.

Licenien's grin melted away and he cast another glance over his shoulder. "Is that so?" he asked.

Dimwater only nodded and started to ascend through the air.

"Then you should turn back," Licenien said after a moment. "Do not cross through this valley."

Dimwater stopped and turned around to face him again. "You gave me your word," she warned. "If you break it, I will banish you."

"It is not me," Licenien said. "There is something far worse than me on the other side of the valley."

"What?" Dimwater asked.

"I don't know," Licenien admitted. "It is on the other side, beyond the border of the valley. Whatever it is, I do not think even you can defeat it. So, I say again, turn back."

Dimwater was not sure what to make of Licenien's sudden concern. "Why would you care?" she asked.

"I didn't, at first," he said. "But if he really is the Champion of Truth, then I would not want him to be destroyed. Turn back."

"But you fought alongside Tu'luh and Nagar," Dimwater pressed.

Licenien took on a grim expression. "I will give you your four days, but I would suggest you turn back."

"The elves in Tualdern will provide us with shelter," Dimwater replied evenly. She decided that Licenien might be trying to trick her somehow, so she dismissed him and ascended up the cliff.

She floated easily until she was near her body, then she stepped down and slid back into herself. All at once a hot flush washed over her and her muscles went slack. Her heart ceased pounding and started to flutter spasmodically. Her stomach flipped and she leaned over just in time to avoid retching on her own lap. She wiped her mouth and spent a few moments regaining her composure before she dared try to stand.

When she finally made it to her feet she noticed that Lepkin was standing near her. No, he was *holding* her. He had one arm around the back of her waist and the other holding onto her right arm, propping her up.

"What did you do?" Lepkin asked.

"I'll be alright, in the morning," Dimwater replied wearily.

Lepkin helped her back to her bedroll. "I don't mind when you use your sleeping spells on Erik, but in the future, I would prefer you not use them on me." Dimwater nodded and eased into her blanket, asleep before Lepkin could say another word. Lepkin backed away and sighed, glancing over his shoulder at the cliff's edge.

Whatever she had done, the howling wind was gone, and somehow the night seemed more peaceful.

*****

Erik and the others broke camp as soon as the first rays of sunlight broke through the sky. Jaleal and Tatev fried up more fish for breakfast while the others packed their bedrolls onto the mules. Lepkin was quick to assist Dimwater with anything that she was doing, and very adamant about making sure she had enough to eat for breakfast.

Erik wasn't sure what to make of it, but Dimwater was moving a bit slower than normal, and even Marlin was watching her carefully. Something had happened in the night, but he thought better of asking what that something was. He finished with his chores, ate the plate of fish he was given, and then fell in line with the others as they descended the steep, rocky path that switched back and forth down the north eastern side of the cliff.

The going was slow at first. The upper portion of the cliff trails were littered with loose shale, gravel, and small branches and twigs. The morning dew still sat upon the grass and foliage, adding an additional degree of difficulty to an already demanding path. The nearby roaring waterfall meant that each of them had to yell if they wanted to be heard by anyone else, but Erik didn't mind that part. It meant that Tatev couldn't ramble on with one of his endless historical anecdotes.

He turned around and saw Tatev's mouth moving. He wasn't sure who the man was talking to, but he was still talking despite the waterfall. Just then, Erik's foot slipped a little. Not enough that anyone else noticed, but enough to make him turn around and focus on the trail. He was grateful that he did, because one more step would have put him in a pile of mule dung. Erik stepped around the steaming brown pile and continued on down the trail.

The pool below glistened in the morning sun, almost making up for the lack of trees or vegetation on the valley floor. The black, dry soil stretched out before them like a thick carpet over the valley floor. Dead, gray trees twisted up into the sky or lay scorched upon the ground. No birds sang, no bees hummed. There was no movement anywhere in the entire valley that Erik could see, other than his group.

After about an hour of switching back and forth down the trail, the group made it to the bottom, near the tear-shaped pool of water. One of the mules went over to the pool to drink, but Marlin was quick to pull the animal away from the water.

"The water isn't good here," Jaleal said casually as he walked up beside Erik and peered into the depths of the pool. "It comes from a good source, but the valley corrupts it."

Erik started to ask about it, but he saw Tatev walking toward them so he thought better of it and quickly moved back into the line behind Lepkin and Dimwater.

The group was silent as they forged ahead over the rough terrain. The trail had stopped by the pool, so now they just picked their way over the barren landscape as best they could. Dust kicked up around their footprints and it was then that Erik realized there were no other prints in the ground. There were no tracks or marks of any kind. He decided he would keep an eye to the ground, looking to see if he could spot any tracks or scat of any kind. After four hours of walking, he gave up the pursuit, realizing there would be no other tracks.

At least there were no beings like what he had seen last night. No howling winds and no ghosts. That was definitely a good thing as far as Erik was concerned. He thought back to the one that had almost pulled him down off the cliff. As he recalled the terrible being, his skin tightened into goose bumps and he couldn't help but look over his shoulder.

Tatev caught Erik's gaze and offered a happy, but tired, smile. Erik returned the gesture and slowed down to let the librarian catch up with him. Perhaps one of Tatev's anecdotes would help him pass the time without thinking of last night's ghosts.

"Having fun?" Tatev asked when he caught up to Erik.

"Not exactly," Erik said. "Any more luck with the book?"

Tatev shook his head. "I have only read a few pages." He fidgeted with his fingers, rubbing the tips together and then he bit his lower lip for a moment. He stopped and grinned sheepishly when he noticed Erik watching him. "I know it is silly, but I have been hesitant to read even the first portion of the book. I mean, I have always fantasized about reading it, but now that I have it, I am a bit apprehensive."

"I understand," Erik said.

"You do?" Tatev asked.

Erik nodded. "I used to day dream about being a mighty warrior, chasing down monsters and earning fame for my family and riches for myself. Now that I actually have that chance, to do something that *no one else* can try to do, I am scared and so nervous I wish I could just go back to Kuldiga Academy." Erik looked to the ground and shrugged. "I guess that makes me a bit of a coward."

"On the contrary," Tatev said with a decisive finger in the air. "The fact that you are scared, but continue on with your quest makes you very brave."

"That sounds like something Lepkin would say," Erik said.

"He is a smart man" Tatev said.

"Are we doing the right thing?" Erik asked. "I mean, what if Tu'luh is right? What if fighting him really just seals our doom, should we continue on?"

"Why are you asking me?" Tatev asked.

"Because you have read *a lot* of books. You always know so much about any subject we happen to be talking about. If anyone will know the answer, I think you would."

"I am flattered," Tatev said with a half grin. "But, to be honest, the books don't teach you everything you need to know in life. They are a good start, but they don't have all the answers."

"Then how do we know what we should do?"

"Well," Tatev said as he looked on down the valley. "What do you *feel* we should do?" he asked.

Erik screwed up his face and snorted.

"No, I'm serious," Tatev said. "What do you feel?"

Erik knit his brow as if he had to think carefully, but he didn't. He didn't need more than just an instant to know what he felt. "I must stop Tu'luh, and destroy the book."

"Some people call that intuition, others call it instinct, or your gut, but I like to think we are all connected to a higher wisdom if we just listen to what our heart tells us."

Erik nodded. "It still doesn't help me figure out what to do about the vision Tu'luh showed me."

"True enough, but if every answer came easily, we would have no challenges in life, and if there were no adversities or hardships, then there would be no satisfaction or triumph. Life would be stale, and we would be stagnant creatures not worthy of the life we have been given."

Erik nodded, half-heartedly agreeing as he turned his gaze back to the horizon. The mountains off in the distance started looming closer and closer. Erik noted that even the tall, hard peaks looked as barren as the valley they walked through. Heavy, thick gray clouds hung in the air near the mountains, drifting lazily toward them. A flash of lightning tore through the sky, followed shortly by low, rumbling thunder. A few moments later gray streaks fell from the clouds, signaling the first rain of the storm.

"Well, at least it will temper the afternoon heat," Tatev commented.

The group trudged through the valley, slowing considerably when they caught the rain. The hard, black ground was turned into ankle-deep muck that sucked their boots down with each step. More than a few times Erik found himself stopping to stuff his foot farther into his boot after the mud pulled it part way off. The mules weren't faring much better either. Their hooves *schlucked* and *popped* with each step. The thunder rolled in steadily and the clouds blotted out the sun.

With the darkness came the howling wind that sent shivers down the back of Erik's neck.

Lady Dimwater moved in beside him then. He looked up and saw her hair clinging to her back and her dress stuck to her skin, accentuating all of her curves. Erik blushed and looked away, afraid that either Lady Dimwater or Master Lepkin might have seen his stare. Then a thought came to him.

"Couldn't you use your magic to keep us dry?" Erik asked.

Dimwater laughed softly. "Every expenditure of magic requires strength and energy, just the same as every use of your muscles requires effort on your part. The rain is not hurting us, so there is no need to waste my energy now when we might need it later."

"But don't you conjure up drinks?" Erik asked, recalling the tea she had summoned after catching him in her office. Erik regretted the words almost as soon as they left his mouth. He closed his eyes and turned away from Dimwater.

She laughed. "Sometimes a person just needs a drink," she said with a wink.

Erik chuckled a bit too, relieved that she wasn't taking offense at his comment.

The two of them talked for the rest of the trip, until the great towers of Tualdern loomed into view and the group found themselves on the brick and stone path leading out of Hamath valley up to the alabaster gatehouse. A deep, wide green moat ringed the tall white walls. The slender, conical towers jutted up into the sky like great spears with windows of rose colored glass.

"I have long wanted to visit the city of the elves," Dimwater noted. "Never had reason to do so until today though."

"Something is wrong," Lepkin announced from the front. He turned and motioned for everyone to stop. "There are no sentries at the gate, and the portcullis is open."

"No, no, no," Tatev said. "The elves in Tualdern have the most disciplined warriors in the Middle Kingdom, they would never leave their gatehouse undefended." The diminutive man jogged up to Lepkin's side, pushing his spectacles up the bridge of his nose and flipping the lenses down so he could inspect the walls.

"The magical wards are gone too."

"Well, we can't camp out in the valley tonight, and we should at least check around inside to see what is going on," Marlin said.

"I have a bad feeling about this," Jaleal commented with a quick glance over his shoulder at the dark and dreary valley.

"Marlin is right," Lepkin said. He moved forward with a determined gait. "We go in." He didn't draw his weapon, but his hand shifted to hover over the handle at the ready. Jaleal, on the other hand, pulled his mithril spear out and swept his gaze back and forth as he followed Lepkin.

"Perhaps I will wait out here," Tatev said nervously.

"You'll be safer with us than alone," Dimwater assured him.

No one else said anything. Erik moved in between Lepkin and Jaleal, keeping his hand resting on the hilt of his sword. They passed through the gatehouse into a wide, slate courtyard spotted with raised planter beds of blue and green marble filled with roses, tulips, and lilies. A fair share of the flowers had started to wilt and dry up, and weeds could be seen sprouting up around them. Beyond the planters was a central well, covered with a brass, conical grate.

"Move the mules next to the well," Lepkin said as he moved off to the nearest door and pressed it open. He motioned for everyone else to wait outside before ducking into the dark portal. What was likely only a couple of minutes seemed an eternity to Erik. The city was quiet, and the previous night's howls and ghosts played on Erik's imagination while he fixed his eyes on the doorway and waited for Lepkin to return.

Thunder rumbled overhead, reverberating on the stone walls and towers through Tualdern. Heavy, round drops of rain fell upon the slate sparsely at first, then the rain thickened and poured out on the group all at once, leaving them little time to scramble under a large second floor balcony for shelter while they waited for Lepkin to return.

A few moments later the door opened again and Lepkin emerged, brandishing his sword.

"Find anything?" Dimwater shouted across the courtyard.

Lepkin scanned the area and then raised a finger to his mouth. He jogged across the courtyard and sheathed his sword just before rejoining the group. "Something terrible has happened here," he said grimly.

Erik and the Dragon

"Where are the elves?" Jaleal asked.

Lepkin shook his head. "I don't know. From the wreckage I saw inside that house there has been some fighting here. We'll need to search the area for more clues, but my best guess is that the elves are likely holed up somewhere taking shelter, or they are dead."

"Dead?" Tatev echoed. "Who could have conquered the elves of Tualdern?"

"Not *who*, but *what*," Lepkin corrected.

"What do you mean?" Marlin pressed.

"Inside the house I saw savage claw marks on furniture and walls. There were also some bloodstains across the floors and walls, but no bodies. Whatever it was, I don't think it was human."

"What is the plan?" Dimwater asked.

"Split into two groups," Lepkin replied. "You, me, and Erik will go to the main hall. Marlin, you will take Jaleal and Tatev and search the houses and shops along the eastern side. You can start with this one." Lepkin pointed to the door behind them.

Marlin nodded and Jaleal went to press the door open.

"Divines be with us," Tatev whispered as he tentatively followed the other two.

"Come," Lepkin said to Erik. "We should be quick, and quiet."

Erik nodded. He felt the same knot in his stomach that he had endured during the battle at his home. It made his gut flip and lurch until he burped a small amount of stinging, pungent vomit in the back of his mouth. He gagged it down as best he could and tried to keep a straight face.

Lepkin must have noticed it, because he turned around and placed a hand on Erik's shoulder. "Nervous?" he asked.

Erik nodded. "Does the feeling ever go away?"

Lepkin drew the left corner of his mouth out into a half-grin. "Fear never leaves of its own accord. It falls to you to conquer it, and banish it from your mind."

"How?" Erik asked.

"By realizing that you are stronger than your fears. Live your life in such a way that you will know that your principles are right and true. Then, you will also know that the only enemies you will have are those who stand against truth. Just as truth and right will conquer evil, it will help you banish your fears." Lepkin paused and looked into Erik's eyes. "Does that make sense?"

"I think so," Erik said. "But, being right doesn't make me stronger than my enemies, especially if there is some monster that wiped out all of the elves."

"You misunderstand," Lepkin said. "A life lived in pursuit of truth will always result in victory. Even if our enemies are stronger than us —even if they should slay us—we can take comfort knowing that we will live in Volganor alongside the just and good men and women of old. So, do not fear death. Also, don't let fear cripple you from doing good in life. It will take practice, but you will understand in time."

"We should go," Dimwater said softly.

Lepkin nodded and the trio walked back into the rain across the courtyard. They checked the myriad roads and alleyways branching away from them as they made their way to the large white and gold palace. If not for the rain and the pit in Erik's stomach, he might have admired the exquisite workmanship more, but he barely noticed the large golden double doors with crystal inlay, or the stained glass cathedral style windows adorning the sweeping alabaster walls.

Dimwater flicked her wrist and the doors opened in a flash. A putrid stench wafted out from the opening and forced them each to gag and jerk their heads away, covering their mouths with their sleeves.

"What is that?" Erik asked.

"Excrement and death," Dimwater replied.

"This must be where they took refuge," Lepkin said. "Come, let's go in."

Erik forced his feet to follow as Lepkin and Dimwater made their way inside. Despite the many windows, the hall was dark and nearly impossible to see in. Lady Dimwater conjured a blue orb of light over each of them to help them navigate the room.

Shadows danced and swung around broken benches, overturned tables, and hunks of armor strewn along the brown floor. Erik looked closer at the armor and realized that some of the breastplates or helmets still had bits of their owners inside. Erik's stomach flipped and he fell to his knees, dry heaving and gasping for breath.

"Stay with him, I will continue on," Lepkin told Dimwater.

The sorceress moved to kneel next to Erik and began weaving

Erik and the Dragon

a quick spell. A second later the stench was gone from the room and Erik's stomach calmed. He looked up to her and met her smiling, compassionate eyes.

"I thought you said it wasn't good to waste magic?" Erik said.

"In this case, I don't think it was a waste," she replied warmly. "We should continue, Lepkin is already pressing on further. Can you stand?"

Erik nodded. It was then, as he looked to the floor, that he noticed it wasn't really brown. It was gray, but there was dried blood covering so much of the floor that it had appeared brown. His stomach threatened to lurch again, but Dimwater placed a hand on his shoulder.

"Look at me," she told him.

Erik nodded, focused on her eyes, and then rose to his feet and the two of them continued on. They passed by the remains of the shattered ivory thrones and into a rear hallway that led up a flight of spiraling stairs to another grand hall. Here, as before, broken bits of furniture and bodies littered the floor. Spear shafts and broken swords were scattered about, and dried blood covered the floor and streaked along the walls.

"They fought hard," Dimwater noted.

The door at the end of the hall opened and Lepkin came out. "Some of them made it out, I think."

"How can you tell?" Dimwater asked.

"More of a feeling I have," he replied with a shrug. "Also, the lock on this door wasn't broken, and the jamb itself shows no sign of forced entry. I think some of the warriors in this room survived, and then they escorted the rest of the survivors out. This room has no blood stains anywhere."

"Sounds plausible," Dimwater said. "Any idea what could have done this?"

Lepkin shook his head. "No, but I think we should go and get the others. We'll make camp here for the night."

"Here?" Erik asked incredulously.

Lepkin nodded. "There are heavy wardrobes and large piece of furniture inside this room we can use to bolster the door. It isn't ideal, but we won't be able to make it through the valley again before nightfall. And if this thing that attacked the elves is still around, we would do best to take shelter here."

"I'll go and get the others," Dimwater offered. "You two can prepare the room."

Lepkin nodded and motioned for Erik to join him.

Dimwater was out in the courtyard within a few minutes, looking this way and that for any sign of the others. Her nose happily pulled in the petrichor with each breath, ridding her nostrils of the horrid odors she had endured in the palace. The darkness was seeping into Tualdern now that the sun hung low in the western sky and the rain clouds still sat over the city. She knew she would have to hurry. After passing four streets she saw a couple of people down next to a doorway in a row of buildings. She turned and went to them, thinking it was Marlin and Tatev that she saw.

Her spine tingled when she realized what it was.

"What are you doing here?" she asked.

The ghastly figure floated toward her. "I mean you no harm," the ghost said. "We have our truce for four days, as agreed."

"Then what do you want?"

"Licenien sent me to warn you," the ghost said.

"Warn me of what?"

The other ghost floated into full view then. "The creatures that have descended upon the elves of Tualdern are still here," the second ghost said.

"If he knew of this, then why not tell me this last night himself?"

The first ghost hissed. "He was not sure what to make of your claim about the Champion of Truth," he said. "He thought perhaps you were simply boasting, or lying to conceal your true intentions."

"What changed his mind?" Dimwater asked.

The second ghost came closer. "We followed you as you traveled through the valley today," he said. "After listening to Erik and the man with the books talk for a while, Licenien decided we should help you."

"Then why wait until now to warn us if you were with us all day?"

"During the daytime we are not able to make ourselves known to mortals, it is part of our curse. So, we waited here until dusk, so we could speak with you."

"What killed the elves?" Dimwater asked evenly.

"Lycans," the ghosts replied in unison. "They came in from the east, and there was a bitter battle with the elves. Now the few elves that are left have gone underground, and the lycans roam the surface at night."

"Will you stay and fight with us?" Dimwater asked.

The ghosts shook their heads. "Our power is in the valley. Even though Tualdern sits on the edge of the valley, we have no power here over mortals."

The second ghost pointed in the direction of the valley. "If you come back to the valley, we can help you."

Dimwater stood there for a moment, trying to discern whether she was being trapped by the ghosts. "Why should I believe any of this?" she asked.

Just then a blood-curdling scream rent the air and Dimwater twirled around in the direction of the scream.

"It is too late," the first ghost said. "They are here."

Dimwater turned back around, but the ghosts were gone. Her heart raced. She glanced at the buildings around her, hoping against hope that Marlin and the others would come out of one of the nearby doorways.

"This way," urged a whisper in Dimwater's ear. She looked up and saw a faint image floating quickly for the end of the street. Despite the doubts in her mind, she ran after the ghost. It turned to the right, down a narrow alley. Dimwater followed and nervously glanced over her shoulder as a terrible howl erupted from somewhere else in Tualdern.

The ghost came into view then, pointing at a large gray building across the street from the alley's opening. "The other three from your party are on the second floor."

"How do I know you aren't lying?" Dimwater asked.

The ghost faded away with the wind, leaving her standing there alone. She stepped to the edge of the alley and peered down the street. Everything was quiet again. Then, a door opened in the gray building across the street and out walked Jaleal, Tatev, and Marlin.

Dimwater smiled and ran over to them.

"Did you hear that scream?" Tatev asked nervously.

The sorceress nodded. "We have to get to Lepkin and Erik as quickly as possible."

"What's that?" Marlin asked, pointing down the street.

"I don't see anything," Tatev said.

Dimwater turned, but she also saw nothing. "What do you see, Marlin?" she asked.

"It is a strange aura," he responded. "Something I have not seen before."

Dimwater conjured a cloud beneath her and grabbed onto Tatev's shoulder. "Everyone hold on," she commanded. They each grabbed hold of each other's hands and the cloud launched them up about twenty feet above the ground. Then the sorceress called in a mighty wind that sped them off through Tualdern toward the palace.

"What is it?" Jaleal asked as they swerved through the rooftops.

Dimwater remained silent, not wanting to say what she thought until she knew for certain.

"There are more of them," Marlin asked. "At least seven have come into the city."

"Seven what?" Jaleal asked with a high pitched, frustrated tone.

"I think they might be werewolves," Dimwater said after a moment.

CHAPTER ELEVEN

Erik almost jumped out of his skin when the window flew open and Dimwater came sailing in with the others. They all tumbled to the floor in a heap and the sorceress was quick to magically seal the window.

"What's the matter?" Lepkin shouted.

"Is the door sealed?" Dimwater asked.

Lepkin nodded and pointed. "We put everything against the door we could find."

"They are only about a minute behind us," Marlin said. "Are there any other ways into this room?"

Lepkin shook his head. "*What* is coming?"

"Werewolves," Dimwater replied evenly. "At least a dozen of them."

"Ever fought a werewolf?" Jaleal asked Lepkin as he twirled his spear around in front of himself.

"Have you?" Lepkin countered.

The gnome nodded. "Twice." He moved to the door and looked at the pile of furniture in front of it. "Send me out into the other chamber," he told Dimwater.

The sorceress shook her head. "We should stand together, here."

"How many of us have mithril weapons?" Jaleal asked. Then he looked down with mock surprise and held his spear up. "That's right, just me!" He pointed to the door. "You know as well as I do that this will not hold. I can do this."

"Mithril isn't the only thing that can kill them," Tatev said. "Fire, decapitation, and stabbing them through the heart will all work just as well."

"Mithril makes their blood boil," Jaleal said.

"I thought that was silver," Marlin commented.

"No," Tatev said. "He is right. Mithril makes their blood boil. Silver does too, but mithril is actually stronger."

Erik pulled his sword and let the white flames engulf the blade. The others looked to him curiously. "Why don't we all go out into the next room and counter attack?" he asked.

"We don't know how many are coming," Marlin told him. "I saw at least twelve different auras, but there could be more."

Erik looked around the room and shook his head. "I don't want to die in here, holed up and cowering in some forsaken tower."

"Interesting time to find your courage," Lepkin noted. Then he nodded his head. "The boy is right, we should stand our ground."

"We will need a plan," Tatev said.

Everyone jumped as something slammed into the door, shaking all of the furniture on their side of the door. Angry snarling and low growls were followed by hot, fierce clawing and scratching at the door.

"Too late for a plan," Jaleal said. The gnome licked his left palm and slicked his beard down as he fixed his eyes on the doorway. "When they break through, I will pierce the first through and then Dimwater can blast them with fire at her leisure."

"I'm not accustomed to taking orders," Dimwater said playfully as she moved into position behind him.

Lepkin drew his sword and moved to stand near the side of the doorway. He motioned for Tatev and Marlin to get into a far corner.

Erik move into position opposite of Lepkin.

"No fear," Lepkin told him with a stern look. "No one dies tonight."

Erik nodded, but as the doorway shook violently and the wood began to crack, he could feel the knot returning to his stomach. He had never seen a werewolf before, nor had he ever thought he would. They were beasts of legend used to scare children around campfires. He knew they existed, but he had always thought they lived far away in the eastern wilds. Never would he have guessed they would venture into the Middle Kingdom.

"Erik," Lepkin called out in a forced whisper. "You trained for this," he assured him.

Not for this! Erik thought.

"Listen to your surroundings, observe your opponent, and control your emotions."

Erik thought about it and everything fell into place. He took a deep breath, calming his nerves. He focused on the sounds all around him, not only the scratching and pounding on the door, but also the crackle of his flaming sword, Dimwater's almost inaudible murmuring as she prepared her spells, and Tatev's whispered prayers.

Erik glanced to Tatev and realized that for all of the man's knowledge, he had no capacity to rationally deal with this kind of threat. This realization helped Erik put things into perspective. He steadied his gaze back on the doorway, realigned his grip on the sword, and listened to the snarling beasts beyond the barricaded door.

After a few moments the door snapped and the top of the pile shifted back, tumbling into the room. The lower half of the door was still intact, and the larger pieces of furniture still butted up snugly against it. Erik watched as Jaleal ran up the mound of wooden furniture and launched his spear through the small opening. A great shriek echoed through the hall and something heavy flopped onto the floor, thrashing and slamming itself around on the marble. The gnome then leapt down from his perch and his spear magically reappeared in his hand a moment later. Erik noticed that bubbling, dark maroon blood covered the top half of the shaft.

"One for me," Jaleal said as he jerked his neck to the side, making a loud *crack*. The gnome moved back into place and readied himself for the next strike. The beasts on the other side of the door relentlessly rammed into the door time after time until finally the door splintered apart and the furniture was thrown down. A trio of huge, black beasts tore their way through the barricade. Foamy slobber dangled from their yellow fangs and their two inch long claws ripped the wooden furniture to bits as they clambered through.

Erik moved in deliberately, stepping to the left and hollering at the closest monster to catch its eye. The beast turned and lunged up at Erik's throat, which is what he had planned on. Erik spun out farther to the left, slicing diagonally down across the monster's neck and severing the head from its body as easily as though it had been a doll stuffed with straw. A silver flash flew in front of Erik and he knew that the gnome had slain another beast.

A gurgled growl emitted from the third werewolf as Lepkin ran his sword through the thing's neck and then quickly pulled out to ram his sharp blade through the werewolf's back and slice through its heart.

"Two for me!" Jaleal shouted out.

"Move gnome!" Dimwater commanded. A massive fireball soared through the air and blasted the doorway, disintegrating any furniture still left in the area. Horrid squeals and shrieks erupted from the doorway as the hot spell devoured several monsters.

Tatev screamed out then as the glass shattered in the back of the room and a pair of werewolves jumped in. Dimwater and Jaleal turned to face them, but two more monsters leapt through the burning doorway, snarling and eager for a kill. One of the beasts landed only inches from Erik. The boy brought his sword down to hack the head off, but the werewolf rolled away and then stood on its hind legs like a man. It rushed forward and swiped at Erik's chest with its claws. Erik backpedaled just out of the way and countered with a swing at the werewolf's unprotected torso. The tip of the flaming blade drew a sizzling, red line across the monster's tight, muscled stomach, but it did no real damage. On the monster came, swinging its claws again before dropping to all four feet and lunging forward with its gaping maw.

Erik leapt out to the right and managed to block the biting attack with his sword. The blade bit into the side of the werewolf's snout, but it only enraged the beast. It came in fast and then raised its torso up to slam its front shoulder into Erik's chest, knocking the boy back into the wall.

It brought its teeth down, but Erik managed to squirm away, dropping down to a squat and then forcing his blade up into the werewolf's chest, wiggling it roughly back and forth hoping he was hitting the monster's heart. The black beast twitched and fell over onto the ground nearby.

Erik jumped back up to his feet and quickly scanned the area. Several more werewolves had infiltrated the room. Marlin and Tatev had even joined in the fighting now. Erik took a deep breath and approached his next target quietly from behind as it circled around Dimwater as she engaged three other werewolves. Erik waited for the right moment, and then, just as the beast hunched its back and prepared to lunge, he sprinted forward and brought his flaming blade down upon the beast's neck. Then he rushed in and helped Dimwater drop another one with a quick thrust of his sword to the beast's chest.

"Dimwater, the door!" Jaleal cried out.

Erik and the Dragon

Erik moved in to defend the open window and the sorceress spun around to whip another fireball at the doorway. A group of seven more were running into the room, but they were halted by a wall of lightning that moved like a living shield, pushing and zapping the monsters back out through the doorway. Jaleal moved around the purple, crackling wall, throwing his spear whenever he had an opening.

Erik couldn't see the others. There were still several other beasts in the room between him and the other side. Not to mention the pair he was still struggling to finish off. One of them was bleeding heavily from its right foreleg, the other had a large, gaping gash in its hip area. Yet still he was finding it hard just to keep up with them. They were so fast, and they timed their attacks just so that one would advance right after the other, forcing Erik to move quickly to avoid injury, and not giving him a moment to breathe. He was in trouble, and he knew it.

Around him the others' shouts and cries told him that they were starting to lose steam as well. Magic fire rippled through the air, followed by hissing, snarling gasps and shrieks, but the growls were growing more intense. He stole a quick glance as he spun away from another attack to see that there were more than twenty werewolves in the room. Bodies littered the floor, but still the savage monsters came on. They would not stop until they had caught their prey.

A sharp pain sliced through the side of Erik's right leg. He flinched and instinctively pulled back out of reach as the beast came in for another swipe. Erik brought his sword down and severed the werewolf's hand at the wrist. The beast howled in agony and curled up against the wall near the window.

The second werewolf lunged forward, but Erik was back in his rhythm. He feigned a step to the left and then darted right after the monster had changed course and thrust his sword down through its hairy back. He quickly pulled his sword out and then took a quick hack at the werewolf's neck. Just as it fell to the floor, another one took its place. It launched through the window and came straight at Erik. Erik swung his sword up to counter, but the beast fell short, sliding on the floor with a grotesque *squeeeeeak* as its upper lip dragged across the stone.

A trio of gleaming shafts protruded from the back of its neck.

Erik looked to the window to see a tall, lean figure leaping through the opening. He had a bow in one hand and a blood-stained scimitar in the other. He whirled the scimitar around and gracefully stuck it through the heart of the three legged werewolf that was still hunkered down near the window. The monster let out a short, high-pitched squeal and then fell limp. The elf's long, silver hair spun around as he danced in through the room with a fury Erik had never seen before. Every flash of the scimitar felled another monster, and even the bow was used to great effect as a staff as the elf rammed the bottom into a werewolf's face to break its guard before coming in with his scimitar.

Another elf leapt in, firing a pair of arrows before Erik could even blink. One of the shafts sailed close enough to Erik's face that it rustled his hair. Erik spun to see a werewolf catch the arrows in his neck and fall to the floor atop another slain monster's body. At that point, Erik noticed that several elves had entered through the door as well. They spun through the battle like green clad, scimitar wielding whirlwinds. In the blink of an eye, the fight was over and the last of the beasts fell.

The elves slid their scimitars into well-crafted black leather sheathes and surveyed the scene meticulously. Lepkin moved toward one of the elves and extended his hand.

"Where did you come from? We feared everyone had perished."

The elf turned and grabbed Lepkin's forearm in greeting. "Many of my people have been slain by these wretched beasts," he said. "But we are not all dead."

"How did you know we were here?" Dimwater asked as she stepped over a crisscrossed pair of bodies. "And where were you?"

"It is a long story," the elf replied. "Better you come with us, and we will tell you along the way."

"Are there more of them?" Marlin asked, staring at a hairy, headless corpse nearby.

"Not anymore, these were the last of them," the elf replied evenly. "I am Talimdur, captain of the Tualdern guard. These are my best warriors." Talimdur's face turned sour as he frowned and looked to the ground. "We, along with seventeen others, are all that remain of the once mighty city." Talimdur signaled for the others to exit the room. "We have little to offer you, I am afraid, but you are welcome to share whatever we have."

Lepkin nodded. "We are grateful for anything you can spare."

Erik and the Dragon

Talimdur smiled. "I was told that you had arrived with someone special."

Lepkin nodded and gestured for Erik to come closer. "This is Erik Lokton, the Champion of Truth."

Talimdur took in a slow breath as he looked Erik over from head to toe. "He is very young," he observed.

"But he is strong," Lepkin said proudly. "He has already been through many battles, and he has even routed Tu'luh the Red at Valtuu Temple."

"Tu'luh lives?" Talimdur asked.

"Well, I didn't fight him alone," Erik said. "I had all of you there with me, and the dwarves were there too."

Talimdur folded his hands behind his back and smiled down at Erik. "Honest, and humble; that is a unique mix in such a young human." It was almost imperceptible, but Erik saw Lepkin puff up ever so slightly at Talimdur's compliment.

"Allow me to also introduce the others with us," Lepkin said. He pointed to Marlin first. "This is Marlin, the Prelate of Valtuu Temple."

"A pleasure to make your acquaintance," Marlin said with a slight bow. Talimdur returned the gesture.

"Next to Marlin is Tatev, the librarian of their order. I would wager he is smart enough to rival any of the best scholars in the Middle Kingdom."

Tatev smiled wide and offered a short nod to Talimdur. The elf smiled back.

"This is Lady Dimwater, the best sorceress in the Middle Kingdom."

"Your reputation precedes you," Talimdur said with a deferential nod of his head.

"And finally we have Jaleal, a displaced gnome who stands shoulder to shoulder with the best warriors in the land."

"He means that metaphorically, of course," Jaleal put in with a wink.

Talimdur chuckled and nodded. "That is a mighty spear you hold."

Jaleal held it out before him proudly. "This is Aeolbani."

Talimdur nodded and turned his gaze back to Lepkin. "Come, let us take you to the others."

Lepkin turned back to Dimwater and looked at her. Despite

their triumph, there was a sadness on her face. Her eyes had lost their sparkle and her mouth was turned slightly down at the corners. He went to her and she looked up at him. "I am sorry," he said. "If it is any consolation, I have a friend in Stonebrook. He has a beautiful garden where we can marry. I know it isn't the wedding you envisioned…" Lepkin's words trailed off.

"That will do," Dimwater said softly. She patted his arm and walked past.

Lepkin watched her for a moment and then caught up to walk beside Erik, letting Dimwater have her space for now. Erik and Lepkin stayed close to Talimdur as they made their way back through the palace and out into the courtyard. The other elf warriors stayed ahead of the group, just to make sure there were no other lingering enemies.

As the group left the city through a man-sized hole in the northern wall, Lepkin paused and looked back to Tualdern. "How is it that the city became so desolate?"

Talimdur stopped and his slender shoulders hung low. "It didn't start with the werewolves," he said. "Let me show you." He led them into the nearby foothills and pointed to several large holes in the ground. "These tunnels were caused by sand trolls."

"Sand trolls?" Lepkin echoed. "I thought they lived far to the east in the wilds?"

"Normally that is so. The trolls are nocturnal, so we didn't notice them entering the valley at first. They burrowed in from the nearby mountains and were able to establish themselves fairly well before we caught sign of them. At first we thought they had come in search of game. They preyed upon rabbits, mountain goats and the like. Then they grew bolder and attacked one of our scouts. Naturally we fought with them and set about exterminating them."

"They stayed to fight with you?" Tatev asked. "Sand trolls would not do that unless they were forced to. They almost always retreat from an organized army."

Talimdur nodded. "We were so focused on ridding our lands of the creatures that we failed to consider that fact until it was too late. The fight was bitter and the sand trolls fought extremely aggressively. Looking back on it now, their desperation should have made it obvious. They couldn't go farther into the valley because they only are active at night, meaning they would be destroyed by the ghosts and ghouls in the valley. We should have realized that they only chose to remain and fight with us because they were afraid of something much worse."

"The werewolves," Tatev deduced. "They were being hunted by werewolves."

Talimdur nodded. "Werewolves are also nocturnal. Usually their clans are small, no more than twenty or so in a pack. This one was different. There were hundreds of them, maybe even a couple thousand. The beasts showed cunning that we lacked. They waited until we had destroyed the last of the sand trolls. Then they scavenged the bodies. By the time we realized what was happening, it was too late. The monsters descended on us at night, catching our fair city off guard. We fought courageously, but for every one we killed, they devoured five of us. Some of our people were turned, adding to the monsters' ranks while depleting ours. We lasted only for three days above ground. Then, we were forced to take refuge in the very tunnels the sand trolls had burrowed."

"The werewolves are too large to fit in the burrows," Tatev said with a knowing nod. "It was a smart move."

"It was desperate," Talimdur corrected. "Every runner we tried to send out was caught and killed. The werewolves started hunting us in the day as well as the night, so that we could never send word for help. We were locked in a losing battle of wills. If you all had not come tonight and drawn the beasts back into the city, I am sure they would have won eventually."

"How did you know we were here?" Dimwater asked, repeating her earlier question.

Talimdur turned to her with a serious gaze. "We had an interesting visitor come to us, a ghost from the valley who told us of your plight."

Dimwater nodded slowly. "And you trusted the ghost?" she asked skeptically.

Talimdur shrugged. "I was alive during the days that Licenien walked among the living. I know his treachery, and the curse laid upon him after his death, but I also know how to tell when he is being honest."

"How is that?" Dimwater asked.

"He swore to me upon the souls of his ancestors, and promised to relinquish his hold on the valley if he were lying. A Tarthun, as I am sure Tatev knows, holds ancestors and land more sacred than anything else. He would not have made the oath falsely. Besides, he also told me about the boy here. There was a fear in the ghost's voice. I don't understand what his reasons are for helping our side after all this time, but his worry was genuine. He doesn't want the Champion of Truth to die any more than we do." Talimdur pointed to a nearby tunnel. "We are in here. It will be a tight fit, but it is best to spend the night here and then we will scout the city in the morning."

Lepkin pulled Erik aside and motioned for the others to follow Talimdur into the tunnel. When everyone had disappeared he looked down into Erik's eyes. "Tomorrow, we will hide the mithril box deep in the well. That way, we will not bring it closer to Tu'luh when we begin to hunt him."

Erik nodded. "Will it be safe here?"

Lepkin shrugged. "The elves will do their best."

"What if more werewolves come?" Erik asked.

"We will just have to pray that they don't."

*****

Al drummed his fingers on the oaken table, staring blankly at the silver goblet before him. Faengoril had finished describing the battle at Valtuu Temple, along with the casualty list. All things considered, things could have been much worse. Even still, losing twenty cavedog riders was a heavy price to pay, and much worse than any encounter the cavedogs had faced as far back as Al could remember. He wondered how Erik was faring, and he couldn't help but feel guilty that he had not been there at the temple to protect him. Worse still, he blamed himself for not seeing through Tu'luh the Red's treachery. It was understandable for humans to be hoodwinked, but he was a dwarf. He should have seen it coming. It all made so much sense now. How could he not have known?

Al felt a foot nudge his leg under the table. He looked up from his thoughts to see Alferug staring at him. Al could tell by the look on his counselor's face that he had missed something. The dwarf king turned to look up to Faengoril. The stocky dwarf held his temper behind a heated sigh, but he regained his composure and repeated what he had last said.

"I believe, with everything that is going on, we have to divide our forces. It is not the best strategy, but it is the only one that makes sense. If the Tarthuns have threatened the northern pass, then we should send a small force up north. However, the bulk of our army should be split. Half of it going to investigate this new pass that the trapper told you about, and the other half going south to aid Lepkin and Erik."

"I still think that is too many warriors to send to this supposed new pass. We don't even know if this trapper was telling the truth," the minister of commerce said.

"Why would he lie about it?" Lady Arkyn said.

Faengoril leaned forward, planting his knuckles on the table. "She is correct, he had no reason to make it up."

"Unless he was a Tarthun spy sent to mislead us," another pointed out.

Al sighed and leaned forward. He had had enough of the debate. "We march according to Faengoril's plan. Keep a reserve in the mountain of two hundred dwarves, so we can either send them where they are needed in case something changes once we are all afield, or If nothing changes, then we will at least have them in addition to our home guard to bolster our defenses. We leave as soon as the supplies are ready."

"*We?*" Alferug echoed questioningly.

Al nodded.

"With respect, I must advise against this, my king. Our people need to see stability."

Al dismissed the notion with a wave. "Our people need to see that stability and hiding in the mountain are not the same thing. You will stay here, acting as steward until my return. I will see to my duty, and help Erik slay Tu'luh the Red."

"I am sorry to say, that I must agree with Alferug," the commerce minister said. "We cannot risk losing our king. You have no heir, and we have only just begun to reopen our trade with the outside world. Things are beginning to change for the better, but we need you here."

"No," Al said. "I am needed on the field. I swore an oath to protect Erik, and that is an oath I must keep."

"With respect," Alferug interjected. "You swore an oath to protect our people, and we need you here."

"My absence will not affect our people. My place as king is on the field protecting our people from the greatest danger. Tu'luh is the most dangerous threat our kingdom faces right now. Commerce and poverty can be wrestled with after we have secured our existence."

"As you say," Alferug ceded.

Faengoril nodded and continued on. "I can have our forces ready to move by tomorrow morning."

"We should go within the hour," Lady Arkyn said. "I understand the larger force will take longer to prepare, but they will also travel slower."

"Agreed," Al said. "I will go with you, Peren, and Gorin just as soon as Peren is feeling up to it."

Alferug opened his mouth to say something, but he stopped himself and sighed instead.

Al rose from the table, his chair squawking against the stone floor beneath as it slid back and away from him. He adjusted his belt and shifted his hammer on his waist. He took in a determined breath and nodded to Faengoril across from him. Faengoril returned the gesture and the meeting was adjourned.

Within moments, Lady Arkyn was beside Al. She remained silent as they made the winding trek through the tunnels of Roegudok Hall. Al appreciated that. It allowed him to let his mind wander through his thoughts undisturbed. He was new at being a leader, and his self-doubt nagged at his heart just as much as it made him furrow his brow and stare at his feet as he walked. What would his father have done with a similar situation? Would he have agreed to split his army? Would he have decided to lead a personal charge to the south?

Al couldn't help but question his own motives. Was he truly doing the right thing? Was he dashing off to the south to defend his friend and his people, or was he doing it to fulfill his own lust for freedom and glory? He had never acknowledged it before, but he knew now that his pride was as much a motivator for him as any other altruistic reason he might try to think of. It always had been. If not for his pride, he never would have turned his back on his father to begin with. He would have studied the way of kings, and he would know what to do now. Instead, he found himself wishing his father would reappear and take the weight of the crown from off his head.

Too bad it didn't work that way.

Al sighed and looked up to Lady Arkyn. She caught his gaze with her blue eyes and smiled gently. He thought of asking whether she thought he was doing the right thing, but he decided against it.

Erik and the Dragon

Instead he kept the silence intact until they reached the chamber wherein they had left Peren and Gorin.

The giant warrior saw them and rose to his feet. "Your healers are very skilled," Gorin commented. He pointed to Peren, who sat shirtless upon a stone altar while a pair of gray-haired dwarves alternated between rubbing a green ooze over his burns and then fanning smoke from a special blend of incense onto the wounds.

"I wouldn't have believed this would work," Peren said. "But, the pain is almost gone, and some of the skin has been restored."

Al nodded knowingly. "We dwarves do not have a great repertoire of magical spells, but those tricks we do have are powerful enough."

One of the gray-haired dwarves *shushed* them all and glowered at Peren. "Stop moving," he said roughly.

Al moved over toward Gorin and looked up to the large man. "We are going to ride out as soon as Peren is ready," he said.

"What is the plan?" Gorin asked.

"My forces will handle the Tarthun threat. We will go south to Ten Forts."

"To help Lepkin?" Gorin asked.

Al nodded. "We have a dragon to kill."

CHAPTER TWELVE

Aparen and Silvi sat on a sun-bleached rock near the apex of a hill overlooking the forest they had just emerged from. The witch took out a bit of flatbread from her pack and offered a piece to Aparen. He shook his head and gestured for her to eat it all.

"You will need to eat something," Silvi said.

Aparen shrugged. "I'm not hungry at the moment." He stared off to the tree tops below and shook his head. "I was certain we would have found him by now," he said.

Silvi chuckled. "It is not simply a matter of finding him," she said.

"What do you mean?" Aparen asked.

Silvi took a bite of the flatbread and swallowed it without hardly chewing and then cocked her head to the side. "He has been here for a long time," she said. "He has had time to alter the island to fit his needs. His magic is powerful enough to mask his presence."

Aparen frowned. "You mean we won't be able to find him?"

"I didn't say that," she countered.

"Sounded like that is what you meant."

Silvi laughed aloud. "If it is any consolation, you should take it as a good sign that we are still alive."

"Why?" Aparen asked.

"Because, I am more than sure he already knows we are here."

Aparen glanced around nervously. "You mean he is watching and deciding what to do with us?" he asked.

Silvi nodded. "The good news is we are still alive, which means there is hope yet."

"When were you going to tell me?"

Silvi shrugged. "I warned you about him before we set out to find him. Fear not. If we continue moving north, I think we shall find him."

"How can you tell? I thought you just said he can mask his presence."

The witch nodded. "From here we can see the valley to the north. When the sun sets there will be a few moments where the light of dusk will help me identify where he is."

"How?" Aparen asked.

Erik and the Dragon

Silvi stood and pointed to the valley. "There are no trees there. It is also nestled in between several large hills which are difficult to traverse. The beaches to the south are best for ships, but the thick forests we just came from would prevent large numbers from being able to easily navigate the land. This valley is the best defensible position. As the light of the sun wanes, there will be a few moments during dusk where I might be able to pick out any structure in the valley. Invisibility spells are like mirrors, there is always a reflection to be found. For these kind of spells, that reflection is noticeable during dusk and twilight."

"Can you teach me to look for it too?" Aparen asked.

Silvi nodded. "Keep your eyes to the north," she said. "Do you know what a mirage is?" she asked.

"I have heard of them," Aparen replied.

"Well, you are going to look for an area in the valley where the ground seems to be wavy, or even wet. Take note right now that there is only one small stream that fades off in the distance. There are no other bodies of water in the valley, so if you see anything that looks like water, or waves, then we will know the direction we have to walk."

Aparen nodded and glued his eyes to the valley. They waited while the sun began its descent in the west. Orange and pink hues lit up the sky as if the clouds were aflame. Aparen glanced at the beauty, and then quickly turned his eyes back to the valley, scanning for even the slightest anomaly. Silvi was silent, also studying the landscape. It seemed hours that they sat upon the rock. For the longest time, nothing happened. Orange and pink gave way to reddish purple hues and the land began to darken. Then Aparen pointed to a point almost in the middle of the valley.

"There," he said. "I see the ground looks wavy."

The witch nodded. She raised her hands above her head and called out in an arcane tongue. A black bolt of silent lightning streaked down from the clouds and dashed itself into the area Aparen watched. Aparen expected a great thunder to rumble through the valley, but instead there was a high-pitched shattering sound, as though a great window had been blasted apart with a metal rod. The waves disappeared from the land to reveal a simple, round tower of black stone.

"Not exactly what I expected," Aparen stated.

"Come on, we don't have much time before he will be able to

repair his spell." Silvi jumped to her feet and began running down the hill face. Aparen was quick to follow, stumbling a bit over the loose rocks as he bounded down after her.

Once they reached the valley floor the two of them began running much faster. The grass *whooshed* around them with each step as the knee-length blades swiped their legs and clothes. They leapt over the brook to land in marshy grass and lilies which slowed them down considerably. The mud and muck sucked in with each step, trailing grime and pungent black goo behind their feet.

"What is that smell?" Aparen asked.

Silvi motioned for him to keep up. "Just keep moving," she said.

A weird, cracking sound caught Aparen's attention and he slowed to turn around. A long, scraggly skeleton arm shot up from the grass behind him. The gray, cracking fingers curled into a fist and he heard a hissing sound. Aparen turned back around and started running faster. "We have company," he shouted.

"Curses!" Silvi spat. She pointed out to their right and Aparen saw two skeletons slowly lifting themselves upright. One pulled a rusty sword from the grass and the other slid its jawbone into place before grasping a javelin and launching it at them.

Silvi waved her hand, disintegrating the javelin with magic and yelled for Aparen to keep up.

Aparen stumbled over a root and fell face first into the muck. The grit and grime rubbed into his skin, pasted on by the thick, cold grime. He quickly pushed himself up to his feet and wiped at his mouth and nose to clear his face. The ooze clung to his skin, almost creating a string of slime between his fingers and face as he struggled to clean himself. Finally he used the elbow of his sleeve and was able to take a breath without fear of the muck getting pulled into his nose or mouth. That was when he heard the loud creaking behind him.

He turned and realized he had not tripped over a root. A skeleton hand was clasped around his ankle even now, and its owner was shakily standing up from the ground, dripping the black ooze from its ribcage and skull. Its left arm held a hatchet, and its right arm was severed at the elbow, with the rest of the arm still holding onto Aparen's ankle.

Aparen jumped to his feet, shook the hand free of his leg and instinctively called his shadowfiend power forth. In an instant the spikes shot through his skin, his muscles bulged, and his skin turned leathery as it had before. He roared mightily and lunged forward, shattering the skeleton with one swipe of his taloned claws. Silvi tried to warn him about something, but he wasn't listening. He just leapt from one skeleton to the next, dodging their clumsy attacks and dashing them apart with his savage blows. Shards of splintered bone cracked apart, flying all around the valley, and yet for each skeleton he destroyed, three more rose in its place.

"Aparen, we have to keep moving!" Silvi shouted.

He ignored her. A pair of skeletons moved to attack. One held an axe and the other held an old, rusty sword. Aparen grabbed the hilt of the axe, ripped it free, and then blasted both of them apart with one swing.

A hail of fire and ice rained down, destroying several of the foul beings in seconds. Aparen then turned to see Silvi standing nearby, weaving her hands quickly as she called down the magical hail. He scanned the area quickly, his heart racing and his breath hot with fury. What had been only a handful of enemies had quickly turned into an entire valley of writhing, stumbling skeletons. There were hundreds of them. Despite the hail, there was no apparent escape route.

Aparen saw Silvi struggling to send spell after spell into the mass of enemies. Seeing the fear and concentration in her furrowed brow and fierce eyes awoke something inside him. A hot fire welled within his chest. He stretched his leathery wings and soared up into the air a few feet. He opened his mouth and out spewed a stream of blue and white fire that disintegrated scores of skeletons in the blink of an eye. Then he turned and dove into the grouping closest to Silvi, breaking them apart with the sheer force of his mass. He rose with a fury, striking some with his wings, others with his claws, and devouring others with the power of his fiery breath.

As he moved through the fray, a pale yellow force rose up from the skeletons and flowed into Aparen, giving him additional strength. Any blows that managed to cut through his savagery only caused small slices which were healed almost instantly as he continued to devour his enemies' energy. Then finally, a great thunder rolled out through the valley and all of the remaining skeletons fell back to the muck from whence they had come.

"What is your purpose here?" a loud voice echoed through the valley.

Aparen turned about, looking for the source, but he saw nothing. The black tower that had once been visible was now gone again, hidden behind a spell. "I have come for help," Aparen said honestly.

The voice mocked him with a cackling laugh. "You come to ask for help? Then why do you come in your true form? Do you seek my power?"

Aparen calmed his nerves and allowed himself to shift back to his human form. As it had before, it drained him of his strength and he was left feeling weak. He doubled over, breathing heavily to catch his breath. "I have no quarrel with you. I heard that you had helped another before, and I wanted to ask for your help as well."

No answer.

Silvi turned to the direction where the tower had been. "Gondok'hr has been slain. This is Aparen, and he has taken over as patriarch of the coven."

"Interesting," the voice mused. "Did you slay him?"

"No," Aparen said. "He and I share a common enemy."

"Why should I help you?" the voice grumbled.

Aparen shrugged and looked to Silvi.

Silvi nodded and took over. "We seek only wisdom and guidance. We don't wish to take anything from you, nor do we wish to be a burden. What price would you name for your help?"

The air before them waved and shook, as if a great reflective cloth was falling from around the tower. The top of the spire came into view, and the spell disappeared entirely a moment thereafter. A large man stood at the base. His skin was dark, almost black. His eyes were brown and fixed intently on Aparen. He wore red silk robes and a pair of green velvet shoes that had long, up curled toes that peeked out from under the robes.

"I am called Dremathor," the man said.

"I am Aparen."

"I know who you are," Dremathor said. "I have been expecting you."

Aparen furrowed his brow. "If you expected us, then why attack us with skeletons?"

Dremathor laughed and a thick, brown staff appeared in his left hand. "I have the gift of foresight. I saw two versions of your visit. In the first, you came peacefully after Gondok'hr is slain in battle by one who wields a flaming sword. In the other, you come to destroy me after killing Gondok'hr yourself and devouring his power."

Aparen looked to Silvi. His thoughts ran wild. "But I couldn't kill Gondok'hr," he said.

Dremathor sneered. "Not this version of you, no," he agreed. "Seeing that you are hardly more than a fledgling, I will answer your plea for help." He took a couple steps closer and pointed to the amulet around Aparen's neck. "You will give me an offering. I will take one of two things. You are free to choose which you give me."

"You want the amulet?" Aparen asked.

Dremathor nodded. "Or, you may give me your witch. The choice is yours."

Aparen looked to Silvi, who simply stood silently looking down at her feet. Then he slipped the amulet up over his head and offered it. "You may have the amulet," he said.

"You don't realize how powerful that artifact is, do you?" Dremathor mocked. "This is what Gondok'hr sought, when he came to me for help."

"I don't care," Aparen said with a shrug. "You can have the amulet as long as I can keep Silvi."

"Silvi," Dremathor echoed with a sly sneer growing wider across his face. He held up his right hand and the amulet bolted away from Aparen to land firmly in Dremathor's grasp. "A shadowfiend who values life above power is a rare find," Dremathor commented.

Aparen stood firm and tried to stand tall to show confidence despite the rapidly multiplying butterflies in his stomach. "So now you will help us?"

Dremathor slid the amulet around his neck. "I have one more thing to ask of you," he said. He pointed to Silvi and a cage of black bars encapsulated her instantly. She tried to struggle against it, but she had no magic that could overpower Dremathor's spell.

"You said I could choose!" Aparen shouted as he rushed forward. He slammed into a solid, invisible wall that knocked him on his rump.

"Calm yourself," Dremathor said. "You can earn her back, but first you must do something for me."

"Why should I?" Aparen shouted.

Dremathor chuckled and shook his head. "Your bravery is

admirable, but if you continue to try my patience, I will destroy you. You live only because I am curious to see what you might become in the future."

Aparen slowly stood up and brushed off his backside. He cast a glance toward Silvi, but even she was standing still and silent now. "Alright, what is it you ask of me?"

"To the north, there is a vampire. He has been terrorizing some of the local villages for the last several weeks. Normally I wouldn't interfere, but his activities have started to encroach upon territory that I like to visit from time to time, and he is drawing attention to the area that I don't appreciate."

"You can't kill a vampire?" Aparen asked.

"I can," Dremathor countered with an impatient tone. "But I want to see if you can. If you complete this task, you will win Silvi back and I will help you."

"And if I fail?" Aparen asked.

"Then you will not have been good enough to waste my time on, and you will be dead."

"No," Aparen said. "Whether I live or die, Silvi should go free."

"That is an admirable thought, but I would not agree to such nonsense. If you want her freedom, you will have to earn it. Bring me the vampire's black heart, and I will release her to you. Fail, and she will stay with me."

Aparen looked to Silvi for a few seconds, staring into her desperate eyes. Then he nodded. "I have little choice. Tell me where I can find this vampire."

"I will do better than that," Dremathor approached Aparen slowly, deliberately. A round, red leather container appeared in the air before Aparen. "In this container, you will find a map of three villages. The vampire lives in the wilderness near these villages, but the map does not show you where exactly. You will have to hunt him."

Aparen nodded and grasped the container. "How long do I have?"

Dremathor shrugged. "Take as long as you need. Silvi isn't going anywhere, so if you abandon the task and run away, no one will be any wiser for it. However, *if* you succeed, I want you to place the vampire's heart in the container. When you do that, it will bring you back to me."

"The container will?"

Dremathor nodded. "It is enchanted. Go ahead, open it."

Aparen twisted the lid and looked inside. A golden, blinding light poured out and enveloped him. His stomach flipped and lurched as he lost his footing and fell over backwards. Instead of hitting the ground, his body spun continually, never touching anything as the light whisked him away to some unknown land. An instant later he was standing in a small grove of ebony trees with green moss hanging low from the branches. The scent of pine and dirt filled his nose.

"Your task has begun," a voice said from behind him.

Aparen turned, but no one was there. He looked down to the container and pulled the map out with his forefinger and thumb. "Alright, let's get this over with." He slid his left hand down to his dagger and looked around. It was dark here. The light of day had fully faded away now. What little light the half-moon gave barely sparkled above the dark trees. Not knowing which way to go, he decided to cozy up to the nearest ebony tree as best he could for the night and wait for the morning to set out on his hunt.

*****

Aparen began to stir as the morning sun broke through the branches above. He hadn't slept well during the night, and his muscles were stiff and rigid from leaning up against the tree. Slowly he pushed himself up and stretched his arms and back. His stomach growled something fierce, reminding him that he hadn't eaten since lunch the day before. He looked around and realized he had nothing with him except his dagger and the small container that held the map.

"Perfect," he grumbled aloud. "In a strange land with no food or water and absolutely no idea where to go." He looked up to observe the moss hanging from the trees. He had heard before that moss would grow predominantly on the north side of trees, but these trees were absolutely covered with the stuff, as if they had been thick webs left by careless spiders ages ago.

So he looked up, through the branches as best he could, to see the sun. It had only just come up over the horizon, so as long as he kept the sun on his right and moved quickly, he could at least be certain that he was headed north.

He set off, picking his way through the brush and clumps of thick trees, ducking under the low hanging moss that smelled both pleasant and musky at the same time. He didn't see any animals, but he could hear birds chirping in the branches above him. The ferns bent gently away from him as he walked through. Soon he spied a blackberry bush and moved toward it, plucking the sweet fruit from the thorny vines and plopping the berries into his mouth. The first couple he crushed with his tongue, pressing them against the roof of his mouth and savoring the sweet nectar, but then he began shoveling them in as quickly as he could, hardly chewing before swallowing as he struggled to bury the rumbling sounds in his stomach with the fresh fruit. The bush was as tall as he was in most parts, some areas were even taller, sprouting thorns as big and wide as his fingernails on the thick vines. His hands became stained purple as he devoured the berries and made his way around the bush, plucking off anything within reach.

As he rounded the back side of the blackberry bush something snorted and the vines shook. Aparen paused and tried to peer around the bush to see what it was. A massive head covered with black fur rose up above the bush. A long, brown and black snout pointed up into the air, sniffing loudly before the bear looked down and locked eyes with Aparen. The round, fluffy ears almost gave the beast a cute appearance, but the boy knew better. Bears in the north were temperamental at best, and not to be trifled with.

His mind raced. What had his father always told him to do when confronted by a bear? Was he supposed to play dead, or was it try to act large and frightening?

The bear's mouth opened and it bellowed a low warning sound as white spittle flung out from its open maw. Aparen took a step back and frowned at the animal's hot, horrid breath. The beast then dropped down behind the bush. Aparen slowly backed away, trying to put distance between himself and the bear. The bushes and vines shook again and the bear appeared around the left side of the blackberry bush, walking on all fours and head low to the ground with its large, black eyes fixed on Aparen.

The thought came to him that he could change forms, and overpower the bear, but something kept him from doing so. Even as the bear stalked closer, he remained still. He watched the bear as it meandered side to side instead of coming directly toward him. It sniffed the air a few more times and then snorted, apparently unimpressed with what it saw, and then turned to walk off in a different direction leaving Aparen and the bush. As he watched the large animal slowly lumber away he felt a different urge come over him. If he had so easily been able to absorb the energy of each skeleton, could he also consume the power of large animals?

His left hand twitched impatiently and his desire for more power bubbled up inside of him the same way greed might overcome a man standing near an unguarded pile of jewels and gems. Another pang of hunger struck his gut just then and he looked back at the berry bush.

"Fruit alone will not sustain a man," Aparen said. He closed his eyes and summoned his true form. The transformation happened within seconds as his limbs broke and grew, wings sprouted forth over his shoulder blades, his skin took on the pale, gray color and the hardened texture and his horns and claws emerged from their hidden places. When he opened his eyes, he not only saw the animal before him, but also its energy swirling around it. He launched into a great leap, extending his wings and gliding over to land atop the animal's shoulders and neck.

He pierced the bear's thick hide with his claws and forced the creature down to the ground. It bellowed angrily and rolled its massive body over in an attempt to either throw or squish Aparen. Aparen released the beast and landed harmlessly on the ground. The bear then rose on its back feet and roared so loudly that it caused a ringing in Aparen's head. A massive paw swung down and connected with Aparen's left shoulder, sending him to the ground. He barely managed to escape as the bear lunged for the spot where he landed, snapping his massive jaws together.

Aparen turned and unleashed a fireball from his right hand that blew the fur clean off of the bear's left side and seared the skin underneath. The bear growled furiously and charged in again. This time Aparen took to the air, allowing the beast to sail harmlessly underneath and then he dropped like an eagle, digging his right claws into the back of the bear's neck while latching onto the bear's massive skull with his left. Aparen focused on the bear's energy as he dug in with his claws as deeply as his strength would allow.

The bear's energy, a strong maroon aura that enveloped the animal, suddenly was drawn toward the beast's head. The animal lost its strength, collapsing onto the ground. Its back muscles twitched and quivered. Then, the beast exhaled loudly and the dark energy released from its forehead to be absorbed by Aparen's hand. It flowed into him warmly, strengthening his limbs and expanding his mind. When it was over, he cleaned the beast using his dagger and then he roasted it with magical fire before eating his fill of the grilled, savory meat.

Mind and body now fed to the brim, he was ready to continue his hunt.

As he changed back into his human form he did not feel weak like he had before. He felt normal, or possibly even stronger than normal. He looked back to the half-eaten carcass and smiled as he now realized there had been no reason for him to fear an animal of the forest. He was now a master over such beings, and the bounds were limitless to what he might become.

Now as he walked through the forest he found himself traveling with purpose, almost as if the forest had become more familiar to him. He changed course by instinct, without regard for the sun's position, crossing over streams, through groves and fields, and around hills until he finally came to a village of seven buildings surrounded by a couple of large wheat farms and pig corrals.

As he looked down from the forest at the old wooden buildings, watching the few visible farmers going about their work, he realized that when he had absorbed the bear's energy, he had also absorbed its knowledge of the forest and the area.

What, then, might happen should he consume the vampire's energy?

The thought was so delicious to him that he almost salivated. Without wasting another moment, he descended from the hill and walked into the village. He got no closer than one hundred yards from the closest wheat field before a bell rang out in the center of the village. The laborers stopped working and pulled rugged, crude short swords from their belts and moved into defensive positions in the main road. A couple of burly men hurriedly drove a horse-drawn wagon up behind the laborers and turned it to the side. Then they jumped into the back and raised some sort of large contraption that Aparen could only guess was some sort of missile launcher.

The large men alternated up and down as they cranked a large wheel. Even from where Aparen was he could hear the gears clicking and straining under the load. One of the men put a large shaft into the contraption.

"Looks like a modified scorpion launcher," Aparen said to himself.

"Halt there," one of the laborers shouted at the top of his lungs.

Aparen paused momentarily and watched the men curiously. "I mean you no harm," he shouted back.

"State your name and purpose," one of the burly men with the scorpion launcher bellowed.

Aparen decided not to use his name. "I have come from the south, I heard there is a vampire that lives in these parts. I have come to slay him."

In unison the men all started laughing hysterically. It took them several minutes to calm down and it appeared as though a couple of them were wiping the sides of their eyes as they tried to stifle their laughing. Aparen resumed walking toward the town and one of the laborers grabbed a bow from the back of the wagon and fired a warning shot in Aparen's direction.

He decided it was time to demonstrate some of his ability. He sent a fireball up and caught the arrow a few yards away from where he stood. "I have more where that came from," he said. "However, as I said, I am here to hunt a vampire. I am in need of food, and information about the monster."

The bowman stepped forward and strung another arrow. "A few paltry magic tricks will be no match for the vampire," he said. "You are a fool if you think you can succeed where so many others have failed before."

Aparen walked toward them quietly, keeping an eye on the men with the scorpion launcher. Once he was within a few yards of them he stopped and folded his arms. "If I fail, it will mean nothing for you, but if I succeed, then it will change your lives." The men glanced to each other and then nodded.

"Alright," the bowman said. "If you are set on throwing yourself at him, then I suppose that is your business."

"What if he makes the vampire angry and he comes after us for revenge?" one of the other laborers asked.

"Sooner or later he will come for you," Aparen said. "You can either help me put him down, or you can slink back to your fields and live out the rest of your days wondering when he will come for you."

The other laborer snorted, but said nothing. The two burly men nodded and stepped away from the scorpion launcher. "Let him do as he wishes," one of them said. Then they climbed back into the front and started driving back into the village without another word.

"I'm Gerald," the bowman said.

"Are you the mayor?" Aparen asked.

Gerald laughed and shook his head. "We don't have a mayor," he replied. "There are only a few families here in the village." The other laborers put their swords away and slowly made their ways back to the fields.

"So, where can I find him?" Aparen asked.

"You look a bit young to be hunting vampires," Gerald said. "You sure you are up to this?"

Aparen forced a confident smile and nodded. "There is more to me than what meets the eye, I assure you."

Gerald nodded and chuckled softly. "I suppose we will find out soon enough." He motioned for Aparen to follow him and then turned to lead him to the nearest farmhouse. Aparen noted the three rocking chairs on the old, gray porch. It appeared that Gerald had a wife and at least one child. As the man opened the door to the farmhouse and walked in, Aparen could smell soup over the fire pit in the center of the house. As he stepped inside he saw a small bed on one side of the room and a larger bed on the opposite side. A round, wooden table was situated near the back wall and a couple of rugged wardrobes lined the front wall.

The man caught Aparen scanning the house and pointed to the small bed. "My son was only six when the vampire came. He was one of the first to disappear in the night."

Aparen looked to the bed and noticed that it was perfectly made up, as if Gerald still expected the boy to come home at any moment. "When was that?" Aparen asked.

"About seven years ago now," Gerald said. "It drove my wife mad. When I gave up searching for the creature, my wife left me. She took the axe we used to chop wood and left into the night. I tried to stop her, but she was beyond reason, and I was the last person she would have listened to anyhow." Gerald paused and a tear welled up in his left eye. "I never saw her again. I assume the vampire got her too."

"You didn't go after her?" Aparen asked.

Gerald shrugged. "By that time there were many other families that had fallen prey to the vampire. News spread that other villages had been attacked also. There wasn't much use in going after the vampire anymore. Anyone who did disappeared."

Aparen shook his head. He could almost understand Gerald's reasons, but he couldn't get past the fact that the man had allowed his wife to go after a vampire. "Where can I find him?"

Gerald went and sat on a wooden chair near the round table. "No one knows," he said. "Some say there is a cave or a castle out in the forest, but if that is true no one has ever found it and lived to tell the tale." Gerald bent down and pulled his boots off, wiggling his toes underneath threadbare socks that looked as though they were about to unravel entirely. "If I were you, I would go northwest. There is an old, dry stream bed that leads up to a gray mountain that is riddled with caves. If I were a vampire that is where I would go."

"Would that give him easy access to all of the nearby villages?" Aparen asked.

Gerald shrugged. "I suppose it is easy enough as any other place."

A thought came to Aparen then. Perhaps everyone had been looking in the wrong places. "Are there any clearings close to the center between all of the villages?"

Gerald arched an eyebrow and folded his arms as he leaned back. "If you take the main road north, you will find a large field about half a day from here. There's nothing there though, absolutely nothing but a few wild flowers."

Aparen nodded. "I'll start there. Thank you for your hospitality."

"How old are you?" Gerald asked.

Aparen smiled and exited the farmhouse without answering. He walked quickly through the village. He waved when he passed the burly men sitting atop their wagon and drinking from flasks. They waved in kind and continued talking between themselves.

If Dremathor had positioned himself in the middle of a valley, then perhaps the vampire had done the same. It seemed a good tactic. All of the villages would send their men to the caves and deep into the forests, all while the vampire would be smack in the middle, within easy reach of the womenfolk whenever the fancy struck to hunt. No one would ever suspect it. If he was wrong, it would only cost him a little bit of time, and he could simply move on to the next village and ask for more information. On the other hand, if he was right, then he might be able to return and free Silvi before the moon rose in the sky.

CHAPTER THIRTEEN

Gilifan pulled his cloak tighter around himself. A cold, biting wind tore in from the north, swiping at the goose bumps on his skin. Nerekar hardly seemed to notice. He just walked on, letting his over cloak flap wildly behind him. The necromancer hated these lands. No matter what time of year he arrived, it was always cold as a witch's heart. Sheets of ice and snow piled high in the winter followed by deceptively bright, sunny summers chilled by northern winds that brought the arctic cold with it. It was not as bad further inland, but here on the coast, it was eternally cold and bitter.

"Do you know the way?" Nerekar asked, pulling Gilifan from his thoughts.

Gilifan nodded. He looked back to the ship they had disembarked from only ten minutes before. The crew was busy casting off from the lonely, long abandoned dock. They were obviously not eager to stay and wait for Gilifan to finish his business.

"I know the way," the necromancer replied evenly. "We go to Och'Duun, a port city perhaps an hour's walk from here."

"If it has a port, then why did we dock here?" Nerekar asked.

"Because the orcs of Och'Duun would sink a human ship on sight."

"But they will not attack us on foot?" Nerekar countered.

"You will not enter the city with me," Gilifan replied. "I expect you to find your own way in. As for me, they will not attack me. Their chief owes me a favor."

"An orc owes you a favor?" Nerekar smirked.

"Don't belittle the orcs," Gilifan snapped. "A favor promised by an orc is worth more than a king's alliance with other men." Gilifan reached down deep into his pocket and pulled out a round coin made of hematite. "Do you know what this is?" the necromancer asked.

Nerekar shook his head. "Child's money?" he guessed sarcastically.

"It is a token of debt." Gilifan held it up in the light to show it off. "On this side you see the face of the first ruler of Hammenfein and the creator of the orcs." He flipped the coin over. "On this side you see the symbol of the Tiger Clan, the strongest orc tribe in these lands. No orc would dare lay a finger on me so long as I carry this."

"Why do you have it?" Nerekar asked.

"Never mind about that," Gilifan said. "You just remember what I told you."

Nerekar nodded grimly. "If a white scarf hangs from the third window in the longhouse, then I am released from our contract. If a red scarf hangs, then I am to strike before the sun rises."

"See to it that you do not fail," Gilifan warned.

"I have never failed," Nerekar growled.

"Neither have you ever tested your mettle against an orc." A howling wind tore through the air then, bending the brown, brittle grass down to the earth and forcing Gilifan to tuck his face into the crook of his elbow. "I hate this wind," he grumbled.

The pair travelled over rolling hills next to the sea as the road wound around some and over others. The beach in this part of the realm was very rocky, and smelled of salt and rotting flesh. They passed by an old oak tree worn smooth by drifting onto the beach and sun bleached so that it might easily have been mistaken for a great bone if not for the still intact branches that now gave roost to a flock of seagulls. The birds squawked loudly, some of them fighting over a couple of small crabs unlucky enough to have ventured into the open and been caught by the vigilant birds.

Gilifan and Nerekar walked on the rocky road for about half an hour before Gilifan pointed out a large, black tree. "In the hollow of that tree you will find a map of Och'Duun."

Nerekar nodded and went toward it. "I will look for the scarf tonight," the assassin promised.

Gilifan continued walking without slowing his pace or even waving to his hired thug. He pulled his cloak in again, warding off the harsh wind as it kicked up for the third time This wind brought with it small, stinging drops of rain that bit his cheek and drove the cold into his bones despite his best efforts to shield himself with his cloak. The necromancer cursed the rain. He thought for a moment to use his magic and dispel the horrid weather, but he knew better. He was in orc country now, and they did not take kindly to magic. Should he use it, some orc patrolman might order

Erik and the Dragon

an attack without bothering to come close enough for the necromancer to display his token. Better to face sharp drops of ice water than to try and deflect an orc's arrow.

As he suspected, a patrol was only a few minutes away. There were four of them, that he could see, and they saw him from afar and started galloping toward him. Being familiar with the orcs, he knew that seeing four meant there were likely ten more orcs nearby that he hadn't yet spotted. Fortunately, he knew how to react so as to not draw their ire. The necromancer stopped walking and held his left hand out to the side as far as possible, empty palm facing out. He extended his right hand out in front of him, displaying the token prominently in his palm for the orcs to see. In all other respects, he stood still and quiet, waiting for them to get to him.

The sharp point of a spear prodded into his back, deep enough to jar him forward, but not so hard as to break the skin.

"On your knees," the orc said in Common Tongue.

Gilifan obliged the orc while keeping his eyes on the four riders galloping toward him. "I have come to see your chief," he said. "I have his token in my hand.

"Quiet," the orc instructed. "Maernok will decide your fate."

Gilifan nodded and closed his mouth. He had hoped for someone else to be the first to find him, but there was nothing he could do about that now.

The four riders pulled their horses to a stop only a few yards away. Gilifan looked up, squinting at the dust the horses had kicked up. The first rider swung his leg over the horse and jumped down to the ground. The many plates of his steel armor jingled together. The necromancer noted how each small plate was attached so that the entire set of armor resembled a skin of scales. Tufts of fur protruded out around the wrists, knees, elbows, shoulders, and around the neck. A pair of sleek scimitars hung from the orc's belt. A bow of wood and bone was slung across the warrior's back, and the feathered shafts of arrows stood out above the orc's shoulders.

The orc's face was a dark green, lined with a scar on his left cheek that ran down under his jawbone. A pair of sharp tusk-like teeth jutted out from his lower jaw, stopping about half an inch below the prominent cheekbones. Blue, cold eyes stared out from under a lock of black hair that had escaped the conical, leather helmet. The orc emitted a throaty growl as it eyed Gilifan from head to toe.

The orc walked with ease, his armor shimmering in the bright sun. "The wizard who plays with the dead," the orc said. "I had hoped not to see you again before we had both crossed over into Hammenfein."

"Maernok, I have many years yet before I will depart from the mortal realm," Gilifan said with a slight nod of his head.

"Why wait?" Maernok asked. He drew his scimitars and flashed them before Gilifan's nose. "I could shorten the time considerably and offer you as homage to my master."

"I carry your chief's token," Gilifan said sternly. "I would remind you that to slay one who bears a token of debt would be considered a great affront to your master. Your promised place in Hammenfein would be stripped from you and you would be discarded to the lower levels of hell."

Maernok stepped in close so that his fetid, hot breath washed over Gilifan's face. "It would almost be worth it, meddler," he growled.

"I have come to speak with your chief. Now that you have seen the token I bear, you are obligated to take me to him."

Maernok scoffed and turned to the other orcs around him. He shouted something in orcish that Gilifan did not understand. The others laughed. The necromancer grew weary of the power struggle. He held the token up in the air and bellowed "Hacht ten mag'nul berak!" The others shrank away.

"Do not recite the command to me, meddler," Maernok snarled. "We will take you to Och'Duun. You will speak with our chief, and then, when you no longer carry the token of debt I will flay you alive, use your skin as a leather cloak and then march up to the dog who gave you life and make her choke upon your flesh."

Gilifan smirked and cocked his head to the side. "My mother has long been dead, by my own hand in fact," he said. "But I appreciate your pathetic attempt to frighten me. Now, move along, cur, and take me to your chief."

Maernok stepped back, jerking his neck to the side sharply, cracking his bones and grunting as he did so. "Let's go," he said to the others. He whirled his scimitars back into their sheaths and jumped up to land in his saddle. The orc riders led the way, and a pair of orc footmen emerged from the nearby grasses to join the other already behind Gilifan.

The first one poked his spear forward, "You heard Maernok,

Erik and the Dragon

time to move."

Gilifan wheeled around and dissolved the spear with a single touch of his left index finger. "Prod me again and I shall remake your spear and dissolve you instead." The orc's eyes grew wide and he took half a step back as he glanced to his empty hands. Gilifan winked evilly and then turned to follow Maernok.

Maernok shouted something in orcish over his shoulder. A warning to the others, no doubt, but Gilifan honestly couldn't care less what Maernok said just as long as they stayed out of his way.

They walked along the coast for about twenty minutes through the biting rain and harsh wind. The orcs seemed almost to grow stronger in the unforgiving weather. The riders sat tall in the saddle, letting the rain sting their faces as the wind howled about them. Gilifan, on the other hand, drew his cloak in as tightly as he could. He also put up an invisible ward to at least shelter himself from the rain.

A heavy fog crept in from the sea, despite the bright sun's attempts to banish it from above. Golden rays mingled with the silvery mist and cast rainbows all around them. Och'Duun seemed to emerge from the fog, as if it slid closer to them along the coast. The stark, black bricks of the wall shone slick from the rain. The heavy, iron gate was open, revealing a thick portcullis guarded by a trio of large orcs holding pikes. Towers rose above the wall within the city, looking down upon the foggy land around Och'Duun like massive sentries of stone and wood. The architecture was not so different from that of humans, and yet it was entirely its own. Each tower was capped with rounded cupolas while the actual tower itself was made with five even sides with precise angles. The orcs' inclination to use pentagons as the basic shape of buildings was a testament to how they lived their lives.

Five sides allows for one more field of vision, one more sentry to sound the warning bells, and one more balcony from which to let loose the arrows of death, or so the old orcish adage says. At the very least, it did make for fewer blind spots, and easier defense whilst besieged.

"Come with me, wizard of death," Maernok said harshly. The others stopped and pulled off to the side before the portcullis. Gilifan followed the large warrior through as the portcullis was raised from inside the walls. The guards all watched Gilifan warily, studying his every move until he passed through the gate and into the city proper.

Then, instead of three sets of eyes staring at him, there were scores.

The orcs walking to and fro upon the wet, slick cobblestone street seemed to freeze in time. Maernok pressed on as if nothing was out of the ordinary, but no one else moved as Gilifan walked behind the orc warrior. Occasionally a small orc child would whisper to its mother, but even then the mother would barely respond.

"Haven't had any visitors since I left eh?" Gilifan remarked.

"It isn't that," Maernok replied. "They are wondering how it is that you are still alive."

Gilifan chuckled softly to himself. "Magic has its advantages," he said.

Maernok stopped and dropped down to the road. The orcs around stiffened even more.

The necromancer looked to the warrior questioningly. "Something else I should know?" he asked.

Maernok drew a curved dagger from his belt and held it up against his armor, indicating to his heart. "I took an oath to slay you, meddler." Maernok slid the back of the blade across his chest, mimicking a slice. "The others are watching you, waiting for me to fulfill my blood oath."

"That was a foolish thing to do," Gilifan said. "I hold a token of debt, and you knew that before you met me."

Maernok stepped in close and placed the tip of his dagger onto Gilifan's chest. "You, meddler, shall die by my hand. I have sworn it before Khullan himself. You will pay for your treachery."

"It is not my fault your father was too weak to rule," Gilifan said. The tip of the dagger pressed into his skin, poking through his cloak. The necromancer looked down and smiled, undaunted. "Go on, Maernok," Gilifan taunted. "Push it in and collect your reward."

Maernok glared down at his dagger, obviously weighing the decision out in his mind. "No," he said at last as he pulled the dagger back. "One day you will no longer carry the token of debt. Then, I will be free to fulfill my blood oath and end your meddling ways."

"Your father squealed like a stuck pig," Gilifan said. "Your mother put up a better fight, but she also begged for mercy at the end."

Maernok spat on the ground and turned away.

"Your younger brother is the one I pity, though," Gilifan called out. "Do you know I brought him back from the dead and made him my slave?"

Maernok's shoulders slumped and the warrior's fists clenched.

"He was the only orc I ever killed twice," Gilifan continued. "You should have heard him cry out your name, it was awful."

Maernok turned back to Gilifan. "Enough of your games," he hissed. "When the time comes, I will make you eat your words, by the blood of my father I will make you pay."

The necromancer laughed out loud and walked on. "You can stay here," he told Maernok. "I know the way to the longhouse."

"You will die by my hand," Maernok swore under his breath, just loud enough for Gilifan to hear as he strolled by.

The necromancer held the token of debt up in front of his face and pretended to polish it. "Think carefully about what you promise," he warned. Then he walked on through the streets, leaving Maernok standing alone in the street.

Gilifan continued on to the longhouse, the traditional seat of power in any orc settlement. The roof was smooth and rounded, almost as if a giant had flipped a massive ship's hull upside down atop the structure. The walls were made of white and gray stone, which had undoubtedly taken more time to find amidst the black and brown soils and rocks of this area, than it would have to build three or four such longhouses made of black stone. But that was the point. The longhouse was the central structure, and as such it demanded a particular kind of stone.

The necromancer stopped in front of the oaken door and looked down to the old, bearded orc sitting nearby chewing on dried meat. "I am here to see the chief," Gilifan said.

The old orc looked up from under his bushy, white brows and spat on the ground as he flipped a mass of half chewed meat over his bottom teeth to rest in his lip like a dip of tobacco. "Go on inside, then," the orc said roughly. "I ain't about to get up and be your personal doorman."

Gilifan gave a half-smile despite himself. There was something refreshing about the strength of the orcs. A pride unmatched by even the haughtiest of the elves, and wisdom too, for those patient enough to look beyond the tusks and swords. He grabbed hold of the iron ring sticking out from the black skull of a small gorlung, a most menacing beast in life, and one of the symbols of the orcs. He pulled the door open and stepped through as he slightly lowered his head so as not to hit the crossbeam. The savory, tempting smell of roast venison filled his nostrils, reminding him that it had been many days without a proper meal at sea.

"I had heard the rumors," a low voice in the left corner of the building said. "I see now that they are true."

Gilifan looked to the source of the words and saw a large orc sitting in a wooden chair and holding a clay bowl in front of him. The orc reached out with his thick right hand and plucked a cherry from a larger clay bowl and plopped it into his mouth. A moment later he spit the cherry pit into the smaller bowl he held in his left hand.

"What was it you heard?" Gilifan asked as he walked up to take a dark red cherry for himself.

"One of our scouts reported seeing a ship heading in to dock. He came back here earlier today to tell us, and to get Maernok."

"Yes," Gilifan started. "I was surprised to see him leading a patrol."

"It is wise to keep your enemies close, is it not?" the chief replied as he took another cherry.

"Sometimes, I suppose," Gilifan answered. "Perhaps I would have found another use for him, if I were chief."

The orc set the clay bowl on the table and went to the fire pit in the center of the longhouse and ladled broth over the roasting venison. "I had expected him to come with the report of what he found," he said. "However, seeing that *you* are here, I can understand why Maernok decided otherwise." The chief set the ladle back into a black kettle, careful to set the handle just right so it didn't fall into the broth. "Did you come alone?"

Gilifan sneered wickedly. "No," he said. "I brought a great assassin to slay you, Gariche."

The chief huffed and looked at Gilifan for a moment before chuckling to himself. "Well, since we both know *that* isn't true, I will assume you are alone."

"You think me a liar?" Gilifan pressed, folding his arms across his chest. "You forget how you became chief."

Gariche waved a meaty hand in the air and went back to his cherry bowl. "I have forgotten nothing of the sort," he countered.

Erik and the Dragon

"As my memory recalls, you came in with an army of zombies. Even then, you needed me and the support of my warriors to finish deposing the previous chief."

"Which is one of the reasons I am surprised you would allow Maernok to lead a patrol," Gilifan said. "You have to know that he has sworn a blood oath to exact his vengeance."

"I do," Gariche said with a nod. "That is exactly why I keep him so close. We may have erred in allowing my predecessor's eldest son to live, but he has proven useful to me since then."

"Ludicrous," Gilifan said. The necromancer leaned in and stared into Gariche's green eyes. "You haven't let him on the council have you?" he questioned.

"Times have changed," Gariche said.

Gilifan shook his head and threw his arms into the air. "The last time I was here, we slaughtered his family so you could have the throne, and now you tell me that you have put your enemy's son on the council, and given him a legitimate right to challenge your rule?"

"He will not challenge me," Gariche said. "He has no need."

"You have grown blind in my absence," Gilifan said.

"In the decades that have past, I have grown wiser." Gariche slid his cherry bowl away from Gilifan and gestured for the necromancer to sit. "You helped me rise in power, for that I am forever grateful, but Maernok has been a great asset to this city. If I were to expel him or kill him, the others would not accept my rule."

"Are you telling me that your orcs have no stomach for blood?" Gilifan prodded.

Gariche rolled his tongue behind his lips and spat a cherry pit out with enough force that it bounced off Gilifan's head. "Do not insult my people," he warned. "We are friends, or at least we were, once, but I will not stomach another comment like that."

Gilifan wiped the warm spittle and cherry juice from his skin and turned an arched brow at Gariche. "The rule of the tribe is not the only thing I gave you," Gilifan reminded him.

Gariche nodded. "I remember my debts," he said. "Even if you did not possess the token, I would never forget how you brought my daughter back from Hammenfein."

"Then, if you remember that, why would you allow Maernok to sit on the council?"

Gariche sighed heavily. "She died, seventeen winters ago," he said. "A disease rolled through our land like nothing we had ever seen before. It was a plague that manifested with purple boils and red rashes. We turned to Khullan for help, but no help came. We tried as many remedies as we could think of. Our shamans danced and made sacrifices, but nothing worked. Once an orc was marred by the first purple boil, they had only three days left to live."

The orc picked up a cherry by the stem and twirled it betwixt his forefinger and thumb. "The orcs in the city began to leave, trying to escape the plague. None of them ever made it more than a day away from the city before they fell victim to its grasp. Those that remained soon blamed me, saying that Khullan was displeased with how I stole the throne, and that the curse was a punishment for me making a deal with you to take my daughter back from Hammenfein."

"And you believed them?" Gilifan asked.

Gariche dropped the cherry back in the bowl and folded his massive arms across his chest as he leaned back and stared at the dirt floor. "Not at first," he replied. "But then my wife took ill. She languished for the three days while I sat by her bed helpless. A week later my daughter shrieked when she found a purple boil on her left hand." The orc's eyes began to water and the focus grew distant. "I will never forget that sound. It still gives me the chills when I think of it." He sat for a moment in silence before continuing. "It was then that a shaman from Oct'Meruus arrived. He said that I should sacrifice my daughter in the longhouse to appease Khullan."

Gilifan frowned. "And did you?" he asked.

Gariche shook his head. "I had the shaman drawn and quartered," he replied evenly. "The next day another shaman arrived and said that if I did not make the sacrifice, all of Och'Duun would be destroyed."

"You had him killed as well?" Gilifan asked.

"I struck him down myself," Gariche said. "The morning after my daughter died from the plague, another shaman came. He said that Och'Duun would be spared if I appointed Maernok to the council, and pledged with a blood oath not to kill or exile him."

Gilifan whistled through his teeth.

The orc chief nodded. "To add insult to the injury, I was to take Maernok and adopt him as my own son, thus ensuring that upon my death, the rule of the tribe would revert back to a proper orc bloodline."

"After you agreed, did the plague stop?" Gilifan asked.

"The instant I drew my dagger across my chest and spoke the words, all who were yet dying of the plague were healed and the plague itself vanished." Gariche shook his head. "So, while I may be in your debt for what you restored to me, I am hardly the same orc that I once was. I know that when I die and walk into the gates of Hammenfein, I will find no glory waiting for me there. So, I have tempered my ambitions in this life, and turned to seek what comforts I could while I still walk among the living."

Gilifan nodded. "I can understand that," he said. "That also makes a bit more sense why the town reacted the way they did to my presence."

"They likely fear that I will make another pact with you," Gariche confirmed. "I imagine they will be gathering outside the longhouse within the hour to inquire about it. I can't blame them though, every family lost at least one member to that cursed plague."

"I do have a favor to ask of you," Gilifan said.

"If I can, I will," Gariche responded seriously.

"I want you to march your army against Ten Forts," Gilifan said.

Gariche reached out and took a couple of cherries in hand while he mulled it over. "To what end?" he asked.

"Tu'luh has returned," Gilifan said. "Join us, and you will see your family yet again in this life."

Gariche shook his head firmly. "And risk another plague, not a chance."

"There will be no plague," Gilifan said. "Don't you see? With Nagar's Secret and Tu'luh in command, we will have the power to shut the gates of Hammenfein forever. The gods of the underworld will have no power here. Your rule can be forever."

"No," Gariche said. "No one would agree to this."

Gilifan slid his token on the table. "Are you going to make me use this?"

Gariche looked down at the hematite stone and shrugged. "It will make no difference. I won't do this."

"You would risk breaking the oath?" Gilifan asked.

"My soul is already damned," Gariche admitted. "Nothing I

do now will make it any worse than it will already be."

Gilifan sighed and nodded. "Then, in that case, I will not use the token," he said. The necromancer slid the token back into his pocket. "A friend does not take advantage of another friend at such a time."

Gariche offered a smile. "Your gesture is very much appreciated," the chief said. "It appears that both of us have become more moderate." Gariche rose to his feet. "Come, the venison is nearly done."

"First I will retire to my room. May I use the guest quarters?" Gilifan asked.

"No," Gariche said. "Orc hospitality is not dead. You will take my room, I will sleep in the guest chamber."

Gilifan nodded and went to the far end of the longhouse. He opened the door to a grand bedroom adorned with prized antlers and weapon racks that each held not only bows and swords, but also a golden plaque with the legend behind each of the revered items. The necromancer walked to the end of the room, unimpressed by the items, and slipped a red scarf into the window.

"Come, my friend," Gariche yelled from the other room. "The food is ready."

Gilifan stroked the red scarf and sighed. "One last meal, my friend, and then I shall bid you farewell."

*****

Nerekar hugged the cold, unyielding brick wall, clinging to the shadows. He peered across the street through the heavy rain and saw the red scarf in the window. He knew what he had to do. A grumpy pair of orcs came around the corner of the building next to him then, cursing the weather and shuffling quickly through the rain.

They didn't see the Blacktongue.

The assassin waited until they passed on and then he skulked across the street to the longhouse. He glanced around and then went up the wall like a spider. Once on the roof he slowly crawled to wait next to the chimney. Thinning smoke still emerged from the hole, carrying with it the remaining smells of the meal inside. Above the pittering rain drops Nerekar could hear laughter from within the building.

Erik and the Dragon

He waited for hours on the roof, ignoring the rain and the night's wind. From his vantage point he watched whenever someone entered or exited the building. Those who left filed away into the night like ants streaming along the ground. As the night wore on, the rain let up, but there were still heavy, dark clouds blocking the moon.

Something stirred below and Nerekar heard the sound of a wooden log smacking against the brick below. A puff of smoke rose up through the chimney all at once, carrying a few small embers with it. He knew they had thrown more wood on the fire. Soon those inside the longhouse would be turning in for the night.

The door below creaked open and a pair of solid looking orcs came out to stand in front of the door. Immediately thereafter the final groups of guests departed from the longhouse. Gilifan was among them.

"You shouldn't go out in the night," one of the orcs said.

"I want to see this contraption you spoke of," Gilifan replied with a hearty slap to the man's back. "If the battering ram is as strong as you claim, then I will have to order one from you!"

The door closed and the sentries moved into position.

"We'll let you back in when you return," one of them said. Gilifan nodded and waved to them as he went with the group.

Nerekar waited for another hour. He wanted to make sure that his target had retired for the night, and give the fire enough time to burn low. The assassin watched the smoke to judge his timing and then, when he was satisfied, he prepared himself. He pulled thick gloves onto his hands and tied leather pads to his elbows. Lastly he put on a pair of goggles, made from the thick, translucent scales of the bortuga fish. Then he clambered over the top of the chimney, held his breath, and descended into the chute.

It was a tight fit, but he was able to squeeze in. The goggles protected his eyes from the smoke so he could see where he was going and his special leather gloves and pads insulated his hands and elbows from being burned. The heat from the fire roiled over his body and within a couple of seconds he was sweating heavily and the oil on his face was burnt away, leaving a naked, hot sensation on his cheeks and forehead.

Nerekar quickened his pace, spidering down the chute and mostly managing to avoid touching the wall with unprotected skin, except for once when he bumped his knee on a small piece of brick that jutted out into the chute. When he reached the hearth's opening he stuck his head down to look about. A couple flames leapt up to lick his forehead, but he paid it no mind. This was not the first time he had used such an entrance.

Noting that the room was dark, and void of anyone, he deftly reached out with one arm and maneuvered himself out of the fireplace without so much as singing his leg hairs. He straightened his back and shivered slightly as his skin tightened and adjusted back to a normal temperature. He quietly let out the breath he was holding and removed his goggles. Nerekar then moved to the far side of the main chamber and bent down to look through the space under the door. He pressed his cheek into the floor and his eyeball darted up and down the narrow field of vision. He spied only a pair of empty boots resting next to a bed.

Next he went up to the keyhole and peered through. It offered him an even narrower vantage, but he spied his target's feet poking up through a green blanket on the bed. He turned his ear to the keyhole and listened to the rhythmic, slow breathing inside.

The orc chief was asleep.

Nerekar opened the door and crept in quieter than a snake in the grass. He closed the door behind him and stepped into the room. He quickly scanned the area and then scaled the nearest wall and grabbed hold of the heavy, thick crossbeams in the ceiling. He monkeyed through them, positioning himself directly over Gariche.

The large orc snorted and his mouth fell open, emitting low, rumbling breaths.

The assassin pulled a small vial out from his belt and gently twisted the cork out. He then pulled a line of silk out of a small pouch on his belt and dipped the end into the vial. The green liquid clung to the silk line and Nerekar smiled wickedly. He rolled his hand around, unwinding the silk line in front of him and lowering the wet end down to Gariche's mouth. No sooner did the silk line brush against Gariche's lower tusk than the green liquid glued it to the tooth.

Nerekar corked the vial and pulled a second glass vial out from his belt. He used his free thumb to gently slide the shellbug cap to its open position and then tipped the vial slowly to the line. The clear liquid inside rolled slowly at first, and then when it hit the silk line several drops raced down to the sleeping orc below.

The drops rolled off the silk and dripped into Gariche's

mouth. The orc snorted and coughed, rolling over and detaching the silk line from his tooth. Nerekar quickly reeled the line in and waited. A few moments later Gariche jerked to the side and a hand clasped at his chest. The orc's eyes shot open and he gasped for air. Then he twitched and fell back in his bed.

The Blacktongue clambered down the wall and went to the side of Gariche's bed. The thin assassin easily lifted the large orc up onto his shoulders and carried him to the door. He shuffled the weight onto one shoulder and then used his left hand to open the door. He walked out into the main room and set Gariche in a chair near the hearth. Quickly, he went and grabbed a half empty bottle of wine and placed it into Gariche's left hand, careful to wrap the orc's fingers around the handle. He then placed the fire poker in Gariche's right hand. Speedily went back to the bedroom and pulled the green blanket from the bed and draped it over Gariche. He then grabbed a couple new logs and put them on the fire.

Then the assassin put his goggles back on and clambered up the chimney before the flames caught onto the new logs.

*****

"Well, it is a fine design," Gilifan said as he admired the plan for the battering ram. "I especially like the fact that it can spew fire from the front. That is ingenious."

Gersimon laughed proudly. "Every piece of the ram is made of iron, so it will not only throw fire, but it will be immune to it, that's why I call it the dragon."

Gilifan nodded. "I appreciate you taking the time to show it to me, but it is late. I should probably be going back."

"There is one more thing I would like to show you." Gersimon motioned with his arm and exited the large workshop. Gilifan ran a finger over the smooth side of the ram again and then followed after the orc. He walked through the small hallway and found Gersimon standing at the end. He put a finger over his lips and then reached into a brass pot. Something clicked and then the end of the hallway swung open, leading to a steep staircase. The orc gestured with his head for Gilifan to go first.

The necromancer quick-stepped down the stairs, hunching over slightly to avoid ramming his head into the uneven brick ceiling. The smell of dirt and cobwebs assaulted his nose and he put a hand up over his face to keep the musty odor at bay as best he could.

A single lamp burned down below, shadows dancing and flicking this way and that as the flame twitched and writhed. A large orc sat at the table wearing simple leather trousers, a sleeveless jerkin, a pair of thick, heavy wrist bracers engraved with the image of a horse trampling a serpent, and a pair of rugged black boots. The orc turned, smiling from behind his heavy tusks, and rose to his feet. The chair scraped across the stone floor as he rose. He was easily a head taller than Gilifan, and his shoulders were twice as wide.

"Gulgarin," Gilifan said respectfully. "It is an honor to finally meet you face to face."

"I will leave the two of you alone," Gersimon said as he returned upstairs and shut the door.

Gulgarin pointed his thick arm to the floor above. "My cousin, and blood-brother since we were only six years old. Both raised by our uncle when our parents were slain."

Gilifan nodded. "He is every bit as cunning as you said," Gilifan commented. "I am surprised he was able to ingratiate himself here in Gariche's clan so easily."

"Gersimon came here a few years ago, after the plague had been wiped out. The clan here was in need of an engineer, and my cousin is the best, so they welcomed him readily."

"Gariche never suspected that an engineer from another tribe might be his undoing?"

Gulgarin growled and his upper lip curled back. "Gariche is a fool. If allowed to rule he would lead this entire clan away from our traditions."

"Fool though he may seem, I can sympathize with his motives for changing his ways. I was told there was a curse," Gilifan said.

Gulgarin waved his hand and shook his head. "The rulers of Hammenfein reward bravery, honor, and above all, fortitude and will. They may have cursed him once before, but *he* surrendered. He stopped fighting for what he wanted. If he was cursed before, then he is one hundred times worse off for it now."

"I see," Gilifan said. He approached a few steps closer. "So, what is it you want to do?"

"The same as I told you in our letters. Were you able to convince Gariche to fight with you?"

Gilifan shook his head. "Gariche has chosen the peaceful exit."

Gulgarin pounded a strong left fist into his thick right palm. "Then he is one thousand times cursed!"

"Let the gods punish him as they will," Gilifan said. "But what about you? Do you still stand with me?"

Gulgarin puffed out his barrel of a chest. "If none of the orc tribes would fight, I would go alone with you to Ten Forts and break down the walls myself."

Gilifan smiled. "That is what I wanted to hear."

"What about you?" the orc asked. "How will you deliver your promise to me?"

The necromancer held a palm up in the air and sneered wickedly. "Let's just say that I think Gariche is going to have a bit of trouble with his heart tonight. In fact, he should be cold already."

"Magic," Gulgarin grumbled. "Never liked it much."

"Maybe that is why the orcs have never been able to retake their homeland from the humans," Gilifan countered.

Gulgarin looked up to the necromancer menacingly and clenched his fists.

"Easy, my friend. It was not an insult, merely an observation."

"Magic is for those who are not strong enough to fight for themselves," Gulgarin countered.

Gilifan bristled and crossed his arms over his chest. "I have taken my share of heads by the sword," the necromancer said. "However, I didn't use magic on Gariche."

Gulgarin raised a bushy black eyebrow and then skewed his face into a grotesque, disapproving frown. "Poison then?"

Gilifan nodded.

Gulgarin snorted. "That's worse. Poison is the way of cowards."

"I recall a group of orcish assassins that rely primarily on poison," Gilifan said.

"Not in *my* tribe," Gulgarin spat.

"Brute strength is well and good, but this matter was delicate. I can't very well walk into town and lop the chief's head off."

"You have the token of debt," Gulgarin pointed out. "The chief of this tribe has to honor it."

"Exactly," Gilifan said. "And now the *new* chief will be bound by it."

A grin slowly appeared on Gulgarin's face. "Oh, but you are an evil viper aren't you?"

Gilifan sniggered. "I will ask the new chief to honor our alliance. However, he has sworn a blood oath to kill me once the token has been spent."

Gulgarin nodded. "I can see to it that Maernok falls at Ten Forts."

"Well then," Gilifan started with a shrug. "Seeing as how Maernok has no heir, I suppose you will also have to assume rule of this clan as well."

Gulgarin's grin widened to reveal his top row of teeth. "It would be the only proper thing to do," he said.

The door upstairs opened and Gersimon ran down the steps. "The guards are on their way here. We need to go!"

Gilifan nodded and went up the stairs while Gulgarin went out of the chamber through a large keg that opened into another secret tunnel. The necromancer and Gersimon had only just returned to the workshop and grabbed the set of battering ram plans when they heard shattering wood and a horde of heavy boots stomping through the house.

"I'll kill you now you measly dung eating worm!" Maernok shouted as he pulled a heavy mace from his belt. The guards at his side each drew weapons of their own.

Gilifan pulled the token of debt out from his robes. "Have you forgotten what I hold?" he shouted. "Gariche still owes me a debt!"

"Gariche is dead!" Maernok roared. "And you will soon join him."

"STOP!" Gersimon shouted. "If Gariche is dead, then *you* are chief. By our traditions you have to honor the token of debt."

"Don't tell me what my traditions are, outsider!" Maernok spat.

"Maernok," one of the guards said. "Gersimon is right. It is our way. You have to honor the debt."

Maernok stormed up to Gilifan and stuck the mace in the man's face. "Come on, wizard, show me your magic and I will end everything right here, right now."

Gilifan took a step to the side. "Gariche is dead?" he asked with feigned concern.

Erik and the Dragon

"Don't act like you don't know," Maernok bellowed. "You are the one who killed him!"

Gilifan put the token back in his pocket. "I came to ask for my debt to be repaid, not to kill him," he said. Then he looked to the guards. "Where is he, how did he die?"

The guards looked to each other for a moment, shrugging and whispering among themselves.

"How did he die?" Gilifan repeated.

Maernok stepped in and slammed the top of his mace into Gilifan's stomach. The wizard doubled over and fell to his knees. "I don't know what you are up to, cur, but it ends now." Maernok raised his mace high over his head.

A crack of lightning flew out from Gilifan's fingers and slammed into Maernok, sending him flying into the far wall and crashing through shelves with tools and bits of metal. "Enough," Gilifan hissed. He snapped the fingers of his left hand and a cord of fire surrounded the guards. He looked to them. "Stay where you are, and you will be fine. Try to leave the ring of fire and you will be turned to ash." Gilifan picked up a large iron strut and tossed it to the fire. The magical flames ate through it faster than if it had been paper, dropping only rancid ash on the floor.

The guards stood still.

Gilifan pointed to Maernok. "If I wanted to kill Gariche, I would have," he said. "I would have walked up to him and plunged a magical bolt of lightning straight through his heart and been done with it."

Maernok rolled to his feet and picked up a large brass plate and moved to advance on Gilifan. The necromancer sent another bolt of lightning through the brass plate, knocking Maernok to the ground.

"I came to ask him to repay his debt," Gilifan said again. He pulled the token of debt from his robes again.

"You are bound to honor it," Gersimon told Maernok.

Maernok looked up and wiped a bit of blood from the corner of his mouth. "Alright, then ask for your payment," he said. "Then, when it is paid, our debt is clean and you are no longer welcome in orc lands."

"I am marching on Ten Forts," Gilifan said. "Gather your armies and fight with me. When Ten Forts falls, then your debt is repaid." Gilifan held the hematite token out in his hand.

"When the debt is paid, I will fulfill my blood oath," Maernok promised.

"Very well," Gilifan said. "When Ten Forts has fallen, you shall give me two days to depart from orc lands. After that, your debt is paid and you are free to pursue whatever you wish."

"One day," Maernok countered.

Gilifan shook his head. "Two days. That is my offer."

Maernok stood and placed his hand over the token of debt. "As chief of the Tiger Tribe, I swear that we will march with you and your men to Ten Forts. We will help you conquer it. From the moment the battle is won, you shall have two days to flee to wherever you wish. After that, I am free to hunt you down and slay you like the rabid dog you are."

"Agreed," Gilifan said with a nod of his head.

A loud ringing emitted from the token between their hands and a great, red and orange light shot out from between their fingers and filled the room.

"The price is set," Gilifan said. Maernok pulled his hand back and all looked down to see the token. It now glowed red and black, as though it were made of roiling lava. The Necromancer placed it back in his pocket, admiring the light as it glowed through the fabric. "Get your armies ready," he said. "We leave soon." He waved his left hand and the ring of magical fire dissipated into the air and the orcs breathed easy.

"You will stay here with Gersimon tonight," Maernok ordered. "You are no longer a guest in the longhouse." Maernok and the other orcs left abruptly without another word.

After they left Gilifan went back to the secret staircase.

"Gulgarin has left through the tunnel," Gersimon said. "You won't see him again until the battle."

"It is not Gulgarin I wish to speak with. Leave me in peace for a while."

Gersimon nodded with a shrug and started to pick up the tools and parts that had been knocked to the floor.

Once Gilifan was in the secret chamber he sat on the cold floor and drew a circle in the dust before him. A small white and orange flame appeared on the floor in the center of the circle. Gilifan waved a hand over it and it grew a pair of leathery wings, skinny legs, and awkward arms and hands tipped with claws. The necromancer gently blew the flame away with his breath, leaving

Erik and the Dragon

only the light brown skin of the creature before him.

"Imp," Gilifan began. "Carry a message to Tu'luh for me."

The creature nodded its bald head and a pair of pointy ears perked upright to listen.

"Tell him that the orcs will soon march on Ten Forts. I will travel with the orc forces." Gilifan then mimed a circle in the air nearby with his right hand and a small, crystalline tunnel bored through the air. The imp flew into the tunnel and vanished along with it.

Gilifan waited patiently for several minutes. The anticipation of Tu'luh's response made the time drag by agonizingly slow, as if each second were an hour. There were not many beings on this plane that Gilifan feared, but Tu'luh was definitely one of them. He only hoped that his new success would outweigh the dragon's disappointment of past failures.

A small sparkle rippled through the air, as if a fleck of silver dangled near Gilifan's face. Then all at once the small tunnel of crystal expanded rapidly and the imp flew back into the room.

"The master says he is pleased with this news," the imp hissed.

Gilifan let out a small sigh of relief.

"He says he will provide misdirection for you. It should delay the boy and his comrades from getting to Ten Forts."

"So the boy lives then?" Gilifan clarified.

"He does," the imp confirmed. "The master says he will send a small surprise for them shortly though, and it should soften them up for you and your army."

"Very well," Gilifan said.

The imp grinned evilly, baring its wicked fangs. "Can I go hunt now?"

"Not here," Gilifan replied. The imp scowled and hissed. The necromancer waved his hand dismissively. "Back to the fires of Hammenfein for you, imp. Go and prey upon the souls of the lowly and damned."

A black flame swallowed the creature and ripped the imp back to its natural plane.

Gilifan sat staring at the ashes for a few moments. He couldn't help but think that perhaps he was outmatched. If the boy was able to escape both Gondok'hr, and Tu'luh, then perhaps he truly was the champion from the prophecies. The thought crossed his mind that perhaps he would be better off in the orcish lands. Here he could make himself reasonably powerful with little effort above what he was already expending.

If the boy slays Tu'luh, then the Wyrms of Khaltoun could continue to exist in Demaverung. Gilifan thought. The volcano is well defended, and the outlying lands of the area are near impossible to traverse. He shook his head. No, the elders would never stand for it. They are too blind to see beyond the power of Nagar's Secret.

"Fools," Gilifan said as he rose to his feet, knees creaking and popping as he stood. "None of them have any idea what Nagar was truly after, or the power he was trying to unlock." He shook his head in disgust and wiped the sole of his boot across the ashes before him. Then he remembered. *Salarion knows. That is why she turned her back on the elders. Perhaps it was time to speak with her.*

CHAPTER FOURTEEN

Erik tilted his head back and opened his mouth, letting the large rain drops plop down onto his tongue and splash into the back of his throat. He breathed in deeply, allowing his eyes to close as the rain fell all around him. His weary, throbbing feet reminded him of how long they had been walking. Tualdern seemed like a distant memory now, despite the fact that he had bid the elves farewell only a day and a half before. If only they had had any horses to spare.

The werewolves had consumed all of the horses and livestock in Tualdern, according to Talimdur. Unfortunately, the monsters had also devoured the pack mules that Erik and his group had been using. The Sand Elves gave them what food they could spare, but it wasn't much, mostly potatoes and greens that the werewolves wouldn't touch. It wasn't that Erik hated a good salad now and then, but the thought of eating another leaf of spinach while marching through the forests, valleys, and hills that still stood between them and Stonebrook made his throat clench up in protest.

A wind howled low, chilling Erik's wet skin. He shivered and futilely rubbed his shoulders. He then noticed that the others were several yards ahead of him now. He jogged along the muddy ground to catch up.

"Nice of you to rejoin us," Dimwater said with a sidelong glance.

Erik smiled, but didn't say anything.

"How are your feet?" she asked.

"I'm alright," Erik said.

"No blisters?" she pressed.

Erik shook his head. Truth be told he doubted he would feel a blister at this point anyway. He was soaked through. His feet throbbed, but the outer layer of skin had long since passed the point of feeling anything so mild as a blister. Erik was certain that if they all stopped to remove their boots, his feet would resemble a white raisin. Then Erik looked up to Dimwater. "Why can't we use the portal that you and I used to get to Spiekery?"

Dimwater grinned slightly. "The first issue is that I would have to physically hold everyone's hand. So it would likely require multiple trips."

"Still, that would be faster than walking," Erik countered.

"The second issue, which is more important, is that we don't want to announce our arrival so blatantly. The enemy has shown on several occasions that they have many skilled wizards in their ranks. Should they have anyone near Stonebrook, using my portal would be similar to ringing a loud gong. It is better this way."

"And you still aren't going to do anything about the weather?" he asked jokingly.

Dimwater laughed. "Why don't *you* do something about it?" she teased.

"I would if I could," Erik promised.

Lady Dimwater opened her mouth to speak, but Lepkin approached then with his raised brow and a stern frown. The sorceress wrinkled her nose and pressed her lips back together.

"Come Erik, we have some training to do," Lepkin said.

"Here?" Erik asked incredulously.

Lepkin nodded. "Here." He pointed to a small brook nearby and the two of them walked toward it. Erik looked and saw that the rest of the group was continuing onward toward the thick forest about a mile off in the distance.

"They aren't going to wait for us?" Erik asked.

Lepkin shook his head. "They will go on ahead and make camp in the forest. We will catch up to them after we are done with today's session."

Erik sighed and his face drooped into a frown.

Lepkin saw it and nodded. "I know," he began. "You have been through a lot, and you have accomplished more than anyone could ever have asked of you, but I still am your master. I still have things to teach you."

Erik nodded slowly.

"I also have a few new scars which, I believe, I am in your debt for."

Erik scrunched up his brow and regarded Lepkin curiously. The big man cracked a smile, stifling a chuckle, and pointed to the brook again. "Come on, over here." Lepkin led them to the slippery bank of the brook and motioned for Erik to look around. "Bring me all of the rocks you can by the time I count to fifty."

Erik and the Dragon

Erik looked down and saw small pebbles and larger rocks half-buried in the mud. "How big should the rocks be?" he asked.

"Whatever size you like," Lepkin said. "Let's see how your strength and endurance are holding up." He held up his hand. "When I drop my hand, your time begins. Go as fast as you can."

Erik leaned forward and bent his knees, preparing to sprint out and gather the closest rocks he saw. He looked up and waited for the hand to drop.

"Now!" Lepkin commanded as he brought his hand down to his side.

Erik sprinted forward, sliding and nearly losing his footing as the first layer of mud gave way under his feet. He bent down and clawed around a fist-sized rock with his left hand while his right hand scooped up a bunch of smaller rocks. Then he turned back to run to Lepkin.

"Put them at my feet!" Lepkin shouted.

Erik ran back and bent low, careful not to plop the rocks onto Master Lepkin's foot. Then he dashed back to the edge of the water and dropped down to gather another load of rocks. As he sprinted back and forth he could hear Lepkin counting aloud.

"Ten, eleven, twelve, thirteen," Lepkin said in an even cadence. Erik rushed out to pull a hefty rock out of the mud. The grime and muck sucked back against his effort, but ultimately relented and the rock *popped* free with a string of mud flying up and sticking to Erik's face. He struggled to keep from dropping the slippery stone but managed to place it at Lepkin's feet before racing back. This time he noted that there were more rocks in the brook than on the bank, so he leapt gracelessly into the cold water and bent low to scoop several stones up. As he came up his fingers stung and burned slightly as small cuts and slices opened in his skin, but he didn't let it bother him. He was going to show Lepkin that he was still in his prime physical condition, despite everything that had happened recently.

Soon the pile of rocks peaked half-way up Lepkin's calf. A sizeable amount by any measure. Erik was breathing heavily and his newly mended leg burned hot deep in the thigh, reminding him of his recent injuries, but he didn't stop until Lepkin held up his hand again.

"Fifty," Lepkin shouted. He nodded satisfactorily and motioned for Erik to drop what he was currently carrying.

"Impressive," he said.

Erik dropped the three rocks in his hands and slowly made his way out of the water.

"No," Lepkin said sternly. "Stay there, in the brook."

Erik looked up confused. "In the water?" he asked.

Lepkin nodded and bent down to pick up a fist-sized rock. "Now it is time for the next part," he said calmly."

"Please don't tell me I have to put them back," Erik grumbled.

Lepkin shook his head. "There will be three commands," Lepkin said. "I will throw these rocks in varying rates and speeds. Your job is to do exactly as I command for each stone I throw. Should you fail, or make a mistake, you will owe me ten push-ups for each mistake."

"What do I have to do?" Erik asked.

"Stand in the center of the brook. I will throw a rock. The first possible command is 'duck' which will cause you to drop down on your belly, catching yourself on your toes and hands."

"In the water?" Erik asked.

Lepkin nodded. "The second possible command is 'dodge' which means you must sidestep left or right to avoid being hit by the rock. The third command is 'catch' and if you hear that, you will catch the rock regardless of where it is thrown, and you will throw it back at me. Do you understand?"

Erik nodded. "Is this to repay me for the scars?" Erik asked half seriously.

Lepkin smiled. "The scars are there because you did not focus enough. You allowed yourself to be hit. In a way, the scars belong on my body, as it was my failure as a teacher that allowed you to get injured. That is a shortcoming I aim to make up for. Are you ready?"

"Well, I guess..."

"DUCK!" Lepkin shouted as he hurled the stone at Erik's face.

Erik's eyes went wide and his instincts took over. His feet shot out behind him and he sprawled out with his hands as his face and chest splashed into the cold water. A second later he struggled to push himself back up.

"Catch!" Lepkin shouted.

Erik hadn't finished wiping the water from his eyes before the

Erik and the Dragon

pebble bounced off his right shoulder.

"That's one mistake," Lepkin noted. "Ten push-ups, right now."

Erik dropped to his stomach and pumped out the ten push-ups in a few seconds, then he rose to his feet and prepared himself.

"Dodge," Lepkin said. He threw a rock at Erik's stomach. Erik jumped to his right. "Dodge," Lepkin said again. Erik jumped left but this time there were two rocks. He hadn't even seen Lepkin throw the second one, but it slammed into his thigh. "Ten more, now."

When Erik finished he successfully made three dodges, one duck, followed by another four dodges. Then Lepkin shouted, "Catch!" Erik stood ready to snatch the rock, but Lepkin threw it wide out to the side. Erik lunged for it, but slipped and landed on his hip in the brook.

"You'll have to do better than that," Lepkin chided.

Erik grunted and did the next ten push-ups before returning to his starting position. He was starting to regret how many rocks he had gathered, and how large he had made some of them. He regained his composure and focused only on his breathing and watching Lepkin's shoulders. As his master moved and shouted, Erik answered effortlessly. The rest of the pile of rocks disappeared quickly, without another mistake until the last rock was thrown.

"Catch," Lepkin said.

Erik leapt up into the air, snatching the rock from high above him like a cat after a bird. As his body descended down he threw the rock back at Lepkin. Master Lepkin whipped out his sword in a flash and struck the stone with the broad side of his blade, sending it back at Erik quick as a bolt of lightning. The stone drove its stinging bite into Erik's solar plexus and dropped him to his backside, gagging and gasping for air.

Master Lepkin sheathed his sword and approached Erik. "When you face the dragon, there will come a moment near the end. You will think the battle is over, and that you have won. If you allow yourself to become overconfident, the dragon will turn that moment against you just as I sent your attack back at you just now. Remember that." Lepkin reached down and pulled Erik up.

"I wish I had known why you wanted those rocks," Erik grunted. "Seems a bit unfair to make me gather them if you were just going to pelt me with them."

177

"Battle is unfair," Lepkin said sternly. "My purpose is to teach you the skills you need to survive." He paused for a second after they got back to the muddy bank. "You still owe me ten for that last mistake."

"Seriously?" Erik asked.

Lepkin nodded. "As serious as a Griporion's belch," Lepkin said.

"What?"

"A Griporion is a large, chameleon-like lizard. It waits for its prey to pass by and then it belches a cloud of paralyzing poison strong enough to take out several grown men at once." Lepkin started to walk away and pointed to the ground. "You can ask Tatev if you want to know more about the creature. It's fascinating, really, and the scary part is you are alive and conscious when it starts to eat you."

Erik slowly dropped to his knees and then toppled over to catch himself with his palms in the mud. Ten push-ups later he rose to his feet and purposefully walked slowly as he followed Lepkin to the forest. Lepkin didn't seem to mind Erik's pace, he just whistled a tune and glanced over his shoulder every few steps.

Each time Lepkin turned back, Erik would quickly avert his eyes half angry, and half embarrassed at how many times he had made a mistake. He soon found his mind wandering back to the battle at Lokton Manor, the struggle with the Blacktongues, and finally to the fight with Tu'luh at Valtuu Temple. At first he thought it bewildering that he could triumph in those conflicts and yet he struggled with rocks being thrown at him. Then he remembered that there had been a couple of occasions where others had saved him from death. This realization helped him understand why Lepkin had done this. He wasn't being cruel, he was trying to prepare him. The battle ahead would require the best each of them had to offer, and even that might not get them all through it.

He nodded his head to himself and resolved to trust Lepkin's training methods. Deep down, he knew that his mentor had never done anything without a solid reason. Even the tournament at Kuldiga Academy proved to be a major help to him in later battles.

"Dodge!" Lepkin shouted suddenly.

Erik instinctively jumped left and looked up, scanning the area. Dimwater stood at the tree line, throwing a blue ball at him. It

Erik and the Dragon

whizzed by harmlessly and Erik looked around with his mouth open. "What's going on?" he asked.

"Catch and return!" Lepkin shouted.

A stick came whirling end over end from the trees. Erik quickstepped to his right, snatched the stick from the air and hurled it back.

"Whoa!" Tatev cried as he jumped down from a tree branch.

"You're out!" Lepkin shouted to Tatev. He turned back to Erik. "Duck!"

Erik sprawled out and hit the ground just as Jaleal jumped up in front of him and swung the shaft of his spear like an axe. The mithril weapon sailed above Erik's head and then Jaleal disappeared back into the grass.

"Dodge!" Lepkin shouted before Erik had gotten back to his feet. A series of blue and red balls flew toward him as Dimwater charged and alternated her arms with each spell. Erik executed a backward somersault, then rolled left and sprang to his feet before jumping right, then back, and then right again to avoid the rest of the spells.

"Catch and return!" Lepkin shouted. Lepkin threw a stone that he had concealed in his pocket.

Erik caught it, and threw it back. Just as before, Lepkin slapped the stone with the flat of his sword, sending it straight for Erik's face. This time, however, Erik caught the stone again, turned around to gain momentum and chucked it back. Lepkin caught the rock with his left hand and nodded with an approving smile.

"Much better," he said. "Much better."

"Well done," Jaleal commented as he emerged from the nearby grass.

"Next time I get a shield," Tatev complained as he rubbed his left shoulder.

Erik, breathing heavily from the sudden exertion, looked around at the smiling faces and then shook his head. "A test?" he asked.

Lepkin shook his head. "Practical application," he replied. "I wanted to see if you were listening to me."

"He is a quick study," Dimwater said approvingly.

"I have a good teacher," Erik said.

"Come," Tatev urged. "I am sure Marlin has prepared our supper by now.

"Salad?" Erik asked.

Tatev shook his head. "Boar," he said enthusiastically. "Found the grumpy bugger out here rooting around. We'll have a proper meal tonight."

"Finally, some good news," Erik said.

The others laughed a bit and they all turned to walk into the forest.

*****

Erik was thankful that the rest of the journey to Stonebrook was during good, dry weather. That way, when he made a mistake during the new types of practice sessions that Lepkin insisted on conducting several times a day, the push-ups could at least be done without the mud. Unfortunately, however, the shining sun did little to help with the several lumps and bruises Erik accumulated from various small stones and sticks. Sometimes he would seem completely untouchable, and other times he was just too slow to avoid getting hit. He soon found himself longing for the old days when all he had to do was swing a sword every three paces.

About a half hour after one of the rock throwing sessions, the group emerged from a pine forest to see several brown wooden buildings. Off in the distance to the west a couple of men could be seen herding a flock of sheep through a green, soft pasture.

"This is Stonebrook," Lepkin said.

The group quickened their pace until they reached the entrance. There was no gate, or high wall. Just a simple horse fence around the perimeter with a pair of guards dressed in leather hauberks and armed with iron swords. They took one look at Lepkin and simply waved the group through.

"I don't see an inn," Erik said as they walked through the main street.

Lepkin nodded. "There is one at the other end of town."

"But we aren't staying there, are we?" Dimwater chimed in.

"No," Lepkin said. He turned and looked to Erik and the others. "I have an old friend who lives here, we will go to his house."

"Is it big enough for all of us?" Jaleal asked.

"It will do," Lepkin replied. He then turned and led them through the town for a few minutes, turning off to the right on a

Erik and the Dragon

rutted dirt road lined with several handcarts and a couple of covered wagons drawn by teams of oxen.

Behind each cart was a man calling out the wares he had for sale. Some had traps, others had spices from other cities, some had cloth and leather, and a few had wine and spirits for sale.

As the group passed by a man with a stack of books on his cart, Tatev started to peel off from the group but Lepkin quickly grabbed him by the arm and pulled him back.

"I think you have enough books for now, Tatev," Lepkin said.

Tatev sighed and glanced back to the books a few times before finally falling back into lockstep with the group. Lepkin suddenly directed them all down a flat road on the left and they walked past several larger houses with neatly manicured gardens of red and white roses, vivid violets, yellow, red, and orange tulips, and vivid red carnations. Some of them even had bougainvillea climbing along wrought iron fences.

Lepkin stopped abruptly and pointed to a large, brown brick home with green wooden shutters flanking each of the tall, slender windows. A huge, lazy dog lifted its head from off its forelegs as it surveyed them from the front porch, but it didn't bark. Lepkin reached over the waist-high gate and pulled the latch to open it. "This is it," he said.

The large, mahogany double doors opened just then and the large dog craned its head around to see its master. Erik watched as a tall, wide-shouldered man with white hair and a thick, bushy gray and brown beard stepped out onto the porch. His boots were black and polished, his trousers made of burgundy silk, drawn together with a thick leather belt held in place by a large, gold buckle in the shape of a shield. A fine black silk vest fastened with pearl buttons covered the pale yellow shirt beneath, except for the pointed collar and the mid-length sleeves. The man walked forward with a limp, leaning upon a thick, black cane topped with a simple brass handle.

"It can't be," Tatev whispered to no one in particular.

"Master Lepkin, an honor to see you down here in these parts," the man said. His cane clicked against the wooden porch with each step forward until the man stood at the top of the stairs. The old dog slowly struggled to its feet, and it was then that Erik could see just how large the beast actually was. Its head came half way up the man's torso, and its shoulders stood well over the man's waist. It appeared that if the dog were to stand on its hind legs, it might very well be a foot taller than the man. It slowly wagged its tail as it gently leaned into its master's side.

"Master Tillamon, the honor is all mine," Lepkin replied with a great smile and a deep bow.

"So this is him?" Tillamon asked as he pointed his chin out, indicating Erik.

Lepkin nodded. "We are hunting the dragon," Lepkin replied.

Tillamon reached up with his left hand and stroked his beard. "Well, you have come to the right place." Tillamon lifted his cane and pointed in a southerly direction. "I saw the creature fly through here not so long ago. No doubt it was headed for Demaverung."

"I thought we might spend a couple days with you, and you could help Erik prepare."

Erik looked quizzically to Lepkin for a moment and then back to Tillamon. The old man's green eyes stared back, piercing into his soul for what seemed like an eternity. Any discomfort Erik had ever felt while Lepkin had locked eyes with him before seemed downright pleasant by comparison.

"I have a few spare beds," Tillamon said after a while, breaking his gaze and facing the others. "What's wrong with him?" Tillamon asked, pointing to Tatev. Erik turned to see the curly red head standing with his mouth agape as if he was looking at a pile of golden books dropped in front of him.

Marlin stepped up quickly and nudged Tatev sharply with his elbow.

Tatev snapped out of his daze and shook his head. His cheeks blushed and he fumbled for the words. "Sorry, it's just that, I thought you were dead."

Tillamon offered a gruff snort. "Not hardly." He turned and started to walk back inside. "Come on in, Hunter here won't bite. He's too old to do anything other than maybe fall over himself and trip you up."

The group moved through the garden space and on into the house. Erik stopped briefly to pet the humongous dog. It whirled around happily, wagging its thick tail in response. Unfortunately the dog was as clumsy with its tail as it was large, it whacked Erik right across the groin and doubled the boy over right there on the porch. Red-faced he looked up, hoping no one had seen the incident. To his dismay he saw Tillamon and Lepkin standing in the doorway looking down at him.

Erik and the Dragon

"Don't worry," Tillamon said. "It happens to the best of us... and to you." The old man cracked a half smile and then turned into the house, shaking his head.

Erik pushed himself up and pushed the dog's head away, careful to watch Hunter's tail as he maneuvered past and into the house. He closed the door behind him and then stood in the entryway, looking up at a grand double staircase leading up to a large, open room underneath a cupola. To the left was a room filled with swords, pikes, spears, axes, and shields, all hung neatly upon well-made plaques. Each one had a small brass plate underneath with writing on it, presumably about the weapon. To the right was a room filled with bookshelves, maps, a bearskin rug, and a spinning globe sitting upon a brass axis. The others all went forward, into a wide hallway underneath the double staircase, but Erik went to the right. He had only seen one globe before in all of his life.

He reached out gently with his right hand and gave the globe a turn. He could see the continents drawn upon the face of the globe, with each of the seas mapped out and the oceans too. Great sea monsters and snakes were drawn in the waters, and beasts of all kinds were drawn upon the lands. He stopped when he found the Middle Kingdom. A golden dragon was drawn within its borders and only Roegudok Hall, Drakei Glazei, and Ten Forts were named on the map.

"It isn't as accurate as it should be," Tillamon called out from behind.

Erik spun around, nearly knocking the globe over in the process. "Sorry, I didn't mean anything by it."

Tillamon raised a hand in the air and shook his head. "An inquisitive mind makes for a much better warrior," he said simply. "That is what I told Lepkin, when I was training him."

"You trained Master Lepkin?" Erik asked incredulously.

Tillamon nodded. "He was my best pupil."

"I don't remember hearing about you at Kuldiga Academy," Erik said. "When were you there?"

Tillamon moved into the library and looked down at Erik. "Oh, I was not at Kuldiga Academy. I was the commander of Ten Forts. That is where I met Lepkin. That is also where I trained him." Tillamon pointed down at the dots signifying Ten Forts on the globe. "It was a different time then," he said. "Lepkin graduated from the Academy, that much is true. Then, he was transferred to Ten Forts as one of my officers. I saw something in him that I had never seen before. So I took him under my care and trained him up beyond what the Academy could ever have done for him." Tillamon glanced over his shoulder. "I had no way of knowing that it would turn out the way it has, but he has done well for himself and for that I am happy."

"What do you mean?" Erik asked.

Tillamon turned his head to the side and reached up to fold his ear forward, revealing a crescent shaped birthmark behind his ear. Erik gasped and Tillamon let his ear flip back into position.

"You are a Sahale?"

Tillamon nodded. "I am." He moved to a wooden chair, picked an old tome off the seat and gently placed it on the side table nearby before turning and falling into the chair. "I am a rather old one at that," he said. "During my command at Ten Forts, we fought orcs, goblins, and dragons. Well, some were dragons, others were those blasted nightwings, twisted by that cursed book Nagar and Tu'luh created." Tillamon's eyes grew hot and a sour frown crossed his face as he said their names. "I trained Lepkin for one purpose, and one purpose only, to slay every dragon he ever saw."

The words slammed into Erik as forcefully as a punch to the gut. "Every dragon?" Erik repeated.

Tillamon nodded and turned his fierce, menacing eyes toward Erik. "Every single one."

Erik stood silently, not knowing where the conversation was going. He fidgeted with his right fingers and bit the inside of his lower lip nervously.

"He was good at it too," Tillamon said. "He was real good. He must have led fifty expeditions. He always came back with the prize. Sure, he lost some men along the way, but we were all soldiers, and we understood the risk." He pointed his cane out toward the room full of weapons. "That room is dedicated to the fallen. The officers who died hunting dragons have their weapons hung here in reverence. Others have forgotten, but I have not."

Why did Lepkin bring me here? Erik wondered.

"I know what you're thinking," Tillamon said with a nod. "But, I don't hate dragons."

"Then why kill all of them?" Erik asked.

"Because they are easier to slay as dragons, before Nagar's

magic warped them into those twisted nightwings," Tillamon looked to the floor for a moment.

Lepkin appeared at the room's entrance then and leaned against the wall. "Go ahead, tell him," he told Tillamon. The white-haired man looked up to Lepkin for a moment silently. "He performs better if he understands people's motives." Lepkin explained.

Tillamon nodded. "My father was a Sahale as well," he said. "Normally, our kind are not affected by the spell as long as we stay in our human form, but he chose to spend his days as a dragon. Ultimately, the book changed him. He became a nightwing." Tillamon's eyes welled up with tears and one rolled down his left cheek to disappear in his thick, bristly beard. He smacked his lips together and cleared his throat. "In his warped state he assaulted Ten Forts. It was my blade that ended his savagery." Tillamon tapped his cane on the floor and glared sourly off into the distance. "I vowed that day that all dragons must die. Letting even one of them live to be twisted like my father was seemed cruel and callous. So we killed as many as we could find."

Lepkin stepped into the room and cut into the conversation. "I spent a lot of time there, at Ten Forts," he said. "However, once we had put down the dragons along the southern border, I was transferred to the east. I spent several years scouting for Tarthuns and ensuring our eastern border was secure."

"The Tarthuns knew how many soldiers we had lost in the south, and they smelled blood," Tillamon cut in. "I also spent a couple years in the east. I had a few encounters, but they were nothing like what we had seen at Ten Forts. Given my experience at Ten Forts, I was asked to guard Gelleirt Monastery," Tillamon added. "The monks there were trying to uncover the location of some ancient texts; historical anthologies about the dragons."

"Why not use the library at Valtuu Temple?" Erik asked.

Tillamon snorted. "Because the temple keeps only the books that put the Ancients in a good light, or at least that is what some of the nobles thought. So the monks at Gelleirt Monastery were looking for other books that might paint a more holistic picture of dragons, and how to defeat them once and for all."

"The monks were also trying to uncover where the Ancients were going during their mass exodus when most of them fled the Middle Kingdom," Lepkin put in. "You have to understand, we weren't sure that Nagar's Secret was limited by range, so we thought any living dragon would eventually turn into a nightwing, no matter how far they fled."

"And a few of us were determined to hunt them all down," Tillamon said. He sighed and wrinkled his nose. "Anyway, after some time I decided the monks weren't going to figure anything out during my lifetime. So I retired. Lepkin was my replacement at Gelleirt Monastery. A few years later, the gods thought it might be funny to play a trick on me, and Lepkin was chosen as the next Keeper of Secrets."

"I thought the monks at Gelleirt were in the same order as Marlin? And, if you had been hunting dragons, why would the dragons choose you to be the next Keeper?" Erik asked.

"Our hearts were in the right place, but our minds were not enlightened," Lepkin said.

"Bah, I wouldn't agree with that," Tillamon said. "I still say the only good dragon is a dead dragon. They only bring destruction, and death."

Lepkin folded his arms, but he didn't bother staring down his old mentor. "I was shown a different path," Lepkin said. "Beyond that, I was the best at what I did, and I was the most respected knight when it came to knowledge and experience with dragons and nightwings." Lepkin stepped forward and placed his hands on Erik's shoulders. "When I was told of the prophecies about a champion, the Champion of Truth, I knew that there was a better way to end Nagar's curse upon the Middle Kingdom."

Erik nodded. He understood. "But you brought me here so he can teach me more about killing Tu'luh."

Lepkin nodded. "I have some preparations to make. I need to see to them personally, to make sure we are well enough equipped for what lies ahead." He looked over to Tillamon and then back to Erik. "There is no one better in all of Terramyr than Tillamon when it comes to killing dragons. Listen to him and do everything he asks you to do. The things he teaches you might just save your life and give you the edge over Tu'luh."

Erik nodded. "Alright," he promised.

Lepkin drew in a deep breath and then turned to Tillamon. "Just start with the dragon's vulnerabilities," Lepkin said. "He has already gone through your DDC challenge."

Tillamon raised an eyebrow in much the same manner as

Erik and the Dragon

Lepkin often did and looked to Erik. "Lepkin threw daggers at you and made you either dodge, duck, or catch them?" he asked pointedly.

Erik's eyes grew wide and he looked to Lepkin.

Lepkin shook his head. "I used rocks and sticks."

"Bah," Tillamon said with a wave of his hand. "Rocks and sticks don't help develop the same kind of reflexes as daggers would, you know that. I used dagger when I trained you!"

Lepkin cocked his head to the side. "Erik is fourteen," Lepkin said sternly.

Tillamon shrugged. "Well I guess two days isn't really enough to get a benefit out of the daggers anyway," he said. "I can show him what I know about the dragons though."

Lepkin nodded. "I am going to go into town. Is Mercer still in command at Ten Forts?"

"No," Tillamon said with a shake of his head. "Mercer was retired early after losing his leg in an accident. His lieutenant replaced him. A knight by the last name of Finorel, I believe. Don't know much about him, other than the fact that he is from a noble house in Pinkt'Hu."

"That's a shame, I would rather have dealt with Mercer," Lepkin said.

"Well, you can call on him if you like. He lives here in Stonebrook. He is in the little white house behind the general goods store."

Lepkin nodded. "I will return as soon as I have gathered everything we need." He started to turn and then stopped himself. "One more thing," he said. "Tomorrow evening, can we use your garden?" Lepkin asked.

"For what?" Tillamon asked.

"Dimwater and I are looking to be wed before we leave Stonebrook. You would honor us by allowing us to use your garden."

Tillamon smiled and his eyes seemed to soften. "Finally ready to do something for yourself for a change?" he asked. The old man struggled to his feet and stepped forward to pull Lepkin into an embrace. "You would honor *me*," he said. "I will spare no expense. Tomorrow night, we shall have a feast to be remembered!" The two hugged for only a moment before Lepkin turned back toward the door and walked out of the house. As the door closed behind him, Tillamon turned and laid a hard, strong left hand on Erik's shoulder. "You and I have some work to do." He started limping to the wall and reached his left hand in over a bunch of books. Erik couldn't see what he was grabbing, but something in the shelf clicked and that sound was followed by rattling chains and creaking gears.

A blast of dust shot out from behind the bookshelf. Tillamon coughed and waved the air in front of him away as he took a couple steps back. The bookshelf slowly swung out like a door, revealing a pathway in the wall behind.

"No matter how many times I clean this room, there is always a bunch of dirt that gets kicked up when I open this door," Tillamon said. "Must be something to do with the draft down below." He limped forward and gestured for Erik to follow. "Well, come on, don't just stand there gawking at the old gimp."

Erik quickly caught up and then realized that there was a metal staircase descending in a spiral. A series of large mirrors caught and reflected light from the library to illuminate the stairs until they reached the bottom. There, Tillamon pulled a large lever that triggered several more mirrors and crystals around them. As the light poured in, reflecting off the mirrors and crystals, Erik could see that they stood in a great chamber that was easily twice the size of the house above, and held up with a complex system of beams and columns.

"That's amazing," Erik commented as the light continued to flow into the area.

"It's an old trick I learned from some of the elves during my time at Ten Forts. They used mirrors to harness the sunlight above and reduce our reliance on torches within the fort. It helped reduce a lot of costs since we didn't need to procure torches and candles as much."

"What about at night?" Erik asked.

"If the moon is out, it's enough to see by. Besides, it helps keep your eyes sharp for the night." Tillamon walked to a large wooden box mounted to the wall and opened it to reveal a series of levers inside. "Now stand right where you are for a moment and don't move. Have to test the system." Tillamon pulled hard on the first lever. An instant later a large log swung down from the ceiling, grazing the floor in the center of the room. Erik couldn't get a good look because it was moving so fast, but he thought he saw

Erik and the Dragon

painted eyes and teeth on the log to resemble a dragon's head.

"What is that?" Erik asked.

"Shh!" Tillamon said. He pulled the next lever and another, equally large, log sailed by in a different direction from the first. This log swung much closer to the ceiling than the first, and had an opening in the front. "Good, that's two," Tillamon commented to himself. He then pulled the third lever. A multitude of loud, echoing clicks and clacks sounded and then wooden poles shot out of the floor, ceiling, and columns. Erik's eyes went wide at the sight.

Tillamon clapped his hands and rubbed them together. Then he pulled three levers below the first and Erik could hear the slithering metallic scrape of chains on stone as everything was retracted into place. "The machine is ready," Tillamon said.

Erik shook his head. He instinctively rubbed his arms where Marlin's gauntlet had given him a beating not so long ago. "What am I supposed to do?"

"For starters, you can lay your sword down over by the stairs, we wouldn't want it to get damaged."

Erik turned and loosened his sword belt, but all the while he was thinking it was ironic that Tillamon was concerned about the sword. "Am I supposed to dodge everything?" Erik asked.

"Of course not," Tillamon said. "If all you did was dodge, how would you defeat a dragon?"

Erik shrugged and moved into the center of the room where Tillamon stood waiting for him. "The dragon has two vulnerabilities. You can't cut through its armor with your own strength, even your magical sword won't help much unless you exploit the beast's weaknesses. The first is the eyeball, strike one of those and I don't care how large the dragon is, it'll go into a frenzy trying to escape."

"I struck Tu'luh in the left eye," Erik said proudly.

Tillamon stopped cold with his mouth open and tugged at his beard. "Well, with one eye down, you just might have a chance to take the demon down." The old man pursed his lips and nodded for a couple moments.

"What's the other weakness?" Erik asked.

Tillamon snapped out of his thoughts and held an old finger up in the air. "The neck!" Tillamon exclaimed.

Erik frowned. "But the neck is covered in scales."

"No, no no, not the outside of the neck, the *inside*!" Tillamon corrected. Unless you have a ballista launcher you are not punching through a dragon's neck, but when he opens his mouth to strike at you, he also opens up his biggest vulnerability. You get a spear, arrow, or axe thrown into the back of the thing's throat and you can drop him within seconds."

"How am I supposed to do that?"

Tillamon pointed to the levers. "Go and pull the top middle lever," he said.

Erik went to the wall and pulled the lever. Down came the log with the opening. Tillamon whipped his cane up in a flash. The outer part fell away, revealing a wicked blade affixed to the cane's handle. Tillamon timed his move perfectly, throwing the cane sword like a dart and sticking it deep in the opening as the log swung by.

"Like that," the old man said. "What do you say, kid, want to try?"

Erik nodded his head. "Looks simple enough," he said.

Tillamon nodded. "There are some practice spears on the far side of the chamber. Go and get seven of them. Erik did as he was told while Tillamon worked the levers to bring the log down, retrieved his cane sword, and then reset the machine. By the time Erik stood back in the center of the room, Tillamon was eagerly waiting for him.

"Lepkin said you already did the DDC training, but it hasn't been something you have practiced for a long time, has it?"

"No, just started on the way here from Tualdern," Erik replied.

"Well, I am going to put it into practice here. I will pull levers, but you are not allowed to watch me. You will have to react and strike either the eye, or the throat, depending on which dragon dummy comes at you. Are you ready?"

Erik nodded. He heard the lever drop, as chains rattled and metal *clicks* echoed through the chamber. Erik looked up, but something jabbed him in the buttocks. Something else swung into his back, knocking him forward. It was then that Erik realized that Tillamon had not pulled either of the targets. He had attacked. The boy ducked just in time to avoid taking a shaft to the chest, then rolled away from a trio of sticks shooting up from the floor. A bag of sand on a rope swung from the ceiling but Erik dodged and continued his dangerous dance until the danger had passed.

"Lepkin was right, you do have talent," Tillamon said. "First rule of dragon fighting, they always use their minds as their primary weapons. If they can sneak, cheat, deceive, or trap you, they will. If they have minions, which Tu'luh most certainly does, they will send them first like pawns in a game of chess. Always expect that they know you are coming, and have prepared for you."

Erik rubbed his backside and nodded. "I understand."

Another lever dropped. Erik looked up, expecting one of the two targets. Again he was surprised to see a pole shooting up near him out of the floor. He dodged it, ducked under a pair of swinging bags, and then jumped away from a series of poles stabbing out from a nearby column. He was so busy dodging the traps that he never heard the next lever. The dragon head swooped down. It missed him completely. In fact, Erik had his back turned to it and never even saw it.

"You're dead," Tillamon shouted above the din.

Erik looked up. "What do you mean, I dodged everything!"

Tillamon pointed to the dragon dummy gently swinging near the ceiling. "He roasted your sorry butt while you were distracted by those sticks there."

Erik's shoulders slumped and his mouth fell open. He stood there staring at the dragon dummy and shaking his head. Another lever clicked and down swooped the other head. Erik pulled himself together just enough to jump out of the way. He clumsily threw his spear at the target, but it bounced off harmlessly, clattering to the ground.

"Maybe I was wrong," Tillamon said. "You are pretty bad at this."

"It's only my first time," Erik countered.

"Well, that ain't gonna stop Tu'luh from ripping you apart is it?" Tillamon pulled another set of levers to reset the machines, then he turned and leaned forward on his cane. "What are you going to do? Will you go up to the dragon and say, sorry but this is my first time, please go easy on me." He waved a hand at him and shook his head. "Get up, try again."

Now I know where Lepkin gets it from. Erik shook his head and dusted himself off. No wonder Lepkin was always quiet. This guy probably beat him half to death.

Tillamon cleared his throat, catching Erik's attention. "If you are wondering whether I trained Lepkin the same way, the answer is no. I trained him harder, and he was better at it."

"He was already a knight when you met him," Erik blurted out before he could stop himself.

Tillamon narrowed his green eyes on the boy and snorted. "You are big on excuses, aren't you?" The old man pulled a lever and Erik turned away, gracefully dodging the shafts and poles jutting out at him from all directions. When a bag of sand swung down he blasted it with the side of his spear, spilling sand everywhere. Out of the corner of his eye he saw the dragon head swinging down. He went to throw his spear into the gap, but a pole darted out toward his side, forcing him to jump out of the way and he missed his shot.

"Pathetic!" Tillamon snarled. "I thought you were supposed to be this all-powerful champion, what is wrong with you?"

Erik threw the spear down and held his hands out to his side. "What do you want? I dodged all the attacks and I couldn't get an opening. What else do you want me to do? Should I just let the traps hit me?"

"Precisely," Tillamon said coldly.

Erik dropped his head back and exhaled in frustration. "You just told me to dodge everything and watch out for traps," Erik shouted.

Tillamon shook his head and approached Erik, leaning heavily on his cane for support and keeping a menacing scowl on his face. Erik felt his blood chill and his heart skipped a couple of beats. He was almost certain that Tillamon was going to run him through with his cane sword.

Just as the old man got within inches of Erik's face he opened his mouth and began to speak in a calm, measured voice. "The DDC challenge is to teach you how to dodge and perfect your reflexes. However, when facing a dragon, you will have to go for the kill every time." Erik shook his head and looked away, but Tillamon grabbed his chin in a vice-like grip and forced Erik's eyes back up to meet his. "The last pole that was going for your side, would it kill you?"

"No," Erik said.

"Was it going to hurt?"

"Yeah," Erik replied.

"Lasting damage or just a bruise?" Tillamon pressed. Erik

stood silent, so Tillamon answered for him. "When facing a dragon, humans are always at a disadvantage. If you have a shot to take, you always take it. Sometimes that means letting yourself get hit in order to score the winning blow." Tillamon straightened up and let Erik go. "Dodge the traps that will kill or maim you, but always take the shot if you can. Some of the most revered dragon hunters I have ever trained offered their lives in exchange for the killing blow in battle. Those are the men whose weapons hang in my hall."

Erik stood there for a moment and looked around the room. Some of the traps stood frozen in place, others had sunk back into their holes. The slashed bag of sand had a drizzle of glass-like grains falling from it still as it twirled at the end of the rope. He sighed. All of his other teachers had been hard on him, even Al and Marlin, but nobody had been this hard on him. Still, the hot anger was little compared to the cold shame he felt creeping into his mind and sapping his confidence. He shook his head. He had to try again. He needed to do this.

"Reset the traps," Erik said.

Tillamon was already at the levers and setting the machines back in place. "That's enough for today," he said. "Let's go upstairs, I am tired and I need some food."

"Let me go again," Erik pleaded.

"Maybe tomorrow," Tillamon said with a wave of his hand.

Erik watched the old man limp away toward the stairs. The guilt of defeat crept into his heart again. The same, crushing doubts that haunted him since his father's death stirred within him laughing and mocking his impotence. The old, crippled man stopped near the stairs where the levers for the mirrors hung. As his hand reached up to reset the mirrors and plunge the training area into darkness, something in Erik burned hot. Erik bent down and scooped up several spears and then he ran to the wall with the three training levers. Even at his fastest speed, he could not reach them before Tillamon pulled the lever that turned the large mirrors and crystals back to their resting places and the reflected light vanished like a ghost in the wind. Unable to see, Erik hooked his arm up hoping to get at least two of the levers. Instead he pulled all three. He rushed back to the center of the room.

"What do you think you are doing? I can't call the mirrors back until they are finished resetting!" Tillamon cried out.

Erik didn't care. In his anger he called forth the same light he had summoned to illuminate Hamath Valley. The orb of light burst into the chamber, allowing Erik to see the myriad shafts thrusting up out of the floor and columns. He dodged a few that he knew would knock him off course, but he let a few others strike him and ignored the pain. The dragon dummy with the closed mouth swung down much faster than the other. Erik lunged forward, thrusting a spear out and jamming it directly into the painted eye. Then he rolled, taking a hard hit to the stomach that threatened to double him over, but coming up just in time to launch another spear in the opposite direction. It sailed straight and true, burying itself dead center in the opening and shaking the log upon impact.

Erik smiled, and then a heavy bag of sand barreled into his chest, knocking him off his feet and flinging him backward a couple yards to land on his back. His breath made a wheezing *whoosh* as it was forced from his chest and he struggled to turn over, clawing at the stone floor as he fought for breath. His lungs and throat burned for the lack of air for what seemed like an eternity. Erik's vision started to go blurry. He could just barely make out Tillamon's frantic voice shouting at him, but he couldn't make sense of the words.

A hand reached down and grabbed him under the armpit, yanking him up into a sitting position. Then he felt a hand seizing each of his elbows and hoisting them up over his head. "Bring your arms up," Tillamon said. "It will help expand your ribcage so you can recover faster."

Erik nodded and blinked, but he still wasn't fully aware of what was happening. Then, almost as if waking from a bad dream, his lungs opened and the air rushed into his body. His consciousness came back in full and he shook his head and groaned.

"That was one of the dumbest, most ignorant things I have ever seen!" Tillamon said.

"Sorry," Erik wheezed. "I just had to try one more time."

Tillamon helped Erik up to his feet and looked the boy in the eyes. "Yeah, that's what Lepkin said when he did the same thing."

Erik looked up at Tillamon curiously.

"Well," Tillamon continued with a shrug. "He couldn't shoot light out of his mouth, so he came out a little worse for wear than you did, but it was pretty much the same."

Erik and the Dragon

"You knew I would do that?" Erik asked.

"Of course not," Tillamon replied. "But, I kind of hoped you would. All the great ones do. That's how I know who is worth training, a true hunter never admits defeat." Tillamon patted Erik on the back. "Come on, I am not sure how long your little light ball is going to last, so let's get moving toward the stairs before we lose the light."

"We're done?" Erik asked.

"Time for a good meal," Tillamon said with a shrug. "After that we will come back down for night training. There are some clouds in the sky today, so the moonlight won't be at its best, but that is the better for you to train with. Just no more cheating with that ball of light. I want your eyes to adjust."

Erik nodded and then the two of them made their way to the stairs.

"It was still pretty stupid," Tillamon repeated as they reached the stairs.

*****

The sunlight on Erik's face woke him long before he would have liked. His body ached all over and muscles still burned from the nighttime training session. Even his head felt tired. That was probably because Marlin had joined them, throwing in his illusions to try and distract Erik even more. Still, he had done well enough that Tillamon was offering nothing but compliments by the time they were through.

Jaleal snored nearby, reminding Erik that he was not alone in the room. He struggled to sit up, rubbing his right side and wincing as a massive cramp worked into his left hamstring, threatening to double his leg up. He quickly jerked his legs over the side of the bed and set his feet down on the floor, straightening his leg and kneading it with his fingertips and knuckles.

A rooster crowed off in the distance somewhere outside. Erik looked to the window and saw the sun was not even fully above the horizon yet. He stood up slowly, mentally checking his leg to see if it was going to seize up on him again. Once he realized he was safe, he stepped lightly over to the door and slipped out of the room. He went through the hall, down the grand stairs, and then made his way out to the glass door that opened into the rear garden. A pair of finches hopped on nearby bushes and then took off into the air as Erik stepped closer. A small, brown rabbit nibbled on some clover growing between a marble fountain and a patch of iris flowers. Otherwise, the garden was still and peaceful.

He walked out onto the grass and flexed his toes among the cool, soft blades, still wet with the morning dew. The air was light and crisp. He held his arms out and leaned his head back, enjoying the cool morning weather.

"Serene, isn't it?" Tillamon said from behind.

Erik startled and whirled around. How could a man with a cane be so quiet?

"From here I can see the plains to the south, the grasslands in the north, and the mountains off in the east. There isn't a better spot in all of the Middle Kingdom if you are looking for quiet mornings and calm nights."

Erik nodded. "I guess so."

"Bah," Tillamon gruffed. "You're young yet, but one day you will see it the same as I do now. While we are young we want adventure, we crave it, but when we get older we want peace, and not just between kingdoms. I mean the kind of peace that comes quietly into your soul and dispels the fears and doubts you harbor deep inside." Tillamon smiled weakly then and looked down to his right foot. Erik followed Tillamon's gaze and noted that Tillamon's foot was scarred and warped, as though the leg had been bitten and held in a fierce fire. He tapped his foot with his cane and it made an eerily hollow sound.

Erik looked up to ask what had happened, but Tillamon sighed and opened his mouth first. "My father did this," he said. "I saw he was turning. The anguish of being driven mad by Nagar's evil curse was burning my father's mind. I tried to convince him to use his human form, but it was already too late. He grabbed my leg in his mouth so fast, like a lightning strike, and then he let the fire roll out over me. Even then I couldn't raise my hand against him. So instead I transformed into my dragon form to escape. I barely got away from him. He chased me for miles through the sky. When I got back to Ten Forts, I told my men that I had been attacked, but not who it was. A Sahale could never expose himself, it was too dangerous." Tillamon sighed. "Eventually, my father tracked me down. He had fully changed into a nightwing by then. My men hurried about, preparing the defenses and firing our launchers. Still

Erik and the Dragon

I couldn't bring myself to join in the fight." Tillamon clenched his jaw for a moment and a tear rolled down his face. "Then, when I heard the screams of my soldiers, dying as my father tore them apart, I did what any soldier would do in my place. I put the threat down as fast as I could."

"I'm sorry," Erik said. His own eyes began to water and a lump formed in his throat. "I also lost my father."

Tillamon nodded quietly and stepped forward to put a hand on Erik's shoulder. "I am too old to fight now," he said. "But you and I understand better than most what this magic will do if left unchecked. If you are the champion that Lepkin thinks you are, then you must put the threat down."

Erik nodded. From Tillamon's standpoint, it made sense. Then again, Tillamon didn't know about the Infinium, or the visions that Tu'luh had shown him. Erik sighed and turned back to look at the fountain and the blue iris flowers.

"Lepkin believes in you, and he believes in this prophecy," Tillamon said. "But I have to ask, what happens if slaying Tu'luh isn't enough?"

Erik turned around with his brow drawn into a knot. "You mean what will I do if the magic has corrupted all of the dragons?"

Tillamon nodded. "Will you have the courage to finish the fight?"

Erik paused for a moment and then gave Tillamon a question. "What if the magic was the only way to save the world, would you have the courage to use it?"

The old man cocked his head back and frowned. His green eyes bored into Erik's soul. "I'm not sure what you are getting at, but I have seen what this magic does. There is no scenario in which Nagar's horrid curse could save anything in this world. It is only madness and abomination. It sucked my father's soul out of his body and replaced him with a twisted monster that craved nothing but blood and destruction. If Nagar's magic were the only way to save this world, then this world is already doomed, and would be better off burning to ash." Erik nodded and ceded the point. The old man tapped the top of Erik's head with his cane.

"What was that for?" Erik asked as he rubbed his scalp.

"Checking to see whether your head is made of mush," Tillamon said.

Just then Tatev came out, tying a robe around himself and

yawning wide. "It isn't made of mush," he said through his yawn. "He is trying to answer a riddle that Tu'luh gave him."

Tillamon snorted. "What riddle is that?"

Erik answered in distant monotone as he recalled the vision with the fireballs. "If I defeat Tu'luh and destroy Nagar's magic, I will save everyone from its curse, but I will condemn the world to destruction. However, if I side with Tu'luh, I can save the world, but only by enslaving it with Nagar's magic."

"Horse-apples, boy, that doesn't even make sense," Tillamon countered. "The dragon is trying to trick you, remember the first rule of fighting dragons?"

"The Infinium confirms the danger," Tatev said quickly.

"The what?" Tillamon asked. "Isn't that the cursed book whispered about around campfires to scare children? I'll not take my wisdom from a ghost story."

"It isn't a ghost story," Erik said. "Tatev has the book."

Tillamon stood blankly for a moment, glancing from Erik to Tatev and then back to Erik. "Come again?"

"Tatev has the book," Erik repeated.

Tillamon turned slowly back to Tatev and stroked his beard. "You have *that* book?"

Tatev smiled from ear to ear and nodded his head.

"That is incredible," Tillamon said. He shook his head and smoothed his hair back as he thought about it. "Have you read it?"

Tatev shook his head. "Only the unsealed portions. It's enough to confirm the possibility of the vision that Tu'luh showed Erik, but not much more than that."

Tillamon nodded. "I have a friend who studies obscure artifacts and books, perhaps he could help."

"Perhaps some other time," Tatev said hesitantly.

"He lives close by, and I was going to suggest you stop by and see him anyway. He is a great scholar, and has essentially turned his entire house into a library. I bet he would give you any book he owns just for a chance to peek at your treasure."

"What is his area of expertise?" Tatev asked, obviously intrigued.

"Orcs," Tillamon replied quickly. "He was the resident expert on orcish culture, language, and history during my time at Ten Forts. More than a few battles were won based on information he could give us about orcish battle strategies and history. He stayed on at Ten Forts to serve Mercer after I left. Then, when Mercer was retired due to his injury, the new commander sent the scholar home as there hadn't been any orc attacks for quite some time by that point."

"What is his name?" Tatev asked.

"Patrical Domnik. I can take you right now, just let me get fully dressed first."

"I don't know," Tatev said. "Maybe we shouldn't."

"Too late now," Tillamon said. "You already let the cat out of the bag, and now I know that Erik here has doubts about whether he can kill the dragon. I think it best to settle the question right here and now."

"He has a point," Erik said. "If this other man can help us solve the question, it's worth telling him about it."

Tatev sighed. "Very well, I'll get my shoes and pants."

"And the book!" Tillamon insisted. "Come on now, let's get a move on. If we are quick we can get back here before the others wake for breakfast.

Only a couple of minutes later the three of them were heading down the street just as fast as Tillamon's leg would let them. His cane making a *click-click-click* in rhythm with his dragging, lame foot. No one else was out yet, except for a couple of round bellied men with white aprons and funny baker's hats on their heads and baskets of fresh bread in their hands. Tillamon excitedly led Erik and Tatev through the winding streets, cutting through unfenced yards when possible, until they stopped at a brown stone building with dark wooden accents around the two windows in the front. They went right up to the front door and Tillamon gave a quick couple of taps with the brass handle of his cane.

A couple of minutes later Erik could hear heavy footsteps approaching from the other side of the door. A metal bolt scraped back out of the way and then the door ripped open to reveal a thin, balding man who looked to be at least seventy. A pair of gold rimmed spectacles sat upon his narrow, humped nose and the man had lines extending from the corners of his mouth that made it appear as though he always frowned. His brown eyes glanced over each of them and then landed on Tillamon.

"To what do I owe the pleasure?" he asked in a high-pitched nasal voice.

"Sorry if we woke you," Tillamon offered.

"Nonsense," Patrical said. "You know I always wake before the sun rises. It's good for the mind."

Tillamon nodded. "We have something to show you. Can we come in?"

Patrical looked to Tatev and Erik once more and then he noticed the book in Tatev's hands. He narrowed his eyes and leaned forward a bit. Tatev turned the book over and showed the front to Patrical. The scholar put a hand up to his chest and nearly fell over backward as he stumbled over his feet and beckoned them all inside.

"Come in, come in!" Erik let the other two go in first. As he stepped inside Patrical pushed the door closed and threw the bolt back into place. Then the thin man scurried back in front of them and gestured for them to follow. "Come to the parlor."

Erik looked around and noticed stacks of books everywhere. Bookcases lined the walls, stuffed completely full so that books laid atop other books, and some hung over the edge of the shelves so much that it looked like they should fall out. Tables and chairs were buried in books. Some were open, while other stacks were busy gathering dust. The hallway, which had once been as wide as Tillamon's entrance, was so narrow that all of them had to turn sideways and shuffle through the hall, there were so many books stacked up.

They passed an open door and Erik happened to spy something inside that caught his attention. It was as if his eye was drawn to a green book in the middle of the room on top of a cherry wood desk. He glanced to the others and then, despite a little feeling warning him not to snoop, he ducked into the side room and went to the desk. The symbol on the spine intrigued him. It was a language he did not know, and yet it somehow felt familiar to him, almost as though it were similar to the dwarvish runes he had studied. He reached up to remove the other books from on top of it and set them on an adjacent stack. He took the green book in his hands and opened it. The pages inside were yellow and stiff with age, but not brittle. Each page was filled with runes like the one on the cover. Every few pages there would be a drawing of stars, or a map of the Middle Kingdom. Then he found several pages that showed drawings of dragons. The first was a great, golden dragon, much like the one that he had seen on the mural in Valtuu Temple. He flipped through the pages, studying each dragon he saw. Beneath each image was a series of runes, but there was no way to know what they said.

"It isn't polite to rummage through another man's belongings," a stern, nasal voice said from the doorway.

Erik jumped and quickly dropped the book. "I'm sorry," he said. Tillamon appeared in the doorway behind Patrical and tapped the thin man's arm with his cane.

"Don't take it too personally, he did the same thing when he came to my home," Tillamon said.

"Did he?" Patrical asked.

"Like I always say, inquisitive minds make better warriors," Tillamon commented with a quick nod and a smile. "Come on, Erik, let's get to the parlor and discuss the subject we came here for."

Erik nodded. "What is this book?" he asked.

Patrical huffed impatiently. "It is an old dwarvish book about the creation. According to the dwarves it details the history of the gods, maps the stars as they formed Terramyr, and also explains the origins of the Ancients."

Erik nodded. "So the dragons in the pictures are—"

"The Ancients, yes. Now, can we move to the parlor?" Patrical insisted.

Erik blushed and stole one last glance at the book as Patrical turned and left the room. A cold fear ripped through him and seized his heart. There, on the page before him, was Tu'luh the Red. He recognized the wicked fangs and downward curved horns as easily as if the beast stood in the same room with him at that very moment. Even as he stretched his hand out to pick up the book his heart thumped palpably in his chest. His breathing slowed, and his mind whirled around in a million different directions.

He raised the book up to his face and stared in shock at the drawing. He flipped back through the images until he found the golden dragon. He looked closely at the image, scrutinizing every detail of the snout, the legs, the fangs, and the body. Could it be?

Erik rushed out of the room, knocking a stack of books over as he brushed them with his hip on the way out. "What is this?" he shouted out after the others. He stumbled into the parlor and flipped the book open to Tu'luh's image. "Why is Tu'luh in this book?"

"Because he is one of the Ancients," Patrical replied dryly.

"No," Tatev said. "He fell from his status. He is no longer included with the honorable ones."

"Are you telling me that he was there when the Middle Kingdom was created?" Erik asked incredulously. "He… he helped create the Middle Kingdom?" Tatev opened his mouth to speak but Patrical beat him to it.

"He was not only there," Patrical said. "He was one of the dragons responsible for establishing Roegudok Hall. He is the second oldest of the Ancients. He is Hiasyntar Ku'lai's son, and heir to the kingdom of dragons."

"Not anymore," Tatev said sourly. "He betrayed the Ancients. He turned on them, and on the Middle Kingdom. He is no longer the heir, he is an outcast."

Erik moved in and dropped the book down in front of Tatev. "It all makes sense now," Erik said.

"What does?" Tillamon asked.

"This is why he showed me the vision. He wants to save the world. That is his motive."

"No, he wants to destroy the world, like all dragons will if Nagar's magic gets to them!" Tillamon shouted.

"No," Tatev growled. "The magic can't go beyond the mountains, it is bound in scope and power. The Ancients who fled to distant lands are safe. The only threat is Tu'luh!"

Patrical clapped his hands together and whistled so sharply that all three of them winced and shied away, covering their ears. "Now that I have your attention," Patrical began, "might I ask what in the name of Hammenfein is going on?"

"I saw Tu'luh, at Valtuu Temple," Erik said. "He told me that if I do not help him use Nagar's magic, then our world is doomed to be consumed by fire."

"You *saw* Tu'luh?" Patrical asked.

"I fought with him, as did many others," Erik replied. Then he pointed to Tatev. "We found this book, The Infinium, which seems to confirm Tu'luh's warnings. Now, we have come here to ask your help in deciphering this book. I need to know whether defeating Tu'luh will result in Terramyr's end."

Patrical's eyebrows shot up so high upon his wrinkled forehead that Erik was sure they were going to get stuck up there. The scholar was silent for a long time, looking to the book in

Erik and the Dragon

Tatev's hands. He pointed to it after a moment and said, "That is not something I can read in a matter of minutes. It would likely take years of careful study by even the most talented of scholars, and even then they should be assisted by a master wizard to ensure they don't lose their minds. The sealed portion of the book contains powerful magic, the likes of which no mere man can read."

"Then who can read it?" Tillamon asked.

Patrical shrugged. "I would say there is only one who walks among the mortal realm who would have a chance at deciphering its pages."

"The Immortal Mystic," Tatev whispered. "I thought the same thing."

Patrical nodded. "I'll admit, I am excited to see it, and it is extremely tempting to open it, but realistically I cannot go beyond the unsealed portion. It would be far too dangerous. If you have already read that portion, and it confirms the vision Tu'luh gave you, then I am afraid you have your answer."

"Tu'luh would enslave the Middle Kingdom," Tatev countered. "Surely it would be better to live as free people, would it not?"

Patrical shook his head. "Who is to say what is right and what is wrong. Good and evil are merely matters of perspective. Is existing in any form, even that of a slave, better than extinction? Is freedom worth the price if all must die to get but a taste of it?"

"I don't remember you being so philosophical," Tillamon groused. "What happened to the scholar who helped me ensnare the orcs at Ten Forts? Where is the man who drew battle plans alongside me that would tear apart our enemies?"

Patrical bristled. "I have changed. Retirement and old age have forced me to ask more important questions. I search for peace now."

Tillamon folded his arms and looked to Erik. "Remember what I told you in the garden," he said. "That is what Tu'luh wants for the Middle Kingdom. Can you call that living? I can't even imagine *existing* like that. Give me liberty and freedom, or put a sword through my heart and bury me down in the dirt for the worms. I don't want what Tu'luh wants."

"The boy brings up a good point," Patrical said. He took the dwarven book from Erik and flipped to the first few pages. "This book is regarded as sacred by the dwarves. If you read it, it paints a vastly different picture of Tu'luh. It shows him as a merciful, loving steward. He helped establish the Middle Kingdom, and everything in it. The Ancients were entrusted with this part of Terramyr by the Old Gods. They have always had a role in preserving life. Perhaps Tu'luh is not the enemy here."

"*That* book only covers the creation period down through the reign of the fifth dwarven king. It does not detail anything after that, nor does it explain how Tu'luh was expelled for betrayal."

Patrical held up a hand. "Save your sermon, priest. I have other accounts here from valid, credible sources that show another side to that episode of history as well. It shows that Tu'luh was trying to warn of humanity's bloodlust, and prevent it from spreading so far that it would threaten the Middle Kingdom."

"Threaten the Middle Kingdom how?" Erik asked.

Patrical turned to him. "I don't know what Tu'luh showed you in the vision, but the accounts I have read said that he tried to warn the other Ancients that humanity's lust for riches, blood, and glory, would consume all of the Middle Kingdom, eventually calling down the wrath of beings the book referred to as the four horsemen. An order of omnipotent warriors who destroy whole civilizations once they have become too corrupted."

"That is nonsense," Tillamon said. "I hate to say it, but you have lost your senses, my friend."

"It's true," Patrical insisted. "I have devoted many years to studying this subject." He pointed to Tatev. "That is the danger you speak of, is it not? The book you hold mentions them. You know it does."

"It does," Tatev admitted. "The horsemen are the reason we have come. We wanted to know whether you could help us uncover the truth behind the legends."

Patrical shook his head. "I can't read *that* book," he said. "However, I can give you a book of mine. It details Tu'luh and Nagar, and it talks extensively about the four horsemen."

"Who wrote it?" Tatev asked.

"Salarion," Patrical replied.

Tatev's mouth hung open for a moment and then he folded his arms and looked to Erik. His brows were knit above his nose and the color drained from his cheeks. Erik wasn't sure who Salarion was, but he could see that the response had shaken Tatev

Erik and the Dragon

considerably.

"You can't trust anything written by Nagar's daughter," Tillamon spat. The disgust was clearly painted across his face. He turned to Erik. "Remember the first rule of fighting dragons? The same applies for dealing with Nagar and his ilk."

"Decades ago, I might have agreed with you," Patrical said. "But I have spent many years searching these books." Patrical continued speaking, defending his position, but Erik was no longer listening to him. He noticed something. It was slight, at first, but it was almost as if a shadow was covering Patrical. He couldn't quite put his finger on it, but something was definitely wrong. Erik quieted his mind and called forth his power. He wasn't sure what he was looking for, but he knew Patrical was hiding something.

Suddenly Patrical stopped speaking and turned to look at Erik. His right brow was arched dangerously over threatening eyes. His cheeks flushed, and he took in a deep, measured breath. Had he sensed what Erik was doing? Could he feel Erik's suspicion? Erik knew he had to act fast. He said the first thing that came to his mind, hoping it would throw Patrical off.

"Can I read the book written by Nagar's daughter?" Erik asked.

Patrical's brow flattened and his expression softened instantly. A slight grin tugged at the left corner of his mouth. "I would be happy to show you the relevant passages," he said.

"What are you doing? Have you lost your mind? Salarion is the enemy, as her father was. There is no truth to be found in that book of hers!" Tillamon shouted.

Erik turned to face Tillamon and Tatev. "I believe that if we are to find the right path of action, then it is best to study the issue from all perspectives," he said. Erik then gave a decisive wink with his left eye, hoping that Patrical was far enough to his right not to notice.

Tatev was the first to pick up on the signal. "Perhaps he has a point," the librarian said to Tillamon. "Let him read the book if he wishes. We will gain nothing by trying to force him to see things our way."

Tillamon's face soured and he scowled menacingly at Erik. Then he glanced to Patrical. "It appears as though the friend and comrade I knew in Ten Forts no longer exists. It was a mistake to come here." He stepped closer to Erik then, standing only inches away from his face. He returned the wink, letting Erik know that he was playing along. "I am disappointed in you, Erik. I would have thought you would understand the peril we are all in as long as Tu'luh lives."

Erik's stomach flipped nervously. Despite knowing that Tillamon was acting, he still found himself shrinking away from the man. "It's like you said in training. You have to know when, and where, to strike. You also have to be willing to take a hit, so long as you know it won't stop you from completing your task."

"Bah!" Tillamon spat. He pushed Erik aside and hobbled out of the house, leaving Tatev and Erik alone with Patrical.

After a few moments, Tatev gripped The Infinium closer to his chest. "Perhaps we should turn to the mystics first," he said. "You could bring the book written by Salarion and I could take this." He held up the book clutched close to his body. "But, you have to promise that once you are sure, you will not hesitate to do what needs to be done."

"It will take quite some time to find them," Patrical said. "But, I believe it is time well spent. Here, take the book you picked up, I will go and find Salarion's book. I will want it back, once you are finished with it."

"Of course," Erik said. "Do you know where we can find the mystics?" he asked.

"No," Patrical answered. "I have devoted much time to trying to study that matter, but to no avail. All I know is that they are hidden somewhere in the east. Many think they have disappeared altogether."

"I have some idea where to begin," Tatev said. "I have also studied the matter extensively. I have always wanted to try to find them, but I never had the time before. My duties at the temple prevented me from other pursuits."

"Mark my words," Patrical said. "The four horsemen are real, and the danger they pose to our world is much worse than anything you can imagine. It may seem illogical, but I believe Tu'luh is trying to save the world from destruction. True, his methods may not be ideal, but it may be the only way." The old man turned to Erik. "If you are the Champion of Truth, then you must be certain that your actions do not make matters worse for the Middle Kingdom."

Erik felt uneasy. The longer he stayed in the room with Patrical, the more intensely his stomach soured and his toes fidgeted. He wanted out, now. "I have been looking for answers," Erik said. "I thought I knew the truth, but ever since seeing Tu'luh, and the vision he showed me, I am not so certain we are on the best path. If Salarion can help me understand the bigger picture, then it is worth the time."

Patrical smiled. "That is wise," he said. He held a finger up and briskly walked out of the room. Erik and Tatev exchanged glances, but neither said a word. They waited for the old man to return. When he did, he held a brown book with a well-worn leather binding.

"This is it," he said as he offered the book to Erik. "When will you head out?"

Erik shrugged. "We were going to leave tomorrow, but now that we might be going east, I don't know."

"Perhaps one more day," Tatev put in quickly. "If we are going east we will have to procure more supplies than we had previously planned." He paused for effect. "We'll also have to convince Lepkin."

Erik nodded.

Patrical placed a bony hand on Erik's shoulder. "Trust your heart," Patrical reassured him. His greasy smile sent a shiver down Erik's spine. The boy nodded and then he and Tatev left as quickly as they could without appearing anxious to leave.

The second they closed the door, Patrical went upstairs to a small room near his bedchamber. The room had no windows, but a red crystal bathed the area in a soft light, allowing him to see everything easily after he closed the door. The old man pulled a white chalk from a small table made of bones and bent over to draw a circle around himself. He then sat cross-legged in the circle and concentrated on his spell. His scalp began to tingle as a warm sensation coursed from the top of his head, over the back of his skull and down the upper half of his back. His hands then grew hot and began to sweat. His breathing quickened and beads of salty water formed on his brow and ran down to the end of his nose, tickling the tip as they grew too large to hang on and ultimately fell from his skin to land in his lap.

A rush of air circled around him and he felt as though he was falling through the floor, down into the belly of the earth, and then he slowed to rest upon black stone. The air around him cooled and the light was pale and gray instead of red. A horned head slowly inched into the light and hideous, sharp fangs shone as pearls. Tendrils of smoke snaked out from the end of the dragon's red snout. It turned its head so that its right eye fixed on Patrical and then it spoke.

"What news have you?" the dragon thundered.

"As you predicted, the boy has come here with Lepkin and others from Valtuu Temple," Patrical said.

Tu'luh sneered. "Takala said you would be useful," the dragon hissed. "What is their plan?"

Patrical stepped forward and smiled. His old skin smoothed and his frame shrunk several inches. His hair lengthened and turned golden yellow. Breasts formed under the shirt and soft, supple hands appeared in place of the bony, frail appendages. "Tillamon still believes that I am his friend, Patrical," she said in her true voice. "They have no idea that I slew him, and had Mercer replaced with Lord Finorel's son at Ten Forts. They came to me for advice."

Tu'luh smiled. "I would not underestimate Erik," he cautioned. "He can see through disguises."

The woman shook her head. "He did not see through mine," she assured him. "They only saw the old form of Patrical." She placed her right hand on her hip and twirled her hair with her left hand. "It seems the vision you gave Erik has indeed shaken his confidence. He doubts his current path, and questions where his loyalties should lie."

The dragon sighed and a plume of smoke flowed out through his fangs, shrouding his face. "Lepkin will not let him turn back now," he said.

"Erik seeks answers about the four horsemen," she assured him. "He seems genuinely concerned."

"As well he should be," Tu'luh noted. The dragon's neck slithered in from the darkness to bring his massive head close to her body so he could scrutinize her more carefully. "There must have been something else other than my vision that made them seek you out," he said. "What was it?"

"One of Erik's companions, a librarian from the temple, has The Infinium in his possession."

Tu'luh reared his head back and roared terribly. The black stone cracked and shook so powerfully that the woman fell to her knees. "The Infinium!" he cried through a blast of fire that rent the darkness. "You let them leave with it?" His menacing teeth stopped just short of her face and the woman held her hands up defensively.

"They said they would go to the mystics, they said they would take The Infinium, and Salarion's writings, to study the matter of the four horsemen. I thought taking the book from them would expose who I am. I thought it best to let them go."

"He has played you. The boy knows who you are and has deceived you. He does not intend to travel east. He intends to march to me. As for the book, they cannot be allowed to keep it!" Tu'luh bellowed. The dragon withdrew to the darkness and his heavy steps paced around the woman. She shook and flinched with each echoing footfall. After a while Tu'luh spoke again. "I have already sent some lesser drakes to Stonebrook. They should arrive tonight, after the sun has set. As soon as the attack is over, I want you to kill Erik and take the book back. Don't bother trying to slay all of them, just get the book and kill the boy. Then bring the book to me. Fail, and I will have your soul."

The woman nodded. A rush of searing hot air swooped in and engulfed her, ripping her back to the circle on the floor in her small room. Her skin had regained its sag and her feminine form had melted away, reverting back to that of her disguise. Her hands trembled and her heart was pounding. She sat there on the floor for a long while, contemplating her mission. Then she looked up to the wall in front of her and laid her eyes upon her assortment of throwing knives and blow-darts. She rose and prepared her equipment.

CHAPTER FIFTEEN

Erik sat on a wooden bench overlooking the rear garden, watching Tillamon and Marlin fuss over the preparations for the wedding. After explaining what he had felt at Patrical's house, all of them decided it was best to keep up appearances and go along as if nothing had changed. Tatev hid The Infinium with Lady Dimwater, and Lepkin was busy continuing with the preparations for the journey. There was nothing for Erik to do except wait on the bench and read the book Patrical had given him.

The book was written in Common Tongue, which he thought strange considering the fact that Salarion was an elf. Their kind usually wrote in Taish, the elven language, unless they wrote specifically for a wider audience. He flipped through the first few pages, glossing over Salarion's lineage and the founding of Tualdern. A great deal of the first portion of the book dealt with her upbringing, Nagar's mannerisms and demeanor as a father, and spoke of their family's noble heritage. It was likely something that would make Tatev drool, but Erik just wanted to find the part about the four horsemen. He still had some doubts about challenging Tu'luh, but they were small compared to what they used to be. He could feel that he was on the right path. Slavery was not an acceptable existence. What is the point of life is everyone is forced to follow someone else's moral mandate? No, it was better to conquer Tu'luh, and then find another way to divert the calamity Erik saw in the dragon's vision.

There had to be a way. If Tatev couldn't find the answer in the Infinium, then perhaps Erik would be able to glean something from Salarion's writings. Thankfully, Lepkin had been more receptive to the idea of studying the book than Tillamon had. Even after returning to the house, Tillamon was dead set against reading Salarion's book. He kept spouting on and on about how anything in there would only be deception and lies. Lepkin, on the other hand, encouraged Erik to study it, cautioning him to make sure he used his gift to try and discern truth from error.

As he flipped through the pages he stopped on an image drawn on one of them. It was a battle scene. Elves fought over the city Tualdern. The page opposite described how the Sand Elves had purchased several shops and houses within the city for a period of decades, slowly moving in and infiltrating the city in a seemingly harmless manner. Eventually the Sand Elves began insisting that their laws be exercised in Tualdern, and as their population began to outnumber the native elves, they eventually turned to the sword to force their law upon Tualdern. All who refused to bow were either killed or expelled.

Erik set the book down on his lap. He tried to use his gift to see if the writings were true. He had done so once before, with Master Orres' journal, so he figured he could do so again now. The result surprised him. The words appeared to be true. It now seemed plausible that Nagar was seeking revenge on them for destroying his home.

"It's hard to fight an enemy that you empathize with, isn't it?" Tatev said as he approached Erik.

Erik looked up and nodded. "The Sand Elves conquered Tualdern. If this account is right, they did it in cold blood, repaying their honorable hosts with murder and deception."

"Keep in mind," Tatev began. "While the Sand Elves may have created Nagar as our enemy by destroying his home, Tu'luh would have found another way to bring his magic about eventually."

"How can you be sure?" Erik asked.

Tatev smiled wide and pushed his spectacles up onto his nose. "I have read her book, many times."

Erik looked at him quizzically. "Why didn't you say anything?"

"I could tell something was bothering you at Patrical's house, so I thought it best to keep quiet and follow your lead. I have read a lot, I mean *a lot*, of books in my time. I believe in you, and I have faith that Lepkin chose the right man for the fight that is coming. One of the tenets of our order is to understand the truth, we couldn't do that if we only read books written by people who were victorious in historical battles. We study everyone's books." Tatev took his spectacles off and offered them to Erik. "Try reading the passage again, with these on."

Erik took them and put them on. When he looked down at the book, the page was not the same as he had seen before. The image before him came to life and played a scene before him. As the image played out, he saw Tu'luh the Red conspiring with several noble families of the Sand Elves to plot against Tualdern. He watched as decades of posturing and maneuvering flashed before him. As the battle scene wrapped up and the last of the native elves were driven out of Tualdern, Erik saw Tu'luh come to Nagar and propose a plan to exact vengeance on the Sand Elves.

"Now read the page on the right," Tatev instructed.

The boy shifted his eyes and saw new words on the page. He read them aloud. "Tu'luh, having been rejected in previous attempts, compelled Nagar to comply with creating the new magic by framing the Sand Elves and kindling Nagar's anger against them. Consumed by hatred, my father lost his judgment, and threw his lot in with the demon, never understanding that he was nothing more than a pawn in Tu'luh's game of chess with the Gods." Erik flipped the lenses up and the pages instantly reverted to normal, as if nothing had changed.

"I may be a bookworm, but I know a trick or two," Tatev said proudly as he took the spectacles back. "The Sand Elves were forced to defend themselves of course, but there is more to it than that. They received an anonymous letter describing Tu'luh's treachery. At the same time, another copy of the letter went to Roegudok Hall, and a third went to Valtuu Temple. These letters were written in Taish, the elvish tongue, but no one knows who wrote them."

"Salarion wrote them," Erik guessed.

Tatev nodded. "That is what I think as well. No one has ever seen her since Tualdern's fall, though there are rumors that she lives somewhere in the south."

Erik sighed. "So, if you have already read this book, does it talk about the four horsemen?"

Tatev's shoulders slumped. "It describes them in detail, but not any more than what I have already discussed with you. Salarion doesn't know how to defeat or prevent them either. Her conclusion is that Tu'luh might have the only answer to preventing the cataclysm that is to come."

"So we are still no closer to solving it." Erik slumped back on the bench and sighed heavily. After a moment he flopped his head sideways lazily to look at Tatev. The red head moved in to sit beside him on the bench. "Do you really know where the mystics are?"

Erik and the Dragon

"I have a good idea of where we can start looking," Tatev replied. "No one knows for sure, other than the fact that there is a castle of gold and crystal somewhere in the east. Few have ever gone there, and certainly none have been there for centuries now. There are books of prophecy that we gathered over the years, many of them are destroyed now, lost forever." Tatev's voice grew sad and he looked down to his feet. "If anyone would know how to stop the four horsemen, it would be the Immortal Mystic, but finding him could take a lifetime."

"Time that we don't have," Erik said flatly. Tatev nodded his agreement. "Well, then I suppose we kill the dragon and let the fates throw the horsemen at us if they will." With that, Erik closed Salarion's book and set it between him and Tatev and jumped up to his feet.

"Where are you going?" Tatev asked.

"Tomorrow morning we are going out to hunt Tu'luh, so tonight I am going to enjoy the celebration and watch my mentor marry his fiancé."

Tatev smiled. "Sounds like a good plan to me."

*****

The sun hung low in the western sky, throwing shades of purple and pink across the cloudy sky. Erik stood in the garden, a few paces off from a large, white stone gazebo in Tillamon's rear garden. Marlin stood in the center of the gazebo, dressed in a new set of white robes one of Tillamon's servants had purchased for him. Lepkin and Dimwater stood in front of him, holding hands and looking into each other's eyes and smiling wide. Lepkin wore a tailored black silk tunic, with black pants and silver boots. Dimwater stood radiantly in a navy blue dress that perfectly hugged her curves, and shined as she moved and caught the light just right. Her hair was done in a neat braid down the back, with light blue sapphires woven in with silver pins. Yet, despite the efforts that Tillamon had gone to ensure everyone was dressed for the ceremony, it was Tillamon himself that put everyone to shame with his fine silks and golden necklaces and rings. He even oiled and slicked his beard into a neat point beneath his chin and wore a large hat with a pair of pheasant tail feathers tucked into the brim. The old man leaned upon his simple cane, clicking his rings on the handle nervously as he watched the ceremony begin. Though this particular cane wasn't nearly gaudy enough to match Tillamon's outfit, Erik knew that the man kept it with him as much for the sword as for the support.

A few servants hurried about the yard, placing the final covered platters on the table and then scurrying back into the house out of sight. Erik glanced around, looking for Jaleal, but the gnome was nowhere to be seen. Erik smiled to himself. He felt a little more secure with the gnome on patrol. No one, not even Patrical, could sneak up on them without Jaleal alerting everyone first. So Erik took in a deep breath and let go of all of his worries as he expelled the air.

"Normally, I would have a book with me," Marlin said apologetically. "Absent that, I will have to improvise some, which is a bit unconventional, but then again so is the couple before us."

Everyone chuckled a little bit.

Marlin looked to Lepkin and Dimwater and smiled. "When I look at the two of you, I don't see the physical smiles, I don't see the stolen glances or the casual handholding between the two of you. As you all know, I have lost my natural sight. What I can see, however, is the love between the two of you. I have always been able to see it, even before you allowed yourselves to express it openly. The energy within you cannot be tamed, and your love flows out of you like water bursting through a dam. The covenant and promises you make to each other today, will enable the two of you to become one, as is natural. Though you have waited many years for this moment, I can see that it is made all the sweeter by your knowledge that this is true love."

The prelate then reached up and wiped a single tear from the corner of his eye. "Forgive me, I don't usually cry at these occasions." Everyone laughed again. "So, let me counsel you to never let anything come between you. Let no man, no obstacle, no enemy—"

"And no dragon," Tillamon put in half-jokingly. Everyone looked to him for a second and he just shrugged and motioned for Marlin to continue.

Marlin cleared his throat. "Let no power on Terramyr break the bond that I see between you now. Cherish each other, promise to support each other, and love each other with all of your heart until the day that you die, and may you spend your silver years

Erik and the Dragon

together in the halls of Volganor." Marlin pulled a pair of rings that Tillamon had given him earlier, out of his robes and held them out to Lepkin. "If you so swear, then take these rings and place them on each other as a token of your affection and promise."

Lepkin and Dimwater took the rings and slid them over each other's ring fingers.

"By the power vested in me by the Ancients, I pronounce you husband and wife, never again to be separated in this world, or the next." Then Lepkin bent down to Dimwater and the two shared a kiss and embrace. Tillamon let out a shout and a *hoot*. Then Marlin put his hands up in the air and whistled loudly. Tatev clapped, and Erik stood silently smiling.

The group went quickly to the tables where Tillamon had set up a feast that would have fed two hundred people, and was far more than the group could eat in several sittings, let alone one night. Servants came out to the garden and played harps and flutes, and then added drums and trumpets as the dusk turned to night. Torches were lit around the garden, lighting the yard like golden stars suspended among them. Erik had never seen Lepkin smile so much in all the time he knew him. For a while, it was as if time had stopped. The world beyond Stonebrook ceased to matter. The only agenda was enjoying the moment.

As Erik watched Lepkin sweep Dimwater into a dance near the fountain, he knew that he had chosen correctly. Life was not about surviving, it was about finding the joy in living. This was something that Tu'luh could never understand.

Erik finished a glass of apple cider and then walked out beyond the gazebo. He looked up to the few stars that had peeked in through the night's dark blanket and wondered where his mother was. As happy as he was for Lepkin, he couldn't help but think of the tragedy that had befallen his family. As he stared off at the horizon, a funny feeling crept upon him. It started at the back of his neck, the hairs tingling and standing on end. Then it moved to his spine and his shoulder blades tightened.

Something was coming.

"Enemy in the south!" Jaleal shouted from the rooftop.

The music stopped instantly. The servants all ran for the tables and lifted large silver platters. At first, Erik was confused. *Why were they going for the food?* Then he realized they were not simple servants. Each of them pulled crossbows, short swords, and tomahawks from the newly uncovered platters.

"Clever," Erik said as he ran back to the doorway.

Tillamon was already there with Erik's sword. "I may be old, but I still have a few things to teach you," he told Erik as he tossed the sword out to him.

Dimwater and Lepkin prepared themselves as well as additional servants came streaming out of the house armed and equipped for battle.

"What do we have?" Lepkin shouted.

"Drakes, several of them," Jaleal replied as he jumped to a nearby tree and then appeared at the ground with spear in hand. "I am going to go and ring the alarm."

"Good," Lepkin replied.

"Come on," Tillamon shouted. "Out to the west. Let's draw the beasts away from the town."

Within moments the small force was jumping Tillamon's fence and sprinting into the fields beyond the town, startling the nearby flock of sheep and nearly giving the two shepherds heart attacks. Dimwater cast a trio of fireballs at the drakes in the sky, catching their attention. The ploy worked. All of the beasts swerved, changing course and flying directly for them.

Marlin shouted to a pair of guards that had fallen behind, but his warning came too late. A black drake, about twenty feet long from nose to tip of tail, dropped down out of the dark sky and crushed the two men in an instant. It finished them with a quick blast of fire and then ripped into one of them for good measure.

"Chew on this, you old vulture!" Tillamon shouted as he leveled a crossbow at the drake. He pulled the trigger and the shaft flew straight and true. As it impacted with the side of the drake's head, the shaft exploded into a small flash of light, scorching the monster's eye and forcing it to recoil in pain.

Erik stood dumbfounded. "What was that?" he asked.

Tillamon winked and loaded another shaft. "Special toy I invented at Ten Forts, it keeps the little buggers away." He leveled and fired the next shot. This time it went down the screaming drake's gullet and the explosion appeared as a tiny blast of red deep inside the beast's neck. It fell violently, flopping and writhing on the ground for several seconds before going completely still. "That's one for me, Lepkin, how many you got?"

Lepkin didn't bother to answer. A trio of drakes were flying

Erik and the Dragon

overhead, circling the group. Tillamon's hired guards took aim and fired their crossbows, but most of them missed. Tillamon swore and cursed at the servants, telling them how to aim better. Off in the distance the town's alarm bell rang loud and clear. Tillamon shouted louder, bellowing orders and swearing that if his men didn't finish the drakes before the town's guard got there, they would all be fired and replaced with three-legged dogs and one-eyed grandmothers.

Erik might have laughed at Tillamon's motivational tactics if not for the large, brown drake that kept diving at him from above. The boy could see that Dimwater and Lepkin were engaged with at least three of the beasts, Jaleal had not yet returned, and Tillamon and his guards were too far away to run to. He had to deal with this one by himself. His mind raced back to the firedrake that had nearly killed him at his home. For an instant, he felt dread and terror grip his throat and seize his feet. Then, as if someone threw water on him while asleep, he shook it off and fell back into his training.

He jumped left, avoiding the drake's teeth, and then he ducked low to the ground, dodging the spiked tail as it swept in and the drake passed by. Erik then jumped up and ran after the creature. He had a plan. As the drake ascended and turned around for another swoop, Erik summoned his ball of light and sent it up straight at the drake's face. The monster balked, turning its head to the side as it descended quickly. Erik then summoned the white fire over his blade and jumped into the air, swinging at the drake's eyes. He connected, slicing through the beast's scales and forcing it to flop on the ground. It thrashed its tail and wings wildly. One wing slammed into one of Tillamon's servants that tried to run in to finish it off. Erik jumped over the tail as it *whooshed* beneath him. Then he somersaulted to the left as the drake's hind leg scraped the air where he had been. Erik then rushed up under the drake, confusing it by jabbing the point of his sword into the monster's metal-like scales. The sword couldn't cut through the drake's armor, but that was not what Erik wanted, he was only trying to distract it. As he ran out from under it, he swung his sword like an axe at the right foreleg. The drake turned and roared, calling up a hot fire from inside its throat. Erik jumped up, thrust his sword up through the roof of the drake's mouth and into its brain. It collapsed, dead as a large boulder.

Erik pulled his sword free and turned to scan the skies.

"Watch out, something is coming in from the west!" Marlin shouted over the battle sounds. Erik turned just fast enough to see a black mass lunge toward him. He jumped left, narrowly avoiding a wickedly large paw and a set of razor sharp claws. Something growled and turned before him. He wasn't sure what it was. It was feline in shape, but it was easily twice as large as any lion or panther he had ever read about. The black cat lowered its head, ears back flat against its head and fangs bared underneath jet black lips.

A fireball slammed into the beast, ripping it apart and reducing it to ashes. Erik turned to see Dimwater offer him a quick nod. He returned the gesture and then took stock of the situation around him. Unlike the battle at Lokton Manor, this one was shrouded in darkness that spells and torches did little to penetrate. He had to listen as much as use his eyes to discern the enemies around him. He summoned forth another ball of light and let it pierce the cover of night. A trio of large, black cats shied away from the sudden brightness and Erik took advantage of the moment. He rushed forward, slicing through one with his flaming sword, then twirling around to run his blade through the second cat's neck. He pulled the blade free and maneuvered toward the third. Something unseen slammed into Erik's chest, knocking him backward and throwing him off his feet. Luckily he maintained his grip on his sword, but the force with which he slammed into the ground stunned him.

The massive cat pounced, and would have landed squarely on top of Erik had Dimwater not seen the peril he was in and let loose another spell. A whirlwind of fire ripped the beast from its trajectory mid-jump and hurled it high into the air, screaming and howling as it disappeared into the night, never to be seen again.

Erik rolled over to his stomach and pushed himself up to his feet. He heard movement coming in from behind. He turned to see a pair of armored men rushing in toward him. At first he thought they must be Stonebrook guardsmen, but once he saw the menacing whites of their eyes, he knew they were not friendly. He quickly raised his sword to a high guard, mentally calculated the number of steps before the men would reach him, and devised a quick plan to counter. The man on the right wielded an axe, and would likely make a diagonal chop in order to hem Erik in and not accidentally hit his partner. The man on the left, however, wielded

Erik and the Dragon

a heavy broadsword and was running at a full out sprint. Erik guessed that the swordsman would likely lead with a stabbing thrust. Erik drew in a breath, waiting for the perfect moment. He watched their feet and it seemed as time slowed down so that each step forward appeared to last for many seconds at a time.

Then, as the men came within range, Erik moved. He feigned to the right, drawing the swordsman's blade over to the side, and then he darted left, arcing down with his own sword and pushing the enemy's blade out wide to the right, and placing the man's arms directly into the axeman's path. The axe came down hard, severing the swordsman's left arm just below the wrist. The swordsman fell in agony and the axeman stood stunned. Erik moved in with a straight stab to the axeman's chest, and then as he pulled his sword back he drew the blade across the swordsman's neck, ending both of them with one efficient attack.

In the blink of an eye, Dimwater was next to Erik and holding him still. Her left hand was up in the air and an opaque, bluish shield formed overhead. The spell sizzled and crackled as black arrows fell from the sky and dashed themselves against the magical barrier.

"Marlin says there is quite a force out there," Dimwater said. Erik looked around, relieved to see that there were similar shields over all of his comrades. He looked up to Dimwater and could almost feel her straining concentration.

"I can try to summon another light ball," Erik offered. The sorceress nodded her head. Erik dug deep into himself, taking a breath and closing his eyes. He opened his mouth and let out a feral roar that sounded far too large and powerful to have come from inside his body. A great heat welled up in his chest and shot out from his mouth to illuminate the surrounding area far beyond his previous two lights had done. All around them were scores of men, several more of the large cats, and above circled many more drakes.

"Look there," Dimwater said as she directed him to the east. Erik looked and saw dozens of men in uniform approaching the battle. Some were on horseback, while others were on foot. "The Stonebrook guard," the sorceress said. "That should help even the odds somewhat." She then set her hands to work, weaving another spell and muttering words that Erik didn't understand. When she finished, she threw another ball of light up to mix in with Erik's.

"That will keep the light burning so we can see," she said with a satisfied nod. "Let's end this." She pushed Erik to the east. "Let's provide Tillamon some support."

He nodded and darted across the field, dropping another warrior that was charging Tillamon's men. Erik heard Tillamon shouting orders at his men, and they responded by aiming their crossbows to the sky. Lepkin and Jaleal were already placing themselves between Tillamon's group and the enemy, dropping any foe foolish enough to attack from the ground while Tillamon and his men worked their crossbows against the enemies in the sky. Dimwater held off the enemy arrows and fired back with spells of her own when the enemy paused to reload. Erik joined with Lepkin and Jaleal, fighting face to face with the warriors that charged them.

They were not Blacktongues, like Erik was used to fighting. These men were different. They all wore full armor, some made from leather and skins while others wore chainmail or steel plates. Even with all of Erik's training, and with Lepkin and Jaleal at his side, it was a struggle to fight through these warriors. Fortunately, the Stonebrook guard proved an effective fighting force as well. They tore into the enemy flank and savagely cut through their lines. Soon Erik found himself pressing forward, wading into the fray shoulder to shoulder with Lepkin and Jaleal as they pushed in, forcing the enemy back.

Jaleal dropped three of the large, black cats by himself. His spear was a flash of silver in the night, bringing death to all it bit. Lepkin was equally as deadly, beheading two of the large cats as they lunged for him and then whirling into the fray, dropping any enemy warrior within the reach of his sword. The two of them worked so efficiently, that Erik almost had time to watch them slice, hack, and stab through the enemy forces. As soon as the Stonebrook guards made their way to the enemy archers, Dimwater soared just overhead on a cloud and rained fire and lightning down upon the enemy, utterly destroying the last of the large cats and obliterating the enemy forces. The last of the firedrakes fell crashing down only moments after the group finished off the final three archers and sent the remainder of the enemy force scurrying off into the darkness.

"Shall we pursue?" one of the guardsmen shouted out.

"No," their captain replied from horseback. "Not unless Master Lepkin says otherwise."

Erik and the Dragon

Lepkin sheathed his sword. "We have no need," he said. "We know who sent them, and we know what they want. There is only one course of action left."

Dimwater floated up on her cloud until she almost disappeared into the night sky above the reach of the magical light floating above the field. Erik watched, wondering what she was going to do. He wasn't surprised when he saw a trio of fiery tornados fly from her position in the sky, darting quickly toward the fleeing enemy. As the flaming cyclones swooped down to devour the remnants of the army, balls of fire fell from the sky overhead, blasting the entire area around the enemy. Within seconds, no one remained alive.

"Your wife has a bit of a mean streak in her," Tillamon said as he approached Lepkin. "I like it."

Lepkin wiped a rivulet of blood oozing from a cut on his cheek and turned back to Tillamon. "Not mean, just efficient," he corrected. "This enemy is not one that we can reason with."

Tillamon nodded. "Well, they should have known better than to crash a sorceress' wedding!" The old man realized that his jest didn't sit well with Lepkin so he quickly changed the subject, pointing to Erik. "What do we do with him?" the old man asked.

Lepkin frowned. "They will be back, very soon. This fight is probably not over just yet. Go and prepare to leave, as we discussed before."

Erik nodded, extinguished the flames on his sword and made for the house. Jaleal, Marlin, and Tatev were quick to follow suit. Dimwater, on the other hand, descended from her cloud and landed near the ruined tables that had been overturned in everyone's haste to fend off the attack.

"By the gods, if I get my hands on that dragon, I swear I will rip him apart with my bare hands!" She bent down and picked up a small hunk of candied ginger and then walked into the house. Everyone inside stopped to look at her. "Everyone else may go about your business, but my husband is expected upstairs. Now."

The group silently turned to look at Lepkin. The man blushed and a frown of dread crossed his face for an instant.

"You are going to follow her, right?" Tillamon teased.

Lepkin's frown vanished, replaced by a boyish grin that would have seemed out of place had Erik not known how long Lepkin and Dimwater had been in love with each other. The man bounded up the stairs without another word.

"Come on," Tillamon said. "We have work to do. Erik will be leaving just as soon as we get their preparations ready.

*****

Erik stuffed the last of the bread into his pack and then went out to the stable as quietly as he could. He looked up and down the street in front of Tillamon's house. During the battle, he had not noticed any drakes in Stonebrook, but now he could see some of the people rushing around to quench fires that had engulfed various buildings. Surely the battle had been much worse than he had seen in the field. That knowledge made his heart heavy, but he could not stop now. He had to follow through with the plan.

He placed his bag onto the back of a pack horse that Lepkin had purchased during the day. He secured the bag in place and then moved to a horse that was to be for him. He checked the saddle one more time. Lepkin then appeared in the stable with him, saddling a paint horse.

"Thanks for coming down," Erik said.

Lepkin nodded. "I wish we didn't have to say goodbye this way," Lepkin said. He stuck his hand out and shook Erik's hand. "Best of luck," Lepkin said to Erik. "Remember what we discussed."

"Don't worry about me," Erik said. "I am stronger than most give me credit for."

Lepkin smiled and nodded his head. "I will go north, with Tatev and Dimwater. You make your way down to Ten Forts. Be as quick and careful as you can."

Erik nodded and jumped up onto his saddle. He tossed a final glance toward Lepkin and then kicked his heels into the horse's sides, galloping off toward the south. He raced by people carrying buckets of water, or others that pulled carts with wounded men. He didn't slow down, there was no time. He couldn't risk being caught. He could only hope that the plan would work.

As he neared the southern edge of the town, he saw just how lucky they had been. Houses here stood in shambles, many of them already burnt to the ground, others simply collapsed in on themselves. Occasionally there seemed to be a random house that stood intact and untouched despite its neighbors being reduced to

Erik and the Dragon

a smoldering pile of orange and red coals. Women and children cried in the streets, mourning their losses, but Erik couldn't stop. He forced himself to push on, without making eye contact with anyone.

Beyond the town he had to slow his horse in order to avoid trampling dead bodies. Most of them were apparently enemy soldiers, but there were many fallen who wore the Stonebrook yellow and silver uniform as well. The farther he went along the road, the more bodies there seemed to be. Fires flared up in the fields and some of the farms and ranches that used to stand outside the town were now rubble and ash.

When he saw a young girl, no more than six or seven years old, hunched over the corpse of her father Erik felt his heart sink. He knew he shouldn't go to her, but how could he not? The raven-haired girl was sobbing loudly and smacking her father's chest, yelling at him through her tears to wake up. Erik dismounted and went to her.

"Are you alright?" Erik asked.

The girl startled and pulled a dagger up from her father's belt, pointing it at Erik. "Don't touch me!" she screamed.

Erik put his hands in the air and dropped to his knees. "I won't hurt you, I want to help," he said. "Are you..." his words stopped in his throat. What was he going to ask? Was she alright, was she the only survivor? How could he ask such a young child a thing like that? "Come with me, I will take you into town," Erik said.

The little girl angrily wiped tears from her cheeks and held her gaze on Erik. "How do I know I can trust you?" The dagger shook in her trembling hands.

Erik smiled and removed his sword belt. He slowly backed away and secured it to the pack horse near the bag with food. Then he returned to the girl. "Come on, I won't hurt you," he said.

The girl smiled and stood up. As she stood, her legs lengthened, her shoulders widened, and her back grew taller. A wicked grin replaced her frightened expression and a pair of cold, brown eyes stared at Erik. She flicked her wrist and a pair of blades tore through the air between them in an instant to sink deeply into Erik's torso. The blades burned as they pierced his body, and he stumbled backward. He barely noticed the long shaft of a blow gun before a sharp sting bit into his neck. His muscles weakened and he fell to his knees.

"The master was so afraid of you," the woman said. "Where is The Infinium?" she asked. "Did Tatev take it to the north?"

"You were watching us?" Erik whispered hoarsely.

The woman nodded. "I have many tricks," she said. Her body then changed form again and Patrical stood before Erik. "This might appear a bit more familiar, yes?"

Erik nodded weakly and grinned slightly. "Do you know what the first rule of hunting dragons is?"

Patrical's face stared at him questioningly.

Erik grinned wider. "A dragon always uses its mind as its primary weapon. If it can sneak, cheat, deceive, or trap you, it will."

The assassin snorted haughtily. "Tu'luh has no reason to deceive me. I am a faithful servant, and I will be rewarded for bringing him your heart."

"I wasn't talking about him," Erik said. A flash of silvery light erupted from the ends of Erik's fingers, poured out from his mouth and eyes, and blinded the assassin. White fire engulfed Erik and then he shifted into his dragon form. Great talons extended from his hands and feet, massive, leathery wings stretched out from his back and a set of wickedly curved fangs jutted out from his snout. The beast wasted no time in lunging forward. The assassin was bitten in half and then dropped onto the ground to be consumed by blazing hot fire, reducing Tu'luh's servant to white, putrid ash.

It was all over in an instant. The dragon form shrank and reduced back, but it was not Erik's form that emerged. Tillamon stood over the pile of ash, with a hand to his chest, his breathing heavy and slow.

"Alright Marlin, I think you can go and safely get Erik and the others now," Tillamon said as he turned away from the ash and looked back to the pack horse. A moment later Marlin appeared atop the pack horse, where he had always been.

"I am sorry," Marlin said. "Somehow her magic was strong enough that I could not see beyond the small girl's aura. This was a powerful enemy."

"It's alright," Tillamon said in his quickly weakening voice. "I suspected the danger, but sometimes you have to take the hit, if it allows you to score the killing blow."

"I have some healing abilities," Marlin said as he jumped

down from the horse.

Tillamon dropped to his knees, clinging to his cane to keep from falling over in the dirt face first. "No, there is no remedy for the poison in my body. It is my time."

Marlin bent down before Tillamon. He took the dart from his neck and sniffed the end. The expression on his face confirmed what Tillamon had suspected. "It is hagroot poison," Marlin said. "I am so sorry."

"Bah," Tillamon said. "This was the plan. It is as it should be." Tillamon winced and lurched forward. Marlin caught him in his arms and tried to make him comfortable.

"I can lessen the pain," Marlin offered. "If you are truly ready."

Tillamon coughed and a spasm arched his back. He could only grunt his ascent.

Marlin placed a hand over Tillamon's chest. The prelate sent a pulse of white energy out from his palm to connect with Tillamon's heart. "It was an honor," Marlin said. Then he shot a quick dart of yellow into Tillamon's heart and Tillamon's energy stopped flowing through his body. Tillamon's aura faded away into the night, and the body lay limp and lifeless. Marlin struggled to put Tillamon's body across the horse and then turned the animals back to town. While he was happy to be able to say that Patrical, or whoever it was, had been defeated and Erik would be safe, he was not looking forward to Lepkin's reaction when the others returned in the morning to Tillamon's house as previously agreed.

CHAPTER SIXTEEN

As Lepkin finished saying goodbye to Tillamon, Erik looked at the newly dug grave and felt his heart sink. He had only known Tillamon for a short while, but the old warrior had left an indelible imprint on him. He could see the same was true for everyone gathered around the grave that morning. Even Tatev was unusually solemn and quiet.

Master Lepkin was the first to break away from the grave. He saluted his trainer and then marched away without another glance back. Dimwater went with him, her arm neatly wrapped around his right elbow and her head leaning in on his shoulder. Marlin and the servants were next to leave. Then the Stonebrook guardsmen that had gathered also departed. In the end, only Erik and Jaleal stood near the grave.

The gnome walked over to the fresh dirt and stuck his forefinger down into it. A moment later a beautiful green vine sprouted from the hole, covering the grave in a blanket of purple and red flowers. Then Jaleal nodded and walked on into the house, patting Erik's arm as he went by.

Erik stood there a while, looking at the grave and thinking about nothing in particular. He just let his mind wander in whatever direction his thoughts took him, and consequently he let his emotions glide along freely. A pair of tears fell down his cheeks, but he felt no fear. There was no dread of the impending final battle with Tu'luh. He wasn't sure if he had finally given birth to a previously unknown self-confidence, or if he finally allowed himself to believe in everyone else's faith in him. In the end, it didn't matter. All that mattered was the fact that he was ready. No more training, no more reading, no more lessons. It was time for action.

Erik turned his back on the grave and joined with the others inside the house. "It is time to leave," Erik said definitively.

Lepkin and Dimwater looked to each other for a moment. Then Lepkin looked to Erik and nodded. "We can make Ten Forts by dawn if we hurry." Erik nodded and walked out the front of the house toward the stables, leaving the others scrambling to catch up

Erik and the Dragon

to him before he tore off through the streets at a grueling gallop.

No one spoke for the entire journey from Stonebrook to Ten Forts. It was as if they could all sense the shift in Erik. Even when the group stopped for meals, no one made a move to suggest food until Erik stopped his horse and broke bread. When he was finished, the others would quickly wrap up their last bites and mount their horses as well. Lepkin and Dimwater still kept on the alert, with Jaleal out in front as the group's scout, but Erik now set the pace and the mood.

They rode hard through the night, and with no ill encounters to slow them down, they did in fact reach Ten Forts just a short while after the sun rose above the eastern horizon and bathed the area in its golden light.

The sight of the fortification was like nothing Erik had ever seen before. Massive, crenellated walls rose sixty feet above the ground, with archers patrolling the tops. Gargantuan, square keeps were positioned every half mile along the wall. Erik could see almost all of the ten keeps for which the border was named. A few to the east were obstructed by the thick forest, but otherwise Erik could see the entire, breathtaking structure.

It took the group another hour from the time they first spotted Ten Forts to actually reach one of the installations. Per Lepkin's instruction, Erik and the rest of the heroes rode for the third keep, the fortification that sat over the southern road, and traditionally served as the command post for the area.

If the structures were impressive from afar, they were absolutely mesmerizing up close. The keep was sealed with not one, but two iron portcullises. A group of ten men stood watch on the northern side, and spoke with Lepkin for a few minutes before agreeing to open the gates and let the group inside. As he passed through, Erik looked up to see countless murder holes above him, with a pair of eyes watching through each one. The inside of the keep was no less intimidating. A massive square building of black stone rose high above the walls, surrounded by stockades and armed guards that made the warriors he had heretofore faced seem like boys playing at swords, rather than seasoned warriors. These men stood proudly, with broad shoulders, thick abdomens, strong arms and massive legs. They seemed to Erik that they were more likely the offspring of giants and humans, rather than any race the Middle Kingdom could have produced naturally.

Beyond the main building, on the other side of the yard was the outer wall, with three portcullises and at least a score of archers manning the top of the wall. Erik wondered what could be beyond the gates that might have the soldiers so on edge. Had they seen Tu'luh fly this way? Had he already attacked? Or had they seen the drakes from the previous day that assaulted Stonebrook? There was no way for him to know, but it made little difference in the end. The only question he really wanted to answer was where was Tu'luh hiding, and when would they set off after the beast?

Lepkin dismounted near the main door on the southern side of the command fort. He motioned for Erik to enter the building with him. Erik jumped down from his mount and left the others waiting outside as he and Master Lepkin went in to speak with the commander.

They were escorted by a bear of a man who called himself Gareth, and claimed to be second in command. He led the duo up two flights of stairs near the doorway and out into a large hall where a thin man sat listening to a much older man talk about orcs. Erik couldn't hear everything that was said, but he could tell by the older man's angered tone that the discussion was not going well.

When the thin man in the chair saw Erik and Lepkin, he dismissed the older man in the middle of his report. The old man fumed as he stormed by them, not even bothering to acknowledge Lepkin, which Erik thought odd considering the usual respect and awe Lepkin seemed to command everywhere he went.

"What can I do for you?" the thin man said in a youthful, somewhat high pitched voice.

"I have come to ask for access to the south," Lepkin said as the two of them stopped beside the table opposite the thin man.

"I am afraid that is not possible," the man said with a shake of his head. "You have only just arrived, but I should make you aware that there is an army of orcs camped just outside our walls. I cannot open our gates or I will risk exposing my men."

"Orcs?" Lepkin asked. "When did they arrive?"

"Yesterday," the man said as he rose from his chair. "They arrived en masse and have since set up some fortifications and are currently making siege equipment, or so my scouts tell me." The man went to the table and pointed to a scale model of Ten Forts. Erik looked down and saw several hundred red wooden pieces placed on and around the walls. "The red pieces are my men," the commander said. Erik then saw the black pieces that were placed in front of the wall.

"Those are the orcs," Erik guessed.

The man nodded. "They are the orcs we know of," he said.

"They seem to run the entire length of Ten Forts," Erik said.

"They have camped along all five miles of our wall. They don't go beyond that, into Verishtahng, but they don't leave us any room to flank them either."

"Have you thought about attacking them before they can complete their siege gear?" Lepkin asked.

The man puffed up his chest and his cheeks flushed. "Who are you to question me? I am Eddin Finorel, first born of my father and heir to his governorship."

Lepkin leaned in on the table. "You know who I am, and you know I have every right to inquire about your actions here. Do not take such a haughty tone with me, Eddin, or I will send you home to your father."

Eddin Finorel bristled and cleared his throat. "The answer still is the same. We cannot open the gate. It is too risky."

Erik looked at the man and felt something similar to what he had felt at Patrical's house. He wasn't sure what it meant, but this time with Lepkin at his side he decided to press the matter immediately. He summoned his power and discerned that Eddin was hiding something. Furthermore, Erik could feel Eddin's hatred for Lepkin. Something was definitely wrong. "Who commanded Ten Forts before him?" Erik asked Lepkin.

Lepkin turned to Erik with an arched brow and inquisitive expression on his face. "Mercer took command after Tillamon left. Mercer was third in command while Tillamon was here, I was second."

"Are there still men here who would remember you personally?" Erik asked.

"What difference does it make?" Eddin cut in. "He can't issue orders that contradict my own."

Erik turned back to Eddin, and trusting in his power, pointed a finger at him. "Was Patrical here when Mercer was in charge?"

Lepkin nodded. "Patrical was here until the accident that injured Mercer, then he retired."

Erik watched Eddin carefully. The man's nose twitched nervously and he bit his lower lip. "I don't have time for this, I have a war to plan, get out!"

Erik lunged over the table and landed a solid kick in Eddin's chest, knocking the thin man backward to the floor. In an instant, Lepkin hopped over the table and was there beside him. Erik drew his sword and summoned the flames. He narrowed his eyes on Eddin and dropped the point of his burning blade to hover inches over the man's face. "Your father arranged the accident, didn't he? He arranged it so that you could command Ten Forts so Tu'luh could have easy access to the Middle Kingdom. That's why the drakes got through in such large numbers last night."

"What drakes?" Eddin shouted. "I don't know what you are talking about!"

Lepkin looked to Erik and furrowed his brow, but he said nothing. Instead he let Erik take the lead.

"Tillamon is dead," Erik said. "Patrical, or whoever it was, killed him last night."

"Really, wow, that is... so sad," Eddin said. His voice cracked and sounded sincere, but Erik could tell the man was lying. He could sense that Eddin was happy about Tillamon's death.

"You knew that Patrical was working with Tu'luh, didn't you?" Erik asked.

Eddin shook his head and looked to Lepkin. "I swear I don't know what this boy is talking about!" He tried to scoot away from the flaming sword, but Erik stepped in closer. "Get him away from me!"

Erik sensed again that the man was hiding something. He had all the proof he needed. "I am the Champion of Truth," Erik said. "I can see through your lies." He pushed the hot sword closer to Eddin's skin. "The only thing that will save your miserable life now is a full confession. Tell us everything you know, and I will spare your life."

Eddin looked at Erik for a moment and then a smile stretched his thin, pale lips. "Go ahead and kill me," he said. "I do not fear death. The master can break its bond and bring me back to the world of the living. You have no power over me."

Erik stepped back and looked to Lepkin. "He is yours," Erik said.

Lepkin drew his sword and stepped in close.

"Wait, you said you would spare my life!" Eddin shouted.

Lepkin reached down and plucked the thin man up with one

Erik and the Dragon

hand. "He said *he* would spare your life. He made no promise that I would do the same."

"My men will stop you," Eddin swore.

Erik shook his head. "No," he told Lepkin. "The men here are valiant and loyal to the Middle Kingdom. They are only kept powerless under this fool's command. Let us take him down to the men below and deal with him in front of his officers."

Eddin blanched then and tried to wriggle free. Lepkin punched him with his sword in fist, doubling the thin man over in pain. Then Lepkin twisted Eddin's arm up behind his back and forced him to walk out to the front.

The few guards they passed seemed unsure what to think, but a glance to Lepkin, and then to Erik's flaming sword was enough to keep them at bay for now. Still, they followed them outside. When the others saw them a few of the officers called their men to attention and Erik saw archers lining up on the interior walls, aiming their bows at them.

"What is the meaning of this?" one of the soldiers shouted as he approached them followed by a group of burly warriors. Erik saw that it was the same, older man that had been upstairs with Eddin when Erik and Lepkin arrived.

Erik stepped forward. "I am Erik Lokton, and I am the Champion of Truth." The old man stopped in his tracks and all the warriors looked around at each other. "You know these others who are with me. Master Lepkin is a man who needs no introduction. He has even fought here as an officer."

"We know him, what of it," the old man shouted. "What are you doing with our commander?"

Erik ignored the question and pointed to Lady Dimwater. "This is Lady Dimwater, the finest sorceress in all the Middle Kingdom. Sitting on the horse next to her is Marlin, the Prelate of Valtuu Temple. All of them are here to help me slay Tu'luh the Red. We are here to end the war that started so long ago."

"Don't listen to him, he is a foolish child!" Eddin shouted.

Lepkin punched the man in the gut again and let him fall to the ground, coughing and gagging. "You know me," Lepkin said. "I say you listen to Erik. He *is* the champion of prophecy, and this man at my feet has committed treason."

The old man took a step forward. "What proof have you that Master Finorel has committed treason?"

"He admitted to working with Tu'luh the Red," Erik said. "That is why he is not allowing you to attack the orcs that lie at your gates. He wants to weaken Ten Forts." The old man looked to the warriors behind him and they fidgeted nervously. Erik looked around, scanning the men before him with his gift and discerning their intentions. "I know you serve your kingdom loyally," Erik said. "I know that you fight here because you believe in protecting our homeland." Erik stepped between Eddin and the other men. "I am asking only that you arrest this man. Have him tried by court as is his right, but as of now he is relieved of command."

"And who do you say should lead in his stead?" the old man shouted.

"I will," a booming voice thundered from the back of the keep.

Erik turned to see a man with salt and pepper hair bouncing gently with each step that his large, black horse took. A great sword hung in front of him, and a pair of javelins were slung across his back with only the slender, deadly points visible above the man's shoulder. His face was disfigured, and a patch covered his left eye. He dismounted less than gracefully, limping toward them with a dragging left foot. It was then that Erik realized who it was.

"You all know me," the man bellowed. "What say you, will you fight for me once again?"

Erik turned to see all the warriors in the yard take a knee and bow their heads. The old man put a fist to his heart and pledged his allegiance. The others nearby quickly added their oaths to serve him.

"If you will not take Lepkin's word, then you will accept mine. I am Mercer, your former commander. I now know that this worm who grovels on the ground before you is responsible for my unfortunate retirement." Mercer pulled a piece of paper from an inside pocket within his green cloak and held it up for all to see. "This is a letter from Eddin Finorel, detailing my schedule and patrols during my time here at Ten Forts. Come and inspect it for yourselves, you will see that it is indeed written by Eddin's own hand, and he is responsible for conspiring to kill me. It was by the luck of the Gods that I survived his treachery."

The old man came forward and took the letter from Mercer. He opened it and read the contents. He then handed it back to him and addressed the others. "It is written by Eddin's hand," he confirmed. "The signature matches all the seals I have carried for him before." The old man then walked over to Eddin and spat on the ground in front of him.

"I am not whole in body, but I am still alive and well in courage and spirit," Mercer shouted. "I say it is time we stop sitting on the walls, and we take the fight out to our enemy!" A chorus of cheers went up along the walls. "Pass the word along, let all of Ten Forts know that their rightful commander is back, and I intend to stay until our mission is finished." Mercer then approached Erik and Lepkin.

"I'm glad to see you changed your mind." Lepkin said.

Mercer nodded grimly and frowned. "After Tillamon's burial, I went to Patrical's house. That is where I found this letter. After that, there was no way I could sit at home in good conscience while this dog betrayed my men." Mercer stepped forward and yanked Eddin from the ground. "Go ahead, Eddin, try and deny that you attempted to murder me. Tell me it isn't so."

Erik watched as Eddin grinned wickedly and laughed in Mercer's face. Mercer pushed him away and motioned for his men to take him away. A trio of burly warriors were quick to step in and remove the traitor.

"That might have gone very differently had you not arrived," Lepkin said.

"What is the situation?" Mercer asked, changing the subject.

The old man stepped up then and answered for Lepkin. "Commander, sir, I am Kranson Millwort. I was transferred here two years ago from the eastern border. I am the officer in charge of the scouts. I would be happy to report on our current situation."

Mercer turned to face the old man. "Then by all means, continue with the report."

Millwort nodded. "Three thousand orcs arrived and set up the main camp directly in front of our fortification here. They are currently building siege rams, catapults, and siege towers armored with shields hung over the front." He then pointed to the west. "Seven thousand and five hundred more orcs are spread along our entire wall all the way along our border in several camps. None of them are quite as large as this main camp before us, but they are all well prepared."

"All from one tribe?" Mercer asked.

Millwort shook his head. "It appears as though there are at

least four tribes working together in this assault." The old man then pointed to the east. "Another three and a half thousand are spread out along the rest of our wall to the east. Though, they are not preparing for assault so much as digging in and erecting fortifications."

"Hemming us in to the middle," Mercer said. The old man nodded. "How long do your scouts say we have until they are able to use their siege equipment?"

"Not long, sir, maybe one more day, maybe less."

Mercer nodded and smoothed his wavy hair back with his right hand. "Well then, what is our situation?"

"Currently Ten Forts is ten thousand strong. We are spread on a rotating basis. Three hundred from each fort patrol the walls at all times, for a total of three thousand men along the walls at any given moment. Another three hundred patrol the inside of the forts, or along the interior of the walls along the forest floor, making sure there are no weak spots. The third set of three hundred will be at rest, so that way we always have fresh reserves."

"That tells me what nine hundred from each fort are doing, what about the remaining hundred?"

"A mix of forward scouts, mid-level officers, dispatch riders, chefs, and porters. The officers usually rotate their duties along with their men."

"Very well," Mercer said.

"Sounds a bit thin to me," Lepkin noted.

"Sir?" Millwort asked.

Mercer nodded in agreement. "In my day I kept no fewer than two thousand soldiers in each fort, and often as many as three thousand. I would never let the total garrison fall below twenty thousand men."

"The orcs have been more docile in recent years," Millwort assured him.

Mercer eyed the man coldly. "I suppose there is little we can do about it now in any case." He turned to Lepkin. "Come, I want to see this camp that is infesting my fort."

"What are your orders, commander?" Millwort asked before they walked away.

"Have you any battle experience?" Mercer asked.

Millwort nodded. "I have endured several engagements with Tarthuns in the east. I have also slain the occasional orc during my scouting duties."

Mercer nodded. "Then gather five of your best scouts. Tonight we are going to see if we can't dissuade our guests from building catapults."

Millwort bowed his head. "As you command."

Mercer, Lepkin, and Erik then walked through the main building, up a seemingly endless staircase that spiraled directly up to the roof. From there the three of them walked to the edge and looked down to the area beyond the wall. From their vantage point they could see thousands of orcs busy about a camp sitting behind three rows of stockades and pikes. Off in the distance they could see a couple of large machines being wheeled into place.

"Looks as though they will be ready just as Millwort said," Lepkin commented. "You could have the archers fire on the camps."

Mercer shook his head. "No, they look to be just out of range," he said. "Our arrows would fall short of the mark. Better to let them think we are waiting, and then sneak out and slit their throats in the night."

"That will take more than five men," Lepkin pointed out.

"I will send some of the junior officers out to assign men from each fort so a similar attack is sent against each enemy camp."

"Even still, that won't put much of a dent in the enemy," Lepkin said.

"What about us?" Erik asked.

Mercer looked at the boy questioningly.

"How do we get to Tu'luh with the orcs here?"

"We must deal with the orcs first," Mercer said.

Lepkin nodded. "We have no choice. The only feasible route to Demaverung is to take the road south into the orcish lands. One must then travel two hundred miles west before a path through Verishtahng will open up."

"Is there no other way?" Erik asked.

Lepkin shook his head. "The fort farthest west from here sits on the border with Verishtahng, and the mountain Demaverung is due west from there, but the way is impassible. The terrain is too fierce, with rivers of lava and animals the likes of which could tear through a small army. To go in directly would be suicide."

Erik's shoulder slumped. "So the dragon has played his hand well, and is still a step ahead of us."

Mercer put a strong hand on the boy's shoulder. "We will cut the orcs down and send them running back to their stone hovels with their tails between their legs. Just give me a couple days."

Lepkin scoffed. "That's optimistic," he said. "Perhaps you don't remember how the last encounter with the orcs went." Lepkin shook his head. "It lasted for two months, and that was in the dead of winter when we thought the orcs would quit for lack of food. I would not bet that this army will be any less committed. The orcs never pull their punches."

Mercer shrugged. "I remember," he said.

"We also had close to three times the number of soldiers garrisoned here during that battle," Lepkin added.

Mercer frowned. "I remember," he said again, this time his voice was soft and lacked the confidence and bravado. "Well, then let us hope the men we have with us now are ready to dig in." Mercer then turned and went back down the stairs, leaving Erik and Lepkin on the roof.

"Couldn't Lady Dimwater use her magic to take us to Tu'luh?" Erik asked.

Lepkin shook his head. "The wizards that have joined with the dragon would sense her magic, and they would lay a trap. It would be less dangerous to jump into a bed of poisoned spikes."

"Well, couldn't you and I change into our dragon forms and fly to him?" Erik asked desperately.

"I admire your courage, Erik," Lepkin said with the resignation clear in his voice. "You are still too young to change safely. Even if you did survive, I would still be subject to the book. If by some miracle we did make it to Tu'luh's lands, his wizards and the firedrakes would descend on us like hornets. We could probably take a few of them down, but eventually we would fall, and Tu'luh would win." He placed a hand on Erik's shoulder. "Our only choice is to fight through the orcs."

Erik stepped to the edge of the building, slipping out from under Lepkin's hand. "Or we could sneak through them," he said. "What if we go with the scouts tonight, and while they attack, we slip beyond the enemy. It would be perfect. The orcs would be distracted and we could get beyond them."

Lepkin shook his head. "We don't know how many more might be on their way here," he said. "It would gain little if we snuck through three thousand only to find ten thousand a few

Erik and the Dragon

miles farther down the road. I'm afraid there is little we can do. If I thought there was any chance to succeed, believe me, I would take it." Lepkin started for the stairs. "Come on, we should get settled in. We are going to be here for a while."

The rest of the day seemed to drag on as though it were a year to Erik. Soldiers rushed about around him, oblivious to his presence. Dimwater and Lepkin planned with Mercer and other officers while Marlin and Tatev carved out a corner for themselves in the great hall to study books and meditate. Jaleal was nowhere to be seen. Erik had last heard that he was volunteering to go with the scouts to sabotage the catapults. Erik envied him. He wished he could go with him, but there was no way he could convince anyone to let him go. Worse still, Mercer and his officers wouldn't even give him an assignment. It was as if they counted him for nothing more than a boy.

When he could no longer tolerate being treated as an invisible liability, he retired to the guest chamber he had been given. He flopped onto the sturdy bed and tucked his hands behind his head as he looked up to the ceiling. What was he to do now? He couldn't very well wait for months while the orcs pinned the whole garrison down. Yet, Lepkin and the others would most certainly be involved with the battle. That would certainly speed up the resolution, but would it be enough? Would Tu'luh be able to launch his attack before Erik's friends could subdue the orcs?

After a while his exhaustion got the better of him and he drifted off to sleep. It was a restless, dreamless sleep that did little more than offer his disquieted mind a reprieve from his worries. He woke, nearly toppling out of the bed as he awkwardly rolled on to his side. He swung his feet down to the floor and reached up to rub his eyes. His left hand was asleep, tingling with fiery needle-like sensations in his palm and fingers. He stood up and went to the window.

The half-moon hung low in the sky, obscured by a thin veil of silvery clouds. He wondered if the scouts had already gone out yet. He silently wished them success, especially Jaleal. He looked along the wall and saw the active patrols walking along the top. He wondered whether the next night would be as peaceful. He had never seen an orc, but he had heard much about their prowess in battle. At Kuldiga Academy he had even read a few accounts of the struggles between the orcs and the humans. Each one was an exceptionally brutal, nasty affair that even made glory-hungry apprentices shudder and shake with fear.

A low, deep rumble came from somewhere in the distant west. Erik looked, straining to find the source of the sound. After a few moments he saw a faint, red glow. At first he thought that a group of scouts had surely succeeded in torching a catapult, but then he realized that it was something far larger. Another rumble shook the very foundation of the keep and the red glow brightened. It was Demaverung, the mountain in which Tu'luh had taken refuge. The volcano was spewing fire into the air.

Erik knew that it wasn't a large scale eruption. He knew that a full scale eruption would cause horrendous devastation instead of a small column of fire. He also knew that many larger volcanoes sometimes emitted smaller amounts of fire and lava on a regular basis. As he watched the red glow fade away he felt a sense of urgency. He knew that Tu'luh was close, and this time Erik knew where to find him, and how to kill him. Erik could almost feel his soul struggling to free itself form his skin and fly out to destroy the dragon.

Something crashed down to the floor behind him. Erik turned and saw his sword, the blade half out of the scabbard and the runes on it glowing faintly. He walked over to it and picked it up in his hand. The handle felt warm to the touch, and the runes glowed brighter as he lifted the weapon from the floor.

"You want to go as badly as I do, don't you?" Erik asked the sword. He then cast one more glance out the window. A fire grew within his chest. In his mind he could hear Lepkin's forbidding words, but his heart could no longer sit and wait.

He strapped on his sword belt and left the guest room. He crept quietly through the halls, hoping not to wake the others. He didn't breathe easily until his skin felt the night's cool, damp air. He raced up a set of wooden stairs until he stood atop the wall. A pair of archers spotted him and stood watching him.

"Where are you headed, out for a stroll?" one of them asked.

"I asked Mercer if I could patrol the walls tonight," Erik lied.

The archers shrugged and went back to talking to each other about whatever it was they had been discussing before Erik arrived. Erik, relieved that they didn't press the issue, continued quickly along the top of the wall. He knew it would take quite a while to reach the final fort, but with any luck he would make it before

Erik and the Dragon

Lepkin noticed he was missing.

He passed scores of archers and guards along the walls. He nodded and greeted most of them, assuring himself that they would take less notice of him if he acted as though he belonged there atop the wall. Whether his theory was correct, or the soldiers simply were too preoccupied to stop him didn't really matter. All that was important was that no one interfered with his goal. More than a few times he had to resist the urge to break into a run. Though it might get him closer to the final fortification, he knew it would draw far more attention than he could afford.

It took almost two hours to reach the final fort. He passed through an arch that led him into a grand gatehouse not unlike the one he had entered when he had first arrived at Ten Forts. Several strong portcullises were locked into place below, sealing the fort off from the enemy. Erik crept to the side of the wall and looked out, spying numerous torches and fires burning a few hundred yards off from the wall.

"Counting orcs are you?" a soldier asked.

Erik nodded. "I wanted to see them all for myself," he said.

"Well, if that hasn't sent you running home to your mother and father yet, I suppose you just might last a day or two once the fighting starts," the soldier said with a chuckle.

Erik curled his fingers into a fist. "My father is dead," he said. "My mother has been run off her land by an army led by one of Tu'luh's servants." He turned to face the soldier. "I have no intention of running anywhere until the dragon is dead."

The man frowned and stared blankly at Erik for a moment before nodding and walking away quietly. After he was out of sight, Erik continued along the wall. He went to the very farthest edge and looked down. He knew he couldn't very well go out through the actual gate. So he searched for anything that might help him descend the fifty foot wall.

"That is not an easy climb to make," someone said from behind.

Erik turned, expecting to see another soldier, but instead he saw Jaleal standing in front of him. "I'm not going back," Erik said. "I have to finish this."

Jaleal nodded and tugged on his long, white beard. "I know you do," he said. "I thought you might like some company."

"You would go with me?" Erik asked incredulously.

"Well, I saw you sneak up onto the wall and I figured you were likely going to need my help more than the scouts I was fixing to go with. Besides, my spear thirsts for dragon blood." He produced his shining weapon and placed the shaft down next to his foot.

"Did you tell Lepkin?" Erik asked.

Jaleal snorted. "No," he assured him. "I figured you had your reason for keeping silent."

Erik nodded and then looked into Jaleal's beady eyes. "Do you think I am ready?" he asked.

"Don't ask me," Jaleal said. "The only one who knows the answer to that is you." Jaleal then took a step closer and brought his spear up to his heart. "What I do know, is that if *you* feel you are ready, then I am willing to follow you into the jaws of the beast. You have my spear, for whatever it is worth."

Erik nodded. "Then, let's go dragon hunting." Jaleal moved to the edge of the wall. "Here, allow me," he said. He stuck his hand over the side of the wall and within a few moments a large vine stretched up from the ground and unrolled massive, soft leaves big enough for them each to stand on one. Jaleal hopped up onto the plant and motioned for Erik to join him. Erik unhesitatingly climbed onto one of the leaves and held onto the stalk. Jaleal then wiggled his fingers and the vine slowly descended toward the ground, bending out to let its passengers off safely.

"That was impressive," Erik said.

Jaleal smiled. "Do you know where we are going?"

Erik nodded. "Demaverung is due west from here." Erik pointed out to where the red glow had been earlier. "We go straight out to it."

Jaleal shrugged and twirled his spear around. "I won't be able to scout far ahead out here. There aren't any trees for me to use."

"That's alright," Erik said. "Hopefully Tu'luh will think that we are delayed by the orcs."

The gnome nodded. "I wish my grandfather was here with us," he said. "He would've loved the chance to hunt Tu'luh."

Erik smiled and then started off through the darkness.

CHAPTER SEVENTEEN

The sun sat above the gray and red clouds like an angry ball of fire, watching over Erik and Jaleal as the two of them emerged from the thinning trees and took their first look at the hardened valleys of Verishtahng. The land stretched before them, covered in red and black dirt. Hunks and patches of pumice dotted the soil between the jagged obsidian spires that stabbed up into the air. Vapors of smoke and steam spewed forth from conical vents that ranged from the size of anthills to some that were a foot taller than Erik.

The vents sparkled in the sunlight, catching Erik's curiosity. When he approached closer to one, he realized that there were rough gemstones breaking through the surface, reflecting the light brilliantly and lending a special beauty to this rugged landscape that Erik could not have imagined before.

"Be careful where you step," Jaleal cautioned. "Sometime the ground near these vents can cave in."

Erik nodded and decided to keep his distance from the vents. They wandered on through the harsh terrain, meandering in and around rocky spires and spitting vents. They walked for hours before they saw any other sign of life. A large bull mammoth stood near a bubbling, clear pond eating the leaves and smaller twigs from a large tree. Several cows and a pair of calves grazed on tender shoots nearby that stuck up out of the dirt.

"Are they dangerous?" Erik asked.

Jaleal shrugged. "I wouldn't worry about the mammoth as much as I would the water," the gnome replied.

Erik turned skeptically. "What do you mean, it looks clear enough."

"In this part of the world, you have to watch out for the clear water. It usually means that the water is boiling hot." Jaleal pointed to the surface of the pond. "Look there, you can see bubbles and ripples breaking the surface. Also, mammoths are usually fond of water, but none of these animals are approaching it." Erik looked closer at the water and then the two of them skirted wide around the herd of mammoths, just to be on the safe side.

The deeper into Verishtahng the two of them went, the hotter the air became, but it wasn't the dry heat from the sun that Erik had experienced before during the summer months. This was a wet, sulfuric warmth that rose up from the vents and holes around them to hang low in the air. It sapped their strength, and pulled the sweat out of them so intensely that they found themselves stopping to rest every couple of miles. The only reprieve they had was Jaleal's magic and knowledge of plants.

Just as Jaleal's water skin began to run low, he put his ear to the ground. A tender, yellow-green shoot of grass broke through the surface and almost connected with the gnome. Jaleal closed his eyes for a moment and then stood up with a great big smile on his face.

"Follow me," he said. "I know where we can get some water."

He started off at a brisk pace. Erik had to almost jog to keep up with the little gnome. They circled around a red plateau, through pillars of wind-polished orange and black stone, and then stopped in a bowl-shaped depression. Near the center, in the midst of a large patch of pumice and smooth flint, stood a large, green tube-like plant with bulbs along the shaft and a couple of flowers hanging from small, vine-like branches that extended a couple inches down along the main trunk.

"This is a special plant," Jaleal said as he removed his waterskin and placed it on the ground near the base of the plant. Erik came in close and put his palm on the side of the plant. It was rough to the touch, like lizard's scales, but there were no thorns. The plant stood almost as tall as Erik, and each of the bulbs were as large as both of his fists side by side.

"What is it?" Erik asked.

"It's called a waterstack." Jaleal reached up and gently twisted the lowest hanging bulb. The bulb creaked and popped as it released its hold and broke free. Clear water seeped out from the severed end. "It gathers water from deep in the ground, and stores it in these bulbs. That is how it survives out here."

"Why don't other animals eat it?" Erik asked.

Jaleal gestured for Erik to watch him closely. "You have to remove the bulb in exactly the way I did, otherwise the plant will attack."

"Attack?" Erik asked.

Jaleal nodded. He took a small knife from his belt and cut

Erik and the Dragon

along the bulb's outer peel, starting at the open end and slowly making his way to the fat end. He then flipped the bulb over and repeated the process on the opposite side. Once he was satisfied, he peeled one half of the thick, scaly skin back. He pointed to a strange, purple sack in the fat end. "The waterstack filters the poisons and minerals out of the ground, and then uses them to create a toxic sack in each bulb. If an animal bites into the bulb, it will puncture this sack and the toxin will paralyze it. The animal will then die, either because another animal will come along and eat it, or it will slowly starve and die at the base of the plant."

Jaleal carefully wiggled a finger between the two sacks. "The plant has created a strong wall between the two sacks, so if you separate them here, you can easily remove the toxin." The purple sack popped free and Jaleal set it on the ground nearby. Then he lifted the clear sack up toward the sunlight, peeling the rest of the skin off so the light could pass all the way through. "Now I will just check to make sure there are no clouds or indications that I accidentally mixed the two liquids." The gnome turned it over in his hands and the sack shined like a gem.

"Well?" Erik asked.

Jaleal grinned. "It's good," he replied.

"Is there an antidote?" Erik asked.

Jaleal nodded. "The plant produces its own antidote." Jaleal moved to the nearest flower and gently lifted it up. "The seeds in the blossoms store a gel that can counteract the toxin." Jaleal put the blossom back. "That way, if the toxin spills into the plant's main stem, it can protect itself." The gnome then put the water sack up to his waterskin and slit an opening at the narrow end. The water poured effortlessly into the container. "There is actually a bird that will eat the seeds, and then burrow into the bulbous parts to drink the water. It is called the fire finch. That is how the first people learned how to avoid the dangerous toxin." Jaleal offered the water to Erik and he took a sip. The water was cool, and had a pleasantly mild, sweet flavor to it.

"That is good," Erik commented.

The gnome grinned wide. "The best we are going to get while here," he said. "I will harvest a few more of the bulbs and then we can continue along our way."

Erik nodded. "Should we take one of the flowers?" Jaleal didn't respond, but he quickly cut one of the blossoms free and tucked it into his satchel along with as many bulbs he could fit into the leather bag. Then he indicated with his spear toward the west.

The two of them set out, climbing up out of the bowl and back onto the hot, muggy plain. Off in the distance they could hear sharp howls, but they didn't see what creatures made them. Erik wondered what other kinds of beasts might inhabit such a place. Eventually they found themselves following a mammoth trail. Most of the tracks left by the beasts were larger around than Erik was tall. Plant eaters or not, he actually hoped they wouldn't run into the herd that made this trail. His wish was granted about an hour later as the trail veered off to the south. Erik and Jaleal continued on in a westerly direction, trying to cover as much ground as they could.

The steam grew thicker in the afternoon sun, casting an eerie red glow over the land. Wind kicked up ash and burning embers from some fire or vent that Erik couldn't see. A few hundred yards in front of them, something roared and split through rocks. Erik could hear the distinct snapping and cracking of stone.

"Maybe we should go around," Erik said. Jaleal nodded his agreement. The two turned south and walked away, but the sound seemed to keep pace with them. It never came nearer, but it somehow always stayed just a few hundred yards directly west of where they stood.

"What do you think it is?" Jaleal asked.

"Maybe a firedrake?" Erik guessed. "Tu'luh could probably break stones with his claws."

Jaleal produced his spear. "Whatever it is, it doesn't sound as though it is going to leave us alone. Do we try and move around, or should we surprise it and go head on for it?"

Erik drew his sword, but thought better of setting it aflame lest the unknown beast spy them all the easier. "Let's meet it," Erik said resolutely. The two of them crept through the dense, sulfuric smoke. Salty, stinging sweat rolled over Erik's eyes and to the corners of his mouth. He casually wiped them away with his left forearm, straining his eyes to see through the dense screen.

Something glowed and writhed near the ground. Erik bent lower, trying to catch a glimpse of what lay before them. A rock, not more than fifteen feet in front of them, broke in two and shook the ground. The immense heat grew so intense that Erik's tunic stuck to his skin and wiping his face now only smeared the sticky sweat across his skin.

Jaleal froze in place and stuck the butt of his spear out to stop Erik. "Not another step," the gnome said loudly. Erik was shocked that Jaleal was using his normal voice, but he obeyed nonetheless. Jaleal tugged on Erik's tunic, bringing the boy lower still. That is when Erik saw it. A massive river of lava, snaking across the surface. It broke rocks and turned them to flaming goo before sweeping them along and building in strength. The gnome chuckled and shook his head.

"Maybe this is why the mammoth trail turned south a while back," Erik mused.

"Well, we sure aren't going to be able to cross it. Come on." Jaleal turned and started to walk back the way they came. Erik stood up and turned just in time to see the smoke bursting apart. Something barreled into Jaleal and sent the gnome flying backward. Erik reflexively reached out and grabbed Jaleal's ankle, preventing him from flying back into the lava flow.

A mass of black fur jumped through the clearing in the smoke. Erik dropped Jaleal to the ground and darted to his right as the beast sailed within inches of them both. Jaleal let out a yell and a moment later a beastly snarl ripped through the air. Erik turned back, sword out and ready to attack, but a mess of yellow, curved fangs lunged at him from the smoke. He brought his sword back in time to deflect the second animal, but he could not get an effective strike. The animal disappeared back into the smoke.

"You alright?" Erik shouted out at Jaleal.

"Just fine," the gnome grunted. Erik heard a snarl, followed by Jaleal shouting something in a tongue he could not understand.

A rock slammed into his side and dropped him to the ground. His right shoulder burned and his arm went numb all the way down to his fingers. The sword tumbled out of his grasp and clattered along the stony ground. Erik rolled to his back and tried to reach out with his left hand.

A massive, black paw dropped down on the hilt and dragged the sword just out of Erik's reach. The leg above the paw was easily as thick as Erik's waist. The immense, snarling maw that broke through the swirling smoke angled down toward Erik's throat. Twisted, yellow eyes fixed themselves on Erik's eyes, sending tingling chills down the boy's spine. The stare lasted only a fraction of a second in reality, but it seemed a lifetime to Erik. The beast stood perfectly still. Then its shoulder twitched and it lunged through the air.

Erik brought his left hand in toward his belt in a flash, ripping a dagger from its sheath and flipping it up so that the business end sat directly in the beast's path. The animal howled angrily as the dagger tore through the side of its mouth and gashed the thick hide in its neck. Erik sat up forcefully, continuing on into a somersault trying to escape. A massive paw slashed at him, ripping the back of his tunic and knocking him slightly off to the left.

Erik scrambled to his feet and faced the animal. Beyond it, he could hear Jaleal still grappling with the first cat-like monster, or at least that is what he hoped he heard. He shuddered to think that Jaleal's grunts and shouts might be his last sounds as the animal ripped him apart.

The boy crouched low, keeping his knees bent and flexible so he could try to dodge the animal's next attack. The black cat stood with its head low, ears flat against its head, and shoulders hunched over. Its massive tail switched back and forth with an angry tick. As it paced around it came to stop on Erik's sword. It looked at Erik and licked the wound in its mouth. Its front paws kneaded the ground, shredding the dirt in front of it.

Erik wasn't sure what to do. If only he had his flaming sword, then perhaps he might have a real chance, but a dagger was nothing to this beast. A hornet would likely have an easier time getting through the monster's thick hide. Then an idea came to him. He reached out to his sword with his mind. He wasn't sure it would work, but what if his power could manipulate objects as well as dispel magic? He had to try.

Just as the cat hunkered down to launch itself again, a mighty white flame erupted underneath it, searing its paw and scorching the fur on its underbelly. The cat yowled horribly and vaulted straight up into the air. Erik ran forward, scooped the sword up, and brought it to bear just as the cat descended back down. The flaming blade bit easily through the beast's neck and lopped off the head. The body fell over to the side, twitching and writhing. Then Erik ran for Jaleal.

He found the gnome standing triumphant atop the first beast, struggling to retrieve his spear from the animal's skull. Despite the danger they had both just gone through, Erik laughed at the sight. The little gnome standing on the cat's head, one foot on either side of the spear which was half-way buried in the animal's head. Jaleal pulled and tugged against the shaft, but it didn't even budge.

"Don't just stand there laughing, come and help," Jaleal groused.

Erik moved in and wiggled the shaft back and forth, shaking the entire head. "Can't you just call it back to you? I thought this was a magic spear."

"It is," Jaleal gruffed. "But this cursed gorlung beast managed to get it stuck in its thick skull!"

"I bet he had some help putting it there," Erik jested.

Jaleal stopped and shot Erik a sour look. Then, he straightened his beard and a grin appeared on his thin face. "I suppose I did help him along with it a little," the gnome said with a twinkle in his eye. "His fault though."

Erik nodded. "I have an idea." He motioned for Jaleal to step back and then he brought his flaming sword up high over his head. With all his might he chopped down with the blade, striking just to the side of Jaleal's spear. A resounding *crack* echoed throughout the area and the skull shifted under Erik's blow. The spear fell over to the side and Jaleal was finally able to pull it free.

"Well, that's one way to do it," Jaleal said. "Are you hungry?"

Erik looked to the gnome and then back at the cat. "Are you suggesting we eat *that*?"

Jaleal shrugged. "A gorlung beast is good eating. Besides, it would be a shame to let it go to waste."

"I don't know," Erik said. "Doesn't exactly look like food. Besides that, how are we going to cook it? We have no fire and there isn't any wood around here."

Jaleal grinned. "Leave that to me." He pulled his knife out and went to work cutting through the animal's hide so he could start cleaning it. The metallic smell of the blood was a little overwhelming to Erik at first, but it wasn't as bad as he thought it would be, and the inner organs didn't smell foul at all. The gnome soon cut a few thick strips of flesh from the animal's haunches and skewered them onto his spear.

"What are you going to do?" Erik asked.

"Erik, my friend, you are about to eat a wonderful treat. Ever heard of shish-kabob?"

Erik sat there and watched Jaleal cautiously walk out to the river of lava. He held the spear out over the hot molten rock. The meat cooked quickly, the dangling bits getting a good char on the edges as the lava reached up with little orange tongues of flame. Jaleal dutifully turned the spear over in his hands so that the meat cooked evenly. When it was ready, he brought it back.

"It is a bit hot, so don't wolf it down all at once, but it is ready now," Jaleal said proudly.

Erik waited until the gnome plucked off a strip of the cooked meat and handed it to him. "What does it taste like?" he asked.

"Like gorlung beast," Jaleal replied matter-of-factly. Then he ripped a large bite off of a piece for himself and chewed happily with a satisfied groan. He rolled his eyes and took another bite. "Oh, dis is goot!" Jaleal exclaimed through his full mouth.

Erik took a small bite. The savory, tender meat almost fell apart in his mouth before he could chew. It wasn't like anything he had ever tasted before. If he had to describe it, he would have said it was like a mix of duck and venison, although that wasn't quite right either. In any case, he was soon taking large bites himself and going back for more.

Jaleal cooked two more servings before they had their fill. Then, he cooked another serving to take with them for later.

As the two of them followed the lava flow to the south, looking for a way to get around it, they exchanged stories about their family. Jaleal's stories were much more interesting, and there were a lot more of them, but the gnome seemed more than happy to listen about Erik's life as an orphan, and his time spent with the Lokton family.

"I knew I was going to like you," Jaleal said after Erik told him about breaking into Lady Dimwater's study and the subsequent adventures. "I knew the moment I saw you that we were going to be good friends."

Erik looked at the gnome skeptically. "Even though I was dying and in Lepkin's body at the time you met me?"

Jaleal shrugged. "Well, yeah," he said. "A gnome can tell these things. We are good judges of character."

Erik chuckled a bit to himself. "Well, I am glad to have you around," he said. Just then a cool early evening breeze blew in from the south and carried away the dense smoke. Behind the wind came a light rain shower. The ground *popped* and *hissed* as the droplets struck the hot surface. Ash and dust puffed up around them, but not so much that it was a problem. Soon the rain became heavy enough that it wet the whole land and kept all of the dust down.

"Interesting place, this Verishtahng," Jaleal commented.

"At least the rain cools it down," Erik said.

"Should we try to find shelter near one of the rock formations?" Jaleal asked.

Erik shook his head. "I just want to find Tu'luh. A little bit of rain isn't going to hurt us."

The gnome nodded and the two of them continued on silently for another two hours before the lava river finally ended. A great hill of pumice and flint rose up out of the surface, and the lava was pouring out from the top. Strings of magma gurgled and shot up in the air above the source and plumes of smoke rose high into the air, carrying ash and hot embers along.

They walked around the mound and then corrected course to move west again. They walked for a few hours, until the rain stopped, the sun had set, and the stars were out in full force, sparkling above almost as brilliantly as the diamonds and gems shone in the rocks below under the red light from the many lava flows and hot vents rising out of the land. The moon was on its descent through the sky by the time they decided to make camp for the night. There was nothing to make a shelter with, or to raise them off of the ground, but they were so tired by then they didn't much care. They just tucked their satchels under their heads and slept. Neither one of them took watch, Jaleal said they didn't need to. He raised another blade of grass out from the dirt and swore it would wake him if anything dangerous approached their location. Erik might have doubted the gnome's assertion, had it not been for the grass earlier that day that had led them to the waterstack.

They woke just as the first light of the sun broke upon their faces. They ate the rest of the gorlung meat, drank from the water skin, and then moved on. They covered more ground the second day than the first. They passed by another herd of mammoths, a large pond filled with crocodiles, and another river of lava that emptied into a deep canyon to the north. For food, Jaleal stole a few eggs from a crocodile nest while the mother was away preying upon a baby mammoth. When one of the eggs hatched in his pocket and a baby croc bit his hip, he cursed wickedly and tossed the wretched creature to the ground. Then he speared it, roasted it on the nearest vent sticking out from the ground, and ate it out of spite. He almost forgot to share it with Erik, but Erik was laughing so hard he didn't mind at all.

Four more days they walked across the desolate landscape of Verishtahng. They stopped and gathered water from waterstack plants, took eggs from crocs and once even took a small juvenile crocodile that had moved into a shallow pool. Erik realized that without Jaleal's presence, he would have died long before making it this far, let alone finding Tu'luh. He vowed then that he would one day pay the gnome back, with whatever riches his family had left, if they ever made it back from Demaverung. Despite doing the majority of the hunting, and all of the cooking, Jaleal never complained. It was obvious to Erik that the gnome wasn't seeking any reward. He was simply there to hunt Tu'luh, and that was enough to keep the little warrior happy along the way. Still, Erik knew that he owed Jaleal much more than the satisfaction of fighting a dragon. He owed him a lot more.

As the sun set upon the sixth day, Demaverung loomed before them. The ground trembled and quaked as the volcano shook. Smoke rose out from the top. The hot fires inside the mountain painted the underside of the smoke red and orange, casting a tremendous glow on all the area around, just as Erik had seen before from Ten Forts.

"Well," Jaleal started. "What is the plan?"

Erik took in a deep breath of the hot, sulfuric air and folded his arms. He could feel anger rising within his chest, giving new energy and strength to his muscles. The sword hummed at his side and Erik could feel its warmth through his clothes. "Now, we climb the mountain and kill the beast."

CHAPTER EIGHTEEN

Erik crept up the side of Demaverung. The black, jagged rocks made it tricky to maneuver, but also provided him with plenty of cover to hide behind. He had expected more firedrakes, or gorlungs, or at least human guards around the mountain, but he saw nothing. Still, he and Jaleal proceeded slowly, always scanning the surrounding area with their eyes and ears. Erik's goal was a ledge about half-way up the mountainside that jutted out from a wide cavern. He assumed that was the entrance to Tu'luh's lair.

The moon disappeared in the sky behind the thick column of smoke rising up from Demaverung's top. The light dimmed, and Erik found himself thankful for the nighttime training session that Tillamon had given him. He picked his way carefully up the mountain until he was able to peek his head just over the lip of the ledge. There were no guards. Just a vast hallway of smooth, shiny stone. Several smaller caverns and doorways dotted the inside of the main hall, but no one was moving around. Erik's eyes followed the tunnel until it curved up and to the left, beyond his field of vision.

"He is in there, I can feel it," Erik whispered.

Jaleal nodded beside him. "Apparently, there are others in there as well. See the doors?"

Erik nodded. "I don't know any other way inside," he said.

"Well," Jaleal started. "You said you used to be good at sneaking out of the orphanage. Think you can steal your way inside here?"

"One way to find out," Erik said. He hauled himself up over the ledge and ran silently to the left side of the wide cavern. He didn't have to turn around to know that Jaleal was only a pace or two behind him. He stopped just at the opening, pulling his body off to the side as he peered in one more time.

A doorway on the right creaked open and a pair of men in hooded cloaks came out, talking to each other and gesturing with their hands.

"Leave this to me," Jaleal said. The gnome sprinted in with blinding speed. His footsteps never made as much sound as a leaf hitting the ground. Within seconds he was upon the two men. A couple flashes of his spear and the two men dropped to the floor. Jaleal then ran to the open doorway and looked inside. A second later he motioned for Erik to join him.

Erik sprinted in and grabbed one of the men, dragging him back into the room. Then he and Jaleal made haste to get the second man before anyone else entered the hallway. After they pulled the second one in, they gently closed the door. Erik looked around and realized that they were in a small bedroom. There were two beds, one on either side of the room, a small table off to one side and a desk at the far end with some parchment scattered across the top.

"Quick, let's put on the robes," Jaleal said.

Erik hesitated. "You are too short," he said. "I doubt there are any gnomes here."

Jaleal nodded. "I could piggy-back on you, under the robes," the gnome said.

Erik shrugged. "It's better than nothing I suppose." He and Jaleal quickly removed the robes from the man closest to Erik's size. He took off his satchel and told Jaleal to do the same. Then he put the robe on over his clothes and Jaleal went in underneath to climb up Erik's back. It was a little uncomfortable at first until Jaleal was able to wrap his legs around Erik's waist and grab onto the boy's shoulders to support himself up. Jaleal even managed to holster the spear through his own shirt in such a way that it didn't protrude through the robe or poke Erik.

Erik then pulled the hood over his face as far as it would go and made for the door. He closed it behind them and walked briskly down the hall. Even with the disguise, he didn't want to risk being caught by anyone and losing the element of surprise. Most of the other doors were closed. Those that weren't led to empty rooms, which relieved Erik at first, but then he realized that meant that the room's occupants could be farther down the hall. Luckily his worries turned out to be in vain. They rounded the corner and made their way up as the tunnel ascended higher into Demaverung.

The air inside the volcano was exceedingly hot, and almost burned Erik's lungs when he breathed. Jaleal stifled a couple coughs. Erik could only guess how uncomfortable the gnome was under the robe, but there was little he could do about it now. Rubies and diamonds glittered in the wall like brilliant stars above

Erik and the Dragon

the stark granite floor. Erik had never seen so many jewels and gems in all of his life, nor had he even dreamed a place like this could exist. He would bet that it would make Al and the rest of the dwarves green with envy if they knew what kind of riches sat in the walls here. Each stone almost seemed to hum as Erik walked by. It was simply breathtaking.

From somewhere inside the tunnel, a slow, rhythmic sigh echoed off the walls. It was followed by the sound of a rumbling snore. Tu'luh was close, and he was asleep. Erik quickened his pace, focusing on keeping his steps as silent as possible so as not to alert the great beast. As the tunnel wound around and around the inside of the volcano, there came a large chamber off to the left. Erik could hear voices coming from within. He stopped just before the opening and peeked inside. Several rows of tables and benches covered the area. Seven or eight robed men sat inside eating and drinking loudly, swapping stories and cursing at each other.

"What is it?" Jaleal whispered.

"A dining hall, looks like," Erik responded.

"Can you sneak by?" the gnome asked.

Erik watched the men for a few moments, studying their mannerisms and trying to time his move. One of the men jumped up suddenly and threw a handful of bread at one of the others. The second man responded by clocking the first with his half-full bowl of soup. The whole group then rose to their feet and laughed as the two men broke into a fist fight and tumbled around on the floor. Erik watched, stunned for an instant, and then made haste farther up the tunnel and away from the hall.

At last, Erik came to the end of the tunnel. It opened into a large chamber. A great hole was situated almost dead center, with hot steam and smoke rising up out of it. To the far side on the right was a pile of gold coins and gems that made the hallways seem like costume jewelry by comparison. Erik's mouth fell open slightly. He had never imagined Tu'luh as a being who cared for wealth. A mighty, rumbling snore snapped Erik's attention to the left. There, almost blending in with the red stone walls of the inner chamber, laid the beast that had haunted Erik for so long. His eyes were closed, the left one still oozing blood from their previous encounter, and his breaths came smoothly as he slept atop a pile of coins and gems. His forelegs were buried in the treasure up to the elbow joint, and the tail curled around protectively holding the gold in place.

"He is alone," Erik whispered. He nudged Jaleal with his elbow. The gnome squeezed Erik's right shoulder to signal that he understood, and then he climbed down and out from under the robe. Erik silently pulled the robe up over his head and laid it on the ground beside him. His hand went down to draw his sword, but Jaleal snatched his wrist. Erik looked down to see the gnome shaking his head and holding a finger to his mouth. Erik understood. Drawing the sword might be loud enough to wake the beast. So he tip-toed in, his hand hovering over the hilt at the ready.

Jaleal went in wide to the left, holding his spear out and ready to throw should Tu'luh awaken. The pair only moved in a couple of paces before the snoring stopped and they froze in fear. The dragon shifted in his sleep and snorted.

"Mmmmm," Tu'luh said in a low, throaty moan. "I smell a gnome."

Jaleal turned and motioned for Erik to get back. Erik shook his head. There was no way he was leaving now.

Tu'luh opened his eyes. The left one was scarred and cloudy, but the right was bright and full of anger and hate. He drew his neck up and peered down at them. "So, you have come to finish our fight?" the dragon asked. In a flash Tu'luh spewed fire at Jaleal, forcing the gnome to sprint away to avoid being roasted. Erik rushed in, drawing his sword. Tu'luh flicked his left leg up, throwing a thousand coins and gems into the air. Then he roared mightily, sending the gold and gems darting toward Erik with such force that they bruised and cut his skin. The dragon then leapt into the air, beating the smoke down with his wings and disappearing from Erik's view.

"You could still join me, Erik," Tu'luh growled.

Erik said nothing. He just ran to the right of the chamber and scoured the smoke with his eyes. He strained his ears, trying to discern Tu'luh's location by the sound of beating wings. Out of the corner of his eye, Erik saw a silvery flash pierce the cloud of smoke. Tu'luh snarled angrily and then dropped out of the smoke, nearly crushing Jaleal with his right foreleg. The gnome snaked between Tu'luh's legs and under his belly, stabbing up with his spear after it reappeared in his hands. The blessed weapon managed to poke through the scales just enough to draw blood, but it couldn't do any real damage. With every poke, Tu'luh roared and snapped his massive fangs down at Jaleal, jerking and spinning around like a savage dog chasing a rat.

Erik sprinted in, focusing on Tu'luh's right eye. If he could just manage to strike it, then he and Jaleal could end this. He saw his moment. Tu'luh lunged in under his left leg, snapping at Jaleal as he stabbed the back of his leg. Erik moved his arm to launch his sword but a massive shock hit his left side and sent him careening for the hole in the center of the chamber. Blue and purple lights flashed before his face and a sizzling pain ripped across his left ribs. He skidded across the stone and stopped just inches before falling down the center chute of the volcano. His vision was blurry and his ears rang wildly.

He shook it off and looked up to see a trio of men in black robes running into the chamber. Erik felt his heart sink. He struggled to his feet just in time to dodge a second bolt of lightning that streaked through the spot he had been standing in and crackled against the far wall. Erik summoned the flames to his sword and readied himself. He sprinted forward, jumping side to side and then somersaulting under a barrage of lightning bolts that the men threw. Then, he changed course and made a dash toward Tu'luh.

Erik strained his ears, listening for the sizzling sound that preceded each lightning bolt, and then jumped to his right or left. Like the training at Tillamon's house, he knew he had to roll with the traps if he wanted to win the prize. A bolt grazed his left leg, burning a line across the side of his thigh, but he didn't pay any attention. He focused solely on the dragon.

Tu'luh leapt up into the air now and blasted the floor with fire. Jaleal sent the spear up into the air and managed to strike inside the dragon's mouth. The shaft soared through the flames to stick through the roof of the snout, but it was not far enough inside to do any lethal damage. Instead, the head of the spear jutted out from midway up the snout. The fire engulfed Jaleal on all sides and the gnome hollered out in agony.

Erik felt a wave of anger rush through him. Just as Tu'luh dropped down to the ground and bent his head low to remove the spear with his right foreleg, Erik rushed in with his sword and slashed down at the dragon's remaining eye. Tu'luh reacted faster than lightning, slamming his head into Erik's chest and whacking him up into the air. Tu'luh then lunged out after Erik, snapping his jaw at him now that the spear was removed. Erik struck out with his sword and swatted the dragon's mouth away, then he landed on his side and rolled to avoid a crushing step of Tu'luh's right leg.

The tail swiped around from the back, spikes aimed for Erik's chest, but he jumped up onto the tail and chopped down with his sword. It bit through the tough scales, showering sparks on the granite floor below. Tu'luh roared and flung Erik from his tail. The boy spun through the air, barely missing the several bolts of lightning that the robed mages threw at him. He managed to land on his feet and ran toward Tu'luh's side.

The beast beat his mighty wings and rose into the air. Erik, not wanting him to escape through the volcano opening threw his flaming sword with all of his might. It spun end over end and struck true, slicing into the dragon's left wing bone. Tu'luh roared in agony, bathing his own mages in hot fire, and crashed down. Erik jumped up, just high enough to grab onto Tu'luh's nearly severed wing as the two of them slid over the edge and fell into the hole.

Intense heat rose up and encircled them both. Tu'luh didn't seem to notice, but Erik's skin felt as though it was seconds from igniting. The dragon latched onto the edge with his claws and managed to stop their descent into the pool of lava below. Erik pulled himself up and ripped his sword free from the half-chopped wing bone. Tu'luh winced and roared mightily. Fire poured out over them. Erik held his sword in his right hand while he used his left to hold onto the spike jutting from Tu'luh's back and climb higher up the beast. Tu'luh whipped his neck around to take a bite at Erik, which is exactly what Erik wanted.

He thrust out straight and true, driving the blade through Tu'luh's right eye and just managing to keep his feet out of the beast's mouth. Tu'luh released his grip on the stone and lurched backward, slamming his side into the opposite wall of the chute. Erik was flung free from the beast. He skittered along the wall and bounced down onto a small, three foot wide ledge about half-way down the chute. Tu'luh slid down farther, clawing madly at the walls and throwing fire everywhere. The massive tail thrashed this way and that, breaking apart rocks and almost spearing Erik's head with one of its wild swings. When the dragon finally lost its grip entirely, it fell to the bottom.

Erik and the Dragon

Tu'luh's tail splashed into the lava, but the majority of his body landed on a red hot, yet solid, outcropping of stone.

"This is how the world will end, Erik!" Tu'luh roared. "It will end in fire!"

Tu'luh raised his head and blindly spewed a column of fire up the chute. Erik hugged the side of the wall, squeezing himself as close to it as possible so the fire wouldn't consume him. After a few moments the fire ceased. Erik could hear Tu'luh snarling below and raking its claws along the wall.

"I am not dead, boy!" the dragon hissed. "My servants will lift me from this pit and repair my wing! Then, I will lay waste to your precious homeland. I will not spend any more time trying to convince you pathetic mortals of the error of your ways. There will be blood!"

Erik peeked over the edge of the ledge and saw Tu'luh up on his feet again. His tail was half burnt and only a stub of what it had been before. His left wing hung limp on its back, like a tooth before it falls out of its socket. Erik's sword stuck out grotesquely from Tu'luh's right eye, the flame now extinguished. Yet, despite all of this, the dragon seemed as strong as ever.

A sharp whistle sounded from above. Erik looked up to see Jaleal. The gnome held his spear over the edge of the chute. "Finish it!" Jaleal dropped the spear down to Erik.

Erik rose to his feet and extended his hand to catch the weapon. Below, he could hear Tu'luh shifting around and the telltale hissing sound deep within the beast's belly that came only moments before the fire.

No sooner had the spear landed in Erik's hand then the boy shouted at Tu'luh. "Here I am!"

Tu'luh cocked his neck to the sound and opened his mouth. Erik jumped from the ledge. The fire gurgled up and then rushed forth from between the jagged teeth like a volcanic eruption. Erik kept his eye on the sweet spot in the back of the beast's throat and waited until the angle was right before he let it fly. The flames washed over him only for a moment before his trajectory took him out of them. His skin and clothes singed and smoking, he felt the sting of the heat growing the farther down he fell. Then the sound he had hoped to hear greeted his ears and made him smile.

The dragon hissed and choked. The flames ceased instantly, and the stifled roar lasted only a moment as the dragon recoiled back and cracked its head against the wall. Then it fell to the ground, wheezing and sputtering. Erik landed a moment later on Tu'luh's broken wing. Bouncing twice before slamming into the hot stone outcropping. Despite his injuries, he jumped up and scampered back onto Tu'luh's wing to shelter him from the heat. The beast tried to shake Erik from its wing, but it was too weak.

Erik saw the glistening red point of the spear sticking out the back of its neck, just at the point where the base of the skull connects with the neck. Tu'luh quivered and trembled. His blind eyes turned toward him and a weak voice emitted from the dying dragon's throat.

"You have doomed us all," Tu'luh said. "The vision I showed you shall come to pass."

Erik Stood and climbed up to the dragon's back. He could feel the slowing breath beneath him. Every ache in his body was replaced by peace as his enemy weakened. He stood tall upon the beast and looked down at him. "No," Erik said decisively. "Our world will live, and we will be free."

Tu'luh ceased struggling and let his head fall to the stone. His last breath whooshed out in one hot, final flame. Erik walked up the dragon's neck and pulled his sword from Tu'luh's eye. He sheathed it and looked up to the top of the chute. The nearby lava roiled and churned around him. Waves of heat drenched him in sweat and sapped what little energy he had left. He only faintly heard Jaleal call down to him, but he couldn't hear the gnome's words.

The triumphant champion sat upon Tu'luh's head and closed his eyes. He sat there, accepting that he would not be able to escape the pit. He knew that Lepkin would continue to protect the book, and at least now Tu'luh was dead. So was the warlock who destroyed his home. He thought about all of the people who had died recently. Numerous Blacktongues, Tukai the warlock, the shadowfiend that Lady Dimwater had slain, Lord Cedreau and Timon, and countless others that had fought against him. In that moment he held no more anger toward them, only pity. Then he thought of his friends who had stood by him. Trenton Lokton and his wife Raisa, who had taken him in and adopted him as their own. Master Lepkin who taught him the lessons he needed to learn in order to triumph in this moment. Al, who had literally given half of his life force to protect him when Janik betrayed him. Marlin

Erik and the Dragon

and everyone at the temple, and then he thought of Jaleal. Erik opened his eyes and looked up to the edge of the chute, searching for any sign of his friend.

He wasn't sure how the gnome had survived Tu'luh's attack. Erik had watched the flames engulf him, but yet he had at least had the strength to give Erik the spear. Erik slowly struggled to his feet and looked back down the dragon's neck. The spear was no longer there. Only a ragged hole remained. Could it be? Was Jaleal still alive? Or would the spear return to its master even if he were dead?

Erik watched the rim of the chute. Then, a coil of rope flew out over the side and dropped down, the slack flopping on the dead dragon's back. Jaleal leaned over the edge.

"Sorry, Erik, but there aren't any plants out here to help you out, so I had to go and find some rope."

Erik smiled and went to the rope. His joy at seeing his friend gave him renewed strength. He grabbed onto the rope and gave it a tug, checking to see if it was secured. Satisfied that it would hold him, he climbed up. It was slow going. His hands were sweaty and could barely hold onto the rope without sliding down. He pinched the rope between the soles of his boots and pulled himself up, hand over hand, until he finally crested over the ridge and crawled to rest on the surface of the great chamber.

"We don't have much time," Jaleal said. "There are others coming."

Erik looked up at the gnome and saw that other than a singed beard, he was intact. "How did you survive?" Erik asked.

Jaleal winked. "I am Jaleal," he said as though that was explanation enough. The gnome then turned and limped toward where his spear was stuck in the stone holding the rope secure. Erik noticed that the back of Jaleal's clothing was burned away, and his skin was sorely burned.

"You are hurt," Erik said. He pushed up to his feet and went to Jaleal. The gnome turned and smiled.

"The dragon is dead, and the spear is happy," he said. He cast a glance to the tunnel. "Come on, we have a long journey ahead." He pulled the spear from the stone and let the rope slip off to slither over the side of the hole. Jaleal pointed to the rear of the chamber. "There is a small tunnel this way. Come, before the others find us." The two of them made haste for a man-sized cavern behind the largest mound of treasure. About thirty yards beyond the main chamber, Jaleal pointed to a small side chamber.

"What is this?" Erik asked.

"This is where I found the rope. There are other supplies in here."

Erik moved in, quickly scanning the racks of weapons and staffs. He spied a pile of chainmail and then his eyes lighted upon a particular item. He went to it and pulled it from the pile. "Feather mail," he said as he held the shirt up for size. He slipped it on and found that it fit him well. Then he rummaged around the table nearby and found a leather apron. "Here, we can use this to cover your wounds."

He turned back around and saw that Jaleal was lying on the ground. He ran to him and knelt down. He could hear the gnome breathing, but no matter how many times he gently slapped his face, Jaleal would not wake up.

"Come on," Erik said. "You can't quit on me now."

Then he heard shouting from the main chamber. Angry voices yelling frantically as they discovered Tu'luh lying dead at the bottom of the lava pit. He knew he was out of time. He hefted Jaleal over his left shoulder and grabbed the spear with his right hand. Then he ran for everything he was worth.

The tunnel flashed by as he descended down several steep sets of stairs, almost stumbling more than a couple of times. Then he picked up the pace as the tunnel smoothed out and the grade of descent decreased. He could still hear the angry shouts echoing through the tunnel, but they were far behind him. He could only hope that this tunnel actually led out of the mountain somewhere, instead of looping him back to the main hall and dropping him in the middle of an angry mob

His prayers were answered when the tunnel wound around a sharp curve and then opened out into the valley near the base of Demaverung. Erik quickly tried to get his bearings, and then he sprinted down the mountainside, hopping over the jagged rocks and falling a couple of times to slide on his backside as loose rocks gave way under his weight and swept him downward at blinding speeds.

Once he reached the bottom he glanced back to see if he was being followed. His eyes didn't see anyone at the cavern's opening, but he wasn't about to take any chances. He ran off into the night, hoping that he was heading east, and praying he would be fast enough to save his friend.

CHAPTER NINETEEN

Aparen moved silently through the forest. He had spent the last several days interviewing the townsfolk about the vampire. Most of them had been too afraid to speak of it, but a couple had given him some idea of where to find the dark creature. Following their advice, Aparen moved east, into the oak forest. He followed a stream up into the rocky mountains nearby. He slowed when he approached the small waterfall that fed the stream. Somewhere around here, there was rumored to be a cave, and in that cave, was the vampire.

He moved up along the cliff wall, scanning the mossy stones for any hint of a depression or hidden entrance. As he slid behind a great, round boulder half-covered with algae, he found what he was looking for. Had he not stubbed his toe on a small, jagged rock, he might have missed it the opening was so small. He crouched down, moving to slide sideways on his belly through the narrow opening. The rock above grazed his buttocks and the back of his head, but soon after he slid his leg in he felt that there was a drop off, and the small opening gave way to a much larger cave.

Slowly he maneuvered his feet so that he held the side of the opening with his hands and cast his legs over the edge to find a foothold below. Once he did so, he pushed his torso back and slowly climbed down. As his eyes adjusted to the dark, he was able to descend more rapidly. He climbed down a series of handholds that had been worn smooth by frequent use. It must have been thirty feet of climbing before he reached the cave floor. Then he turned and peered into the darkness before him. His natural eyes were not strong enough to pierce the shadows, so he decided to transform into his more powerful form.

Once his body was done changing, he easily discerned everything in the cave. He could count the bats hanging from the small stalactites above, spot the large spiders crawling along the wall to his right, and, more importantly, see his way through the cave. He walked forward, mindful of the sheer drop to his right that descended into a crevice roughly fifty feet deep. To his left were a couple of smaller caves branching out into the belly of the mountain. He sniffed the air cautiously, and then decided to continue onward through the main cave that ran along the crevice.

As he went deeper into the cave, his nose caught the unmistakable scent of blood. The odor became stronger as he continued to stalk among the shadows in search of his quarry. After a while another tunnel branched off to the left. This time he followed the new route. The ceiling was tighter in this area, forcing Aparen to hunch down to avoid striking the jagged stone.

Suddenly the tunnel opened to a large chamber filled with bones, as if a great beast had discarded its meals for hundreds of years. The smell of blood was almost overwhelming now, but there was a new scent too. Something sweet, yet it also held a hint of musk. Without needing to think about it, Aparen knew that he smelled the vampire. He crept into the opening and searched the area. There was no sign of any movement.

To the right the floor inclined up to a small landing of stone, upon which stood a man with silver hair that hung down to his buttocks, but was kept neatly in a single plait and held together with a series of silk bows. He wore a leather vest over a silk shirt tucked into wool trousers that were in turn tucked into mid-length leather boots. The man seemed to be standing in front of a desk or pedestal of some sort and reading something. Aparen took one more step into the room and the man raised his head as if suddenly aware of his visitor.

"Do you know why I have the bows?" the vampire asked in a surprisingly low voice for such a wiry frame.

Aparen didn't answer. He just kept his eyes on the vampire.

The man turned around calmly, revealing a disfigured, gaunt face accentuated by long, sharp fangs that hung over his bottom lip. Void, black eyes stared out at Aparen and a thin, gray brow arched high on the vampire's forehead. "I have one bow in my hair for each century I have lived."

Aparen still remained quiet.

The vampire folded his arms. "In all those years, how many do you think have come to slay me?" the vampire asked. "Many have come to test their mettle against me, as evidenced by the piles of bones you see around you here. I have taken pleasure in devouring each and every one of them. What makes you think you can succeed where they have failed?"

Aparen readied himself. His muscles tightened and he

stretched his wings. He let out a feral roar that shook the entire cave. The vampire stood still, unimpressed. He locked eyes with Aparen and then launched off from his perch with ethereal grace and speed, baring his fangs and hissing. Aparen lunged to the side and threw a yellow bolt of lightning at the vampire. It sizzled and crackled through the air, illuminating the chamber, but it did not hit its mark.

The vampire disappeared in a puff of smoke only to reappear next to where Aparen landed. He seized Aparen's shoulder with inhuman strength and bent down to strike with his fangs. Aparen quickly reacted, shoving his talons into the vampire's chest and then sending a bolt of lightning out from his palm, connecting immediately with its target. The vampire was thrown back to crash through a pile of bones.

Aparen then opened his mouth and sent flame after the vampire. Again the vampire disappeared in a cloud of smoke. This time Aparen leapt into the air so that he was above the vampire when the creature reappeared. He rained down a pair of fireballs at the vampire. One of them struck the monster on the shoulder and the other missed. The vampire howled in agony and jumped back to his landing.

The vampire hissed, baring his fangs at Aparen once more, then he turned and pulled a wickedly curved scimitar from a mount on the wall that seemed to appear when the vampire reached for it. The vampire slowly drew the blade out from its scabbard and dropped the scabbard onto the stone floor.

Aparen let loose a massive ball of lightning. The vampire stood calm waiting for the spell to come in range, and then he sliced through it with his sword. The lightning dissipated harmlessly and the vampire grinned.

"You shall die as all the rest," he hissed.

Aparen reached around his back and pulled his magic dagger out. He watched the vampire descend from the perch once more. Aparen floated down to the ground and waited for the right moment. The vampire came within a few yards and then halted. He flashed an eerie smile and then charged forward. Aparen sent a bolt of lightning straight out. Just as he expected, the vampire disappeared in a cloud of smoke. Aparen then took a big step toward where the vampire had been and whipped around with his dagger, launching it directly behind where he had been standing.

Erik and the Dragon

Just as the vampire reappeared, the dagger pierced through his chest. Aparen seized upon the vampire's shock by lunging forward. He threw two more lightning spells, blasting the vampire in the stomach and face. Then he reached out with his left hand and stabbed his talons through the vampire's sword hand. A massive kick to the vampire's abdomen dropped the vampire to his knees and then Aparen placed his right palm on the vampire's forehead.

The vampire looked up with wide, dead eyes. Aparen wasted no time sending all of his magic through his right arm and crushing the vampire down to the floor with a massive psionic blast. The vampire moaned weakly and struggled to rise up again. Aparen then bent down and placed his knee squarely on the vampire's back. He then pulled the scimitar free from the vampire's grip and rammed the blade through the vampire's upper back to pierce its heart. The vampire cried out in agony and went limp.

"You can't kill me," the vampire hissed. "I am immortal."

"No, you are undead," Aparen corrected.

Aparen pulled on the vampire's braid, lifting him up enough to grab the handle of his dagger that still protruded from the vampire's chest. As he wrapped his taloned hands around the handle, he felt his dagger pull the vampire's magic out of him. The energy and power then transferred from the dagger, into Aparen and he felt his own power strengthen. He also felt his wisdom and mind become enlightened with the vampire's experience, like it had when he had consumed the bear's energy. A smile crossed his lips and he closed his eyes as he drank it all in. The feeling was indescribable, like drinking from a crystal clear spring after wandering in the desert for days. Then, in the blink of an eye, it was over and the vampire turned into ash, leaving only the dagger, the scimitar, and the vampires clothes.

"Now you are just dead," Aparen said smugly. He looked down into the pile of ash and found a hard, black mass. He picked it up and inspected the petrified heart. He shifted back into his human form and then he put the heart into the container that Dremathor had given him. In an instant, he was whisked away.

He found himself standing in the middle of a small room with marble floors, bronze pillars, and a pair of chairs facing each other. There were no doors, and no windows, yet the room was as bright as if it were a solarium during the bright afternoon sun.

"Have a seat," a voice said.

Aparen turned, but saw no one. He assumed Dremathor was either in the room, or nearby. "We had a deal," Aparen said.

Dremathor appeared in one of the chairs and smile devilishly at Aparen. "And I see you have completed your task, and quicker than I expected I might add."

"Where is Silvi?" Aparen asked.

Dremathor nodded and snapped his fingers. Silvi appeared in the room, shackled at the legs with iron bands. Her eyes were wide with surprise, but she seemed unhurt. "She is fine," Dremathor said.

Aparen tossed the container to Dremathor. "Here is what you asked for."

Dremathor opened the container and removed the petrified heart. "Did you consume his energy?"

Aparen nodded. "I did."

"It felt good, didn't it?" Dremathor inquired as he turned the heart over in his hand. "You gained some insight from his experience, some additional power from his strength, and yet none of the vampire's undesirable traits were passed on. It's incredible, isn't it?"

"Can we go?" Aparen asked.

Dremathor nodded and motioned to the chair. "First I would speak with you. Have a seat."

Aparen moved to the seat, setting the vampire's scimitar across his lap. He noticed Dremathor's thirsty eyes upon the blade like a child might look upon a chocolate cake left unguarded on the kitchen table.

"That blade is mine," Dremathor said.

"The vampire had it, I killed him. Now it is mine," Aparen said sternly.

Dremathor cackled. "No, you don't understand. The vampire stole it from me. I want it back."

Aparen looked at the blade. "Why would he steal it from you?"

"Well," Dremathor said with a shrug. "He didn't steal it from *me* so much as he stole it from the man I gave it to. I sent another to slay the vampire. I gave him the sword. When the vampire killed my champion, he kept the blade." Dremathor held his hand up in the air and the blade flew out to meet its master before Aparen could blink. Dremathor slid his fingers along the blade and admired the way it shone it the light. Then he set it adrift next to him and it disappeared from the room. "For returning it, you have my eternal gratitude."

Aparen frowned, not sure what to think of the whole mess. He glanced to Silvi. As he did so, her shackles fell from her ankles and she was set free. Then, as the sword, she disappeared from the room. Aparen jumped up from his seat. "What have you done with her?" he shouted.

Dremathor motioned for Aparen to sit. As he moved his finger, an unseen force shoved Aparen back into the chair and held him there. "I am a man of my word," Dremathor said. "Don't worry about that. She is free and waiting for you. Once we are done chatting, I will send you to her and you may do as you please. I have the amulet, and you have brought me the vampire's heart. You even returned a precious item of mine that I had counted as lost. I want to offer you something in return."

"What?" Aparen asked.

"You seek power, I can see it in your eyes, and I can smell it on your breath," Dremathor said. "I can grant you the power you seek, and I can help you establish a new coven so you can build upon your power."

"Why would you do that?" Aparen asked.

Dremathor shrugged and pulled the amulet out from under his robes. "Have you heard of the Black Fang Council?" he asked. Before Aparen could answer, Dremathor shook his head and waved the notion away. "Of course you haven't," he said. "Let's just say that it is a powerful group of shadowfiends. I used to be one of them."

"Used to be?" Aparen asked.

Dremathor nodded. "I now have everything I want. I don't need the council any longer. Besides, I am afraid that the group will not last much longer now that..." he paused and put the amulet back in his robe. "I suppose it matters little to you."

"What?" Aparen asked. He was utterly confused and unsure what Dremathor was alluding to.

"Maybe I will tell you one day, but I am not sure you are ready just yet. For now, tell me whether you would be willing to accept my help. If you are, I can send you to a place where you may learn how to increase your power, and you will be able to build a new coven, would that interest you?"

"What is in it for you?" Aparen asked skeptically.

Dremathor grinned. "You have already given me so much," he said as he patted the amulet. "What do you say, will you accept my help?"

Aparen thought it over silently.

"I know the hunger you have for power," Dremathor said as his grin widened. The man leaned forward. "I know the ecstasy of feeding upon another's energy. Don't sit there and pretend you don't want more."

Aparen nodded. "Where will you send me?"

Dremathor slapped a hand to his knee. "I have friends far in the west that will teach you all you need to know. They are an interesting lot, but if you can get past the smell, they will grow on you."

"The smell?" Aparen echoed questioningly.

"They're satyrs," Dremathor replied.

Aparen started to open his mouth but a blinding light made him flinch and hold his hands up over his face. Air rushed around him, chilling his skin and causing goose pimples to appear. Then, as quickly as it appeared, the light was gone and he was sitting in the chair in a lush, green forest. He blinked a couple of times and saw that Dremathor was sitting a few feet in front of him.

"This is it," Dremathor said. "My friend will be here soon to greet you. Treat him with respect, you may be powerful, but the satyrs are a savvy bunch, and wield powerful magic. If you anger them, I will not come back to rescue you."

Aparen glanced around. "What about Silvi?"

Dremathor chuckled and clapped his hands. "She is on her way," he promised. Then he shook his head and stood up. The chair disappeared behind him. He started to walk away and then held up his hand as if he had forgotten something and turned back to face Aparen. "Oh, and, in a while I may come back and ask you for a favor. From one gentleman to another, I trust you will honor my request." Before Aparen could say anything, Dremathor disappeared as he walked away. A sphere of golden light appeared to Aparen's right, and then Silvi stood next to him, smiling widely as she placed her hand down on his shoulder.

"You came back for me," she said.

Aparen nodded. Then he heard a strange instrument from some distance down the path in the forest. It was somewhat like a

Erik and the Dragon

flute, but not quite as sharp. It was softer, and smoother. Around the bend in the path came a most unusual animal. It skipped along on two hooves that resembled the hind legs of a goat. The fur was brown and came up to the creature's waist, where it changed to resemble that of a man's torso. A thick patch of hair stretched across the belly and up over the chest, fanning out to touch cover the shoulders. A thick, red beard hung below the creature's chin and its lips were pursed together as it blew into a set of wooden pipes the likes of which Aparen had not seen before. Long, pointy ears stuck out from the side of the satyr's head and it stared at him with beady, brown eyes beneath a mat of reddish-brown hair that curled around a pair of stubby horns.

All at once it stopped skipping along the path and put its instrument down. "So, you are the one that Dremathor wants us to teach eh?"

Aparen looked up to Silvi and she shrugged back at him.

"Well, come on, we can't very well stay out here in the forest. The prowlers will be along come nightfall. We should be back in Viverandon before then. Come on, up, let's go." It turned on its hooves and began skipping back down the path, playing its wooden pipes as it went.

Silvi nudged Aparen. "What should we do?" she asked.

Aparen rose out of the chair. No sooner had he done so than the thing vanished from behind him. He looked down to where the chair had been and then up to the creature disappearing back behind the trees. "We follow him," he said decisively.

*****

Gilifan walked to the edge of the pit and looked down. His face soured and he turned away from the sight at the bottom. "When did this happen?" he asked.

"I called for you just as soon as I found out. The acolytes summoned the other elders, who had been out gathering firedrakes for an assault on Ten Forts."

"Where were you?" Gilifan asked.

"I was also out in the valley," Takala replied. "I was gathering some of the mercenaries we had hired."

Gilifan nodded. He turned away from the pit and looked at the other elders of the order that stood nearby.

"What do we do now?" one of them asked.

Gilifan stood silently. He knew of the egg, but none of the others did. He turned to Takala and looked at the man for a moment. "Where do your loyalties lie, Takala?" he asked.

"You have the power to raise men from the dead," Takala said quickly. "Couldn't you raise the master back?"

Gilifan sighed. Even if he still had the amulet, raising a dragon was beyond his power. He would need the book for that. The only problem was, he needed a dragon to use the book.

"I knew this was a waste of time," one of the elders spat. "I have been sitting here waiting for the master's return for all of my life, only to have him come back just in time to die at the hands of one man! This is ridiculous."

Gilifan reached up with his hand and a magical vice wrapped around the elder's throat. "It was your job to secure the lair."

"No," the man sputtered as he wiggled against the unseen choke-hold. "We were out on the master's errand. We weren't here!"

Gilifan released his spell and the man fell back a couple of steps. "We go after the book," he said definitively. "Our order still serves the same purpose."

"How will we use the book without Tu'luh?" the same elder asked.

"You let me worry about that," Gilifan replied. He then turned back to Takala. "We will need strong warriors to accomplish our goal now. The orcs at Ten Forts will need our help."

"Orcs won't fight with us," one of the other elders said. "Their witch hunters will come after us. That is why we hide here in Verishtahng. It is too dangerous even for the orcs to come at us here."

Gilifan placed a hand on Takala's shoulder. "I asked you before, but now I need a direct answer. Where do your loyalties lie?"

Takala met Gilifan's eyes evenly and set his jaw. "Command me, Master Gilifan, and I will obey. I, and all other members of the Black Fang Council, will serve you as we did our master. I have lived long enough to know that there is still a chance for victory as long as we are strong."

Gilifan nodded. "I was hoping you would say that." The necromancer then turned and walked to the five elders. "Come here," he instructed them. "Join hands with me, and I will show you the visions that Tu'luh showed me."

The elders looked to each other nervously and then formed a circle, holding hands and then closed their eyes. Gilifan looked at each of them and then mentally called forth a spell to paralyze them. He sent it out in a wave through his hands. It coursed through each of the elders faster than the blink of an eye. Then he pulled himself free of the circle and turned back to Takala.

"To win this war, we will need to rebuild our order. I need men who are strong, and unwavering in their determination." Gilifan held out his hand, indicating the five elders behind him, still frozen in place. "If you wish, you may consume their power, take it as a token of my appreciation for your loyalty, and a promise to reward you for future endeavors."

Takala grinned evilly. "I think this new arrangement will work well."

Gilifan started toward the exit. "I will cull the rest of the weak from my order, and then you and I will begin rebuilding. It will take some time, but we will come back stronger than before. Tu'luh may have died, but his legacy lives on."

"Glory to the strong," Takala said.

Gilifan stopped in his tracks and turned back. "Tomorrow, I will have a special errand for you, Takala. Do you know Salarion?"

"I know *of* her," Takala replied.

Gilifan nodded. "I will send you out to find her. I wish to speak with her." Takala nodded quietly, and Gilifan turned and left the chamber so Takala could enjoy his reward. There was much work to be done, but all was not lost for the Wyrms of Khaltoun.

About the Author

Sam Ferguson has a sword collection so large that Wolverine has blade-envy.

He once fought a bull with nothing but a fencing panel and won.

He has enough sons to create his own 3 on 3 football game and still be all-time QB.

When Russian, Latvian, and Hungarian didn't confuse him enough, he moved to Yerevan so he could learn Armenian.

He once drove through an earthquake while all others were too afraid to come out from hiding.

He used to hunt cougar with a baseball bat.

While others use a .22 for target practice, he uses a Russian RPD.

He can curl more than 200 lbs, without cheating.

He also draws the BEST darn stick-figures you have EVER seen!

Now, he won't admit to being Batman, but no one has ever seen him and Batman in the same room at the same time...

When he is taking a break from being awesome, he is usually at home with his wife and kids and learning from them how to become even AWESOMER!

(Yes, "awesomer" is a word. The toddler says so!)

If you enjoyed this book, then join Sam Ferguson's Facebook page, sign up for alerts on his Amazon page, and by all means leave a kind review!

Other Books by Sam Ferguson

<u>The Dragon's Champion Series:</u>
The Dragon's Champion
The Warlock Senator
The Dragon's Test
Erik and the Dragon
The Immortal Mystic (Spring 2015)

<u>The Netherworld Gate Series:</u>
The Tomni'Tai Scroll
The King's Ring (Autumn 2016)

<u>The Dragons of Kendualdern</u>
Ascension

Tales from Terramyr

Made in the USA
Las Vegas, NV
09 March 2023